"I can't decide whether you are one of the fae folk or a little bird."

LEIFMAN BOOKS
Porterville, Ca, USA

This is a work of fiction. Its characters, places and incidents are a product of the author's imagination and any resemblance to actual persons, living or dead, or real events or locales, is entirely coincidental.

Copyright © 2023 by Tess Bentley
www.tessbentley.com
Instagram: @tessbentleyauthor
Twitter: @TessBentley47

Cover Design and Book Design by Franziska Stern
www.coverdungeon.com
Instagram: @coverdungeonrabbit

All rights reserved. No part of this publication may be reproduced in any form or by any means, electronic or mechanical, including photocopying, recording, or any information storage and retrieval systems, without prior written permission from the author, except for the use of brief quotations in a book review.

Paperback ISBN: 979-8-9882792-1-1
Hardback ISBN: 979-8-9882792-0-4
eBook ISBN: 979-8-9882792-2-8

*For my boys, you are my sunshine.*

*The human heart has hidden treasures,
In secret kept, in silence sealed;—
The thoughts, the hopes, the dreams, the pleasures,
Whose charms were broken if revealed.*

*—Charlotte Brontë, "Evening Solace"*

# VALE

The Former Things

# CHAPTER 1

"And God shall wipe away all tears from their eyes; and there shall be no more death, neither sorrow, nor crying, neither shall there be any more pain: for the former things are passed away. Revelation 21:4"

*Clara A.*
*Wife of J. F. Twitchell*
*Died*
*June 27, 1883*
*Aged 26 YS. 4 MOS. 15 DS.*

I found myself staring at this grave for quite some time. I have always had a fascination for cemeteries. Rarely, though, did I find the luxury of time to wander through the consecrated grounds. This day, however, I drifted mindlessly through each row, studying each headstone, getting to know the inhabitants who lay sleeping beneath my feet. There was an eerie juxtaposition between the sleepy little cemetery and the bright spring day. This section of the cemetery contained many older trees; they were not tended to very well and were probably much older than the graves they sheltered.

It was a beautiful day. There was a cool breeze, calm and forlorn, that said "Summer will be here all too soon, so enjoy me for today." Summer always came early for us in this part of the country, and by mid-May it would be hot and uncomfortable. I took a deep breath, delighting in the sweet spring scent of fresh-cut grass and cypress trees. For the first time that day, I felt the urge to smile. The gentle moment was fleeting, though, as my heart was heavy. This cemetery was well-known to me as most of my own relatives were spending their eternal rest here. Being a rather small city in the middle of California, there was only this cemetery and an even smaller Catholic cemetery a few miles away.

I had often wished to wander around and examine the headstones, especially here in the older section. My hometown was founded at the beginning of the twentieth century, so the oldest graves were still quite young compared to some of the larger cities in the state and not nearly as old as those on the East Coast or in Europe. Clara's grave, however, was one of the oldest and best-preserved headstones I had found during this short visit. Clara was barely past her twenty-sixth birthday, a tragedy in my time but a more common loss in hers. I had been lamenting my own mortality—at least the part where I was getting older. With my thirty-sixth birthday only a month before, I now felt a little guilty for being sorry about getting older when other lives were cut short. I wondered how she died. Did she succumb to consumption, like so many of her time? Or perhaps it was childbirth, robbing her of the little joy that life had to offer? Again, I felt guilty, for I knew my thoughts were bleak.

It was not my intention to visit the cemetery that day, but I had needed to escape from my house for a momentary reprieve. The best excuse I could muster was that I had to take flowers to my grandfather's grave. I did take the flowers, a fresh bouquet of white lilies, and laid them upon the stone grass marker where he was buried with my grandmother. The powerful fragrance of the flowers permeated the air around me. I closed my eyes as I briefly went to another place in time, when the two lying before me were more than a beautiful memory.

I soon found myself wandering row after row, looking at the old graves and monuments, many of which were cracked, aged with dirt, and had grass growing between the open spaces. Others, however, were splendidly preserved and were as easy to read as the day they were laid down.

I felt the familiar sting of tears in my eyes as I reread, *"for the former things are passed away."*

I was indeed having a bad day. No, it had been a few bad *years* if I was honest with myself, and honest I was, standing at another's grave on Resurrection Sunday. Easter had begun with me waking up extra early to get myself ready before I dressed and groomed my two little children. I struggled in the shower; I was tired and my motivation was low. I took longer than necessary, allowing the warm water to wash my tears away. I can still recall the morose look upon my face as I caught my reflection in the glass shower door. I had a mental discussion with myself: *Do not fall apart, focus on your children, take it one day at a time.*

And so I did.

I said a quick prayer, finished my shower, did my hair and makeup in record time, and put on the new light blue dress I had been looking forward to wearing. Once I was ready, I took on the tasks of wrestling my seven- and two-year-old, combing their hair, brushing their teeth, fighting to convince one to wear his sweater vest and the other to wear her shoes on the correct feet; all the while trying to be cheerful and excited for the long day ahead: church, Easter baskets, egg hunt, and a family barbecue.

Dear reader, I sound ungrateful; it isn't lost on me. My love for my children was infinite, and to be their mother was the delight of my life, but I was emotionally exhausted, not because I was a mother, but because I was a wife. Did I sound like a single mother? I felt like one. It was not a new feeling—it was old, tired, and repetitive. My spirit was so low that I no longer recognized myself. For the first time in my life, depression was beginning to surface. The seeds were planted on my wedding day—tiny shoots of loneliness, sadness, infidelity, dismissiveness—and all had been watered, often with my own tears, over the last decade.

I couldn't help but be angry, mostly at myself. I'd ignored so many red flags. Why had I wanted a peaceful home so much that I had swallowed all my feelings, ignored my own hurt, and given so much of myself to my husband that I had nothing left for me? Walking on eggshells had become my story and I loathed it. I desperately wanted another story, one where my children and I were holding each other, felt at peace, and played happily, with only joy ahead of us. When my husband had finally decided to wake up, with only himself to get ready, the constant disapproval began: the house was a mess, the children were loud, there was nothing for breakfast, he couldn't find the car keys, and "is that what you're wearing?" The good mood I was so desperately trying to maintain faded. I knew immediately how the next few moments of the day would go.

I would be criticized for looking moody and, in his most mechanical way, he'd say, "What's wrong with you? Is this how the day's going to go?"

I didn't have the energy to fight anymore. "I'm fine. It's Easter, and it's a beautiful day." I attempted a small smile, though it felt strained.

"Right. Go put the kids in the car," he replied.

What bothered me more than his attitude and treatment of me was how I could so easily predict it, so clearly see the pattern in his behavior. Yet no matter what I did, I could not stop the outcome.

Mechanically, I did as he said and placed my children in their car seats, attempting to pick up the stray toys scattered about and buckle myself in the passenger seat before he sat down. The familiar beat of anxiety thrummed in my chest; knowing that my own husband shouldn't be the cause added to the sadness within.

Lost in my thoughts as I stared down at this young woman's grave, I unconsciously removed my wedding band. I looked down at the pretty gold ring, not with sympathy but apathy. I turned it to see the engraving written inside the band, "the best is yet to be." I couldn't suppress a small, sarcastic laugh. The engraving had been my idea—stupid, romantic girl!

I dreaded going home to him. I thought of my children again. They had wanted to come with me, but I thought it best they stay behind and play with their Easter baskets. I didn't like them to see me upset. I needed this break—I needed to make a decision.

Consumed by my thoughts, a stranger stood quite close to me before I noticed he was there. He saw me startle but offered a warm smile and gently lifted his hands, almost as if to say, "No harm meant."

I smiled back, a little embarrassed he'd caught me brooding. Instinctively, I made to move away and acted as though I hadn't been caught unaware. I wanted to avoid looking weak and decided to head back to my car parked not so many feet away. There were a few people visiting the cemetery that day— it was Easter, after all—but this section was long past the time of survivors placing flowers on their loved one's graves. As I was turning to go, the stranger spoke.

"How are you, Vale?"

He knew my name. I'd never seen this man before, and even if he'd been someone I failed to recognize, I knew I would remember being acquainted with an Englishman, for his accent was easily recognizable. He must have read the puzzled look upon my face, for he quickly added, "I'm sorry. I'm an *old friend* of your grandfather's. I recognized you from pictures."

"Oh?" I remarked, more articulate words failing me. "You seem young to be an old friend of his."

I mimicked his saccharine smile as I said this, not wanting to seem rude or distrustful. I was always aware of how people might perceive me and my intentions, a trait I disliked about myself. He was young enough, perhaps mid-forties; far too young to be an old friend or even acquaintance of my eighty-six-year-old grandfather, who had recently passed.

"Well, yes. We were not childhood friends or anything of the sort."

His eyes were a clear blue, but I couldn't quite call them friendly, despite his smile. This gentleman wore a fine tailored suit. His brown slacks matched his jacket, and underneath was a plaid, khaki-colored vest with wooden buttons and a black tie tucked into it. It was a smart, modern look with a touch of nostalgia.

He went on, "Your grandfather and I are kin. We shared some correspondence, building the family tree and such. He was a great help. I had not heard from him in some time, so I took it upon myself to make the trip to see him. I was sorry to find he had passed. I should have liked to have met him in person."

He seemed genuine. I, too, was sorry he had missed the opportunity to meet my grandfather.

"Yes, I'm sure he would have liked that. He did enjoy researching his ancestry. He never mentioned you though, Mr..." I paused, realizing he hadn't given me his name.

"Ah, Mr. Emberley—Mr. John Emberley."

He stretched out his hand to shake mine. Here was a distant relative I knew nothing about. I was interested. I didn't know as much as I would've liked about my family tree and wondered if he was a third cousin or an even more distant relation than that.

"Nice to meet you, Mr. Emberley." I extended my hand to shake his in return. As I went to give him my full name he interrupted, both his hands encircling mine.

"Ah, Vale, a lovely little thing you are too." Instinctively, I tried to pull back my trapped hand, but Mr. Emberley's tight grip prevented this. "Do not struggle so, little dove. I mean you no harm, not if you work with me. I am in need of your help, and as fate has shone down on me and finally led me to you, you will indeed provide assistance."

Fear and panic had replaced the anger and sadness that had earlier occupied my mind. "Let go of my hand! I don't care what your needs are!"

Once again, I tried to regain my hand, to no avail. I felt the panic mounting within. Yet my rational side couldn't comprehend him having bad intentions. Here was a well-dressed, previously polite Englishman claiming to be my relative—my mind couldn't keep up with such a sudden change.

The nice act was over. "Now hush, and be a good girl. You will help me. I have spent too many years here in this Godforsaken century for you to refuse me now that I have found you."

*Godforsaken century.* What an odd thing to say. Doubt was removed, and I was now sure he must be ill. I became determined to get away. As I went to pull my hand back with all the strength I could gather, he did the same. I was petite and it didn't take much for a man of his size to overpower me. He pulled me close to him in a partial embrace at his side, with my left hand turned palm up.

"Let me go! Let me go *now!*"

I could no longer think clearly. I didn't know how to fight, and fear had arrested my voice. I began to pull and tug and was about to kick and bite when my senses were drawn back to my hand. This Mr. John Emberley had taken a small dagger, one he must have kept out of sight, and made a long cut in the palm of my left hand. The sting was sharp and severe, and seeing so much blood come gushing out, I suddenly felt lightheaded.

Before I had time to completely process this assault, he had pulled another object from the inner pocket of his coat. It was some sort of pendant necklace with a gold chain and a purple stone hanging from it, perhaps amethyst. Mr. Emberley took the necklace, placed the stone against my still-bleeding left palm and began to utter some words from a language I was not familiar with. With the final syllable of his strange speech, I forgot the pain in my hand.

Something was happening.

As we struggled against each other, a new sensation enveloped us both. It was as though we were two caterpillars sharing the same cocoon, an invisible one that separated us from the rest of the world. I looked up at him in strange wonder; he had a wild gleam in his eyes that said he was both amazed and pleased with himself. We both grew still, watching in amazement the changes taking place around our invisible cocoon. For a split second, it was as though the world around us was on fire, bright and oppressive, then suddenly the fire began within. My lungs grew hot, and I could not breathe. With each passing second, Mr. Emberley's grip on my hand tightened. It was as though the whole of life was closing in on us.

Whatever was happening internally was making an outward impression as well. A chill ran down my spine as I noticed my hand take on a more youthful appearance. My thoughts did not linger on this peculiarity long. The pressure within began to increase. My head was swimming, my lungs were burning, and I felt my life fading: suddenly, it was as though the pressure must be released. The thin-veiled cocoon was spent, and after what seemed like an eruption of life, all was still.

Out of the Vale

# CHAPTER 2

As I regained consciousness, the sensation of burning in my lungs dissipated. With my right hand, I could feel soft, damp grass, but my left hand was immobile with pain. I took in a deep breath, grateful to be breathing freely again, and then I opened my eyes. An overcast sky mixed with large dark and light clouds greeted me. I gently turned my head as I lay there in the grass and saw my newly acquainted assailant lying unconscious several feet away. I pushed myself up as best I could. I was dazed, and my hand was beginning to ache unbearably.

Mr. Emberley started to stir, and I was determined not to be his victim again. Confused and frightened, I stood as stead as possible. I quickly scanned my surroundings—my God! This must be how Dorothy felt upon realizing she was no longer in Kansas. This was certainly not my little hometown, with its mixture of pines and palms; low hills and large mountains majestically framed in the background. This was miles upon miles of greenery, small rolling hills in the distance and the unmistakable look of the English countryside.

To my left stood an old and elegant manor house. Its gray stone exterior rose tall and stately, with large windows and a pretty garden surrounding it. To my right, several yards away, was the entrance to an old orchard. I needed to get away and think. I knew I was in trouble, and instinctively began to develop a plan of action. This plan, however, would require some serious thought to ensure self-preservation. To accomplish this, I needed to get away from the man who had inflicted this situation upon me so rapidly. As Mr. Emberley began to rouse in earnest, another sight caught my eye. Three individuals, standing close to the house, were staring in our direction. That look of utter bewilderment could not be mistaken; they had seen something supernatural take place. I felt sick. I needed to get away before I found myself deeper in trouble.

I took a good look at the three people, two men and a woman, who were slowly and calmly walking my way. I glanced back at Mr. Emberley, who was beginning to rise to his knees. Without any more hesitation, I turned and ran. I pulled up my dress to prevent a fall and ran as fast as I could towards the orchard. I was breathing heavily and not from exhaustion, no, I was far too awake for that. I believe I was beginning to experience my first panic attack. *I need to calm down,* I thought; *find a safe place, and quickly.*

I cannot say how deep into the grove I ran. I zig-zagged at least twice, crossing over the small mounds of the neat rows that allowed for water runoff to protect the roots of the trees. Great fruit trees I was familiar with; they were plentiful where I came from. My mother and I had taken many walks through tree groves when I was a child. Then, as an adult, I had pulled my own children through them in an old metal wagon. My children—the anguish struck like a hot sword, cutting me from my stomach to my heart. *Not now,* I thought. *Get somewhere safe, make a plan and get back to them.* After a few minutes of panicked running, I found a single old oak tree. It sat in the midst of the other trees, interrupting their perfect pattern. It had a low branch, with a large knot below it that I climbed up. As I had never been athletic, this exertion was a struggle. Fortunately, I was successful. The tree was old, and the branches were well-developed, thick, and strong. I was able to maneuver myself up another branch or so and position myself where I could see the row of trees in front of me. I was not completely hidden but well enough that one would have to be intentionally looking up to see me. It was still early spring; the trees in the orchard retained their beautiful pink blossoms. It would be another week or so before the leaves would replace them.

I attempted to pace my breathing. I closed my eyes, inhaling deeply. As I began to calm, I allowed myself a moment to take in my surroundings. It was a beautiful sight to behold. Spring was alive and in her prime. The whole orchard looked like a fairy garden, with the blossoms sprinkled all over the ground, resembling pink snow. With the overcast sky casting its soft glow against the trees, the whole place felt ethereal. I thought I recognized the trees now as apple. They were beautiful.

I had finally calmed myself down enough to begin to try to make sense of my current situation—impossible! None of it made sense. For a moment, I questioned my own sanity. I reflected on my morning, the very natural and mundane morning. I thought of the drive to the cemetery, and then my encounter with Mr. Emberley. Despite my disdain for my marriage, it wasn't a new stressor; I was all too familiar with the feeling. I knew I was indeed sane. Once I was assured of my own mental strength, I questioned Mr. Emberley's purpose. Who was he and why did he need me? I leaned back against the branch, holding my left hand with my right.

The blood had dried, but my hand looked red and offended. I noticed my marriage line was literally severed. "I am so facetious," I said to myself. I always made light out of everything, perhaps only mentally, but still—there had to be more tolerable ways to cope. I looked down at my dress. The light blue material moved with the gentle breeze. It did not fit me as well as it had when I was at the cemetery. I ran my right hand down my body from my neck, stopping momentarily at my breasts. Something was different there. I continued down to my stomach, which was smoother and smaller. Some strange wonder had indeed occurred.

After securing the bottom of my dress so it did not drift in the wind, I rested my head between my legs and finally let the tears run. My thoughts rapidly jumped from subject to subject: the recent events, who John Emberley really was, where I was, and where I could find help. I thought of the three individuals emerging from the manor house. It was impossible to ignore how they were dressed. I recognized the style at once—why they were dressed that way was a better question. I had studied English literature at university, and now taught a few courses at the local community college; I could not claim to be an expert on the era, but I could certainly recognize it.

The strangers had been wearing clothes that looked to be from the nineteenth century, most likely mid-1800s I considered the possibility they belonged to some sort of literary society and were having one of their meetings, though I was unconvinced. I had to focus and seek help, but how and from whom still perplexed me. Perhaps I should have waited for them to approach, but I could not take the risk. I had panicked initially, and I considered that they might have been in a panic as well, seeing what they did. They could have caused me more harm than good, and I had to also consider the possibility they were working with Mr. Emberley. And this Mr. Emberley—was it conceivable that he was planning on using me for human trafficking? It seemed plausible enough at the time. I had no intention of being any use to that man. As I sat there with one thought running into another, trying to process my current situation and attempting to keep a grip on my vast array of emotions, I realized someone was coming through the orchard.

I carefully leaned to my left side, still hidden by the low-hanging tree branch in front of me, attempting to see who or what was coming through the trees. Not too many yards down the very row I was in, a concerned-looking man was walking through, obviously looking for something or, more likely, someone. I recognized him as one of the three people who saw me appear. This was the taller of the two gentlemen, and a gentleman he was, wearing a long, dark brown cloak, inner vest over his white shirt, brown cravat, top hat, trousers, and tall boots to complete the look—he was exactly like the daguerreotypes I had seen. I feared he was working with John Emberley. Mr. Emberley knew enough about me that I had to assume there was some intention behind all of this, whatever that might be. The gentleman drew closer and began to call out.

"Miss, I know you must be taking refuge somewhere in proximity. Do not be afraid. I mean you no harm."

The gentleman had a refined, gentle voice with a familiar accent. His serious tone was mingled with a genuine expression of curiosity. Half of me wanted to surrender immediately and get it over with, the other half was too afraid to speak at all. The latter was still in control.

"I know you are frightened. We saw you run. Let us meet and understand each other."

I had leaned back into my prior position, holding still as best I could. Despite his soft words, he had an austere look about him. He seemed confident in his mannerisms and in control, the complete opposite of myself. I was nervous—terrified, really. As he walked nearer, a cool spring breeze wafted through the orchard, sending small blossoms through the air, causing my dress to drift in the breeze which caught his eye. His gaze drifted first to my dress, then settled into eye contact with me. I was found.

A Little Bird

# CHAPTER 3

I knew my current location on a large branch of an old oak tree was not ideal or even well hidden. I had, however, imagined I would have more time before I was discovered. I'd had just enough time to myself to process some of what had happened. This led to more questions than answers—answers that someone else would have to supply.

Feeling deeply distressed, I was in no mood to talk, but that was not an option anymore as my new acquaintance probably had as many questions as I.

The gentleman, with his fine clothes and confident stride, came closer. It was obvious to me that he walked carefully and deliberately, as one would do when trying to approach a frightened animal. With his eyes locked on mine, he gave an amused half-smile that was more becoming than it should have been. I could not help but look away as I felt the blood rush to my cheeks.

*Why is he not terrified of me?* I wondered. I was sure that he had seen Mr. Emberley and me suddenly appearing out of nowhere. *He must have known what was going to happen,* I concluded. A knot was beginning to form in my stomach.

He was now at the base of the tree. He could easily have pulled me down if he had wanted, though he did nothing of the sort.

"Are you well?" he asked.

All I could do was nod my head. I was not well, however; I could barely breathe, let alone converse. He considered me for several moments.

"I can't decide whether you are one of the fae folk or a little bird. Since you have taken refuge in my tree, I would surmise you to be a bird—but then I am sure you have just come from fairyland, have you not?"

He leaned against the tree as he asked me this. I could not tell whether he was teasing or not, and I didn't know how to respond. This was one of those excruciating moments in life when one does not know how to adequately respond in a conversation, and though the context seemed odd, I knew he was testing me somehow. Before I could respond, no doubt rather stupidly, he began to speak again.

He nodded his head as though he had worked it out. "I have decided on a little bird presently. You have naturally found your home in a tree, are rather little and fair, and you are very frightened. If I were to attempt to approach any further, I believe you would spread your wings and fly away in much haste. Is that not the case, little bird?"

His half-smile had returned, but his large brown eyes had a look of concern in them. He seemed a peculiar person. I did my best to respond, though I doubted I could sound as clever.

"No, sir." Intuition told me to mirror his speech and speak as formally as possible. "I doubt that I could fly away at the moment. I don't have any feathers and my hand is injured."

I lifted my left hand to show him the bloody mess that it was. I struggled to hold back tears when I saw my hand; it was in vain, as a couple escaped and ran down my cheek. I knew my hand would heal, but the scar left behind would run deeper than the surface.

The gentleman winced upon seeing my hand.

"You are injured. How did this happen?" he asked.

"The man I was with before—Mr. Emberley—intentionally cut my hand. Do you know him?"

It was hard to pull rational thoughts together at this moment, but this was my best chance of gathering what information I could.

He looked angry now. "Yes, I do *know* him. More than I would prefer to admit. Care for him, I do not. Even less now. John and I have never got along well."

I felt some comfort in his words, and he did know Mr. Emberley's first name, proving to me that he was not trying to hide the ill acquaintance. If what he said was true, I at least had something in common with this gentleman. He must have read my mind.

"You are not the only one with the displeasure of being acquainted with John Emberley, who is now, I am sure, making up some excuse for his sorry behavior to my sister."

"Your sister? Was she the lady with you coming from the house?"

I was curious about who these people might be. Brother and sister, that was somewhat more comforting.

"Yes; you saw my sister, Anne, and her husband, George Ellis. I am Edward, not that you asked."

With this, he allowed a teasing half-smile. *I would have eventually asked,* I thought, a little embarrassed.

"That manor house you speak of is my home, Avenhurst Manor. This is my estate, my orchard, and, in fact, my oak tree that you find yourself neatly perched upon."

I was deeply engrossed by his conversation. His words rolled fluidly; his accent handsome. I hadn't noticed him come closer. He had stepped up, probably on an old root he used as a stool, and had his arms crossed gracefully over the branch I was still sitting on, leaning towards me like we were two old friends in casual conversation.

"Now you know all about me, or at least what is necessary for the present moment. Does the bird have a name?" he inquired in earnest.

"Vale—Vale Leifman," I offered nervously.

I had given him my maiden name. I felt a hint of shame, but I had been detaching myself mentally from my husband for some time and inwardly preferred to think of Leifman as my last name. I meant no falsehood. It simply felt right.

"Leifman—that is an unusual surname. *Leofman* is an old word for beloved."

I knew he was correct about the meaning—my grandfather had once told me about it. Like many other American families, our surname had likely altered over time.

Edward continued, "Your accent is rather peculiar. You are a native English speaker, certainly, but it is not an accent I am familiar with, and I have traveled extensively. Though now is not the time to inquire more about that, I see—that hand of yours needs attention, and the expression on your face looks as though you are in a great deal of pain."

He was correct in his assumption on this point. My hand was throbbing, and fiercely so. I knew I needed to clean it at the very least or else I would soon have a nice infection. I was still hesitant, though, and unsure how to proceed. I simply nodded my head in agreement. This was enough.

"Very well, come down from your perch, then, and we will get you some aid. Here, take my coat and put it around you."

He took off his dark coat and handed it to me. I noticed him glance at my legs. I blushed in spite of myself. My dress was not short, just pulled up slightly from my sitting position. My legs showing, especially my calves, had never in my life made me blush. Somehow, though, I think I was responding to his feelings about my legs. I wrapped the coat around me; his scent lingered, masculine and strangely comforting. I looked to him for the next move. He understood.

"Do you think you can get down easily enough?" he asked.

"I think so," I said.

Putting too much pressure on the palm of my left hand, however, was out of the question. I tried with difficulty to move myself into a position to get down from the branch, but Edward stopped me.

"No, you are going to injure that hand more, or fall. Here, just move yourself closer along the branch to where I'm standing. Use the backside of your left hand and put pressure on your right to pivot to the side."

With these instructions, he held out a white embroidered handkerchief he'd pulled from his pocket.

"Wrap this around your hand."

I obeyed and moved closer to him.

Before he had time to give further instruction, I asked, "Mr. Emberley, is he still out there?"

Edward looked at me with some concern. "Yes, Anne and George are dealing with him presently, I suppose. He will not leave so easily, is my guess. You needn't worry, though; I will not let him hurt you. I would rather shoot him now and end his misery, except we need to get some information out of him. I have questions, as I am sure you do."

I would have been sure he was teasing if I hadn't been so nervous already. He considered me again. "My sister—she will make a pet out of you yet!"

Edward said that with a friendly smile, which I am sure was meant to give me some comfort. I returned the smile as much as I could; it was weak at best. I resumed my attempt to get down, now feeling slightly dizzy. Between the pain in my hand and ache in my head, not to mention my heart, I was struggling. Looking at me with pity, Edward recommenced his assistance.

"I am going to have to help you down—I'm going to lift you up off the branch. Do you object?"

I shook my head, amazed at the politeness of it all. Edward reached up and took hold of my waist, and just as quickly removed his hands; he looked surprised. Whatever alarmed him, he dismissed it, because he immediately resumed grasping me by the waist and lifting me from the branch while making a comment about me being "light as a feather." I now stood in front of him. He was several inches taller than me. He had a broad chest and slender waist—and his arms were strong. I could still feel where his hands had touched me. Maybe I would have been more embarrassed, but the staggering pain in my heart was becoming insistent.

"That is a lovely locket," Edward stated, pulling me out of painful thoughts.

I realized I was absentmindedly tracing the oval shaped necklace. It was a gold cameo locket, decorated with a cream-colored lily of the valley flower on the outside. I dropped it immediately.

"Thank you," I said, without another pathetic attempt at a smile.

Edward did not pry. He placed his arm out for me to hold, and together we made our way back to the courtyard in search of answers.

✦

As we were exiting the old apple orchard, Anne, Edward's aforementioned sister, seemed to be having a heated discussion with Mr. Emberley. As soon as she saw us coming, she walked away from him without another word. Anne looked to be near the same height as I, maybe an inch taller but not as petite as my own stature. She shared the same dark eyes as her brother and the same dark brown hair. I noticed her hair was combed smoothly on the sides and pulled back in a low bun, whereas Edward's was loose and wavy. He kept his hair several inches longer than the styles for men that I was accustomed to.

Upon meeting me, Edward had been careful and cautious. Anne had her own approach; she was less guarded and more captivated. Anne had a round and pleasant face that was filled with fascination as she looked me over head to toe and back again. She was wearing a speckled white-and-gray dress with long pleated sleeves. It was tightly fitted at the waist, with possibly several petticoats underneath due to the volume of the bottom of her dress, and she wore black leather boots. I thought she looked rather lovely; old black-and-white photos did not do this look justice. In contrast, I must have seemed ridiculous. My long, light brown hair was down, with large curls. I was wearing makeup. It wasn't a lot, but Anne wore none. My light blue chiffon dress had short, loose sleeves and was also fitted at the waist, but lacked the several modest layers of petticoats underneath it. In fact, it only went a few inches below my knees. My dress was light and flowy, perfect for spring—Anne's was stately yet feminine. She wore boots; I wore small, strappy, tan leather sandals that revealed painted toenails. Thankfully I was still wearing Edward's coat, so I felt less naked.

"You are a living, breathing fairy, I am sure of it!" she exclaimed, looking at me with amazement.

I tried to respond, especially since she seemed warm-hearted, but it was increasingly difficult to force a smile or speak; the head, hand, and heart pains were taking their toll.

"What is your name, darling?" Anne asked me.

"Vale Leifman," was my simple reply.

"You can get better acquainted inside, Anne. This little one needs care. John, it seems, attempted to butcher her hand, and she is getting paler by the second."

As Edward stated this, I felt myself start to sway. Anne noticed, too, and put her arm around me for support.

"Well then, let's get her inside. Besides, I think it best we all be seated."

Anne said this while looking over her shoulder at John apprehensively. John was only a few feet away, increasing the anxiety I currently had. Anne, I felt, deliberately situated me between her and Edward as we walked into the large house. A man, who I supposed was George, walked on the other side of her. John trailed behind, looking rather irritated, even disgruntled.

We entered the manor house from a side door and traveled through a small stone hallway illuminated by candles in large sconces along the wall. We turned and walked through another much larger and brighter hallway before entering what I imagined must be the drawing room. It was, indeed, a very fine room. There were several large pieces of furniture. The sofa was made of dark mahogany and upholstered with what my grandmother would have called a "dusty rose" color. The chairs were also of dark mahogany and styled in the same floral design. The stately furniture could have been right out of a museum, for all I knew, except it looked new and in its prime. On the far wall there was a large, splendid fireplace, alive with flame and heat; the crackling sounds were a small comfort.

"Take a seat here, dear, and wrap this around you."

Anne situated me on the love seat near the fireplace and then wrapped a soft, woolen blanket around my shoulders. I was grateful as the temperature was several degrees cooler than earlier that day and the blanket allowed some coverage as it was obvious I was underdressed compared to the others.

"Thank you." I said.

I received a small, reassuring pat on the shoulder from Anne. I watched her walk over to a table and ring a bell. Within a minute, someone I imagined must be a servant came in and took an order from Anne. She then came and took the spot next to me on the love seat, once again offering some comfort.

"I will tend to your hand, and then we will have some hot negus soon. That will warm you and perhaps lift your spirits a little."

Anne had a friendly smile, and it was pleasant that she cared how I felt as I had done nothing to earn her kindness. I had no idea what hot negus was, but I was not going to admit that. I had enough peculiarities working against me.

"Thank you, Anne."

With a squeeze of my right hand, Anne and I turned our attention to the men in the room. The three gentlemen stood by the opposite wall near the window. Edward and John were about the same height: both tall and slender, yet athletic in stature. Edward's chest was broader than John's, and though he had been kind, his aspect appeared moody. I noticed that he had a natural frown, as though his features were regularly lost in thought. John, in comparison, was fair and blond, light eyed, and distrustfully handsome, more so than I recalled from earlier in the day. Even though John looked to be in an ill mood himself, his youthful appearance spared him the habitual look of melancholy that Edward shared. I pondered the idea that John might have lived a less taxing life than Edward. The third gentleman, Anne's husband George, was a friendly-looking man. George was not so handsome as Edward or John, but not unattractive either. He had smooth cherub-like cheeks, wispy brown hair, and the same long sideburns as Edward. George was a couple of inches shorter than Edward and John, and slightly rounder around the middle.

Edward was leaning on the wall with one foot set against it, his arms folded into himself. His dark eyes were cast down at the floor as he listened to the conversation between the other two men. While they were not whispering, they were certainly speaking low. Straining to hear, I overheard a curse word or two, "the future," "younger, much younger," "hateful and careless man"—the last was spoken by George. The next speaker was John, and these words were audible enough for us all.

"Say what you will, but I do not owe anyone here any further explanation than what I have already stated." John then turned his attention to me. "Come, Vale, we are going!"

With that exclamation, all eyes looked towards me. A wave of fear and dread coursed through my body, and I involuntarily grabbed Anne's hand. Anne took my hand in hers, and she gently wrapped her free arm around me in a defensive position.

"You are not taking this girl anywhere."

Anne stated this with such resolve and such calm, matter-of-fact speech that for a moment my fear subsided. Though Edward did not look so calm, his voice was checked as he spoke.

"You, John, are most welcome to take your leave immediately, if you will. As it is, your presence now and as always is like poison: destructive and foul. But please, rest assure—Miss Leifman is not now or ever taking leave with you. Let this young lady here become absent from your mind upon leaving this place."

Edward stated these words with such authority and conviction that I found myself incredulous when John continued to argue about my going with him. With a curious look, John turned the conversation to include me.

"Miss Leifman, is it? Using your maiden name already?"

My cheeks were on fire; I felt dishonest, though I was not intentionally so. Edward and George shared the same quizzical look.

Edward spoke first. "Maiden name? She appears far too young to already be a widow."

This statement was made about me and not actually directed towards me for an explanation, so I gave none. I was already at a loss for words. I did not know enough about my current situation to enlighten anyone else.

Before any more conversation could commence, a young servant came into the room with a tray of what I assumed must be the previously mentioned hot negus and a bowl of water with some cut rags. The girl wore a plain dress with a white apron and a white bonnet on her head. She could not have been more than twenty. Quickly and quietly, the servant handed Anne and me our cups. We thanked her, but before she could make her way over to the gentlemen, Edward dismissed her.

Anne quickly tended my hand. Once cleaned, I could see that the cut wasn't deep, and would probably heal neatly if wrapped properly. Anne was no nurse, but my grandmother had been. I was able to guide her through the process. Though still sore, I was glad it was wrapped tightly and no longer an exposed wound. I thanked Anne, who then insisted I take a drink. I did and was pleasantly surprised by the taste and comfort of having a warm drink in my hands. I had been cold since I arrived at the estate. Edward's jacket, the blanket, and fire were immensely helpful, but a warm drink brought a sense of comfort that one usually feels at home. Having the friendly Anne next to me aided in this feeling. The hot negus had a hint of lemon and fine wine. This lovely moment of comfort was short lived as the conversation was continued by John, who stared directly at me.

"No, she is not a widow. In fact, her husband is yet to be born. You recall him, yes, *Miss Leifman?*"

I struggled to understand his tone. To my knowledge, I had done nothing to cause offense, yet he seemed to hold me in contempt. My own feelings of contempt were mounting. I began to feel the injustice of my situation. I was innocent of any wrongdoing towards John Emberley, and here in a room full of strangers, with no straightforward explanation of anything that had happened, he continued to cause me embarrassment. I had always hated being the center of attention, so I checked my growing anger and resolved to keep my naturally reserved and modest temperament; at least while I had an unfamiliar audience. While I ruminated over these thoughts, I continued to stare back directly at John.

"I supposed you would be proud."

As John stated this inaccurate fact, he turned back towards Edward and George; I noticed neither gentleman bothered to be discreet in their looks of disdain for him. John was unaffected.

"Miss Leifman here is not too young to be a widow, at least that was the case a little while ago. As you see now, she cannot be over twenty."

"Not so many years as that," Edward interjected.

Meanwhile, I grew more bewildered and anxious with each passing moment.

"No, perhaps not," John retorted.

"What are you getting at? Speak directly." Edward was demanding answers that I also wished for.

"What I am saying is that this girl, Miss Leifman, as she is, is much younger than she was when I made her acquaintance earlier today, in her own time."

*Her own time.* My heart and stomach both sank deeply as fear and despair set in. Those three words confirmed what I had already known to be true. How it could be so, I had no clue, but I knew enough of history and the past to be fairly confident that I was no longer in the twenty-first century. I believed I must be in the nineteenth, but could not confirm the year without asking, which I was not ready to do. Yet I could feel it was; when I awakened on the lawn, I inherently knew that the world felt different.

"How much younger?" It was Anne now who posed the question to John.

"Miss Leifman doesn't look quite twenty years younger; then again, she looked young to begin with. The people of her time are very good at retaining their youth, often by any means necessary. I cannot be sure of the exact number of years we lost."

My heart was racing. There was a ringing in my ears, and I felt nauseous. What was he implying? I knew I must have looked ill because I had the attention of all three men, though only two of them looked concerned. Even though I had no desire to be the center of attention, my resentment was now becoming greater than my shyness.

"What do you mean?" My voice was not as well controlled as the others. "What do you mean, *younger?*"

Despite my utter confusion about my situation, inwardly I knew something was different, and I had already taken note that my clothes were looser than they had been that morning. John did not immediately respond. With a couple of long strides, he made his way over to where an oval-shaped mirror framed with carved wood was hanging; there was a monogrammed "E" etched on the top piece. John removed the fine mirror and placed it directly in front of me. I saw Edward and George shift uncomfortably as John approached me, but I was far more concerned with the image staring back.

Humans have long yearned for the fountain of youth, to try to regain their younger appearance, always in vain. Sure, we can slow signs of aging, and we can certainly appear younger than our foremothers and forefathers by the care we take to protect our skin, but what appeared before my eyes was not the result of some well-injected toxin or expensive night cream.

The look upon my face might have been humorous had it not been for the shock and horror I felt within my soul. Unnatural!—I internally screamed. Though familiar in every way, I was staring back at a face that was altered from what it had been that very morning. John had been correct, I had looked young for my age; between the precautions of my generation and my mother's good genes, I was often mistaken for around twenty-five; even then, I did not look *this* young. I very specifically remembered looking at the soft fine lines that were just beginning in the corners of my eyes; probably only noticeable to myself, but they were there. Not now, however—now my former self was looking back at me. No wonder Edward had thought I looked too young to be a widow. I could not be sure of my age. Somewhere between seventeen and twenty would be my guess. My cheeks were still full, as always, but my face seemed generally smaller, the small crease in my forehead had ceased to exist, and that random gray hair I debated plucking was yet to be born.

The changes to my face, though, were far less prominent than the ones to my body. First, I looked at my hands. Almost childlike they now appeared; they were smooth and supple, even my palms had fewer lines. My newly young hands made their way to my mid-section, which this morning had been a little softer, the hips slightly wider. My hands were naturally heading upwards to explore more when I remembered that I was not alone; I then returned them to the cup of hot negus. I was intrigued, horrified, and humiliated. I sat there for a moment, speechless, before telling John I had seen enough.

Once the mirror was removed from my view, I was grateful that I had stopped my hands from further exploration as I had an audience watching me.

"It is true, then? You see a younger version of yourself?" Edward asked me directly.

"Yes—I do," I replied, still suffering the shock.

"What was the purpose, Mr. Emberley? What did you hope to gain by restoring her youth?" George asked in disbelief.

"Gain?" John stated, loud and obnoxious. "I had naught to gain. I could not have known."

"But you yourself claim to have brought her here from the future," Edward pursued.

"Yes, that I did. And for a purpose that has nothing to do with any of you. Yet you keep me here."

John took the amulet out of his pocket, looked at it, and shoved it back in. I noticed it seemed dull now, the color no longer a soft purple but more of an opal. Seeing it again caused my heart to flutter.

"I will have to ask another about her age. I will give you

answers later." John directed his last sentence to me alone. I was too astonished to reply.

Seeing I was troubled, George asked gently, "Do you have any idea of your age, Miss Leifman?"

I thought for a moment. My mind still said thirty-six. I went to shake my head no. Then it occurred to me that right before my eighteenth birthday, I had burned my inner left forearm reaching over a hot curling iron. I turned my left arm, and sure enough there was the light pink scar. The wound had healed, but the scar tissue was still pink and ever so tender as I touched it. I looked towards my new friend, Anne (for so I claimed her in my nervous mind) and asked for the date.

"It is the fourth of April, Easter Sunday," was her response.

Anne searched my face while I pondered my thoughts. I could not bring myself to ask her for the year.

As I turned my arm for Anne to see, I stated, "Then I must be about eighteen. I received this small burn a few days before my eighteenth birthday, which would have been in March. It's still tender."

I felt it a minor victory to have worked that out when John abruptly extended his hand to me.

"Come, Vale, it's time we go. I have had enough of Avenhurst with its gloom and forsaken master."

I regarded him in disbelief.

"Are you mad?" Edward questioned, his dark eyes dangerous and violent. "Do you truly believe we are going to let you walk out of here with this girl, especially after all you have inflicted upon her?"

"This is none of your concern, man. You are still so *exceedingly* arrogant. You imagine that at the snap of your fingers, all will follow your orders. I brought her here, and with me she will go!"

I had had enough of John Emberley. He was hostile and heartless, and I was in no way consenting to go with him.

My voice was shaky, but as stern as I could command it to be, I stated, "I'm not going anywhere with you. I don't even know you, except that you have been cruel, hateful, and violent with me! I don't know what I could have done to you, but I will never choose to be alone with you again!"

Had I not been so irate and on the edge of passion, I might have been terrified at the look of rage that entered John's light eyes. Mentally, I damned him to Hell while outwardly, I attempted to regain the false calm I had been portraying.

For the second time that day, I felt true terror at the hands of John Emberley. Without another word, the man suddenly lunged forward and grabbed onto me, taking hold of each one of my arms, and pulled me from the love seat into a standing position. It happened in a moment, but George and Edward overtook John. They had been on their guard; the former struck him squarely in the face, and the latter caught him as he lost his balance and then used the opportunity to strike him once or twice more. Neither gentleman persisted in continuing the assault. Once they had put John in his place, the fight ceased. Between being grabbed by John and the ensuing physical altercation, I felt overwhelmed with anxiety. I looked towards Anne to see if she shared my shaken nerves, and she was indeed paler than before. I gently placed my hand on her shoulder and asked if she was all right.

Anne's own hand overlapped mine as she replied, "Yes, dear. I am fine—but we have company."

I followed Anne's eyes to the window. All three men had regained their composure. Edward and George were nursing their right hands, while John was wiping blood from his nose and mouth with a handkerchief; all three noticed the shift in our deportment and turned towards the window as well. The sun was swiftly setting, and dark rain clouds covered the sky, but the objects of our attention were the three women walking up the cobblestone pathway to the manor house. Two of the women looked to be midway between thirty and forty; the seemingly younger of the two had a head of bountiful blonde ringlets. They walked alongside an elderly woman, possibly their grandmother, who was a good deal shorter than her companions. The blonde woman was dressed in a similar fashion to Anne. Her dress was less refined, but not unattractive, just more colorful. The other two women wore skirts and buttoned blouses, with bold kerchiefs tied in their hair. It was a familiar look, one I had seen exploited by others in my time.

I did not know what to think of the scene before me, but seeing Anne pale and Edward with a look of antipathy upon his face, my feelings began to falter, then quickly turn into dread as I noticed John Emberley's glower turn into a smug smile.

**Gheata**

# CHAPTER 4

The large fire burning in the elegant fireplace cast its warm glow over the three additional faces in the drawing room. One of the servants who had come into the room to light the candles quickly stepped out with a bewildered look upon her face; the same look the doorman had when he informed Edward of the newly arrived company. The women were seated across from Anne and me. Edward had taken a seat in one of the mahogany chairs on my left near the fireplace, and George on Anne's right. John was still standing, in a rather cheerful manner despite his bruised face and lip; he remained near the three ladies. My anxiety was rising, and I could feel my right leg trembling. I felt Anne place her hand on my knee.

"Steady now, do not let them see that you are nervous." Her attempted whisper was unsuccessful as this drew a comment from the youngest of the three ladies.

"Miss Leifman need not fear us." Her kind green eyes were sincere and friendly as they turned towards me. "My mother here—Eldria—has been looking forward to meeting you. It was never a surety that you would come, but it seems it was meant to be, after all."

I wasn't sure how to take these comments. I wondered why they were here for me and how she knew my name. My eyes turned towards her mother, whom I had been previously sure was her grandmother. The older woman had a soft face, not too different from the blonde woman except that it was much more weather worn, with deep lines in the corners of her eyes and her lips. The old mother stayed quiet. The third woman, who I supposed to be the older daughter, didn't share the kind, soft face of her family; hers was haughty and proud, and her dark, piercing brown eyes never stopped gazing in my direction. I wanted to ask her what her problem was but thought that would be unwise.

"She's not much to look at, is she?" the lovely lady commented. "She barely has any bosom, and she's rather thin."

I felt my cheeks burn and heat fill my chest, more from embarrassment than from anger. I was far too emotionally exhausted to be angry over someone whom I didn't know insulting me, but not too tired to be embarrassed in front of seven strangers about my small bosom! I didn't dare look in the direction of the men and was spared further insults by the younger lady speaking up against her.

"Emilia, keep your crude remarks to yourself, if you will. You needn't have come if you intend to be meanspirited. Miss Leifman, I do apologize for my sister's comments."

"Please do not apologize on my behalf, Gildi, and my place is here with John. Long have I waited for his return."

As Emilia said this, she got up and John placed one arm around her. My cheeks stopped burning and my embarrassment turned into disgust. *Well, they definitely deserve each other, the horrid little couple,* I thought. I wanted to tell her that she had greasy hair, but now was not the time to be petty with insults, and I was sure she could be a lot meaner than I. Emilia was beautiful, though. She had fine dark eyes and raven hair. Oily as it was at the moment, the color complimented her fair skin. Her eyebrows were naturally shaped, a look that women of my time continuously sought. The fine lines near her eyes were there, though no smile graced her face. In the light, I believed I saw a few glimmers of gray hairs mixed within the raven tresses. Emilia had one of those irritating faces—when someone is much prettier than they deserve to be, much like her lover John.

Emilia continued, "And perhaps you needn't have come, Gildi. This girl is none of your concern, nor mother's. John brought her here, and you are all just wasting his time."

I was wrong. I did, in fact, have enough energy to become angry. It was difficult, as I was trying to stay composed for Anne, Edward, and George; I knew if I was too spirited, it could frighten them and make them doubt the kind of person I was, and I needed their help. I felt I already had so much working against me, so I swallowed my pride once more. As I controlled my emotions, the old woman began speaking to Gildi in a language I didn't understand, but it was the second time I had heard it that day. The language had a familiar sound, perhaps Latin, I guessed, but I couldn't speculate on what she was saying, and I didn't need to as Gildi was her translator. Gildi and Emilia were both solemn as they listened. Gildi, it seemed, was the elected speaker on her mother's behalf—a just choice, I surmised.

"My mother wishes to express her gratitude to you, Mr. Emberley, for seeing us tonight with such short notice; due to the circumstances of our visit, she hopes you will excuse our intruding on your evening."

I was momentarily puzzled. Gildi spoke of Mr. Emberley, yet her eye contact was with Edward, not John. Edward gave a small, polite smile and accepted her niceties.

"Of course, Miss Gildi. I am pleased you and your mother have come. Perhaps one of you will be able to give us some explanation of today's events as my cousin John has not been so forthcoming."

I had not realized they were cousins. I wondered why Edward did not tell me at our first meeting when he introduced himself. Gildi's mother began to speak again, and while the language was foreign and meant for Gildi to translate, this older woman looked at me as she spoke.

"Yes—my mother hopes to provide some clarity and perhaps even some comfort, especially for Miss Leifman." Gildi turned and spoke to me directly. "She would like for me to tell you that she sees the pain and fear you are battling within." Gildi paused as her mother continued. "You are anxious and desire some explanations of your purpose here. Yes?"

I nodded in agreement.

"While she may not have the answer to all of your questions, at least not tonight, she hopes to give you enough so that you may have some peace of heart."

This gave me a little feeling of hope.

"Mother also says to tell you that all will be well—what was lost has been restored—the innocent will no longer pay for the sins of the father. I suppose that makes but little sense to you, however."

She supposed correctly. While I certainly appreciated their efforts in clarifying my concerns, her last statement sounded more like a riddle. I looked around the room to observe the others' reactions. Edward had a concentrated look upon what had been a solemn face. He was giving me the same look he had when he first saw me; almost wonder. Anne shared a similar look of wonder yet she seemed a bit more animated, and once again she squeezed my hand. Meanwhile, John and Emilia both seemed to have had their feathers ruffled, as my grandmother would say. Emilia was whispering in John's ear, his scowl only deepening.

"I am sorry, Miss Gildi. I do appreciate all you have said

regarding my feelings, and you and your mother are certainly right." Unhappily, I felt the tears burning in my eyes, but I couldn't stop now. "I don't doubt for a second that my father was a sinner—believe that—but what does that have anything to do with today? Why am I here and how did Mr. Emberley manage all of this? And why, what was the purpose? Besides, I was not lost; I meant to go to the cemetery today!"

All the emotions I had been fighting overwhelmed my frame. I sobbed, too distressed to be ashamed. I wanted to go home. I wanted to be back there with my babies; I knew they had to be missing me as well. I felt so much guilt. They would wonder why momma was gone; they would question why she had missed Easter. I felt almost nauseous for a moment. Suddenly I could feel Anne begin to gently rub my upper back to console me, and it did. I was able to compose myself rather quickly. I had another handkerchief in my hand, but I wasn't even sure who had handed it to me. I looked at Gildi through blurred eyes. She had a deep, compassionate aspect about her.

Gildi shared a small, soft smile. "Of course, you do not understand. How could you? We are not speaking of the sins of your father from your time, dear, but the sins of the Emberleys. Specifically, Mr. William Emberley, whose inequity was so great to my family that a curse was placed upon his family by my grandmother. You, perhaps, have been most affected by this curse, though you could not know it. My mother believes that once you understand, you will see how love can be restored."

Gildi had the full attention of the room. My own sniffles were stilled, and I, along with the rest, were ready to hear what Gildi and her mother had come to say.

"This story, your story—in fact, our story, all that are present here tonight—began almost fifty years ago. The impact of those events was just as significant to my family as they were to yours, and because of that, it has been with us all this time. You see, my mother was there when it began. My grandmother, Claudia, who was once full of goodness and altogether lovely, made sure we knew what transpired as a way to protect us from the charms of men, especially the powerful and rich, but also to remind us of who we were, or who she thought we should be. My mother did not dare attempt to stop her from telling my sister and me, but she has always believed in forgiveness, and so she has used these events to show us how powerful forgiveness and love can be."

Both Gildi and her mother seemed to project peace. I was almost ashamed of how nervous I initially was. Then I looked at Emilia, and wished I hadn't. If looks could kill…

"At the end of the last century, Mr. William Emberley, grandfather to the present Emberleys in this room, Edward, Anne, and John, lost his beloved wife. Mother says every servant in Avenhurst and the surrounding area grieved for Mr. Emberley over the loss of his Catherine as his pain was evident to all. Catherine Emberley was his great love, and together they had three children: Master James, Master Thomas, and Miss Eleanor, the girl being the youngest child. It seems it was no secret that Masters James and Thomas were not friends, not the way brothers ought to be. Mr. Emberley, the father, did not wish to divide his wealth, as most was held in Avenhurst, so it was arranged for his second son, Mr. Thomas, to become a clergyman, with a parsonage near the estate. Mr. Thomas was not happy and resented his brother and father; however, they all shared in their adoration of little Eleanor. During the year 1800, the fates of our two families were intertwined in a most, as these fine people may call it, indecorous way. Mr. Emberley became infatuated with my mother's older sister, Maria, who was very spirited and beautiful. My grandmother, Claudia, along with my mother and Aunt Maria, lived at a nearby cottage, about a mile from Avenhurst Manor. It was not long before infatuation turned to desire and, in turn, Maria found herself quite enchanted by Mr. Emberley. Claudia tried in vain to stop Maria; she warned her that a gentleman of Mr. Emberley's rank and wealth would never marry her. Alas, Maria declared that she loved Mr. Emberley and believed that he felt the same. Maria was but eighteen, young and naïve, and Mr. Emberley was older, stately, and handsome. It was only a matter of time before Claudia found Maria to be his mistress.

"Much to my grandmother's dismay, Maria was soon with child. Claudia took it upon herself to plead with Mr. Emberley. She begged him to marry her daughter and make Maria and their child, her grandchild, legitimate. Mr. Emberley requested to see Maria that same day. My mother here recalls how anxious Claudia was, as she waited for Maria's return from the manor. Maria did return; she walked into the cottage, dripping from the rain that had plagued the skies that day. She said not a word and went to her and my mother's room silently. They wondered, why would Mr. Emberley send her back without a carriage, the mother of his unborn child? My grandmother found Maria sobbing, holding onto an opened envelope, stamped with the Emberley seal. According to my mother, her sobs were so deep and desperate that it was hard to distinguish between Maria and the wind during the storm. After a time, Maria told my grandmother that upon seeing Mr. Emberley at the entrance to Avenhurst, he had denied her any further access to the estate. He then denied the child was his and stated he would not further degrade his children and his Catherine's memory by marrying a *gypsy*. Mr. Emberley gave my aunt an envelope with some money and told her she should leave Yorkshire.

"As you may imagine, Miss Leifman, my grandmother was disgusted, but Claudia had expected no less from a gentleman of his rank and supposed superiority. The same could not be said for Maria, who was disappointed and heartbroken; both her mother and sister attempted to provide some comfort. The three made plans to move to Edinburgh, a busier town where Maria could start anew and away from the charms of English men. Maria agreed and seemed at peace with their plan. The only request she made was to sleep alone that night so she could finish her tears in private. This was a grievous error that neither my grandmother nor mother ever forgave themselves for. When they went to wake Maria in the morning, they found she had hanged herself during the night. Claudia took Maria down by herself. She wouldn't allow Mother to help or retrieve anyone. For the next several hours, she rocked her firstborn like she was a toddler and wept bitterly for her and the grandchild she would never see. Our family was altered that day. My mother here has seldom spoken English since Maria's death. My grandmother, though, she was changed completely. The magnitude of her grief had awakened the power she was gifted at birth, the same power she had fled from with her daughters.

"Claudia had been good. She wanted natural, happy lives for her children, and she roamed the kingdom to protect them—now she grieved that she had led one of them straight to her doom. It had been about a week since the cold autumn day that Maria was put into the ground when Claudia and my mother were walking back to the cottage from town. Along the way, they saw the three Emberley children in their fine clothes, each on their own horse, enjoying a day of riding despite the overcast sky. Claudia watched the young men for a moment. They were handsome like their father—tall, with dark eyes and hair, but it was the youngest Emberley, Miss Eleanor, that she found herself fixated on. It had been common knowledge that this young lady was the favorite Emberley, favored by all but especially by their father, for she was a reflection of her mother's image, with long, golden hair in ringlets and fine brown eyes. She was small and dainty—like a bird.

"Claudia, who was a sibyl and now open to her gifts, allowed herself to see this child's future. Claudia saw the girl blossom into a beautiful lady, she saw a fine marriage—her father would be pleased—then she saw a baby, a daughter. Claudia could not stop the anger that was mounting within her. The female child would also grow beautiful and was also destined to love an Emberley. This baby would marry her cousin, the male heir to Avenhurst. In just a few moments, Claudia saw it all: the injustice of losing her first born and what would have been her first-born grandchild, also an Emberley by birthright. As Claudia ruminated over her dark thoughts, suddenly Miss Emberley dismounted her horse to retrieve her bonnet. Claudia approached; she offered the child a flower. The young men hissed at her to leave, but Miss Emberley gladly went to Claudia to accept the flower. Once within reach, Claudia placed her hand upon Miss Emberley's head, spoke the enchantment, handed her the flower, and released her. Miss Eleanor was a little surprised, but otherwise unharmed; the child said her thanks and ran back to her brothers.

"Master James and Thomas witnessed the interaction but made no comment, and the three Emberley children rode back towards Avenhurst. Claudia and my mother walked home in silence. My mother remained outwardly calm, but internally she feared that her mother had just damned her soul. They had rarely practiced their gifts and never intentionally harmed another soul. My mother did not ask Claudia what had transpired between her and Miss Eleanor, but she would soon be made aware. Late that evening, a loud knock awakened my mother. Claudia had been sitting at the table and had not moved in hours; she had been waiting. It was Mr. Emberley. Claudia gladly welcomed him into her home. He, however, refused to enter.

"'My sons, they saw you lay your hands upon my daughter's head. Eleanor says you muttered something in another language as well. I attempted to repress thoughts of the evil you might have imposed until I heard my daughter scream. I found her sobbing in her room, her little finch dead in its cage. Eleanor swears her little bird was happily chirping until she placed a pretty flower in its cage. The bird was dead before her little hand could fasten the lock on the cage.'

"Mother remembers that despite the fury in his voice, you could see the fear in Mr. Emberley's eyes.

"'Tell me, Madam, what have you done? What did you say when you touched my daughter?'

"This was exactly the reaction my grandmother wanted, and she explained with a song in her heart.

"'I saw your happy children; I saw the beautiful life that awaited your daughter. I saw her pretty babe, the beautiful little girl she would raise, and I saw the happy union between your future grandchildren, your son's heir, and your favorite child's daughter. I could see it all. The Emberley legacy would strengthen, and you would die having everything you ever wanted. And then I saw my Maria, my most beloved daughter, and her unborn child cold in the ground. I asked you to do what was right by the girl who *loved* you, and you *abandoned* her, you *shamed* her, and ultimately *cursed* her life. When I saw your children and your children's children, I knew I must repay the kindness you bestowed upon mine. Little Eleanor was more than willing to accept her gift. The little darling is used to nice things. Since Maria's legacy is not to be, then neither shall Eleanor's. To prevent the union of your grandchildren, I have made Eleanor barren; she will never have children. Eleanor did not lose just one little bird today. Your heir's heir will also go through his life without his love, without his little bird. A generational curse as grand as the Emberley name and as plagued as the grounds of Avenhurst I have bestowed upon you.'

"Mr. Emberley stood horrified, but silent; he left without saying a word. After that night he avoided our family, and the Emberley children never came near the cottage again."

The room would have remained in complete silence if it had not been for the crackling coming from the hearth. The flicker of the light from the fire cast shadows across Eldria's face; I could see she had shed some tears. It was a difficult story to hear, and it was hard to look at the current Emberleys or the Gheatas and be unaffected. My heart had been aching for my own family all day, but now it ached for those present as well. I did not know who I hurt for more, Maria or Eleanor. Both deserved better than they received. Though I would not say it out loud, I could not help but think that Claudia Gheata was no better than Mr. William Emberley in the end. The story had disturbed me; I needed to know more. I turned to Anne.

"Have you heard this story before? Is it known to you as well?" I needed to substantiate what I could, and I was most comfortable asking her.

"Yes, darling, I know the story well, as does Edward. I first overheard it told as a myth of Avenhurst when I was a child. Servants love ghost stories, you know. It is true that my father loved Aunt Eleanor with a great depth, and that he did believe her to be cursed."

Anne's voice was somber; I sensed she was choosing her words carefully.

"Your father was only capable of loving himself, just like his father before him," John interjected bitterly.

"Well, his father was also your grandfather, and if anyone lacks the ability to love, it would be you," Anne retorted, her emotions visibly rising.

Anne struck me as someone who was usually very in control.

"It is the same with all of you, arrogant and self-righteous…" John was about to go tit-for-tat with Anne when Edward put an abrupt end to it.

"That is enough. Anne, you need not engage John. It will only encourage his ill temperament."

A small look of irritation crossed Anne's sweet face, but she obeyed. I held her hand. It was all I had to offer her, and she gently squeezed it.

"Miss Gildi, I am all too familiar with my family's unfortunate story, and I am most sorry to hear by your own personal account how it has affected yours. I really am. Please tell us, how does all this affect Miss Leifman?"

Edward was direct, yet not cold; I could see he was used to being in charge. There was a certain level of agitation in his countenance that I observed. He was leaning forward, not fidgeting, yet I knew he was not relaxed; his dark hair kept falling into his face and he would brush it back habitually. After a thoughtful pause, Miss Gildi responded.

"It is as I said, Mr. Emberley. For Miss Leifman to understand why she is here, she needed to know what had transpired before." Miss Gildi turned towards me and took both my hands into hers. "My mother is gifted as well, and after Maria's death, she learned her craft. For reasons of her own, she lifted the curse."

I was perplexed. "Lifted the curse? How? Eleanor has since passed, hasn't she?"

I looked towards Anne and Edward for confirmation: the way they had spoken of her, I had assumed. They both nodded their heads in unison.

"Yes, Miss Leifman, she did pass, but that doesn't change the fact that my mother did release the curse several years ago. That is why John was able to bring you here today." Gildi spoke as if she had given me the last piece of the puzzle—far from it.

"All right"—*How do I proceed politely* —"your mother ended the Emberley curse. That was quite kind, but what does all of this have to do with me?"

I tried my best not to sound impolite. I really did feel bad for both families, but I was nowhere nearer to understanding what had happened earlier than I was before. Miss Gildi's large green eyes were animated and an incredulous smile crossed her face. *Surely, I must be dense,* I thought.

"Miss Leifman—Vale." She paused. "*You* are Eleanor's little bird! You are the child she would have had."

I was sincerely at a loss for words.

I looked at Anne, who upon making eye contact with me stated, "I knew it must be so. You resemble her so much, and with all that happened, I think it must be true. Do you think so as well, Edward?"

Anne seemed elated now, but Edward was emotionless. I knew there was a mistake, and Edward's reaction validated this thought.

"I think there has been a mistake, Miss Gildi. I think you have the wrong person." I tried to let her down easy, but she was quick to reply.

"No, Miss Leifman." She almost chuckled. "We have not got the wrong person. You could not have come otherwise. I know it is quite a bit to accept right now, but it is the truth. You belong here."

I could only shake my head. It was all so ridiculous to me. How could all of this be? I had a life, a childhood, memories—for God's sake, I was a nineties kid who watched Nickelodeon and ate Gushers. I looked to Edward for support, to back up my argument more eloquently than I could. Edward was looking directly at me, like he was seeing me for the first time; he no longer looked emotionless. I blushed deeply in remembrance of Gildi's story, which implied that I was his predestined life partner.

Desperate for any conversation, I engaged Gildi again.

"How was the curse reversed, and how was your mother able to do that? Did she help John bring me here?"

I caught John's eye as I said his name. He smiled in a way that was more disturbing than his glares. Eldria began to speak to Gildi, whose blonde ringlets bounced as she nodded, listening.

"My mother will only remark on this. Eighteen years ago, she crossed paths with Mr. Emberley here." She directed her gaze towards Edward. "Another event between our families had transpired—an event she was quite unhappy with. Upon meeting Mr. Emberley in town, mother recited the *anahex* to remove the curse. It was done similarly to the curse itself."

Eldria whispered in Gildi's ear, who then held Edward's gaze. "She asks if you still have it?"

Edward took a moment, maybe to guess at her meaning,

then reached inside his coat pocket; he didn't withdraw whatever it was.

"Yes, I still have it," was his only reply.

Eldria seemed pleased; she smiled and grunted in pleasure. Edward glanced at me again. I could tell he understood; I did not share in this enlightenment.

"What is an *anahex*? Is that a spell?" I asked.

"Yes. Even with our gifts, good or bad, there are certain rules. One of them being balance. For every curse or hex, if you want to call it that, there must be an *anahex*, or a way to reverse it; otherwise the curse will not work. All our spells must be balanced. It does not mean that the *anahex* will be used, I should say, but it must exist."

I pondered this. Eldria whispered to Gildi again.

"Mother feels it is time we part, at least for now, Miss Leifman. She wishes you well, all of you."

"Wait! There's so much you didn't explain! And besides that—how do I go back? I must go back; I'm not trying to be rude. I have—"

I stopped; I knew my voice would fail me. I could feel the texture of the flower on my locket as I traced it. The pleased look on Gildi's face was replaced with a look of true pity. I dreaded her words.

"I am sorry, Miss Leifman. You cannot go back—not to the time you left. When John brought you here, the *anahex* reversed time before allowing you two to be fixed here in this time. Do you know how old you are?"

I was numb. "I believe eighteen."

"Yes—that makes sense."

I looked at her like she had gone mad.

"It's been eighteen years since Mother completed the *anahex*," she continued.

I guessed that was meant to provide more clarity.

"In what year did you turn eighteen?"

Gildi's question threw me for a second. None of us had discussed actual years; it felt like the elephant in the room.

With a deep breath, I whispered, "2003."

I felt the warmth creep into my chest, then my cheeks as I heard hushed sounds of surprise come from the others.

"You cannot return to your time." Gildi responded. "Your soul belongs to the present century, which is why our magic allowed John to seek you. And every year you lived past 2003 no longer exists."

The floor grew closer. I was hot all over. I felt several hands grab both my arms and sit me back on the sofa. I had not realized I had been standing. I could feel my pulse begin to race, it was difficult to breathe, and hot tears spilt from my eyes helplessly. Anne rubbed my back, whispering gentle comments in my ear, though I couldn't comprehend them as my ears were ringing. Gildi came to where I was sitting and knelt in front of me.

"Please don't despair. I know you want more answers, and in time you will have them." She patted my shoulder. "You are home now."

I was not comforted, and my eyes continued to burn.

"She is not home, Gildi. She is to come with us," John projected, still determined in his plan with regards to me.

Before I could object, Eldria spoke. Though I knew not what she said, it was enough for Emilia to hush John and gain his compliance.

"We will all go," stated Gildi. "Thank you, Mr. Emberley, for taking your time to speak with us, all of you. Miss Leifman, we *will* speak again."

Gildi gave a small curtsy, as did her mother, while John

stormed out indecorously with Emilia by his side. It was just the four of us once more.

A Wife No More

# CHAPTER 5

As I heard the large front door close behind John Emberley and the three women, my eyes, which had grown tired, rested on Anne's equally exhausted face. Anne, with her gentle way, had come and encircled my arm in hers to lead me out of the drawing room. I intentionally avoided making any eye contact with the two remaining gentlemen; I was far too aware of what Gildi had said when she referred to me as Eleanor's little bird, and what that future had looked like. As I went to walk with Anne, I suddenly felt very warm again. The familiar warmth encompassed my whole body. I believe I attempted to steady myself on the sofa, but with a sudden intense pressure in my head, all went black.

"Quickly Anne, try the salts once more," I heard a muffled, concerned voice state. "There she is. Easy now."

"Shh, there you are. Take a moment, darling."

I recognized Anne's voice as I came back to consciousness. It was not a dream. My head now ached with pain; it was all too much to bear. I felt hot tears streaming down my face, betraying the emotions I had unsuccessfully tried to hold back. Aiding me in my distress, Anne handed me a handkerchief and had me use the smelling salts once more. I was surprised at how well they revived me to my senses. With that revival, however, I became very conscious that someone was holding me, not in a complete embrace, but enough to keep my head off the ground. Anne became aware as I did, for her eyes moved from me to the one holding me. I looked up to see that it was Edward, and likely it was his voice I'd heard upon awakening. To my surprise, Anne was smiling. I looked at her quizzically, for I was not sure what could be humorous.

"What is it?" I asked, massaging my temple.

"Honestly, Vale, I am just surprised you didn't faint sooner. I certainly would have."

Anne gave a small laugh. At least one of us was not too traumatized. Edward ignored his sister's well-intentioned but ill-timed sense of humor.

"Do you feel you are recovered enough to stand, Vale?" Edward asked.

I nodded my head, anxious to recover from the embarrassment I'd caused myself. Gently, Edward lifted me up to where I could stand, making sure I was in no danger of fainting before handing me back to Anne.

"Come, Vale, you must rest for a while." And with that, Anne led me back down the long corridor, the flickering of the candlelight bouncing off the dark walls.

✦

Anne had led me to a large chamber room, as she called it, where a great fire lit up the space. I realized it was rather bright in this room when I noticed an oil lamp burning on the nightstand next to a very elegant four-poster bed. The bed had long, burgundy curtains pulled to each post; the same dark mahogany I'd seen in the drawing room. The bed was beautiful, with many pillows of various sizes cluttering the top of the comforter. Anne interrupted my tired thoughts on the furniture.

"Here is a nightgown you could use. Do you need help to undress?" she asked.

"No," I said, out of habit of refusing help. "I'm sure I can manage. Thank you, though."

Anne politely moved away to give me some privacy. As it was, I was wrong to refuse her help. My dress was difficult to put on, let alone take off, especially with my invalid hand. After two failed attempts, I called Anne back, and sheepishly apologized for bothering her.

"It is no bother at all. I never used to dress myself. It has only been recently that I have become more independent."

I was not sure which question to ask first—why she never dressed herself, or why was there a sudden change? I decided to ask both. Anne looked at me curiously.

"Do you not usually have help getting dressed, Vale?"

"No, I have always dressed myself."

"Did you keep a lady's maid? Is that not typical of your time? Or—was that not a priority to your husband?"

Anne spoke the last part rather carefully. I wasn't sure if it was because she was gently accusing him of being cheap, which would have been true regardless, or because she mentioned him at all.

"It's not typical of my time, Anne. I can't exactly say why. I guess I would have to think about that a while. People in my time—well, we don't usually have servants at all."

Anne's eyes widened. I couldn't help but give her a small smile.

"We do have housekeepers, and people that take care of our gardens," I continued. "At least for those who can afford it, but most people, including the well off, don't have servants who live in the home the way they do here."

"How do you manage it?" Anne asked sincerely. I didn't know how to respond properly. It was a genuine question, but I was mentally and physically exhausted, and even on a great day, that question was difficult to answer.

"Not always so well. Perhaps we can speak about it some more another day?"

Anne smiled and carried on with removing my dress. Dear reader, the look that graced Anne's face in that moment is forever etched into my mind. A look that at first startled me, I now think back to fondly, and not without a good laugh. In all my exhaustion, it did not occur to me that my underwear would be so extraordinary to Anne Ellis.

"My God! What are those garments that you are wearing?"

My bra and underwear, which were quite loose on me now, were completely foreign to my new friend.

"They're called underwear. A bra and panties, to be specific."

"Which is the bra and which are the panties?" she asked, half-bewildered and half-amused.

I explained which piece was what and the purpose of both pieces, and made what I felt was a solid defense of the modern-day woman's underwear.

Anne laughed. "Well, they are certainly pretty, but they look terribly uncomfortable."

Anne bit her lip, shook her head, and laughed again. Even in my exhausted state, I could still appreciate a woman's judgment of female undergarments. If only I had the energy to explain to Anne a century's worth of prejudice against the corset. As it was, I had a feeling I would be making my own judgment on that particular piece soon enough. After placing the soft, pretty white gown on me, Anne took my clothes and placed them in a drawer inside a wardrobe against the far-right wall of the room. She locked the door and told me we would keep them hidden there so no servant would come across them. I was grateful she was still able to think solidly.

"Rest a moment, Vale. I'm going to run to the kitchen and get us some supper. I know you must be famished. I certainly am." Before she stepped out, Anne addressed me again, "Vale, I meant to ask you before, which part of England are you from? Edward and George will need to know."

It took me a moment to understand why they would have that need, then it dawned on me that they would need to make up a story for my sudden appearance here at Avenhurst.

"I'm not from England, Anne. I'm from the United States."

Anne raised her eyebrows; she did not hide her emotions well. "That is quite a distance." I could hear the pity in her voice, but she didn't push. Before she let the door close, Anne added, "Also, I know you must be uncomfortable by now. You see that small door right there?" She pointed to one that looked fairly new, unlike much of the house I had seen so far. I nodded. "That's where the commode is kept. I'll soon be back."

I was uncomfortable to be sure, and had assumed I would be using an ugly metal chamber pot. I opened the door, and inside was the prettiest little commode I'd ever seen. It was—no surprise here—carved wood, though lighter than mahogany, and the inside was a decorated porcelain bowl with blue flowers. It actually resembled a little toilet, complete with a wooden lid. Feeling better, I made my way to the bed. As I was walking, I crossed a full-length mirror. For the first time since my arrival, I was free to look at myself without reserve. I could hardly believe who it was that I saw. Though I recognized the figure before me, I was nevertheless looking at a girl, not a woman—at least, not a woman to me. I touched my face again. It was surreal. Knowing Anne would be back at any time, I quickly pulled back my gown, careful not to injure my hand, so I could see myself fully. I didn't know what to think. It was like having one of those dreams where someone who is deceased is alive once again in your mind. You know they shouldn't be alive, but in your dream it just makes sense. This body of mine once existed, but two children had altered it, given it a few stretch marks, and softened my mid-section. I knew it to be a fact, but the little body reflected back at me was young, with no signs of carrying my darlings. I had always been small, even at thirty-six, but I had developed a womanly figure, small as it was. Guarding my sore hand, I quickly replaced the old-fashioned gown.

I went and lay in bed; Anne was taking longer than I had expected. I stared up at the ceiling, my mind all over the place. All day I had fought my true feelings, stifled my tears and sobs as best I could, not wanting to give too much of myself away. Now that I was alone, I could not cry. Nothing felt real. Perhaps it was the exhaustion, or maybe I was in shock. As I lay there, my children came right to my mind. I would probably be brushing their teeth right now, removing all the Easter candy they would have overindulged in. They would have been exhausted—they always were after a holiday.

✦

I woke up sometime during the night. It was completely dark, except for the glow from the embers burning low in the fireplace. It took a moment for my eyes to adjust and to recognize my surroundings: I lay there a moment, stunned this was my reality. I had to breathe deeply and slowly, trying to remember what I had once learnt of anxiety attacks. Fortunately, the breathing released some tension and, after a few minutes, my pulse slowed. I realized I wasn't alone in bed; the soft form of Anne was asleep next to me. I was grateful to have her there, for the beautiful room at night felt frightful. I had always loved old furniture and items from days gone by, but not as much in the middle of the night.

As I looked around, I noticed that the only bed-curtain that was pulled back was the one closest to the fireplace. It occurred to me that these curtains were probably not for aesthetics, like in my time, but helped keep the warm air in and cold air out. I crawled to the foot of the bed and pulled back the curtain to look around. It was pitch black in the rest of the room, where the firelight did not reach. Even the window was black. I assumed that the moon was covered by clouds, or it was not yet big enough to provide light. It was an odd feeling, knowing I couldn't get up and flip the light switch on. Solemnly, I crawled back to my spot next to Anne. My mind was awake for the moment.

I watched Anne sleep. She looked peaceful and like a little girl in her long nightgown and with her hair down. I wondered if George was upset that his wife was in here with me. I knew some men were less easygoing than others. I thought of my own husband. He had been furthest from my thoughts that day, though he had always dominated them previously. Despite everything that had happened in the past several hours, I could not bring myself to miss him. A thought occurred to me at that moment: I had struggled in vain to avoid the idea I was no longer a mother; it occurred to me I was also no longer a wife. I married my husband when I was twenty-five and, at eighteen, I was still a few years from even meeting him. Habitually, I went to twist my wedding ring—it was then I realized I'd lost it, most likely dropped during my struggle with John.

1847

# CHAPTER 6

If I thought of much else, I could hardly say what. The next time my mind was conscious, I was awakened by Anne and a servant having a discussion next to the bed. What I gathered from their conversation was that the servant, Margot, was ordered to draw a bath for her new young lady—I guessed that was me. Margot was also instructed to bring some tea and toast. When she made her exit, Anne approached.

"I'm sorry I took so long last night. When I came back, you were fast asleep. I felt awful about it because I knew you had to be hungry. Margot will bring some toast. That way you won't look so famished at the breakfast table."

When Anne mentioned the breakfast table, a strong feeling of dread came over me. The idea of sitting with strangers after such a day was the last thing I could see myself doing, and despite Anne's concerns, I was not famished. I had no appetite at all.

"Please don't be sorry, Anne. Honestly, I wasn't hungry. I'm still not. If you think it would be possible, I'd rather not go to breakfast. My head is aching and so is my hand." I looked away, unable to keep eye contact. "It's a lot, Anne."

Anne came and sat next to me on the bed; she took my bandaged hand in hers.

"Very well, Vale. I will make your apologies to the gentlemen. Let Margot help you to the bath and please eat the toast—for my sake. I will feel better excusing you if you promise to eat."

I agreed to the toast.

"Margot can also help with your headache. She has applied the vinegar to mine in the past, and it works well. Once you have bathed, I can come back and rewrap your hand."

Anne kept her place next to me but was quiet for a few moments, lost in thought, I imagined. Finally, she spoke.

"Vale, I understand you must be miserable right now. I—I know you probably miss your husband."

I looked at Anne. She blushed.

"Anne, it's not my husband I miss." I found myself running my fingers over my necklace again; Anne noticed too.

"A child?" Anne almost whispered this.

With a lump in my throat, I nodded. "Two. I have—had two. A son and a daughter." The tears I couldn't find last night found me now. I lay back down. "I will try to eat the toast."

◆

I did my best to keep my promise to Anne. I ate half of my toast and I drank the tea. After I kept my word to eat, I crawled back into bed and remained there for another couple of hours. Before she left me to my misery, Margot did indeed give me a vinegar compress for my head. I didn't enjoy the scent; however, it did work, and Margot seemed pleased to assist me. She was a kind enough girl, I thought, but timid and quiet; or perhaps it was me.

After what must have been deemed an adequate amount of time to wallow, she returned and prepared my bath. I was missing most of the products I was accustomed to using when I showered at home. I had soap though; for now, that would be enough. I had feared that a bath would be a once-a-month event, but I asked Margot in a roundabout way how often she was expected to draw my bath. The response was it would be drawn every other day, and she would prepare my toilette in between. I considered the prejudices my contemporaries had against Victorian bathing habits and, seeing how many times history is viewed with an incorrect lens, I realized I knew just enough of history to cause myself more harm than good. I decided I had to stay as open-minded as possible if I were to survive the nineteenth century. There were moments, though, when I was unsure if I wanted to survive.

Margot mentioned that Anne had instructed her not to dress me, that Anne would do it herself. The maid seemed a bit confused by Anne's request but stated that she would at least do my hair for me. On this point, Margot was especially gifted. The amiable maid seated me near the fire as she could see that I was easily chilled. I tried my best to refrain from shivering, but no matter how great a fire was burning, these large chamber rooms were drafty. My hair, still somewhat damp, was braided from one side of my head to the other, almost like a headband, while the rest was pulled back into a loose and delicate-looking bun. Margot explained that the hair always dried very nicely when braided and pulled back in this fashion. I had seen enough of the daguerreotypes, and Anne's hair, to know what I could have looked like. I thanked Margot, and as she walked out, Anne came in.

Anne smiled as she saw me.

"Now, you do look lovely with your hair back!"

I glanced in the mirror, more skeptical than not; I was used to wearing my hair down. The hair did look very pretty, but I felt my face needed the soft shield of loose hair to help it.

"Thank you. I usually prefer to wear it down, though."

"Ah, but wearing your hair pulled back shows you are a lady. It is clean and smooth on the sides, and pleated elegantly. That is indeed a nice touch—one I cannot do myself. Besides, why would you want to hide your lovely face? If I had one like yours, I would always make sure to show it off," Anne said with a playful smile.

"I don't know about all of that. I think I'm sort of plain."

I meant what I said. I didn't see myself as a great beauty, nor was I hideous; regardless, I definitely did not have Anne's enthusiasm.

"Plain?" Anne looked at me with an expression that told me she was uncertain whether I was joking or not. "If only I were as plain as you, then, Vale! You almost look like a porcelain doll."

Oddly enough, I agreed with her on this; however, I always thought those dolls plain, too, at least the ones I had as a child. I couldn't help but smile at my own inane thought. This encouraged Anne to continue.

"You have that nice, smooth, high-set forehead, not small and square like mine. Not to mention, you have dark eyebrows and lashes and fine eyes. I have never seen someone whose eyes are truly the color of the sea. They fade from green at the center to blue. Your cheeks are well-developed; a small, straight nose and a small, pretty mouth." Anne looked at me very seriously. "And your teeth, Vale—I am honestly not quite sure they are real. Are they?" I laughed a little at this. I would miss twenty-first century dental work perhaps more than twenty-first century plumbing, and that was saying something.

I responded, "They are very much mine, Anne. I have had

the good fortune of having a very skilled dentist since I was a young child."

"That is fortunate. I once had my tooth pulled at the barber. I have refused to go back ever since."

Anne proceeded to show me her missing tooth in the back of her mouth. She was lucky though. From what I could see, most of her teeth were in decent condition.

From here, Anne assisted with my getting dressed. Margot had laid out several items and as I looked at them, I realized it was a very good thing Anne was here: I had no idea how to wear them nor in what order to put them on.

"I assumed you would find this task a bit puzzling as you were only wearing a dress and underwear—I think you called them. I did not want Margot to see you confused about something so simple as getting dressed."

I told her that was a wise decision on her part and that I was indeed bewildered with so many pieces of fabric before me. Gracefully, Anne explained as she went. First, the shift, which was similar to my nightgown, but shorter in length and short sleeved as well. The shift was cut low in the front. Next, the corset. I was most interested in this part. I awaited the oppression I immediately expected to feel—to my relief, none came. The corset was clasped in the front by little eyelet hooks I was familiar with and then tied in the back: Anne did this part. I thought it would have been tighter, to get that famous eighteen-inch waist. Even as small as I was, eighteen inches was out of the question. Anne laughed and explained that women rarely wore their corsets tight, unless they were attending a ball, for which yes, they were tightened a little more than usual and could be terribly uncomfortable. For a regular day at home, the corset was only meant for support. I was amazed at how much better the corset felt than my bra.

My back had more support, and my chest was still pushed up. The biggest difference I noticed was that the corset gave a flatter look to the breast, except for the cleavage, whereas a bra gave the entire shape of the breast. Both were nice, in my opinion. Next came the petticoats. Anne debated on three or four as the petticoat gave the dress its fullness and the contrast made the waist look smaller. I argued that my waist was small enough and that, since I was new to wearing so much material at one time, less was more. I eventually talked her down to two petticoats.

"Just keep in mind, men like a small waist and full skirt." Anne's eyes glittered mischievously.

I laughed at Anne's small joke. "That hasn't changed in…" I was going to say in one hundred and fifty years, but then I realized I didn't know what year it was.

Anne saw my countenance change.

"What's the matter? You were almost enjoying yourself!"

I hesitated and then replied, "I—was going to make a comment on how long men have enjoyed our full skirts, and then I realized I couldn't count the years." I took a breath, "I'm still not sure what year it is, Anne."

Anne continued to adjust my second petticoat. "I wondered when you would ask. It's 1847. There, you already look more voluptuous. Imagine four petticoats!"

I couldn't imagine anything at that moment. I also lost the ability to count momentarily. Anne must have read my mind.

"One hundred and fifty-six years, Vale. Well, between this year and, I believe you said last night, 2003. Though that's not the year John found you in, is it?"

"No," I replied. "It was 2021."

Anne took in a deep breath as she processed my statement. To change the subject, I told her I was impressed with her ability to subtract so quick.

"No." Anne smiled. "After I found you sleeping last night, I went and spoke with Edward and George for a little while. I counted the years then. It's a lot for us, too."

I shifted uncomfortably. I knew it must be so, and I felt awful for it. I apologized, but it felt weak.

"You have nothing to be sorry for. I didn't mean to imply that. I just meant that these are new waters for us as well. However, we are in our own time, with our comforts and even our dislikes—they, too, are at least familiar. That is not the case for you, and I promise you have our every sympathy."

Anne completed my being dressed. Once she had finished lacing the back, she turned me to the mirror to see myself. My dress was just slightly too big, not enough to fuss over. Anne explained that Mrs. Miller was rushed to take in one of her dresses. I was aware then that the house knew something of me. Despite my internal struggles, I certainly looked like I belonged to this century.

"See how beautiful you are."

I knew beauty to be in the eye of the beholder, and so I surmised that Anne had a different opinion on beauty than my generation. Anne spoke to me through the mirror.

"We have invented a story for you. Some of the servants, such as Margot and Mrs. Miller, are aware you are here. George said that we need to keep to the truth as much as possible. Obviously, it will be stretched, but what we can keep to, we will."

I agreed completely.

"We will need your help to fill in the gaps," Anne stated.

"I can do that," I stated. "Anne, what year were you born?"

"1822. I'm five-and-twenty," was the quick reply.

"That's how old I was when I was married. Though I think it is best not to dwell on that. Of all things, not being married is the best part of being here."

I immediately regretted my words as I saw Anne's face fall. I hadn't considered how she felt about her marriage. I didn't doubt that I had more choice in my mate than she did hers.

"I'm sorry, I didn't mean to imply—"

"No, no, it is fine. It's just, well, it hurts a little to know you also have sad feelings about your marriage. I would have hoped that in one hundred and fifty-six years, marriage would be based more on love and affection; a mutual understanding of each other and what that means. It is not like that now, why should it be the case then, correct?"

Oh, it was just too much to explain. How could I tell her that yes, we did marry for love and mutual affection, but that it easily wanes in my generation? I would need to ponder these feelings and thoughts for a while before I told her any more about marriage in my time. It was too complicated. Instead, I squeezed her hand and thanked her for her help, intending to revisit the topic another time.

Avenhurst

# CHAPTER 7

Anne and I had lunch alone that first day. I was relieved. Anne was warm and gentle; it was easy to be with her. It was the men I was apprehensive of. I had always been shy around men. I never really dated, and when I did, it was always with a group of friends. I was also highly aware that Victorian men were different from the men of my own time. I anticipated that they would assume I was ignorant. Women of the nineteenth century were educated in a very different way; it occurred to me that currently, they would be right. Of course, I was educated far beyond their imaginations, but on day-to-day life, in this time, I was severely ignorant, and it terrified me. Still, I held on to the hope that Edward and George were not quite so austere as the men I had read about in novels. They had been generous in their defense of me the night before, but it had been an exceptional night; all were caught off-guard. Now that the crisis was over, I worried what they might think. I was anxious that I was a burden thrown upon them all, especially Anne and Edward; but as much as I hated to be a burden, I had nowhere else to go and no money to help myself.

◆

I had eaten what I could of lamb cutlets and rice pudding. The lunch was not bad, but it was not exactly good, either. My appetite was suppressed from stress, and the cuisine was so different from what I was used to that a few bites was all I could manage. I had never eaten lamb before, but if I told that to Anne I risked being thought of as picky. Tea was the most familiar part of the meal, which made me appreciate it all the more and also made me a little more relatable to Anne, who insisted I have a second cup. I could see she wished I would eat more, stating that I took little bites like a bird.

After lunch, at about half past one, Anne and I took a stroll through the grounds of Avenhurst. Anne carried on the conversation for the most part, complaining about a servant here and there, or praising another one and wishing she could take them back to her home, which she referred to as Highgarden. As much as I tried, I couldn't focus on much of what Anne said. I was far too consumed by my own miserable thoughts. I could not shake the feeling of guilt: I felt like my children were waiting for me and that they would feel abandoned. Gildi's words replayed in my mind, and my own body was proof the last eighteen years of my life no longer existed. Still, the guilt lingered. I listened more attentively when Anne spoke of her family, explaining that she and Edward were half-siblings and that their father remarried a few years after the death of Edward's mother. I was sorry for them both, yet this only furthered my despondency.

Anne's careful voice broke through my thoughts. "Vale, you are very quiet. I am doing my best to keep you busy today, but perhaps it would be better for you to rest—you are somewhat inscrutable."

I felt a small sting at her words. I had often been told I was hard to read.

"I'm sorry, Anne. I don't mean to be difficult. It's just—everything here is new to me. All of this is new."

I felt the tears begin in my eyes: half sadness, half frustration. My melancholy was interrupted by a sudden change of weather. Cold rain fell upon us. Anne took my arm and led the way back to the house.

"Oh, Vale, I am sorry. I did not mean to upset you. I know this is a new place for you and you are missing your family."

"No, Anne. It is so much more than that. It is that, *too*, mind you, but like I stated before, it is everything! Even the rain coming on the way it did just now. That doesn't happen back home. In fact, it probably won't rain for several more months."

Anne had a peculiar look on her face. "I have never heard that it doesn't rain much in America."

I smiled at Anne. She was a good soul. I could see her innocence, loneliness, and kindness, all at once. There were few people in the world I could ever speak to freely, without putting up a guard, and Anne was one of them. I inherently knew that she was genuine and true, and so, then, was our friendship.

"Anne, there is plenty of rain in America. It's just that I'm from California, central California, and we don't get much rain, except sometimes in spring, if it is a good year."

Anne and I had made our way to the parlor room, more familiar to me as the family room. It was smaller than the great drawing room and cozier as well. The furniture was not quite so grand, but it was just as lovely. We took a seat on the sofa near the fireplace. Anne placed a blanket over our laps. The rain had brought a drop in temperature with it. I momentarily abandoned our prior conversation to ask Anne about Edward and George. Anne informed me that George had gone back to their cottage. He had some letters to write and send off. Anne had an air of indifference when she spoke of George; it was hard not to observe. Edward, she said, had to go see some tenants. Apparently, there had been some trouble between a few of them. Anne assured me they would both be back in time for dinner, which was at a rather late hour, I felt, eight o'clock in the evening. My shyness made me uneasy at the thought of dinner. I wasn't looking forward to seeing either man again. I felt a twinge of guilt at this.

"Well, Vale, now that we are nice and warm, why don't you tell me more about your California? I'm not so familiar with it; though I do believe I have heard of it."

I had to quickly revisit my state's history before proceeding.

"Well, you may have heard of it, Anne. I believe that many people, pioneers they call them, are heading west and that California will be ratified as a state in 1850. Someday it will be a very popular place to live. I'm from a small town in the middle of the state."

Anne took my hand and placed it in hers. "California is quite far from here, is it not?"

"Yes. Something like five thousand miles, I believe."

She squeezed my hand. "I cannot believe that you lived that far away. I can't even fathom what it would be like."

Anne looked deep in thought.

"What's wrong, Anne?"

"Nothing is wrong. I just feel bad. Not only are you in another time, but another country. I am surprised you agreed to get out of bed at all."

"It was with great effort," I stated softly, "but you have made me feel very comfortable. I still feel like this is all a dream, I'll admit. But you have kept me calm, and for that I am grateful."

"Well, you will have to speak up when you need me to explain something to you. I am sure there are some things that have changed between now and your time."

I laughed, perhaps more bitterly than I intended. "It's better if you presume that everything has changed. That will be easier on all of us."

Anne looked baffled. "Are things so different?"

"Yes," was my simple reply. Though I was glad for us to discuss the elephant in the room, for it helped me feel more authentic, it was exhausting.

✦

For the next couple of hours, Anne showed me around the interior of the house. The first floor consisted of the parlor room, the drawing room, the dining room, the library, and the kitchen. As I had seen most of the first floor already, we quickly peeked in on the library, which was vast with copious amounts of books. I was more than a little pleased at this great room, and I told Anne so.

"Just be sure to have a servant light the fire for you or you will surely freeze," was Anne's response.

Next, we visited the kitchen, where the cook was busy cutting up a recently butchered chicken; I tried not to watch too closely. It was a spacious room with a large table in the middle. Wooden cabinets and counter space wrapped around the room, and at the far side was a large, red-brick fireplace. I was impressed to see two large old wood-burning stoves. I remembered seeing one when I was young at my great-grandmother's old house. To see an object I had seen once before as an antique, but now in its prime, caused an uncanny feeling to overcome me. As we moved about the house, I was always left with a feeling of familiarity.

Several chamber rooms occupied the second floor, including Mrs. Miller's, to whom I was briefly introduced. Mrs. Miller was a quaint and stout little white-haired woman with a white cap upon her head. I could see she once was a redhead as she still had a few sprouts of the flame-colored strands throughout her white hair. Her small green eyes were kind, yet serious, and she had an air of sincerity to her person. I thought her the epitome of a matronly woman, with her black Victorian dress and white apron. Besides the chamber rooms, including mine and Edward's, which were right next to each other's, was Edward's study. The door was partially open, and I could see French doors that led out to a balcony as we walked past the room. I felt a little relieved he wasn't there.

The hallways in this old house were wide and dark, even when the candle sconces were lit. In the main hallway on the first floor and the hall where our chambers were on the second floor, the candle sconces had been replaced with hanging oil lamps; this made the hall much brighter and was somewhat closer to a modern lightbulb. I wished Edward would replace them all. The candlelight flickering against the dark walls cast many shadows. Before, I might have considered it romantic; now, it seemed dreary and affected my spirit. As for the third floor, Anne desired to keep away as it was now the servants' quarters, along with some spare chamber rooms. The Emberleys once had grand parties when friends and relatives stayed for months at a time, usurping all the spare chamber rooms on the third floor, but Anne had never known such a time, and neither, she said, had Edward.

Throughout the tour, as I became acquainted with Mrs.

Miller, the butler, and a few of the other housemaids, Anne thought it a good time to inform me of my own personal tragedy, which was slightly different from the truth. It was a sad state of affairs indeed: I was on holiday with my American side of the family when they all took ill with typhus on the ship between New York and London. With no other relatives to turn to, my short trip to see my Emberley relatives became permanent. This explained my being all alone in the world, though I asked Anne if it was not odd that they had never heard of an American cousin before. Anne assured me that it did not matter, really. The servants, including Mrs. Miller, would not break propriety and ask. They would take the master at his word.

"Besides," Anne said, "Mrs. Miller and the butler are the only ones who know any of the Emberley family history firsthand, and Edward explained you were a second cousin. And no offense, darling—and I mean that sincerely—they will not question the Emberleys not bragging about having American cousins."

I almost questioned the need to be honest about my nationality at all when I remembered what Anne said of George about keeping to the truth whenever possible. Besides, I knew my mannerisms would be odd, even when I tried my best, and it was much easier to blame my being American than being from another century. Anne insisted this would quell any rumors amongst the servants, as eventually the rest of their circle would be aware that Avenhurst had a new tenant. My injured pride aside, the house itself was beautiful and large: one could get lost in it.

Once we completed the tour of Avenhurst, I asked Anne if she minded much if I laid down. With keen discernment, Anne did not hesitate to agree. I made my way back to my chamber, wary that I should see Edward in the hall. I no longer had an accurate concept of time. I didn't know how long it took to get anywhere by horse or carriage; I had no idea how many miles away anything was. I felt like a novice to life, and it left me unbalanced. I needn't have feared. Edward was nowhere in sight.

I was unable to stifle the sobs that erupted before I closed the door behind me. I had to hold onto one of the bed posts to anchor myself as I shook from head to toe. Oh—this was misery. I felt the deepest sting of despair at that moment. Reader, I could not enjoy the beauty of this fine house—what was it to me? Not *my* home. My home had my children, it had messy walls that I wiped down every few days, it had a kitchen with gas appliances and electricity—it had bathrooms with showers and plumbing! I must have wept for an hour, until exhaustion settled in, and I fell asleep right there on the ground where I had sat, too unhappy to settle myself in bed. Margot found me lying there, as I awakened to her shouting for Anne. I knew I gave her a fright and that she probably thought I was dead—*if only*, I bleakly thought.

Anne rushed in and saw the mess I was. I half-expected her to demand courage from me and to tell me to wash my face, but once again, my expectations were inaccurate. Anne dismissed Margot for the time being and came and sat next to me on the floor. I didn't say anything; I just wept. Anne pulled my head into her lap and stroked my hair, remaining silent for some time. She finally spoke when I was more settled.

"I cannot pretend to understand the insurmountable loss you are feeling. And I know loss. But, Vale, these circumstances are extraordinary, darling. All I can do is promise you my loyalty and love."

I felt her wipe my tears with her hanky.

"The Gheatas say we were—are cousins, but think of me as your sister now. And try to think of Avenhurst as your home if you can. It will help alleviate some of the fear you inevitably have." Anne's kind eyes were solemn, her cheeks wet. "Edward and I would do anything for you, anything to give you comfort. You will see after a time, I promise."

I closed my eyes, still fatigued. "Please, Anne, don't mistake my breakdown for ingratitude. I'm more than grateful to you both." I began to sob again. "I'm scared, and I'm homesick. Mostly, I miss my— ".

Anne began stroking my hair again and bent down to kiss my cheek.

"I know, I know," she whispered.

My gratitude towards Anne for her love and care in my early hours at Avenhurst could never be fully repaid. Never could one find a friend so in tune with another's misery, so careful to not accost, as Anne Ellis. Anne promised that I could remain in my chamber room for the rest of the evening if I wished. I accepted this offer and remained in bed until the next morning.

A Rose Without Thorns

# CHAPTER 8

When I awakened that morning, I was surprised to find that Anne had stayed with me again. I asked her if George would mind, but Anne insisted that he understood my delicate state.

"How are you feeling this morning?" my dear friend asked.

I tried to smile. "All right, I suppose. A little tired. Perhaps tired of being tired."

Anne gave a small laugh. "Well, that I can understand. May I offer some advice, Vale?"

I couldn't get over how much younger Anne seemed with her hair down.

"Of course," I replied.

"I know my situation is not the same, and I wouldn't dare compare. But I do understand what it is like to miss someone and to also be very homesick. My advice is this: you need to get out of bed and try to stay busy. Not all the time, but if you allow yourself to stay in bed all day, you will feel worse, and then you will be worse."

I watched Anne twitch her face nervously as she awaited my response; I imagined she thought I would be upset. I knew she was right, though I didn't like it. I felt the sadness in my heart beginning to oppress my every nerve, and if I didn't heed Anne's advice, she was correct: I would only get worse.

"I know you're right, Anne. Maybe we can take a walk

later." I must have spoken straight to her heart, because her whole face lit up.

"Yes! We shall! Come, I'll ring for Margot so we can get ready for breakfast."

Seeing Anne so happy at my feeble attempt to be normal was somehow slightly encouraging.

Much of the new day went on as the one before it. Edward and George had left before breakfast, and I mostly focused on making it from one hour to the next. Anne and I spent much of the morning in the parlor near the fire. Anne read to me from a novel I had never heard of, written some time at the end of the eighteenth century, while my mind continuously wandered. I was curious now to see Edward again. I knew I had missed him and George at dinner the night before, but Anne had said very little about their reaction to my absence; in fact, she said nothing at all. I worried that I had already offended Edward. He was the owner of Avenhurst, after all, and I was a guest in his house.

Around four o'clock, we were to have tea in the garden. Anne thought the fresh air and sun would do us well. We were set up just inside the garden gates, where a gorgeous table spread awaited us. A servant, one whom I had briefly seen in passing, pulled out a white floral-patterned chair for me. The metal chair was heavy, and I could not pull myself closer without assistance. I could see from its legs that the table matched the chairs. This little bistro set was similar to one my grandmother had. A white tablecloth covered the round table and in the midst of the cut meats and cheeses was the loveliest tea set I had ever seen.

The pieces were made of fine white bone china, lined with a gold embellishment around the top. There were red-and-gold roses painted on the sides of each piece. The tea set was so finely made that I was almost afraid to touch it.

It was odd to sit there and be served. I had spent so many years taking care of myself and others that to sit and be idle felt like a burden. This was not the case for Anne, I considered, who had always lived this way. I watched her as she drank from the pretty little cup. Several strands of her soft brown hair had escaped from her bun and were gently blowing with the breeze. How odd, I thought, to sit here with a woman who lived one hundred and fifty years before me. And yet, she was real.

Once our teatime was spent, Anne wanted to show me the rest of the garden. The entrance alone was breathtaking. The garden gates were tall, black wrought iron with a flower design that made up the structure. The entrance had a cobblestone path that eventually gave way to grass as it led farther into the garden. Where the cobblestone ended stood a wooden arbor with what looked like a mix of jasmine and English ivy growing around it. A breeze drifted through, confirming it was jasmine. Hanging over the brick walls were beautiful wisteria plants that were matured and whimsical. There were even potted young trees along the edge of the wall and several rose bushes.

Before Anne and I could follow the path down any farther, a servant came up to speak with her. The servant made a small curtsy and then told Anne there was a need for her in the house and that Mrs. Miller had already been informed. Anne did not question her further but replied that she would be right there. I declined Anne's offer to go with her. I preferred to be alone in the garden. I took any alone time available to me.

With Anne gone, I looked around the garden and admired its beauty. I walked towards the arbor and noticed that right outside of it was a very beautiful wrought-iron bench, similar in style to the garden gates. Going through the arbor was almost like entering another room. Here the garden seemed almost wild. It was obviously manmade in design, but it was overgrown in the most charming way. I saw a lonely-looking rose bush with large, bloomed white roses all over. Eyeing the thorns carefully, I reached in to pluck a rose. I was startled by a man's voice behind me.

"Let me get that for you, Vale."

It was Edward's voice; I recognized the way he said my name before I looked around at him. It rolled off his tongue in such a way, it was as though we were old friends. In one long stride, Edward reached beside me, breaking off a rose at the stem; he removed the thorns before handing me the flower. I took the rose and thanked him, attempting to make eye contact the best I could. He had caught me off guard; I had mentally prepared myself to see him that evening, but here Edward was, in his riding boots and all.

"Why are you alone?" he inquired.

"Anne was just with me. A servant called her to the house. I told her I would wait here." I hesitated a moment. "She was going to show me the garden."

He slightly nodded his head. "This was my grandmother Catherine's garden. Our grandfather had it designed for her. There were plenty of trees and flowers all over the grounds of Avenhurst, but she wanted a garden that was enclosed. Somewhere she could let her children play out of sight more comfortably." He also seemed to briefly hesitate. "I could show you the garden. I spent much of my childhood playing here."

I nodded my head in agreement, and he led the way.

"Your grandmother sounds like she was a lovely mother. Your grandfather, he didn't hesitate in building this garden?"

"No, he was very devoted from what my father told me. He would never have denied any pleasure he could bestow upon my grandmother Catherine. I, unfortunately, never knew her. As Gildi mentioned, she passed when my father, uncle, and aunt were just children."

I was unsure how to proceed. I did remember what Gildi said, of course—all of it.

"Did he have this bench made for her, as well?" I asked, pointing to the rose-patterned bench near us.

"No," he replied, walking towards the bench. Edward ran his hand along the back of the metal bench, reflecting on something. "My father had it made for my mother. He wanted her to have her own special place in this garden."

I smiled; at least the women of his family were well-loved. We continued through the garden slowly. It was breezy again, but no clouds lingered in the sky. As we were walking, I noticed he glanced at me a couple of times. I began to feel insecure. *Am I wearing this wrong?* I considered I might look ridiculous, or maybe needed those extra petticoats.

"You keep looking at me. Am I dressed wrong?" I looked down at myself, smoothing out my dress.

"No." He smiled. "I was just admiring how you look. I thought you would look like a different person compared to what I saw a couple of days ago, but no, I think you are still in there. Same blue eyes. You would never know you were from another time."

I felt my cheeks get warm, but I could not help smiling. I began to thank him, but we were suddenly joined by Anne again. Anne hooked my arm in hers, and the three of us continued in our walk.

"I didn't expect to see you until this evening, Edward."

An enigmatic look appeared on Edward's face. "Yes, well,

one can only spend so much time with the tenants." He looked at Anne. "But they are settled."

Anne gave a small nod. "Yes, very well."

"I did not expect to find an abandoned little bird when I returned, however."

Anne furrowed her brow. "I did not abandon her. Two of the servant girls had an argument. It sent Mrs. Miller into such a tizzy that I had to become involved. Vale did not need to see that."

Edward looked more irritated now, and I was curious.

"What were they arguing about?" he asked.

"Mrs. Miller found one of them with a penny blood. One girl blamed another girl and then they both argued over who really owned it. Neither wanted to confess."

"Good God. I assume you took proper care of this?"

"Of course."

"And Mrs. Miller? Did the good old woman need any salts?"

"No. She excused herself to the parlor and opened her Bible to Leviticus."

They both began to laugh. I had to assume that Mrs. Miller must be somewhat of a character despite her serious manner. I made a mental note to ask Anne what a penny blood was later. I did ask about Mrs. Miller's character, if there was not more to her than what I had seen.

"You will see soon enough, darling. Mrs. Miller has already mentioned that she would be glad to have you read to her." A smile crept across Anne's face.

"What else does she like to read?" I felt almost relieved to have a small occupation, even if it was reading novels to this little old lady.

"Well, besides Leviticus?" Anne and Edward were both

smiling. "She really enjoys the New Testament too!"

I couldn't help but laugh a little. "I mean besides the Bible, Anne."

They were both fully amused.

"Well, when Mrs. Miller is feeling exceptionally open-minded, she may let you read the Apocrypha!"

Anne laughed heartily at Edward's comment. I would have laughed, too, if I had not been the one destined to read to her.

✦

After our stroll through the garden, we all retreated to our own rooms for a couple of hours. Edward was tired from his ride, and I needed to be alone for a while. Anne ensured I was well before retiring to her own room and reminded me that Margot would dress me for dinner. It was odd to have to change for dinner. I knew it was common for Victorians, but it was a far cry from getting fast food on the way home from work. Margot had removed my dress since I would be changing later anyhow, which was a nice break from all the clothes I had on. I closed the curtains around my bed, closed my eyes and allowed myself to indulge in the pain I had fought back all day.

With my eyes closed, I could swear I was home in my own bed. Often, we would lie down together, my children and I. I could feel my four-year-old son embracing me on one side. He liked to lie in my arms. Sometimes he would sing "You are My Sunshine" to put us to sleep. My two-year-old girl would lie on the other side. I could still feel her rubbing my eyelashes as she drifted off to sleep. I could almost hear the soft humming of the ceiling fan. For a moment, I felt joy, and then a severe sensation of despair waved over me. I sobbed myself to sleep. I had taken what felt like a very short nap when Margot cautiously woke me up.

"Miss, it is time to dress for dinner. Would you like me to fix your hair?"

Margot's soft blue eyes were focused on the mess on top of my head. I agreed, and rather quickly she tamed my wild hair. Margot replaced my day dress with a much more elegant and formal evening dress made of light blue silk, similar in color to what I had worn the day I arrived. Margot added a pretty broach to the dress and some gloves. I almost felt as if I were attending high-school prom. After Margot left, I sat down at the small desk in my room and placed my face in my hands. It had been such a long day already. I didn't know how to carry on—it was hard. I already felt like an imposter. Everything felt like an effort, as well. There was so much for me to learn about this new life, and I did not want to learn it. I wanted my children and to be home with them. I knew Gildi said it was impossible, but I was also sure there was more to all this than what Gildi had already disclosed. This thought planted a small seed of hope in me. Gildi. I knew then that I needed to speak with her. *But how?* I wondered. Anne had been my primary guide so far, but it was Edward's home and his rules. I knew enough of the Victorian era to know it was a patriarchal society. I would need Edward's permission to see Gildi, and I was determined to get it or find another way. I wasn't sure where to start, but knowing that I would find a way to see Gildi put enough hope inside my heart to even give me a little appetite.

✦

Anne met me at my chamber door as I was exiting. I was nervous, but having Anne by my side was a comfort. Together we made our way to dinner, where the gentlemen were waiting for us. As we entered the room, both George and Edward were standing by the fireplace in what appeared to be a serious conversation. Upon seeing us, they both performed a small bow and assisted us to our seats at the table.

Dinner was more pleasant than I had expected. The three of them kept up the conversation, discussing tenants and trivial gossip. Dinner was five courses, and though it felt formal to begin with, I quickly realized I had overthought everything. I was just as good at using a knife and fork as anyone else, and I didn't choke on my water or wine, so it felt like a success. Once dinner was over, Anne and I left the men behind as we made our way to the parlor. I did not need Anne to explain this, as I was familiar with the custom: the men would have a drink or cigar while we entertained ourselves elsewhere. I also was not surprised when Anne offered me a sampler and some thread. Here I sent a silent thank you to my grandma for teaching me to embroider. At least in this most important female occupation, I was well-trained. Anne was even a little impressed with my fishbone stitch.

Soon the gentlemen rejoined us. I was so occupied at dinner with attempting to blend in that I hadn't really taken in my surroundings. The parlor was much more well-lit than the drawing room had been a few nights before. It was pleasant and warm. Edward and George were both wearing their evening clothes, which consisted of black coats and white cravats. Edward filled out his jacket with a much broader chest than George. Edward walked over to the piano and began to play. I didn't recognize the song, but I couldn't believe how well he mastered it. Anne asked me if I played.

"I took lessons as a child, but I didn't practice like I should. I wouldn't remember much now," I responded.

"I had lessons for years, and yet I am still awful. Edward does not mind telling me, either."

I noticed Edward smiled, but he didn't look up or speak up. It was a nice scene: Anne sewing, Edward playing, all seemed comfortable until my eyes rested on George. He was standing a few feet behind Edward at the piano, drinking another glass of wine, deep in thought.

"Is your husband all right?" I asked Anne.

"He's been in a bad temper since he came back from Highgarden. He said it's nothing, so I did not press."

I looked back towards the piano and caught Edward's eye; he looked away gently. Out of embarrassment, I looked back at George, who was also watching me. In this case I was the one to look away first. Edward finished his piece, and then sat down across from me and Anne. Soon George came and reclined in a chair beside him. Edward spoke first.

"Anne told you that we discussed inventing a story about you? One to explain how you came to England so suddenly and alone."

"Yes—she did. I believe she mentioned something about typhus."

Edward's lip twitched a little, giving in to a small smile.

"Yes, glad you were spared. We all agreed that would be the most believable story. People are less likely to inquire as it would be rather indecorous to remind you of your loss."

I nodded in agreement.

"What we need to clarify with you are some concrete details. For example, when is your birthday, Vale?"

"March 12—1985." I had hesitated to give the year and rightfully so. Each face in the room reacted ever so slightly at my response. It was as hard for them to hear a twentieth-century date as it was for me to hear it was 1847.

"See, that is a problem. Of course, your date of birth need not change, but you were born in 1829. At least that's what you need to practice saying."

I did not know what to say. 1829. I would need to write that down a few times.

"All right, the twelfth of March, 1829."

"Good girl. Now, if at any time anyone begins to question you on where you are from, feign discomfort if you must—they will leave the subject."

"I will not be feigning."

"No, I suppose not."

◆

I was to sleep alone for the first time that night. Even though I had fallen asleep without knowing she was there both nights previously, it still felt lonely knowing she wouldn't be there now. Anne kindly spent some time with me in my chamber room before bed, though, and she and Margot made sure I had a strong fire before they left me alone. Before Anne left, she admitted that the men had purposely found other occupations away from Avenhurst to give me some time alone with her and to get acquainted with the estate in a more comfortable manner. As aggrieved as I was, it did bring some comfort that I was probably in the best care that one could hope for.

The Essence of the Nineteenth Century

# CHAPTER 9

The next two weeks passed much like the first few days at Avenhurst, with the exception that the men were present during all meals. I often sat quietly as the three of them discussed current events or the day's happenings. I didn't have any clever comments to contribute, so I listened instead, occasionally asking a question.

Edward and George were busy much of the day. I didn't know what business they attended to, but often Anne and I were left alone to entertain ourselves. Sometimes I sat on my window ledge while alone in my room. I would watch as Edward left on his horse for a few hours. Sometimes, I would happen to be there as he came back home.

Edward was a commanding man, that was easy to see. From the impressive way he handled his horse to the way he delegated to his servants with a firm but benevolent authority, Edward was indeed Master of Avenhurst Manor.

George seemed to come and go between Avenhurst and Highgarden. I wondered about the importance of his visiting Highgarden each day. I could have asked Anne, but despite my efforts to stay occupied, a depression was growing inside of me, and the more it grew, the less I cared about the comings and goings of others. In contrast to the travels of the men, I took note that Anne was always home, at least; always grounded here at Avenhurst. The farthest Anne and I roamed was through the orchard and around the outer edges of the estate, where a river ran past. I knew my state of mind was deterring my desire to roam, but I questioned if Anne was always so confined. She had no other occupation and no children to tend to. Together we sewed, walked, read, and talked; for now, that was enough for me. It was Anne who kept my spirits somewhat alive, but even then, her kind disposition was becoming less effective against my growing melancholy.

◆

I awakened to Margot pulling back the curtains to the bay window. Even though I had pulled all my drapes around the four-poster bed, it was such a sunny day that the whole room was bright. My fire had died, and the room felt cool, even with the sun out. The low temperatures of northern England would take some time for me to get accustomed to.

Margot informed me she had prepared my "toilette" and would be back in twenty minutes to help me dress. She had left a cup of coffee, prepared how I liked it, on my nightstand; this was one of the few pleasures I really enjoyed. I managed to wash up, and though I felt reasonably clean, I knew I would need to improvise with some modern customs if I were to feel like myself—at least as far as cleanliness went. Luckily, my grandmother always insisted on keeping to the many homemade remedies she grew up with. I could still hear her sweet voice telling me how much better vinegar is than Windex and that baking soda is the best for whitening. I wasn't concerned with cleaning windows, but I was considering how I could get my hands on some baking soda. I had a toothbrush, one made from soft boar hair, which took a moment to get past, but I had only used water on my teeth since getting here. I knew there were apothecaries that had some ointments for the teeth, but only God really knew what was in them, and I was not about to put plaster in my mouth. Baking soda would not only clean my teeth, but I could also use it as a deodorant: it might not smell like baby powder, but it would be much better than nothing at all, especially when summer came. I busied myself with these thoughts, purposely avoiding the painful ones that stayed just below the surface. I felt for my locket. I hadn't opened it since I had arrived here, but the desire was growing. I wanted to look inside, but I dreaded it too. Here Margot returned and pulled me out of my thoughts.

I was about to descend downstairs for breakfast when Anne met me at my chamber door, a big smile on her face.

"We are going to town today after breakfast, Vale. Make sure to grab your bonnet."

"To town?"

I was surprised to feel a twinge of excitement. I hadn't seen any of England save for Avenhurst, and even then, I had only roamed the grounds within the estate.

"Yes. Edward and I agree that you need some day and night dresses, ones that fit you properly and are not hand-me-downs. Your bonnet is my old one, and your shoes are as well."

I was slightly uncomfortable.

"Anne, I—I don't have any money. I mean, I wouldn't even know what anything costs or what is considered a lot of money."

Anne gave me a quizzical look.

"Of course, I would pay you back if I could. I was a teacher—I could get a job teaching. Women are allowed to teach, correct?"

Now Anne was looking at me like a second head had sprouted from my neck.

"Just a moment, Vale. First, there is no debt, and to be clear, it is Edward who will pay for your wardrobe—gladly, mind you. And you will certainly not work! I think my grandfather would roll over in his grave to think of an Emberley woman working!" Anne laughed, kissed me on the head and walked away. "Come now, come eat!"

The conversation did not amuse me or relieve my feelings of shame. I had been a teacher, and a rather good one, I thought. I was not used to others paying my way. As it was, I had a hard time living under someone else's roof and not helping to clean, cook, or do anything besides roam the gardens; I hated feeling useless. I told myself over and over it was custom; this was the expectation. It was also not lost on me that she called me an Emberley. Though I knew this to be the truth, according to Gildi and her family, to myself, I was a Leifman. And that feeling I associated with my maiden name had been stronger than ever, especially after seeing the younger version of myself every time I glanced in the mirror. At first, I avoided looking too long, but each passing day I began to feel more acquainted with my former self.

✦

The four of us—Edward, Anne, George, and I—were to visit the local town of Weston, which was said to be about six miles away or a thirty- to forty-five-minute trip: a *short* ride to town. The carriage had been brought around to the front of the house and the coachman had taken his seat. Though I knew what to expect, the sight of a two-horse carriage still affected me. I had ridden in an open carriage once at a theme park, but this was certainly a different experience, one somehow mixed with nostalgia and reverence.

George stood at the door, assisting Anne in, then me. The gentleman took their seats after us. The grandeur of the interior was beyond magnificent. The seats almost resembled the sofas in the drawing room, except these were a cream color; they still had the wooden border. The roof of the carriage was painted with cherubs, similar to what one would find in the Sistine Chapel. The inside doors were also painted in this fashion. I had never seen a more beautiful car in my own time.

With a small jolt, we were off. To avoid feeling awkward and to give myself a moment to take it all in, I occupied myself by looking out the window. I was interested to see what lay outside of Avenhurst. As we left the large iron gates that closed off the estate from the rest of the world, within several yards was an old church and, just like the ones I'd seen in pictures, an accompanying graveyard. I could see it was very old. A small thrill of excitement ran through me. I immediately made up my mind to explore that graveyard—in the middle of the day, of course. I admired the endless sky, which appeared royal blue with many cumulus clouds laid against it. I did not trust that cheery sky, however, as I had quickly learned how fickle the weather could be this far north.

Soon I became aware of the other carriages increasing in numbers as we drove closer into town. For reasons I couldn't understand, my stomach was turning with knots: seeing dirt roads gradually blend into granite-paved ones, vehicles of different sizes—some with two horses, some with just one—then there were several lone riders. It was surreal. I didn't know what was making me so anxious, except that this dream was beginning to feel real. I focused my attention back inside the carriage for a moment, and realized I had been far more interesting of a subject for my companions than anything outside of the carriage.

"You look as though you are seeing the world for the first time," Edward stated, surveying me with amusement in his eyes.

"I am," I replied, slightly self-conscious.

Edward simply smiled. I suddenly noticed he was wearing a top hat. I thought it becoming on him.

We soon arrived in Weston, which looked more like a village than a town to my eyes. Weston looked nothing like the little cities, or big cities, I was familiar with, and it was also nothing like the old Western towns I had seen so much on television. As we began to descend from the top of a small hill, I could see the village below. Beyond the main road, most of the community lived in small, terraced houses made of brick. Just past the terraced homes, I could see perhaps a few cottages that sat alone, but most of the humble homes seemed attached to one another. It was only another minute or so before we came to the center of town. I imagined we were somewhere like a Main Street, or perhaps it was the *only* street. Weston was a quaint little place, with an old cobblestone road down the center and a few gas streetlamps spread out every few feet. Charming little shops were lined up along both sides of the road and busy carriages were passing both ways; though it was small, the center of this town was lively. I wondered at how these modest villagers could have such a nice little district. Edward explained that much of the middle-class and nearby gentry use Weston as it is the closest shopping center before one of the larger northern cities, such as Manchester.

Besides the nice little shops, there were people out selling various produce and other goods, almost like a farmer's market, with chickens loose while children chased them, to complete the picture. My interest couldn't help but be piqued by the mix of elegance and farm life. This reminded me of home. Shopping was usually my favorite pastime, but today I just wanted to make it through without looking out of place, not with the strangers, but with my current company.

Edward assisted Anne and me out of the carriage carefully; our dresses were an accident in waiting. Today especially, I felt my dress was remarkably heavy and difficult to walk in. Upon my descent, I noticed that George offered Anne his arm. She took it very mechanically. Edward extended his to me. I took it and felt my cheeks burn as I did—I hoped he didn't notice.

Seeing a town such as this in person was, once again, strangely familiar. I was accustomed to Victorian museums and old photos, but to breathe in the scent of the era was quite another experience. The air was fresh but mingled with the scent of horses and the aroma of food cooking nearby. I had almost forgotten the scent of horses; it had been some time since I had been around one in person. I had noticed it when I entered the carriage earlier that day, but now, in this small place where there were so many of the large animals close by, the odor was overwhelming. I humored myself to think that if I could bottle the essence of the nineteenth century, it would be a mixture of horse, roasted chicken, and smoke from the fireplace. It was not necessarily displeasing.

The people on the little street were bustling about, men and women alike. Immediately, I saw the class distinction. In my time, it was difficult to distinguish class based on clothing alone as mass production had made clothes affordable. Here it was quite different. There were many middle-class people about and they looked well enough with their pretty dresses and long coats, but Edward stood out amongst them. He was tall and stately, debonair even. Most of these men couldn't be more than five-foot-seven and their clothes, though clean, lacked the decorous detail of Edward's. I hadn't noticed it before, but now I could even see the difference in detail between his and George's vest and coat. There were a few seemingly upper-class people as we walked down the street. The men all had black top hats and walking sticks and the women with them had large, flowered bonnets and what seemed to be at least four to five petticoats. I decided it was a slight distinction between the middle- and upper-class as far as fashion went. I guessed that the upper-class had more fine outfits to choose from and, perhaps, better quality. But the distinction between the working class and the others was most severe. The only equivalent I could imagine was to compare the working class to the homeless I had seen in my time. These unfortunate people, though, were working and struggling. One woman was wearing what I assumed to be a dark brown dress, that is until I watched her lift her apron to wipe her face and saw that the dress had been a light blue at one time. I felt a pang in my heart; her dress was too short. I could see her torn stockings and a rip at the seam of both her boots. My heart was hurt more when I saw a young girl dressed in the same fashion, maybe her daughter, run to her and give her a wilted flower. I felt guilty at being depressed over my own situation. I did my best to dismiss the feeling as I walked with my party.

A Beautiful Promise

# CHAPTER 10

Our first stop had been a hat store—Edward insisted I have a new bonnet. I left with two. The first was of light-blue silk, with pastel flowers lining the edges, and the second was an everyday straw bonnet with brown ribbon and some neutral flowers on the side. I preferred the latter, whereas Anne preferred the silk. As we were leaving the shop, a man resembling a beggar approached another gentleman who had been walking in our direction on the sidewalk. Before the beggar could even speak, the gentleman, and I use that term loosely, came down upon the poor man with his walking stick, administering several hard strikes. I was astonished and appalled. I looked towards Edward and George for support; the latter kept walking and the former shook his head slightly in disapproval, but also to say, "None of our business." Once more I reminded myself of the year in which I now existed, though it was of little comfort.

We visited a couple more stores. Anne led me into a shop full of fabric while the men made their way to the cigar store. Here, I was measured and fitted and subsequently told by the mistress running the store that I ought to eat more. I had to choose various fabrics for my day dresses, evening gowns, petticoats, nightgowns, shifts, and corsets. The fabrics were beautiful, even elegant, but my heart was far away, so I left most of the decisions to Anne, with the exception of one pattern. The cream-colored material with small pink flowers, little green leaves outlined in a chocolate brown, and small hints of yellow scattered throughout caught my eye. Despite Anne's earlier argument, I knew this was quite a bit of money to spend all at once, and it bothered me. I pondered ways I could pay Edward back, but nothing came to mind. I relayed my troubles again to Anne, who appeased me once more, though more sincerely.

"We are responsible for you, Vale, and you have need of a wardrobe and materials as much as anyone else. Edward would not bother if he did not want to, I assure you of that."

I nodded and left it alone. I walked to the counter, where I had viewed the various designs, patterns, and colors of the fabrics for my clothing and was amazed at the amount needed to dress oneself. I could only imagine what the owner thought, seeing a young lady have need of so much in one trip. Anne was one step ahead: she later told me that she had quietly let the woman know of my great loss and how all my belongings had to be burned. The lady gave us her great pity, and we left her with more money than she probably saw in a month's salary. Because everything was custom made, my new wardrobe would be delivered at a later date.

The last store, and the one I had most anticipated, was the apothecary. I had explained my desires to Anne while we shopped at the previous store. Together we sought baking soda, apple cider vinegar, and scented soap.

"What scent do you prefer, Vale, lavender, or lemon?"

Anne had found the soap. They were carved, pretty little things. I breathed in both scents, choosing the lavender for its soft floral aroma. Soon we had every item we sought, including witch hazel, a pleasant surprise. There were many different potions, tonics, cleansers, and medical remedies on display throughout the shop: I trusted none of them. I sought out items that I knew were pure and that my grandmother would have heard of. As we paid for our items, I noticed Edward and George waiting outside for us. We joined the gentlemen once more. Edward teased me, asking if I'd spared any of his money; I could see he was pleased. As uncomfortable as it had been initially, I was beyond grateful for his generosity. Edward did not question any of our purchases but trusted us to get what I would need for comfort. He offered his arm to me again; as I took it, I thanked him.

"I know this must have cost you a small fortune—thank you, Edward."

I received a satisfied smile. "You are quite welcome."

We took a stroll down the street before heading back towards the carriage. I was listening to Anne ramble about the most hideous bonnet she had ever seen: "…and on a matronly lady to boot."

I was mildly entertained by the sheer passion in her voice when I felt something, or someone, tug on my skirt. I looked down to see a giggling toddler boy.

"Mama, mama!" he exclaimed.

I was startled and momentarily confused. Instantly, his mother was at my side, grabbing her son and apologizing. I noticed we were both wearing light-green dresses. It was an easy mistake; the boy became very bashful once he realized he had the wrong skirt. The mix-up was laughed off, but as we continued on, I discreetly pulled my bonnet forward to hide the few tears that escaped.

✦

The ride back was quiet. I could see the gray clouds moving in, the promise of rain within them. I kept my eyes out on the landscape, actively avoiding my companions. I sensed their pity, but I knew they were far too polite to say anything. Still, their eyes said enough. We were passing through the wooded area, which now I knew meant we were getting nearer to Avenhurst. I noticed a small house that I'd missed earlier that day, the dense foliage easily obscuring its view from the road. I felt a sudden jolt of shock. I saw a familiar blonde head come out the rustic little place, closing a wooden door behind her. Our carriage passed as she turned our way, so I couldn't be sure if she knew who went by and what her reaction may have been. As for mine, I kept my composure. I glanced back in at the others, who were all absorbed in their own thoughts. Anne attempted a small smile my way, I smiled back gently. Perhaps Anne thought I was recovered, but I was not. I was determined, and now I knew where to find Gildi.

✦

I sat alone in my room, watching the rain drizzling down the windowpane as I pondered all I had seen that day, when I heard a soft knock. I welcomed Anne into my room. Margot had just made a fire; its heat was fresh, and it crackled loudly, so I knew the room felt inviting. Anne came and sat next to me on my bed.

"I imagine today was exhausting for you. However, I am glad that you will have your own personal items to enjoy. I think you will feel more at home now."

Anne sounded cheerful, but her small smile seemed forced.

"I'm sure you're right, Anne. Thank you."

Anne looked at me with more unease than I felt prepared for. I always hated seeing others upset; I felt it was my job to rectify this for them.

"Is something the matter?" Anne stood up and paced a step or so and then turned towards me and spoke with a defeated voice.

"Vale, George and I are returning home tonight. George is ready. Honestly, I'm surprised he's complied this long. We never meant to stay here at Avenhurst after Easter, but with all that happened, he wanted to be supportive."

I struggled to keep the look of disappointment from my face. A knot developed in my stomach. I felt a mixture of feelings: confusion, dread, and sorrow, to name a few.

"You're leaving for Highgarden? I mean, I knew you would one day, but so soon?"

I felt the sting of abandonment, like a child who has just found out their parents are to divorce.

"Oh, darling, I am sorry! I'm not happy about this arrangement at all. By all rights, you should be going home with me."

"What do you mean?"

"You're underage."

"What do you mean, Anne? I'm th—eighteen."

Anne gave me a quizzical look. "I know. Until you are twenty-one, you must be under the guardianship of a female relative, which is obviously myself. And technically, you still are. However, Edward refuses to let you leave Avenhurst. He insists that your home is here."

Anne sat down again and held my hand. "And he is correct about that. This is your home. You have been through too much as it is, and it may do more harm than good to move you away from here. Besides, you are Edward's…"

Her voice trailed off as I looked at her. I felt my cheeks burn. We had yet to discuss what Gildi had stated that first night. I didn't want to circumvent the topic any longer.

"Edward's what? Say it."

"You know what was said. Well, what Gildi said." Anne began to play with the hem of her sleeve. "We knew of the curse—Edward and I, that is. I am not sure either of us truly believed in it. I know it was but a myth to my ears. Perhaps Edward feels differently; he has never said. I knew it was a sad story, hearing of what Aunt Eleanor had lost and what that meant to the family. My father believed in it." Though Anne's face was flushed, I could see that she was relieved to speak. "The day you came, that morning, Edward and I both felt odd. We had been in the parlor; he was at the piano, and I was busy with my sampler. I felt a peculiar sensation run up and down my arm. I looked up because the piano had stopped. Edward was rubbing his arm vigorously. I questioned him, and he described precisely what I felt. I think that was the beginning. Neither of us could let it go: the very atmosphere had an intense energy in it that day, much like the feeling you have when you know a thunderstorm is coming before the rain begins. Edward and I are both susceptible to supernatural beliefs, so naturally George teased us that we'd gone mad. Edward even said it felt like a presentiment."

"That is strange indeed, Anne. The sensation in your arm, did it feel as if you had pins and needles running through your veins?"

My mind was now full of questions. I was intrigued and, for a brief moment, forgot we were to be parted.

"Yes, Vale. How could you know that?" Anne asked, her soft face now animated.

"When John cut my hand, he put a lavender-colored stone

against it and repeated something in a language I didn't know. Well, I felt that same, strange sensation you described, but through my entire body. At least at first, that's what it felt like."

I shuddered when I remembered the intense pressure; what I could only describe as a painful rebirth.

"How odd," Anne stated. "There must be a connection."

"I'm sure there is," I agreed.

We both sat in silence for a moment.

"How often will I see you?" I asked with sudden anxiety. Anne had been my comfort since day one. I dreaded her leaving.

"Often. I came over frequently before, despite it being to Edward's chagrin at times. I know he tends to be lonesome, though he would never admit it, so I make the trip. I may not be his first choice in a companion, but all the same, he has always accepted my company."

Anne spoke of Edward's loneliness, but I considered hers.

"You know to always guard yourself, Vale?" Her dark brown eyes were serious. I immediately thought of John Emberley.

"Yes. I'll be careful when I'm outside."

"Yes—of course—you must keep Margot with you if you go for a walk, or near the village, I know you understand this"— Anne was watching me closely—"even here at Avenhurst, you should not be alone, including inside the house. Keep to the parlor with Mrs. Miller or spend time with her in her apartment if you like. You have your sampler; it will keep you busy."

*I don't know about that,* I thought. I wasn't pleased with the idea of always having company with me. I was a person who enjoyed her alone time, especially when my mood was foul, which presently was often the case. Anne seemed to be making a suggestion, though, so I didn't argue. Then it occurred to me.

"You mentioned the other day that Edward spent a few

years in Europe. Do you think he has any plans to go back?"

Anne contemplated my question for a moment before answering.

"I don't believe so." Anne sighed. "I believe Edward is quite possibly done with the continent—for now." Speaking more softly, she continued, "Edward hasn't always made the best decisions, yet neither have I, so I don't judge his past. I know what Gildi said about you and Edward must weigh on your mind. But understand this: what Claudia saw was a vision of the future that no longer exists. You were not born here, nor raised with us. You are not obligated to anyone, and Edward has said as much to me."

I now felt enlightened to Anne's dilemma regarding myself.

"Then why are you concerned with my being alone with him?" I blurted it out before I had time to think it through.

Anne, however, did not hesitate to answer.

"You are not obligated, but he is still a man—a gentleman, full of decorum, propriety, and pride—but a man. Gildi laid out a handsome future, did she not? Edward is careful, but you are a beautiful promise that he did not know existed." We looked at each other. "It is just—it is unwise to be unguarded around men, for any of us. Do you understand?"

I told her that I did understand. I understood all too well.

"Will you miss being here? This has been your home all your life, right?"

"Yes. It was nice being home for a while. But Highgarden is my home now, and the more time I spend there, the more like home it will feel. I need to focus on George too. He almost seems jealous." Anne furrowed her brow as she said this.

"Jealous?"

"I don't know exactly. I think he just needs my attention.

We are newlyweds still. He has been understanding. We must remember that this is new to him as well, and he doesn't have the familial connection that you, Edward, and I share. So, with that, I think he has done quite well."

I agreed that he had. Anne held my hand and we sat in silence for a little while longer.

Lights Beyond the Gates

# CHAPTER 11

I woke up the next morning to a very dark room. I would have thought it night, but my body knew better. I went to the window and saw an unhappy sky for miles. Today promised more than the typical drizzle. I sat down at my desk and let the dark and solemn sky determine my mood. I knew it was going to be bad enough now that Anne was gone, but with a storm approaching, there was no way I would be able to go outside. I felt trapped; I had wanted to test myself, see how far I could walk or run without being missed. I was mentally preparing for a visit to Gildi. As I sat brooding, Margot made her way inside my chamber room.

"Miss, your fire is out." Margot set down my coffee and went directly to the fireplace to relight it.

"Thank you, Margot. I would freeze to death if it weren't for you."

I must have sounded moody.

"Oh, miss, don't be so down. Anne will be back. She never stays away for too long. Drink your coffee. It is still early. I will come back and prepare your toilette in a little while."

Once Margot left, I moved closer to the fireplace, grabbed a blanket and nestled myself in the large comfortable chair beside it. *The sky looks like I feel*, I thought. I felt the familiar hard flower of my little necklace. I knew I shouldn't do it. Not today, not when Anne was freshly gone, and the weather was miserable. I ran my thumb down the edge where it was clasped, testing its strength to see if it opened. I felt my heart flutter in strange anticipation.

Without another thought, I opened my locket. Staring back at me were my two little babies. On one side, my daughter. Her round little face and smiling eyes stared back into mine: she still had that soft, wispy baby hair, and a little button nose. My daughter was the ideal toddler, full of energy and feisty, yet apologetic too. The other side, my boy, my firstborn. My son had large, intelligent brown eyes, warm and careful—he was so careful. I always teased that he was born this little old man. People told me he was an old soul like me.

Despite the pain erupting in my heart, I was relieved—they had been real. Reader, after some time at Avenhurst, I had begun to wonder if my old life had actually existed. It was as though I had died, along with everything and everyone I knew. It certainly did not help that every time I saw my own reflection, a young lady stared back. At first, I was in denial. Now I wasn't sure which life was really mine. Seeing their little faces, though, this was concrete—this was real. Oh!—how I loved them!—how I missed them! My heart broke again and again. My courage was lost, and I wept bitterly.

I wasn't sure when Margot had returned, I only became aware of her when I felt her put another blanket around me and ask if I was ill or if she should fetch Mrs. Miller. I was able to excuse my grief with missing my mother and father. Margot believed them recently deceased; it was an easy explanation for her to accept. I refused to get out of bed for the rest of the day. Without Anne for comfort or motivation, I surrendered to my grief.

✦

I slept on and off throughout the day, sobbing quietly while awake, until my mind drifted off back into a restless sleep. I awakened once to a very loud thunderclap. It drew me out of bed. The fire was going strong, so I knew Margot had been in to check on me. I lit the candle at my bedside and went to the window. I could see lightning dancing in the distance: large bolts streaking across the sky, revealing large shadows of the trees they illuminated. The whole north of England seemed to light up. I had never seen a display such as this. The lack of electricity blackened the night sky in a way I had never known, and there weren't any mountains to block my view. It was breathtaking and terrifying all at once. I slowly moved away from the window, as if by moving too quickly, I might gain the attention of nature. I suddenly wished I hadn't stayed in bed all day. I was too ashamed to leave my chamber now, yet I desired the company of another human as the storm made the old manor house that much more frightening. Avenhurst, beautiful as it was, felt very old and like it had a life of its own. During the day I had always been with Anne, so I'd done little exploring, but even now that she wasn't around, I was not yet brave enough to wander far. I wasn't sure when the manor had been built, but I knew that Edward and Anne's grandfather grew up in it; therefore it must have been built at least as far back as the mid- to late eighteenth century. I also considered that it was normal for people to die at home at this time, so I figured that left room for the possibility of several ghosts.

Just as my dreary thoughts were taking hold, I heard a small creaking sound. I had worked myself up thinking of ghosts and felt my heart flutter. Before I had time to prepare myself for an apparition, Margot knocked and proceeded to come in.

"You startled me, Margot!" I exclaimed, more annoyed with myself than her.

"I didn't mean to, miss. This storm has made you nervous."

"Yes, it has. I'm sorry. Margot—what time is it?" It felt late, but sleeping the day away made me a poor judge of the hour.

"It is nine o' clock, miss. I came to see if you would like some supper. Master insists you have something."

The mention of Edward made me feel a little guilty.

"Yes, thank you."

Margot nodded her head and went to leave.

"Margot?"

"Yes, miss?"

"Never mind, it's nothing. Thank you."

I wanted to inquire after Edward but remembered how inappropriate that likely was. Servants knew their place. I needed to keep that in mind. I needed to remember everyone's place, including my own. I knew Edward was probably upset I hadn't left my room. How could he know the pain I felt, how lonely I was?

Perhaps he did know. Anne had mentioned his loneliness: she also mentioned they both had made mistakes. I wondered what those mistakes could have been and if it was their loneliness that led to them. I had mixed emotions. I felt bad that Anne and Edward had struggled, though I wasn't sure how exactly, but then I was angry as well. I wasn't angry with them, but all I could think was that I was brought here for them, or for Edward. Was I nothing? Just a token to please others and fulfill their happiness? I knew this feeling all too well, and I despised that it was creeping into my thoughts. I reminded myself of Anne's words—that I did not owe anyone anything and that Edward had told her "as much." My guilt for that man returned. Edward had thus far been gentle and patient; I sensed that was not always his way, either. I was determined not to appear ungrateful. I decided that the next day, I would face the world head on and show Edward some kindness back. I felt determined as I sat in my chair and waited for Margot's return.

✦

Every part of me that was resolute on being a good Victorian girl was out of the question. I woke up feeling worse than I had the day before. I had dreamt of my children all night long. Sleeping the previous day away had only increased my despondency; my mind and body had been restless, and I paid for it by having what felt like the worst night of my life. After I drifted into sleep, I found that I was running from room to room, looking for my children. I would see signs of their presence: a little toy train or a small doll. I knew they had to be there, but I couldn't find them. I fought with my husband. I begged him to let me see my children. He never spoke a word. Somewhere in the distance I could hear their little voices—it sounded like they were playing. When I finally woke up, I was sweaty and had been crying in my sleep. I had to crawl out of bed to gain my composure.

Sitting down at my vanity, I crossed my arms and cried into them. It was torture; my mind would not rest. I cried until I felt drowsy, then went back to bed. I lay there a while, staring up at the molding that decorated the ceiling. It was beautiful and elegant, I thought, yet it was meaningless beauty. I wished I had been staring at my son's ceiling, where at least fifty tiny plastic stars glowed back at me. When morning finally came, I could feel that I had continued to have uneasy dreams. Margot came to dress me, but I dismissed her for the rest of the day. I no longer felt sorry for Edward or anyone else. I was haunted by my dreams and struggled to recover.

◆

I remained in bed, though sleep was elusive. I was drained from the night before, but I dreaded closing my eyes and chancing a reprise of my unhappy mind. It was currently sprinkling, but the clouds would break, with some sunlight shining through every so often. I lay facing the fireplace, watching the flames die away, when I heard Margot open the door. I didn't want to seem rude, but I also didn't want to be bothered.

"I'm fine Margot," I stated before she could ask. "Just let me be for a while, please."

"And how long will *a while* be, Vale?"

This was not Margot. I was mortified that Edward had come in. My twenty-first-century self was not so surprised, but the new nineteenth-century girl in me, who knew enough about propriety and what it meant for Edward to break it, was surprised. I also knew I didn't look my best and that kept me staring into the fire, horrified. I answered back without moving.

"I'm not sure," I replied rather meekly.

"Well, you can be sure that lying in bed for two full days will do nothing but torment you. Margot told me of your need to be alone. I do not believe it wise to do so."

I didn't know how to respond.

"I'm sorry," was all I could say. I was sorry, but I felt crippled all the same. I heard him sigh.

"I know—I know you are suffering. I wish I could fix that for you. Stay in here today if you desire it so, but tomorrow you must come out—for your *own* sake. You will continue to feel worse if you lock yourself away and give in to your depressed state."

"Yes. I'm sure you're right."

I still hadn't moved, then I heard the door close. I looked over and saw I was alone once more. Instead of relief, as I expected I would feel, I felt lonelier than ever. I wept, full of self-pity and hatred.

✦

I was awake and sitting at my vanity when Margot came in that evening, supper in hand; this time, she didn't bother to knock.

"What are you looking at, miss?" Margot saw me gazing out of the window, trying to focus.

"What are those lights? They almost seem like candles or lamps."

I could see some glimpses of light flickering in the distance, outside the iron gates. It frightened me a little, but I couldn't stop looking. Presently, Margot stood beside me to look too. The kind maid reached for the window and opened it. A cool, gentle breeze came into the room and the scent of wet dirt with it. My spirit was momentarily revitalized.

"For sure, miss, those are lamps. There are people out there."

Instantly, I felt nervous.

"Hmm, I think they are travelers."

"Travelers? Like visitors from another country or town?" I asked.

"No, no, miss. Travelers, you know, gypsies. Look, there's the caravan moving! What could they be doing in this part, so close to Avenhurst?"

I felt a drop in my stomach. "Should we go get Ed—Mr. Emberley?" I asked.

"No, miss. You eat your supper. I will go get his butler; he will notify Mr. Emberley."

Without hesitation, Margot left. I was too nervous to eat. What could they want? I wondered. I tried to reason with myself—they would have no need for me, yet the fear remained. I waited for Edward to come, but he never did. I questioned whether he would do anything or just let them be. At last, however, Edward appeared outside my window. I felt a mixture of emotions: fear for Edward and disappointment that he did not send for me or ask me along. He wore his coat and top hat as he walked towards the iron gates.

✦

I wasn't sure how long I had been waiting for Edward's return. It had to have been close to an hour. I had started to doze off, sitting there at my desk. My head was resting in my arms when I heard a soft knock at my door. I looked out my window—still no sign of Edward. I went to the door, expecting to see Margot, who was probably checking in on me one last time before retiring to bed. I was surprised to see Edward standing there in the dark hall, holding a candle. He gestured for me to stay quiet.

Edward spoke in a low voice: "Vale, get dressed quickly. I will wait for you in the parlor. Don't forget your bonnet and cloak. I will explain when we step outside the house."

And with that, he retreated down the hall. I got dressed as fast and best as I could. My hand was still sore, but much more functional now. I took my candle from my nightstand and made my way down to the parlor. Edward was standing by the mantle, pushing his boot against the brick in an agitated manner.

"I'm ready," I stated softly.

I proceeded towards him, unsure of what was happening. He took my hand and led me outside. We were walking to the stables when he asked me to wait a moment near a close-by tree while he went inside. A moment later, he returned with a horse, a beautiful gray mare.

"Is this a new horse?" I asked.

I had watched him from my window, and I knew he usually rode a chestnut-colored steed.

"We are going to ride together, and I feel better with a mare. This one has a sweet temperament."

I nodded my head, not knowing what to say. Edward mounted the horse and then assisted me up right in front of him into a side-saddle position. I smiled to myself. The antiquity of it was somewhat entertaining. I dared not say anything, though. This was all he knew, and since I was no horsewoman, I had no claim on how to ride. Edward handed me a lantern to hold out in front of us so he could see and then set the mare off into a slow walk. I waited at least a minute or two before my patience was spent.

"Where are we going?" I inquired. I added, "Have you tired of me and are sending me on my way?"

Edward made a sort of half-grunt, half-chuckling sound.

"No, my little bird, I would not have spent so much money on your wardrobe just to see you off like this." He had a humorous edge to his voice.

Hearing him call me his *little bird* caused a surprising flutter in my stomach.

"What's wrong, then?" I asked more seriously. He was silent. I could sense he was trying to determine what he should say. I pushed a little more. "I saw the lights outside the gates. I saw you leave to see what was out there."

This garnered a response. "Did you? Well, I assume you know what the lights were from?"

"Yes, travelers, or gypsies. That's what Margot said."

"Gypsies, in this case. I have never known them to stop at Avenhurst, so you can imagine my concern. I assumed they were heading towards the Gheatas' cottage, which they were indeed doing." He was quiet for a second. "But they had stopped for you."

"Me? What for? How could they possibly know who I am?"

The idea of strangers asking about me was unsettling.

"I imagine Emilia told them, or possibly John. I am not completely sure. The gypsies have their own ways. I have little experience with them, save for the harm they have done to my family—to you."

I felt his grip tighten slightly.

"Are we going to their caravan?"

"No, to the Gheatas' cottage. There had been a message from Gildi; apparently, she has a promise to keep."

I then understood why Edward had agreed to take me, but

I was surprised he would at this hour; I asked him about it.

"They insisted, Vale. I don't care to take orders, especially from them, but as they have proven that they keep their word, especially on the point of cursing others, I thought it best to comply. Mind you, I have my revolver with me, just in case—though I doubt it will come to that."

"I hope not," I stated. Edward's voice sounded more sarcastic than fearful.

The whole situation had me unnerved, but the prospect of speaking again with Gildi excited me, and I was relieved I didn't have to sneak off to see her. I needed more of an explanation, and I knew she was the only one to provide it. I still hoped there was a way back to my own time, perhaps one she didn't want to mention in front of the others. Just thinking that caused a wave of guilt; Edward and Anne were good to me, but the thought of my children overwhelmed every other feeling I had.

The weather was chilly, but the sky was now clear; the clouds were spent. I looked up and was taken aback by the night sky. Without city lights, I knew the stars were always breathtaking, but here the heavens were ever so brilliant. I looked for a while, waiting for a familiar light to creep across the sky, but it never came. Reader—only one other time in my life had I watched a night sky where no airplane made an appearance. Edward made a comment about my fascination with the sky; I promised I would tell him another time.

We could see multiple caravans situated near the bushes right outside the little cottage, in what Edward called bivouacs. Smoke filled the air as several large bonfires were burning, each with people gathered around them. With only the moon and fire for light, the beings seemed like shadows dancing in the dark. The scene was surreal: some of the people were wrapped up in their cloaks, whispering one to another as they used the fire for warmth, and somewhere in the near distance I could hear a fiddle playing and people laughing. I had never seen such as the picture before me, nor heard such strange tones from an instrument: my spirit was affected, and despite the presence of my brave companion, my courage began to falter.

"Edward," I whispered, "maybe this was a mistake."

He dismounted and reached for me, drawing me closer to him. His hands were firmly on my shoulders.

"It will be fine, Vale," he stated. "I will die before I let them lay a hand on you."

"That is not comforting!" I looked at him sincerely. "I need you alive."

He smiled. "We shall live, I promise."

I nodded in agreement, but I wasn't completely reassured. Edward took my hand, and together we walked past the bonfires and watching eyes.

**Clairvoyance**

# CHAPTER 12

Together, Edward and I were welcomed into the small and humble Gheata cottage. The first room seemed to function as both the kitchen and living room, with a tall wooden table in the center. There was a small fireplace where a young child sat, playing with her doll; near her sat an elderly woman in an aged rocking chair. There were a couple of younger ladies, perhaps sixteen or seventeen years old, who were busy kneading dough in another corner of the room. I saw them look at our clothes and whisper to each other; Edward and I most certainly looked out of place. Our discomfort was not long-lasting, though, as Gildi soon emerged from one of the other rooms. I could hear faint voices as the door opened and closed behind her. Gildi looked full of anticipation, with her big, green eyes darting from my face to Edward's.

"Thank you both for coming. I apologize for the late hour."

Neither I nor Edward said anything, but I did offer a small friendly smile to Gildi.

"I am sorry I have not come to see you. I wanted to speak with you again. My mother though, she insisted I wait—that was, until today. Mother is waiting and would like to see you once more; she is just beyond the door I came through. I would like you to accompany me, please. Just you."

Gildi looked only at me; I felt the awkward pull of power. Edward, a gentleman, was not used to being dismissed, and I highly doubted he was in the mood to take more orders. I was correct.

"Gildi," he stated with a frustrated breath, "I cannot let Vale leave my side tonight. If it were just you, then perhaps I would consider it, but I will not allow her to be put in any danger."

I was moved by the passion behind his words, but also feared losing my opportunity to speak with Gildi. I looked at him in the small firelight. Even with the shadows, I could see his handsome face was grim and stern. I felt his grip on my hand strengthen, as though he thought I might be pulled away from him at any moment. I returned his grasp, trying to think of how best to respond. To my surprise, Gildi looked amused as she shook her blonde curls and smiled in disbelief.

"Mr. Emberley, Vale is the safest person in this cottage. No one here means her any harm. Quite the contrary, to be sure—they have come in admiration of her. I think many of them were just as surprised as we were to see Vale restored to this time. As I said before, I had planned to speak with Vale once more, and mother believes tonight to be the right time."

Edward didn't look convinced, but I interjected. "I'm sure it will be fine, Edward. Gildi wouldn't have brought me here if she thought there would be danger."

Gildi reinforced my argument. "I would not have, Mr. Emberley. You have my word—Vale is safe." Looking at me and taking my free hand into hers, she said, "Vale, you will want to hear this alone."

I nodded in agreement, much to Edward's chagrin.

I turned to him. "I trust Gildi."

Edward broke eye contact with me and looked up towards the ceiling, perhaps for guidance or out of frustration, and then agreed with a nod of his head.

"I suppose I shall wait outside, then."

Edward hesitated a moment before dropping my hand and exiting back out the front door; I immediately missed his presence as I looked around the room again.

Gildi, still holding my hand, led me to another small room. Inside were three women. Two were familiar. Several candles burned around this small room, giving just enough light so I could read the expression on Emilia and Eldria's faces. Eldria still had a kind, knowing face; with her, I felt welcomed. Emilia, however, watched me not with hostility but with interest. Gildi guided me to a small chair with a low back and indicated I should sit; it was then that I could clearly see the third woman. The familial connection was easy to see. This woman had long dark ringlets tied back in a scarf; her face resembled Gildi's, especially the green eyes.

Said woman spoke to Eldria in their foreign tongue, and they conversed for a few moments. Whatever she was saying, Eldria nodded enthusiastically. Both old women looked to Gildi. Eldria must have given an order, for Gildi nodded her head as though she understood what to do. I felt Emilia's gaze, and with the memory of her opposition and the current atmosphere of the little room, I debated on whether yelling for Edward would be appropriate at this point.

My thoughts were disturbed by the two older women and Emilia abruptly standing to leave. Before any of them had fully retreated, the unfamiliar woman came and stood in front of me; she took a small bag out of her pocket, dipped her fingers inside and then proceeded to run her thumb down my forehead. Being so far out of my element, I resisted the urge to pull away, even as I felt her touch me. I then heard the light muttering of words I could not understand. Lost in the moment, I was slightly startled when Emilia stopped in front of me.

"You need not fear us. *Ai la fel de multă gheață în sânge precum focul.*"

"*Să plecăm*, Emilia," stated the unfamiliar woman, "Gildi has work to do."

Gildi and I watched the three women leave. I feared what might have been said. I wasted no time in questioning Gildi.

"What did Emilia say? And what did that woman put on my forehead?"

Gildi gave me a patient smile.

"That woman's name is Revekah, my mother's cousin, and she gave you a blessing, Vale."

I felt a little ashamed. I had allowed my fears to make me prejudiced.

"As for Emilia, she said, 'You have as much ice in your blood as fire.'"

"What does she mean by that?"

"Let me just say, she has had a change of heart regarding you."

"How so? Mind you, I don't believe I did anything to offend her before."

"No. But she saw you as an object to be removed from the Emberleys; the fulfillment of Claudia's curse. Emilia still holds the Emberleys in contempt, but she has been given some new information regarding you."

I examined Gildi, waiting for her to continue.

"Though that is not why I asked you here tonight, Vale. Mother and Revekah gave Emilia some clarity. I am here to give some to you." Gildi was right, and I was ready.

Gildi took a moment to herself. She had something in her hand I hadn't noticed before. It reminded me of the stone that John Emberley had used, except this one was deep blue. Gildi looked up and saw me eyeing the stone.

"Nay, Vale, your blood needn't be spilt for this. And I promised—did I not?—that no harm would come to you."

Gildi resumed her thoughts, rolling the stone from palm to palm. It took me a moment, and then I realized Gildi was mumbling something under her breath; it was not quite a chant, but similar. I questioned my imagination, but the stone seemed almost brighter than before. Gildi looked up at me once more, seemingly pleased with herself.

"I know you have questions, Vale. Many questions. I cannot answer them all for you, but I will tell you what I can, and I believe that will be enough for you."

I began to worry that there was no way she could satisfy my needs. I thought of my children again. Gildi, still holding the blue stone in one hand, reached forward and took my cameo in her free hand; she opened it without effort. I was surprised by the emotion this evoked in me. I hadn't willingly shared it with anyone yet; I wasn't ready to discuss them. Gildi looked at me with wonder in her eyes.

"Their portrait—it is in color. I hadn't expected that."

I began to stroke the locket as a habit. "Yes, that's common in my time."

"You guard that necklace."

"It is all I have left of them in the world."

Gildi had an aspect of deep compassion. "It is almost like two different worlds, I imagine."

I nodded my head in agreement.

"But Vale, they are not two different worlds, even if it feels that way now. You are where you belong. Before you get upset, as I see you are beginning to now, let me show you something. This will give you great comfort and allow you to live your life."

I was very doubtful of her in this moment, and angry that

she hadn't surprised me with a way home. Yet I was curious and deep down, I knew I should take any comfort offered to me.

"Vale, I told you a little about my grandmother's gifts."

I winced at the idea of them being gifts.

Gildi ignored this and continued, "And I told you about my mother's gifts as well, correct?"

I nodded in agreement; she had told me the night I met them.

"My grandmother did all she could to sway Emilia and me—turn us against English society and to embrace all that our family had to offer."

"Do all gypsies have magic, then?" I was baffled about the possibility of magic in my time.

"No, Vale. My family *is* exceptional. It is not because we are gypsy that we have powers, it is because we are"—Gildi struggled with the word—"what you would call...witches, though we rarely use the term. Most people confuse this. We just happen to be both, and sadly, both have long been persecuted."

I looked at Gildi with new eyes. I lamented how little I knew, though I was unsurprised about the persecution she spoke of.

"My grandmother, my mother, Emilia, and I are also English. We have often felt we do not belong. We were not Romanian enough before, and we are certainly not English enough now. That is why we have stayed mostly secluded in our little cottage. This has been our longest home—my *only* home. Fortunately, we do have some family who are rather fond of us, as you saw before when you arrived."

I smiled warmly at Gildi. "As they should be. Well, of you and your mother, at any rate." My feelings for Emilia were not changed.

Gildi laughed. "I do believe that you may have the gift of discernment—yet it is underdeveloped. Over time, I feel it will mature and bear fruit. Having said that, I ask now that you not allow your hurt feelings to blind you to truth. Emilia is difficult and complex, but she does not mean you harm. And if it is of any comfort, not all of us inherited a gift. Emilia being one of them."

"So, Emilia has no powers?" This was a consoling thought.

"Well, hers is of a more worldly power, one could say. But no, not gifted like Claudia, Eldria, or me."

I thought of her influence on John and believed I knew what Gildi was hinting at.

"My gift isn't the ability to curse or perform an *anahex*. I see visions and I can share those visions, Vale. I would like to share one with you, if you are willing."

Gildi offered her hand, the one holding the stone. When we enclosed hands over it, a warm and safe feeling came over me. This experience was different from the last. Instead of pressure, I felt light and free.

"Close your eyes," Gildi said.

When I did, I could see then that I was in her vision. I was standing next to her; we were outside somewhere. I looked at my surroundings. The trees and shrubs were real and substantial. The leaves waved with the wind, and I could smell the honeysuckle and jasmine. I was conscious that I felt no fear, though it seemed like I should. This was sublime. I looked at Gildi in anticipation.

"Follow me."

I did as she said. As we continued to walk, I realized we were on the grounds of Avenhurst and very near the entrance to the garden.

Gildi turned to me once more. "I want you to walk in first."

I obeyed and walked in ahead of Gildi. I followed the cobblestone path, past the now-familiar arbor and into the area of the garden where it became wilder. In the short distance, I could hear children laughing. I knew those sweet sounds. I felt my entire heart well up with a mixture of excitement, love, and grief. I followed the sounds now, doing my best not to fall as I ran. As I turned the corner, passing large shrubs that obstructed my view, I saw them. There was a large quilt on the ground and sitting on it, playing together, were my two babies: my son with his large brown eyes and my daughter with her wispy hair, as real as I was standing there. Shock alone grounded me where I stood. I saw Gildi move to my side out of the corner of my eye.

"Will they disappear if I go to them? Are they a mirage?" Tears ran down my face, my sight becoming blurry.

"They cannot see us, Vale. It is a vision. It may or may not be your future."

I was confused. I looked again at my children. In my surprise and anguish, I hadn't noticed their clothes. In this vision they were not wearing T-shirts and shorts—no, they were dressed like little adults. My son wore trousers, boots, and a little jacket; my daughter, I could see, wore a small white dress with bows on the shoulders. I couldn't help but smile, then it dawned on me what Gildi had just said.

"Wait, may or may not? How is it possible, and what would prevent it?" I had already gained too much. Fear reminded me I could be left empty once more.

Gildi took me gently by the shoulders. "The souls of children are attached to the mother. No matter what, they belong to you."

She looked at me. I couldn't quite take in what she was saying. I was in disbelief.

"Time was reversed, correct? Your children are *yet* to be born. The only obstacle to their existence is *you*. You were meant to be in this time, so your children, too, were meant to be in this time."

A wave of emotion came over me. I watched my children play; I yearned to go to them. Gildi's words reverberated in my mind, *Your children are yet to be born.* The pain in my chest was lightened, though not eradicated. I closed my eyes, overwhelmed with joy and a sense of relief, I think. I put my attention back on Gildi. This time, I took her by the shoulders.

"Let me make sure I understand. You are telling me, Gildi Gheata, that I can have my children back?"

Gildi smiled and said yes. I may have startled Gildi as I sobbed and laughed, a mess of emotions.

After a moment of collecting myself, I had a thought.

"Wait, though—how would I prevent it? How am I the obstacle?"

Gildi had a smirk on her face. "Well *Miss* Leifman, you'll have to take a husband."

I blushed, then laughed. Even that didn't ruin my current elation. "Small price to pay," I teased.

Gildi laughed and then offered her hand once more. I hated to leave. I took a long look at them playing there in the garden, joyful and happy. My heart was content—for the moment.

"Come, Vale. I have one more vision for you."

"Another one?" She had been right before, when she hoped this would be enough. As long as I had my children, I could be content.

"Yes, I think you should see this other possibility."

Gildi explained that *whilst* she was confident that I would be fine, she suspected I might need a push in the right direction.

"My mother has a sense about you. She believes there is a fire inside of you—one that has been suppressed for many years. It is time to reignite the embers smoldering within."

I was more than a little curious now as to what she was about to show me.

"This vision is not a guarantee. It is, as I said before, a possibility—a likely one, if you please."

We had come to a door—it was familiar. It led to Edward's chamber room.

"I will wait for you," stated Gildi; she gestured I should open the chamber door.

I slowly turned the handle and walked in alone. The room was dark, but not completely without light. I first noticed that his room had French doors that led to a small balcony, much like his office. The moonlight was low, but present. I felt nervous and excited. I didn't know why. I could see his four-poster bed to my left. The curtains were closed. I walked closer, quietly. I felt like a voyeur, but I was compelled to look. I walked around to the other side of the bed, and I saw that one of the curtains was drawn back to allow the heat from the fireplace, just like my own bed. I stopped before I passed the foot of the bed. On a sitting chair, a dress had been laid across and the floor collected what seemed to be the remnants of Edward's clothes. I glanced in the direction of the bed; I felt a warmth run throughout my body. I could see myself in Edward's bed, in Edward's arms. I watched him run his hand gently across my forehead and then kiss me. I saw his strong arm wrapped around my waist, lifting me to meet him. I watched myself holding the back of his head with one hand and running the other down his spine until it stayed at his lower back. I backed away quietly, as if I might disturb this happy couple. My cheeks were on fire, as was everything else.

I closed the chamber door behind me and leaned back against it. I closed my eyes, trying to compose myself and yet trying not to forget, either. I opened my eyes and found myself sitting alone with Gildi again in the small room.

"Gildi!"

Her innocent face shared a devilish grin. "A possibility."

**Anachronism**

# CHAPTER 13

I sat there a moment in awe of all I had just witnessed in Gildi's visions as she made to open the door.

"Just a moment, Gildi—I have a question."

Gildi gently nodded her head for me to proceed.

"Before—at Avenhurst—you said it made sense that I was eighteen as it had been eighteen years since your mother lifted the curse. I still don't understand."

Gildi gave me a soft smile. "I apologize, Vale. I assumed you understood, and I had no right to. My family—myself, mother, and sister, that is—have long anticipated you. I forget that others do not share the same insight as we do—it is so often on our minds."

I watched as Gildi walked over to a small wooden desk. It looked old and worn. She pulled a small drawer open, retrieving what looked to be a small painting.

"This was my grandmother, Claudia."

The woman resembled Emilia. Her features were slightly softer, but the resemblance was quite astonishing.

Gildi smirked, seeing my surprise. "They are alike in many ways. They both have the ability to be quite harsh, but I don't believe it to be their true nature."

Gildi seemed so sincere as she spoke that I felt guilty doubting her.

"Please explain."

"Claudia and Emilia have both been taught to be cold; for Claudia, it was a reaction to William Emberley's treatment of Maria. For many years, Claudia attempted to believe that she could be happy in England. William's dismissal of Maria and the bleak outcome only validated her inner fears, contributing to her horrific reaction. In Emilia's case, she was taught by Claudia; we both were. Fortunately, the little voice inside me sounds much more like my mother. Between you and me, Vale, I can hate no one, not even William Emberley. My mother encouraged our good nature, but Emilia longed for Claudia's admiration, which she often received."

Gildi placed the portrait back where she had found it.

"To answer your question, for many years my grandmother avoided her gifts; she was aware of the harm she could cause, but she was quite skilled, and once she lost her sense of morality, she wielded the curse that she believed would most hurt the Emberley family. And it seems to have worked well. Even with the curse being broken, here stands before me a very wounded Emberley."

I felt a tear escape at Gildi's words.

"Mother performed the *anahex* in 1829—eighteen years ago. Eighteen years is how long your soul has belonged to this time, here with us. When John used the stone to bring you back, the magic reset your age. I am only sorry it couldn't reset your memories—that is a terrible burden to bear."

"No Gildi, for that, I'm not sorry at all. The pain is almost unbearable at times, but it is something I'm willing to accept. The memories of my children are far too precious—I never want to forget."

Together, Gildi and I made our way out of the rustic little cottage, where Edward was at the bottom of the steps, waiting for me. The frown hadn't left his face. I couldn't stop from blushing when I saw him; thankfully, it was dark. Gildi embraced me and then left for one of the bonfires in the distance. I couldn't be sure, but I thought I saw John Emberley out there.

The journey home was quiet, much more than when we'd departed for the Gheatas' cottage. I knew Edward was curious, but I didn't know what to share with him. I could feel his arms resting against my side as he held his reins. Finally, he spoke.

"It seems Gildi kept her word and didn't let any harm come to you—but was she able to provide you with any comfort?"

I thought of my children in the garden. "Yes, Edward. More than I thought possible."

"That is well." Edward seemed appeased with that small amount of knowledge. I would tell him of my children I decided, just not this night. For now, I wanted to keep that sweet vision to myself and ponder the possibilities.

"Vale—"

"Yes?"

"You mustn't come back here. I know you have a soft spot for Gildi, and I believe she and her mother are good…" He hesitated. "They're a dangerous sort, Vale. You out of everyone should know that."

I wasn't sure what had brought this on, though I could guess. I was still on cloud nine from my visit with Gildi, but I knew Edward had a longer history, or at least the Emberleys did. I thought about Claudia and all Gildi had told me. Though I could never hate anyone either, I could empathize with Edward.

"I understand."

When Edward and I returned, my mind was far too full of new ideas and thoughts to simply go to bed. For a while, I paced the floor, reliving Gildi's vision in my mind. I smiled every time I thought of my children, and I blushed every time I thought of Edward. Suddenly, I became overwhelmed with emotion; I dropped to my knees where I had been standing and began to pray. First, I thanked God for my safety and for my new friends, despite what I had already been through. Next, I begged him to please let Gildi be right—let me have my children back. My prayers were neither eloquent nor beautiful. They were desperate.

My long nightgown made it difficult to get up off the floor, but I eventually managed. This life—this Victorian life—was not easy. From the clothes I wore, to the food I ate, having to plan my bathroom habits, or simply needing some light, it was always an effort. Yet, I knew I had managed well. Having my children taken from me—that was the true battle. For some time, I assumed my grief had overshadowed the discomfort I should feel, being in a different time. And though that might still be true, I now believed there to be something more.

I blew out the remaining candles on my nightstand and crawled into my soft bed, pulling the covers around me. I could hear Gildi's voice: *Eighteen years is how long your soul has belonged to this time, here with us.* I felt haunted.

"Perhaps this is why..." I said out loud to myself as I was flooded with memories.

I had never felt as though I belonged in the twenty-first century. I tried not to dwell on the feeling too long. I knew it to be a common one, but for me, it was also persistent. I had long gravitated towards old buildings and ancient towns. At museums, I felt drawn towards anything from the nineteenth century. I could never pinpoint a year, but it always felt familiar. Because of this, I was often called an old soul and was even told that I should have been born in another time. I used to roll my eyes at the statement, I heard it so often.

I became overwhelmed in my thoughts and knew I needed to put my mind to rest, at least for the moment. I wrapped my arms around my pillow and closed my eyes, hoping to fall asleep quickly. Instantly, I saw Edward in my mind again. I smiled to myself as I entertained this vision, wondering if he really did have a small beauty mark on his lower back.

A Paradox

# CHAPTER 14

The next few weeks were happy ones. There had been but little rain, just a few sprinkles in the early morning which gave way to abundant sunshine. This pushed spring into full bloom and encompassed the entire grounds in a lush, cheerful green. When I viewed the front of the estate from my bedroom window, I was able to appreciate the full grandeur of the English countryside, to my mind a juxtaposition of serenity and melancholy.

During the day, Edward was kind enough to give me some time alone. I would often see him in his study writing or speaking with other gentlemen about what looked like business transactions. I spent much of my time wandering around Avenhurst, becoming more familiar with the people who came and went as they worked to keep the estate in motion. I learned the old orchard, how far it went until it met with the river. I memorized each grove and knew where to find the old oak tree Edward had pulled me from. I found it comforting to read as I sat against the base of this tree. As much as I enjoyed wandering the grounds and keeping to myself, I particularly adored the garden. I found myself returning to it each day. It was an impulse I couldn't resist. I was always alone when I walked through the rose-patterned gate. I wanted to relish in the vision, so I would make my way back to the spot where I had seen my children. Once there, I would lie in the grass and close my eyes: I indulged in the fantasy of seeing their sweet faces and hearing their light voices. I could see them so clearly in my mind, and this, for a time, was enough. I made it a habit to pick flowers while in the garden and then spread them around the parlor and drawing room in little vases. I wanted my newfound happiness to be felt by others.

My eagerness to visit the garden was my first thought upon awakening. This anticipation, much like desire, consumed me. I would delay the visit until midmorning as it increased my excitement. It was like a drug, and the anticipation was half of the pleasure—and, like the high you receive from a drug, one day I realized it left me empty.

It was difficult to define the sudden loss of joy in my visits. My routine had not changed. I went to the garden, just like I had every day that past week, but suddenly, this time, the excitement was gone. I was disappointed. I sat down where I had each day in the same place I had watched my children play. I felt the familiar sting of grief. I thought I had put it to rest, but I was wrong. This grief—this agony—was like a fog. Gildi had given me the sun and it kept my pain at bay for a time, but slowly, the fog began to creep in, and once again I felt its dense oppression take hold of my heart and attempt to blind me to joy. I had been happy because I had hope, but it wasn't concrete. As I sat there, I realized that each day the vision and the emotions tied to it faded, until it felt more like a dream.

✦

Dinner was, as usual, just Edward and me. After Anne had left, I initially dreaded eating alone with a man I barely knew. As fortune would have it, Edward was as easy to get along with as Anne ever was. I didn't doubt that the unusual circumstances that had formed our acquaintance allowed us to bypass the usual discomforts of getting to know one another. As it was, Edward had already seen me at my lowest and had also put himself out to help me. This, thankfully, removed the need for small talk.

Conversation between the two of us was effortless. Sometimes, Edward would tell me about his favorite cities in Europe, ones he thought I would like, with museums and operas. Though travel was much easier in my time, I was not well-traveled, and hearing Edward's experiences was fascinating, especially the way in which he toured the continent. In turn, I would tell him small details about the twentieth and twenty-first centuries, like theme parks, automobiles, and, eventually airplanes. When Edward demonstrated a shadow of doubt, I reminded him gently of how much change had taken place since his grandfather's youth.

Edward had a fine mind. It was obvious he was well educated, but more than that, he was insightful and intuitive. I noticed he often got lost in his own thoughts—a trait we shared. This was why it was natural to be with him. We could both appreciate sitting in silence with no pressure to speak, and when we did speak, that was just as easy. We were different too. Edward tended to be more direct and blunt—not rude, but he didn't dilute his thoughts or feign his feelings. I knew that pretending I was fine when I wasn't was my biggest flaw. He enjoyed debating certain topics, to deconstruct his own opinion to see if mine would influence his. I appreciated this part of him. It was deliberate, even provocative, but always playful. I knew by default I was the most educated woman he had ever met, and instead of rebuking me, he encouraged me. I would banter and vex lightly when I could, but like Edward, I was naturally good natured. I might have had a more formal education, but much of it was based on history that was yet to happen and science that was impossible to discuss with others. Where I could prove my wit was my propensity to be philosophical at times, and that I did study literature as well as teach it. I had plenty to learn from Edward, though. He knew rhetoric and studied philosophy in depth; where I was theoretical, he was empirical. Edward did not get a rushed lesson in history as I did; he knew an incredible amount about the ancient world; about religion, music, and art. Where one of us was blind, the other could see.

I was quiet tonight; my mind was occupied, and I couldn't keep up a decent conversation.

"Where is my loquacious friend? Though you are sitting so near me, I am sure you are hundreds of miles away."

I forced a small smile. "I'm just tired."

Together, we retreated to the parlor once dinner was finished. I breathed in Edward's rich scent as he walked near me. I couldn't be sure of what he used to wash with, but the hint of citrus mixed with his own particular fragrance was hard for me to ignore.

It was Edward's custom to have tea with Mrs. Miller, and now mine as well. I noticed that, without Anne around, Edward relied more on Mrs. Miller's company than perhaps she realized. Anne had commented on Edward's loneliness—I could see it.

Mrs. Miller, I noted, kept a watchful eye on the interactions between Edward and me; Anne's doing I supposed. Edward sat down with a book, and I had my sampler. I was carefully working a backstitch when Mrs. Miller brought the tea in. I got up to help. It had become my habit to make Edward's tea. I felt it the least I could do for all his generosity, though he asked nothing of me. Besides, I enjoyed our little ritual. It felt most like a home at this time of day. As I passed the teacup to Edward, our eyes met, and I could see he looked wounded. I didn't know what to think. Nothing out of the usual had occurred in the last twenty minutes.

"What's the matter?" I asked, genuinely concerned.

Edward just shook his head and then looked towards Mrs. Miller; he didn't want to speak in front of her. I expected him to let it go, but he spoke up and dismissed the elderly woman.

"Mrs. Miller, if you will please, do you mind leaving Miss Leifman and me for a few moments? We have a family matter to discuss."

The surprise on Mrs. Miller's face must have mirrored my own. Not knowing quite what to say, she bowed gently and took her tea with her. I looked at Edward, who was looking back at me rather unhappily. *Oh, hell,* I thought. My mind began to search for any possibility I had said or did something wrong. I hated this feeling and decided to be direct for once.

"What have I done to upset you?"

Edward set his tea down and leaned forward. "Why did you feel the need to lie to me?"

I didn't understand. I asked softly, "When? When did I lie?"

"At dinner. You have been inside that head of yours all night, which usually bears some interesting fruit to pick at a later time, but tonight I could see you were upset. And then you denied it. I don't understand. Have I given you a reason that you feel it necessary to dismiss me?"

I understood. It hadn't occurred to me that I had been dismissive, but I had. Instead of telling Edward I would rather not talk, I simply lied. The truth was, I had been met with confrontation in the past whenever I chanced being upset, and so it was my natural tendency to push my feelings aside so as not to make others uncomfortable. Though he was upset, I felt pleased—pleased that he understood me and took note of my disposition. That small sympathy we shared was enough to put me at ease, and for once, I didn't mind being vulnerable.

"I'm sorry. It wasn't my intention to be dishonest or dismissive. I didn't want my foul mood to ruin your dinner. I should have said so."

Edward gave me a small but encouraging smile.

I continued. "I am upset, but—" I looked at him. His face had softened quite a bit; he was a handsome man, in my opinion.

Not in the perfect and symmetrical way we are all taught to admire, but in that rare combination of brooding beauty where the soul mirrors one's aspect. Fortunately for Edward, his melancholy soul was naturally good. His dark brows were furrowed in concentration, but they were friendly. I didn't know how, but I understood him. Despite being born a century and a half apart, I knew this man. I couldn't help but smile at these thoughts and *that*, I could see, caught him off guard as his brows lost their tension and were replaced with something of animation.

"…I have been struggling with something for some time. I think you have an idea of what this struggle may be."

He nodded in agreement.

"Gildi did give me some peace of mind, or heart, perhaps. For a little while, it was enough. Recently though, that peace has begun to wane. I visit the garden every day—in search of that peace."

"Why do you believe this feeling of peace is beginning to wane?"

I thought for a moment. "It's starting to feel more like a dream. Or like when you are beginning to forget what the dream felt like. Does that make sense?"

"Yes, it does. Perhaps if you spoke it out loud, it would no longer feel like an old dream."

I smiled again; I knew he was right. As much as I understood him, I knew he also understood me. Dear reader! This was a new feeling, and one I quite enjoyed. I took my tea and moved closer to Edward. I explained the pain in my heart. I tried to explain how the loss felt more like the grief you have when a loved one passes; not after a long illness, but suddenly, like an accident. I then explained Gildi's first vision, detail by detail, and her promise that all children are spiritually attached to their mother, and that I would have them in this life, where they, too, were meant to be. I watched Edward's face move from pity, to concern, to wonder, and then to something I couldn't be sure of; I think it may have been longing. We were quiet for a moment after I finished. Edward sat there, seemingly collecting his thoughts as his gaze moved from something in the distance to my locket. I had been absent-mindedly touching it again.

"I notice you often touch that little necklace when you are in deep thought."

"Yes…"

I meant to explain, but couldn't trust my voice. Instead, I removed it from my neck and passed it to my benevolent friend. Edward gently reached forward and held my locket in his hand. He didn't attempt to open it, he just held it, knowing it was important. I took it and opened it for him. I could see the amazement in his eyes. There may have been a little astonishment at the two little colored pictures he saw: for him, photography was in its infancy. He gazed at the photos for several moments, running his thumb on the outer edge of the locket. It was as though he was trying to learn their faces.

"They are beautiful, Vale, just like their mother."

I smiled, feeling my cheeks burn a little. They felt real once again, and my mind and heart had been lightened immensely by sharing them with Edward in particular. I looked up at him; he was now looking at me. I recognized this look, though I hadn't seen it from him until now. My pulse quickened and my breath grew shorter. I felt a sense of anticipation.

"Sir, have you finished your tea?"

I startled and nearly spilt my drink. I swallowed my irritation and, perhaps, some disappointment, though I quickly regained my humor. Mrs. Miller had returned and looked completely frazzled. God knows what she feared; I was certain now that Anne must have warned her of something.

"Yes, madam, thank you," stated Edward, who could not hide his annoyance so well.

Though I was disappointed myself, I knew it was best that Mrs. Miller interrupted us when she did. I was still too emotional, and that vision Gildi gave me was revitalized as well. I bid them both goodnight and went to bed. As I lay there, thinking over all that had happened, I felt giddy and full of hope. I opened and closed my locket, taking in my children's little faces. It no longer pained me with the unbearable anguish I felt before; now I was able to look forward to seeing them again. I repeated these thoughts for a while until another crept into my mind: Gildi's second vision. I thought of Edward. He was a source of both comfort and stress. I felt my chest get warm every time I recalled the look in Edward's eyes.

✦

Margot brought my coffee to me a little earlier than usual the next morning. I drank it in bed as I watched the little soul bounce around my room, humming a tune I had never heard before. It was overcast now, but Margot swore that was the sign of another sunny day. I enjoyed her spirit. It hardly ever seemed to be down.

"I laid out your new riding habit that the master had tailored for you. You'll look quite handsome on your ride, I daresay."

"Riding habit?" I looked over to see a beautiful dark green dress set out for me to wear.

"Yes, miss."

"When did he have it tailored?"

"I'm sure he had it done when your other dresses were ordered, miss. I've had this put away until he requested you wear it, which happens to be this morning. The master said you are to ride with him after breakfast."

"Are you coming with us, Margot?"

"No, miss. Mr. Emberley said he'll be escorting you alone this morning."

I didn't ask any more questions. I remembered what Anne had told me. I had been too depressed to worry about being alone with Edward when we went to visit Gildi, but that seemed like a different time already. I reminded myself that Edward was a gentleman by birth and character, and I would just have to be on my guard.

I made my way down to breakfast and found Edward waiting for me, anxiously it seemed, as he was pacing near the fireplace. Upon seeing me in my full riding habit, which I now knew to be a special dress and hat just for riding, a proud smile broke across his face.

"Anne was right, you do look splendid in green."

After breakfast, I walked with Edward to the stables. He told me I would ride the mare. I was nervous. I had next to no riding experience, but fortunately Edward was a seasoned horseman, and he insisted that the mare was perfectly safe, especially since I had already ridden her once. As we approached the stable, there seemed to be a problem. Edward's horse was saddled and ready for him, but the mare was nowhere in sight. Edward asked me to wait outside the stable while he went and spoke with one of the stable boys. When he came out, he looked flustered.

"The mare hurt herself during the night. She'll have to rest for several days before she can ride."

I assumed we were to return to the house when he took his steed by the reins and asked me to follow him. We walked to the outside of the orchard until we were out of sight from anyone at Avenhurst. Edward was in full riding gear: boots, coat, hat, and whip. I was about to ask what we were doing when he stopped and mounted his horse.

"Come, Vale." He put out his hand to help me up. "Our morning ride will be shorter than I would have liked."

I obeyed and was soon situated in front of him like I had been the night we went to see Gildi.

"I think it's important that you get some exercise and get out of the house every morning. I would like to teach you to ride, and I will soon. For today, we will ride together, unless you object?"

It was a little late to object now, I thought, not that I necessarily wanted to.

"I don't mind," I replied.

I tried to act like I was relaxed, but in truth I was quite nervous. As much as I was enjoying being with Edward, I could see Anne and Mrs. Miller in my mind. Not only were we out alone together, but I was sitting so near him. I knew very well this broke all rules of propriety, and I could see why Anne was concerned. Edward didn't mind breaking the rules—at least not when I was involved. I felt him get his horse to start in a slow trot as I held on to the saddle, trying to look more natural than I felt.

Despite my first apprehensions, I was soon at ease with Edward. We spoke of our favorite poets, and we happened to have many in common. We moved from Coleridge to Byron to Burns, and I even made a case for some of his contemporaries over the Romantics; of course, he could not appreciate the poets of his own time as much as I could. I told him of my favorite poet who was yet to be born, Robert Frost. Edward listened intently, and then asked me if I had any of his poems memorized. I did, and fortunately it was short:

*Some say the world will end in fire,*
*Some say in ice.*
*From what I've tasted of desire, I hold with those who favor fire.*
*But if it had to perish twice,*
*I think I know enough of hate*
*To say that for destruction ice*
*Is also great*
*And would suffice.*

Edward was quiet for a few moments, then he whispered in my ear, "I, too, hold a preference for fire."

✦

We moved away from the more densely covered part of the countryside and could now see the open fields full of tall grass and green hills in the distance: the moors, Edward had called them. We stopped for a moment to take in the view.

"Edward?"

"Yes, little bird?"

"Do you ever come out alone and just ride at full gallop?"

I imagined the feeling I used to get when I rode down a hill on my bike as a child.

He chuckled. "I have certainly been guilty of it, yes."

I smiled to myself. "I can almost imagine the feeling, even though I have never done so myself."

I felt his arms tighten around me as he took hold of the reins. He took a moment before speaking again.

"I want you to stand up as best as you can. Go on, stand on my boot."

I was confused, but did as I was told. I was standing with both of my feet balancing on his left boot. I looked back at him curiously. He was grinning.

"I'm going to lift you up. I want you to throw your right leg over and straddle the horse."

"Are you serious?" Now I knew he cared nothing for decorum.

"Yes! Some experiences in life are worth breaking a rule or two for, are they not?"

I was afraid to answer.

"Besides, this is a mere break of propriety that only you and I will know about."

With that, Edward lifted me up by the waist so I could straddle the horse while adjusting my dress and multitude of petticoats. Once I was secure, Edward told me to hand him his reins. He took the two reins and placed them both in his left hand, in a Western fashion. With his right hand, Edward took hold of my waist again, holding me closer to him. I felt a wave of warmth course through my body.

Edward put his face near mine. "Are you ready, Vale?"

I nodded my head nervously and told him yes. I was terrified and excited all at once. We started in a trot as before, then I felt Edward shift slightly, and we began in a steady canter. I could feel the energy in the horse and man change as we picked up speed. The beat in the horse's gait felt different and Edward—ever so slightly—held my waist tighter.

As we made our way to the open landscape, Edward whispered in my ear, "Are you ready to fly?"

Before I could answer, I felt Edward's legs tighten around his horse as he spoke something to him; the steed accelerated his pace as Edward moved his hand from my waist to hold me in a partial embrace as if his arm were my seatbelt. I held on to his arm as tightly as I could and took in the moment, feeling my stomach flutter just as I had anticipated.

Together, our bodies moved in harmony, bouncing gently out of our seats in response to the horse's gait as his hooves touched the ground. I felt the wind hitting my face, and I watched in amazement as we passed through the moors, the tall grass moving like waves in the ocean as a breeze rippled through. I was secure against Edward, and I felt safe in his embrace. Once my stomach recovered, I couldn't help but laugh. This was exhilarating. At that moment, I promised myself I would learn to ride and learn well.

Edward soon began to slow the horse, not wanting to overexert the creature. We settled into a nice slow walk as we turned back towards home.

"Well, was it what you imagined?"

"It was better."

We made it back to where the trees became thicker again, and Edward decided to let his horse rest a moment. The river ran near, so we walked him over so he could drink.

"This is one of my favorite parts of the county. The land changes so—woods and moor—and yet both are equally stunning."

I could see Edward felt at peace. I knew he enjoyed riding, and I thought perhaps he felt more rejuvenated afterwards.

I agreed with him. "It's true, the trees and the moors are both beautiful in their own way. It's strange how nature can be both joyful and melancholy all at once."

"Yes, she's a paradox. Quiet, haunted, and serene—yet bursts of bliss to awaken the soul and relight the fire that dwells within."

I looked away from my shoes, to which my gaze had settled, towards Edward, who was regarding me sincerely. He began to walk towards me when the sounds of another rider caught both of our attention. We were mutually relieved to see George was the horseman who startled us. He had just come from one of the villages nearby and was on his way home to Highgarden. George was slightly reserved in his mannerisms. I accepted this was his nature, one I could appreciate. He did make sure to acknowledge my presence, though.

"Have you enjoyed your morning, Miss Leifman?" he asked.

"I have, thank you."

I was Miss Leifman now. This sudden formality was not lost on Edward—I could see it on his face.

"How is my sister doing, George? I'm surprised she hasn't been back to Avenhurst yet to check in on her friend."

George looked back towards me.

"Ah, yes, but she has thought of her."

"Bring her to dinner tonight. It's still early, and Anne is not one to fuss over her evening attire. Vale would love to see her."

"Well, causing this little one displeasure is the last thing I want to do. I will tell Anne we have dinner plans."

With that, George tipped his hat to us both and mounted his horse once more. I waited for Edward to mention his shift in using my name, but he must have thought it less important than I. I was accustomed to people greeting each other informally and the use of one's first name in most settings. I was aware that in this century, they usually only called one another by their *Christian* name when they were of the same class and only after they were more closely acquainted. My quick adoption into this family had bypassed any normal formalities, or at least so I had thought. Edward had intentionally used his first name to avoid scaring me off by offering the Emberley surname. I wasn't sure why George seemed to waiver with me. I was determined not to think too much about it and to recognize that for George, I was still very much a stranger, having had but few conversations with him. I decided to try to get to know him better when they came over later. My mood, elated at the thought of seeing Anne again, was temporarily deflated when I realized that George would probably report finding me and Edward alone in the woods. Some guilt began to sink in. Maybe that was why he seemed reserved; perhaps he thought Edward and I inappropriate in our actions. While pondering my thoughts, I watched Edward mount his horse and beckon me near him to do the same.

"We had better get back. Anne may not fuss about her dinner attire, but I know you desire some time to prepare."

I could tell Edward took delight in teasing me.

"I'm not fussy either," I replied in faux defense. "I just have long hair, and it's trying for Margot sometimes."

He laughed.

"It probably takes you an hour just to decide which cravat to wear!" I continued.

He laughed harder still, not fazed by my comment.

"Too true, my friend. I'm not quite so vain as my father was, yet still, I do try to make an effort. Especially in the company of such a fashionable little bird."

It was my turn to laugh. "I don't know what you are talking about."

"I've not forgot what you were wearing when you first came to us. I don't need to see one hundred and fifty years into the future to know that you were well-dressed for your time."

I looked back at him to see his face; he was smiling. I tried not to blush, remembering how revealing my dress must have seemed to his genteel eyes.

"Never mind that now. I'm not so vain, I just like to look presentable. Besides, you would take your time whether I was around or not." To push our friendly banter, I continued, "Do you know the story of Narcissus? Beware of the river lest you should fall into it, Edward."

"It is not my own beauty that would be my ruin." And with that, I received a friendly tweak to the ear.

"Ow, you horrible man!" I said through my laughter. "Wait until Anne hears how cruel you are!"

"She will not be surprised! She will repeat that I am both cruel and vain, and you two will vex me the rest of the night. I can already see this play out."

His words did not match his tone, which was playful. We carried on our teasing until we made our way home to Avenhurst.

**Canon in D**

# CHAPTER 15

Margot had finished dressing me for the evening and had retired from my room when I heard a soft knock on my chamber door. It was my dear Anne. She looked more beautiful to me than ever. She quickly entered the room, embracing me before turning me about to get a good look.

"Look at you, darling. You've filled out some, and your dress fits splendidly!"

I just shook my head and laughed. "I'm so happy to see you Anne, now I feel I can really say I'm happy." I embraced her again and kissed her cheek. "I have so much to tell you!"

"I do not doubt it! Come now, I've been dying to know how you've got on. George kept me home so you could learn to survive without me. I almost hated him for it, but perhaps he was right. You seem well."

I couldn't help but feel a little sting at her words. Oh—how I had suffered! I made myself swallow my first instinct of distaste for George. *All is well,* I thought. I took Anne to my chair by the fireplace and sat her down in it, while I sat near her feet.

"You arrived early tonight, so I will indulge you with everything. But Anne, I was not well at first."

I recalled my depression; my feelings of hopelessness and anger. I admitted that my anguish for my children nearly destroyed me and how I would not leave my bed. I told her how

Edward requested I leave my room, but I didn't tell her that he did so in person. I then relayed to her about the lights and the caravans; how Edward felt obligated to take me to the Gheatas' cottage at their request. Anne looked concerned. I wasn't sure if it was because of the Gheatas' involvement, or because Edward took me out alone after dark. I avoided the topic and kept moving forward in my story.

"The vision, Anne, it was so clear. I could see them as clearly as I see you now. Their little voices had the same quality to them that I remember so vividly." My eyes streamed with tears. "After seeing them in the garden and Gildi explaining that their souls are attached to me, that I get to be their mother again, it is a miracle. Anne, it was like someone flipped a light switch on inside of me, and hope returned. I still have my moments—there's an undercurrent of sadness that may never leave completely—but I am hopeful, and my faith is intact."

Anne also had tears in her eyes; she had been holding my hand affectionately in hers.

"It hurts me to know that you were so hopeless and so full of despair, but I am relieved all the same. I will always be grateful to Gildi for sharing that vision with you. To see your children again; children I may get to see—I can hardly believe it, but how happy I am!" We were both tearfully smiling.

"Vale?"

"Yes," I replied, wiping away my tears.

"What is a light switch?"

Once again, I just shook my head and laughed.

✦

Together, Anne and I began to walk down the hallway towards the dining room, passing an old portrait of a weeping woman; I often wondered what plagued her. Anne took my arm and slowed our pace to a near crawl.

In a most casual voice, she said, "How was your ride with Edward this morning?"

I avoided her eyes. "It was a fine ride. Edward is a very skilled horseman."

"Yes, skilled, indeed. George only saw one horse. Did one of you walk? That couldn't have been comfortable."

I could feel her eyes burning through my temple. I returned her gaze, attempting to suppress a nervous smile.

"The mare was injured. Edward and I shared his steed. It was a short ride, just enough to get some air. Edward was worried I wasn't getting enough exercise, and with all that had happened, some fresh air was exactly what I needed."

I realized I had begun to ramble as Anne looked at me curiously. Thankfully we had arrived at the dining room doors and continued to dinner.

✦

After dinner, the four of us proceeded to the drawing room together, the men insisting on taking their brandy with them. I was glad of this change of routine as it kept me from being alone with Anne. I noticed all through dinner that she watched my interactions with Edward closely. Edward, however, never blundered in his decorum and was the perfect gentleman. I had missed Anne terribly, but her suspicious nature regarding Edward was beginning to annoy me. I reflected on all of Edward's behavior towards myself and could see no wrong. It was true, Edward did pick and choose when to follow societal conventions, but he was always respectful. Presently, Edward began to play a lively tune on the piano, and Anne and George started a card game I was familiar with. I watched them play as I worked my sampler. I was glad to see they were playful with each other. Anne gleamed as she hit twenty-one perfectly, and George, teasing, called her a cheater. I noticed that Edward was watching them as well, seemingly pleased.

Edward ended his lively tune and began another song; this one I was familiar with. I set my sampler down and walked over to the piano. Seeing me come near, Edward moved over so I could take a seat next to him, so I did. His hand moved gently across the piano keys, just a few notes at a time. I knew the song would become more complex. I joined in slowly at first, letting the song build between the two of us.

As the melody of Pachelbel's "Canon in D" began in earnest, we were a solid duet. Anne and George stopped their card game and listened from where they sat. Together, my fingers and Edward's danced around the piano keys, instinctively knowing when and where to land. As his slowed, mine slowed; when his hastened, mine followed suit. Occasionally they danced close enough to touch, and then flirted away once more. When we finished, the silence of the room was heavy. George and Anne resumed their card game and acted as though they hadn't heard a thing.

Edward leaned towards me and whispered in my ear, "I thought you didn't remember how to play?"

I smiled sheepishly. "I lied. I was afraid I would be asked to play that night—I didn't want to refuse."

Edward took my hand into his. "You are full of surprises, my little bird."

I nudged him with my elbow in teasing.

"Let's take a walk, shall we?" Anne called out from her seat. I saw she quickly placed her cards back in their box and proceeded to grab her shawl.

"Get your shawl, Vale," Anne stated, eyeing me curiously. "The evenings are still chilly in May."

✦

Together, the four of us walked out towards the front of Avenhurst. Anne had my arm in hers as she led the way. We made our way through the front gates, heading in the opposite direction of town.

"Why are you taking us this way, Anne?" Edward asked.

"Just a change in scenery, I suppose."

The days were beginning to lengthen. It was still light outside, even though it was half-past nine in the evening. We came upon the little church with the graveyard that was situated near Avenhurst. Though I was curious to explore it, the sun was getting low, and I was thankful we walked past it. I asked Anne where this road led, to which she replied that it could either take us further up north or down towards London. I remembered the assembly of caravans had come in on this road. George and Edward stopped and took a seat at the base of the large gates that wrapped around most of the estate, lighting their cigars; I made a mental note to break it to Edward about cigars and lung cancer. Standing with the gentlemen at a distance, I took the free moment to tell Anne what I hadn't confided in Edward during my visit with Gildi, excluding the vision of him.

Anne seemed most concerned on one point: "I'm not so sure I can believe Emilia has had any change of heart for you. She has long hated the Emberleys and done much to prove so. You are everything she resents."

"How could I be? She doesn't know me."

"I told you before, my darling, that you are a dream Edward did not know existed. Emilia did know—and wanted to use you to punish him."

I considered her words carefully. "How could you know that?"

"Do you remember, the night of your arrival, how she stood by John's side, so smug?"

"I do."

"While you were yet in the woods, and Edward had gone to seek you, I watched John yell and curse his foiled plans. What those plans were is still a mystery to me. I am certain, though, that he did not intend for you to come to Avenhurst, and certainly not to deliver you to Edward."

I began to adjust Anne's shawl. It was a nervous habit of mine, a nit-picking one I did to my children when I felt anxious, like my hands needed to work.

"You're right. John kept wanting to leave, and for me to go with him. Do you think he would try again to take me?"

I watched Anne shift uncomfortably at my question. "I don't know," she stated. "Stay close to Avenhurst, Vale. Maybe I shouldn't have brought you out this far. Come, let us get back."

The men, seeing us retreat towards the house, followed.

"What happened, Anne?" Edward inquired. "Did you lose your sense of adventure so soon?"

"Does she have one?" George asked as he chuckled to himself.

I watched Anne lose the color in her face. I made eye contact with Edward, who was walking near my side.

"Don't be fooled, old man, Anne has a feisty streak. I ought to know," Edward said teasingly, but in her defense.

"Yes, yes—Anne is certainly lively at times. I don't deny it." George responded warmly.

I could see Anne had not recovered. It pained me, so I attempted to help.

"Anne is one of the most spirited people I know, as well as warm and kind." I held her arm tightly. "Avenhurst is not the same without her." I received a smile of gratitude.

"Yes, thank you, Vale. My darling Anne is missed dearly when not at Highgarden, just as she is missed at Avenhurst when she is absent from there. Come dear, let us walk."

George proceeded to hold Anne's arm gently, and they continued their walk farther into the grounds, leaving Edward and me alone. I was at a loss for words. I wasn't sure if it was just that George was awkward or if he was intentionally insensitive. Thankfully, Edward lent me some insight.

"It was somewhat of an arranged marriage," Edward said as he had me sit on one of the benches.

I wrapped my shawl around myself. "Arranged? Why?"

"It's a bit of a story."

"Did you arrange it, Edward? I know your father has been gone a while now, and they are still within their first year of marriage."

He looked bothered. "I did. I had to, Vale. Anne needed a husband, and George wanted a wife."

I suppressed the sick feeling in my stomach. "I'm having a hard time understanding. Why did she need a husband? You were tired of her living here at Avenhurst?"

"Yes." He laughed lightly. "As her brother, of course I grew tired of her, but that's not the reason why she needed a husband."

Before he could say more, Anne and George were walking back to where we sat. We stood up and walked them to their carriage.

"Edward, my dear Anne is lonely without her little friend. What say you to Anne spending the day here tomorrow? As it is, I have business in town, where I will spend most of my day."

"I will send my carriage for her. I will be gone tomorrow, as well, so Anne can keep Vale company."

Anne grabbed my hand and squeezed it before climbing into their carriage.

George stopped, gave a small bow to Edward, and took my hand as he stated, "You are good to my Anne. Thank you."

And with that, they were gone. I was glad to have made some progress with George and even happier to have Anne to myself the next day. Edward and I made our way back into the house to find Mrs. Miller asleep in a chair, Bible in hand.

Emberley

# CHAPTER 16

Edward left on his horse shortly after breakfast the next morning. I didn't expect Anne for another hour or so: Mrs. Miller was making her rounds on the servants, and Margot was cleaning my chamber room. Waiting on someone had always made me restless, so I decided it was a good day to explore the side of Avenhurst that was most desolate and, as it was morning and everyone was busy, it also felt less foreboding.

I made my way down the unexplored passageway, which was much darker than the main hallway. The daylight from the chamber room windows was unable to reach this far, and there were no lit sconces to guide my way. I was not a fan of the dark, so I prepared for this small journey by taking a candle. There were several unoccupied chamber rooms on this side; I remembered Anne telling me they used these rooms for guests. I peeked in each one as I went; they were all handsome and large, full of old furniture that might belong to a museum. None were as warm and comfortable as my room on the main hall, but I could see how appropriate they were for guests. There was one room that attracted me more than the others. It was at the end of the hallway and to the left, the only one on that side. It was dark, but with my candle I could see the door was carved beautifully on the outside. I half-expected it to be locked, but it opened easily, taking away some of the suspense I felt.

The room was covered in a carnelian quatrefoil-patterned wallpaper and had dark wainscoting throughout with a matching carved ceiling. There were several large, life-sized portraits hanging on the walls and a few smaller paintings scattered throughout the room. Some were laid against each other carelessly, and others were covered and well protected. I glanced around, disappointed to find no window, so I prayed my candle stayed lit. I ambled around the room quietly, noting that my admiration for the portraits was similar to that of old gravestones. I knew some of the paintings were likely a century old by the gray wigs and short trousers the men wore. One painting showed two aristocratic-looking women, one with a flower in her dewy white hand, the other holding an embellished book. Several looked to be portraits of men who held titles. Leaning against the back wall was a handsome portrait of a prestigious and harsh-looking couple. Between them was their young son, a wispy-haired boy of three or four, holding a small toy in his hand. Not too far from it was another portrait of a handsome yet severe-looking young man about twenty-five years old. It was the same boy. I noticed the same dark eyes; the wispy hair was now thick and parted to the side. I thought it interesting—he did not use the gray powder like the others. This young man's sideburns were long, but his face was bare. I wondered about him, about what had happened to make him so hard, if he was indeed as severe as he looked.

As I turned away from the unhappy young man, my attention was drawn elsewhere. In the middle of the room stood a large, covered canvas on a black easel. I walked to it slowly, unnerved by how strong I felt its pull. I was too short to reach the top of the tapestry and didn't want to risk knocking the painting over. I looked around until I found a piano stool, using it to gain some height. I gently pulled the curtain off, revealing a noble-looking family of five. There again was the severe-looking gentleman, older this time, but just as handsome. It seemed as though he retained the austerity of his youth, yet he had an air of happiness in his slight smile. His wife appeared kinder. Her beautiful, long golden hair pulled to one side served as a halo around her gentle face. She wore a pink dress trimmed with gold rope. This handsome couple had three children. Two were fine-looking boys, both dark-headed with piercing brown eyes. The third child was a girl, beautiful like her mother except that she, too, had her father's brown eyes instead of the blue hues of her mother. The little girl had inherited her mother's golden-blonde hair and shared the same ethereal grace the poets attributed to seraphim. I knew without being told that I was staring into the eyes of the previous Emberley generation. I could see both Edward and Anne in this portrait. I was moved in a way I hadn't anticipated. I felt akin to this portrait. I was held by Eleanor's eyes. I hurt for her; she was very young here, and I thought of her finch. I felt drawn to Edward's father, as well. He looked so young and already shared the austerity of his father.

I was entranced for several moments, unable to take my eyes off them all; this portrait was done in their likeness, not with soft colors and curvy lines like that of an artist's fancy. No matter how hard I tried, my eyes kept meeting those of William Emberley: they haunted me. Though unyielding, I felt comforted, and this disturbed me. I was deep in this trance when somewhere nearby, I heard something fall. Against the silence of the room, it seemed to resound in the walls. Startled, I was arrested on the spot—I'd had enough. I gathered my courage and made to leave. I went to step down, trying to control the panic building within my chest, and I dropped my candle on the floor. It was fortunate that the floor was hard wood, as it did no damage, and the candle was still burning. Unfortunately, in my haste, I put my finger in the hot wax and lifted it too fast, extinguishing the flame. I felt my pulse quicken and my chest tighten. I forced some more courage and made to move back to the door like I had not a care in the world, as if anything that should like to haunt me would only do so if fear were detected. As I opened the door, I heard a creak in the floor behind me. I lost my courage and ran.

Sitting in the parlor room in broad daylight, my rational side prevailed. I wasn't sure if I was more amused or annoyed with myself as I envisioned what I must have looked like running from the empty chamber rooms. Thankfully, no one else was around to see such a sight. After grounding myself back in reality, I realized the creaking was just the house settling, and I took note that the maids were on the upper floor cleaning around the time I was in the portrait room.

Still, as I sat there, I could not shake the sense of longing I felt when I observed the family portrait. I was also a little saddened that Edward and Anne's entire family were already deceased. Many of my relatives were still living in my own time. It was harsh reality to acknowledge the short life spans of this century.

"Why such a gloomy face so early in the day?"

I looked up to find Anne smiling as she observed me. I was both happy and relieved to see her.

"Oh, I'm not gloomy, just a little lost in thought."

"With what or whom are you lost in thought over?" she inquired.

"Not whom—well, yes, whom, I suppose."

I relayed to Anne my adventure in the portrait room and the feelings evoked by the painting, to which she listened intently. Anne was quiet for several moments before standing and taking me by the hand.

"I want to see, Vale. It has been a very long time since I have been in that room. Will you come with me?"

I was taken by surprise; I didn't expect to revisit the scene so soon.

A few moments later, I was staring back into the eyes of William Emberley, and was still oddly comforted by this.

"Edward looks so much like grandfather—I hadn't realized it until now."

When Anne stated this, I was relieved. Yes, Edward certainly resembled William Emberley. He was less severe, but there was no denying the familial connection.

"Yes, he does, and his father—your father—does as well. But I see his mother in him, too; something in the brow."

Anne nodded her head in agreement. "Yes, I see it. They were all very close to Grandmother Catherine. And poor Edward, he was also quite attached to his mother; she kept him home and raised him without a nurse."

Anne eyed me seriously. "He doesn't speak of it, but Mrs. Miller has told me in recent years that Edward suffered greatly after her death. Naught could comfort him."

My heart weighed heavy for Edward as I thought of my own mother. I suppressed the lump in my throat as I watched Anne touch the portrait, running her hand gently near her father's face.

"How old were you when he passed, Anne?"

"I was twelve."

I felt sorry for Anne. I knew her mother had died when she was only ten.

"All you really had was Mrs. Miller and Edward, then?" I asked.

Anne looked at me with a rather sad look. "Ah, mostly Mrs. Miller, dear. My father sent Edward abroad when he was eighteen, not long after our grandfather passed. I might have been about seven. And he returned for a few short months when my mother died, then left again. Edward was in and out of England for several years, actually; he's only been back steady for a few years now. I remember Father said he would never be content due to the Gheatas. That's when I first learned of the family. I asked Mrs. Miller what she knew of them. Of course, she would tell me nothing of it."

"Then how did you find out about the curse? It seemed as though you knew something of it the night Gildi and the others came here."

Anne smiled. "I did. It can be difficult to fall asleep at an early hour here during the summer, as the sun does not set until after ten, and my nurse, Fanny, would put me to bed around seven. Well, I used to lie in my crib and stay very still until Fanny left me. Often, I would get up and play with my toys until dusk. This night I did the same, except that I heard Mrs. Miller and Fanny speaking outside my room. My question must have reminded Mrs. Miller of the happenings at Avenhurst, and it gave her a good story to share with Fanny."

"How long has Mrs. Miller been a part of this household?" I knew she was an elderly woman, but to be with one family so long was impressive to me.

"I'm not exactly sure. She had been my aunt Eleanor's governess, though." Anne's gaze moved to Eleanor's little face. "Edward once told me that Eleanor couldn't part with her, especially after her mother died, so grandfather kept Mrs. Miller on as housekeeper. He also said that Mrs. Miller was not quite the same once they lost Eleanor. Poor Edward, he was still young when she died too. I remember him saying that it was like all the joy in this house was extinguished with Eleanor's death."

"That makes me rather sad to hear." I meant it: a feeling of melancholy came over me as I gazed back at the lovely family who were looking at us.

Anne nodded in acknowledgement and continued, "I was born two years after Aunt Eleanor passed. Mrs. Miller, though not my nurse, took to me, from what I've been told. Of course, being the only baby, and a girl, I can imagine that it was no special merit on my part. I think Father had finally begun to recover from the death of Edward's mother when mine passed. In my opinion, that's when all joy was truly extinguished from this home. My mother was gone, my brother had abandoned us, and then in three years, father was gone too. I have spent so much time alone, Vale, so much time. I'm not sure why I should care at all about propriety, society, or… any conventionalities." Anne looked at me with bitter tears rounding her eyes, stifling a sob. "Now that some joy has finally entered these walls again—I don't belong here."

The tears made their way down her fair cheeks. I took Anne into my arms and let her sob to her heart's content.

**M'eudail**

# CHAPTER 17

Anne and I sat in my room for the next few hours. Here we took lunch and our tea, away from any ears that might hear us. Anne admitted her grief at being married to someone she didn't love, someone with a different spirit than her own.

"I will not deny that he is a good man; it isn't that. But we are so different; I cannot explain it exactly, but our souls are not aligned."

I did not struggle to understand her feelings and, knowing she had less of a choice than I did, my heart broke for her.

"Has George grown on you at all? Is there anything you like better about him now than you did before?"

"Well, he is very much a gentleman, and he does work hard to consider my feelings. Take last night. He realized he upset me, and he did apologize. George is never severe with me, even though he knows I am not exactly happy. It makes me feel so guilty, knowing that he is doing his best as a husband, and I cannot be his wife the way he wants me to be."

I could see a bigger issue developing between them; she must have interpreted my thoughts.

"I have never refused him, mind you. I would not do that. I'm lucky he married me." Anne placed her chin on her hand with a small sigh. I was puzzled at this statement, just as I was when Edward alluded to the same idea.

"Why are you the lucky one?"

Anne stayed quiet for several minutes, shifting her weight periodically. I knew she was deciding what to say to me. I didn't push. Finally, she spoke, avoiding eye contact as she did.

"Vale, I consider you my sister now. I hope you have come to realize that." She caught my eye, and I took her hand and squeezed it gently. "I have allowed myself to make poor choices in the past. I am quite ashamed. I will tell you though—because I know you will not judge me, and because we already share so much more. Despite this, it is still a difficult subject for me to share."

"I can understand if you would rather not."

She shook her head. "No, I think I should tell you the truth. You are a part of this family. I told you before that Edward was in and out of England for several years. During that time, after my father died, I was alone quite often. Fanny went home to her ailing mother when I turned sixteen, and my governess left about that time too. That was difficult, to lose everyone I knew in one way or another. I understood that they had lives waiting for them elsewhere; it just seemed that I did not. Most girls of our class would still have been attending balls, traveling to London and Bath to be amongst their peers, but Avenhurst had been left desolate so soon that I was just an afterthought. Edward, being the new master of Avenhurst, made sure I had the money I needed, and that Mrs. Miller could act as a surrogate guardian in his stead, as I had no other living female relatives.

"Shortly after my twentieth birthday, a young Scottish man came to help at the estate. I didn't mind him much at first. He blended in with the rest of the help, except that he did seem more genteel in his mannerisms. He was polite to me and would acknowledge my presence when he saw me outside or sitting in the kitchen with some of the servants. I spent more time with the hired help than anyone would like to admit.

Who else was I to be with? Malcolm, for that was his name, came to understand that I had no one else but Mrs. Miller for company. Our housekeeper was watchful of me, certainly, but I don't believe she ever questioned my sense of propriety; perhaps she should have.

"It started with a small gesture. It was raining outside; I had ventured out too far on my walk and hadn't thought to take an umbrella. Malcolm met me halfway, covering me with his coat as he led me inside Avenhurst. I then took notice of him; he began to tease me, just little things, but they soon became little jokes between just him and me. I remember lying in bed and realizing for the first time that I wasn't lonely. The next day, despite my better judgment, I made sure to see Malcolm alone. I noticed him standing just outside the front gate. I, of course, knew he had been anticipating my appearance. I made like I was walking to the cemetery; he went with me. That is where we first kissed."

Anne smiled to herself. "We began to pass letters back and forth. He called me *m'eudail,* my darling in Gaelic. I was madly in love with him, Vale. Malcolm spoke of marriage. I reminded him that I wasn't of age, I couldn't agree to marry him without my brother's consent, and I knew very well Edward would not consent to my marrying beneath my class. That is when he told me about hand-fasting—a wedding ceremony without an officiant. We left for Scotland—I was both terrified and thrilled to start my new life with Malcolm."

Anne needed a moment. I watched her stand up and go to the window, wiping tears as they fell.

"God—I am so ashamed to tell you this. I was not there three weeks before Edward arrived. I will never forget the look on his face. I would have thought him severe and cruel, but he was full of pity, and that was so much worse."

Anne turned back to me. "Malcolm was a married man, Vale. He had abandoned his wife, his wife that he married in the Church. Edward had a copy of the marriage certificate with him."

"How could Edward have known? He was in Europe, was he not?"

"It seems I was not quite so abandoned as I presumed. One of the workers became aware of the relationship between Malcolm and me; his loyalty was to Edward, and so he wrote to him and warned him early on. Edward, who approves all hires here at Avenhurst, knew of Malcolm, and was aware that he was a married man. By the time Edward was informed of my situation, he knew it would be too late to stop us before he got back to England. With keen discernment, my brother believed that I would not listen to him without proof—he was correct. Edward requested a copy of the marriage certificate between Malcolm and his wife from the Church of Scotland; with such an argument, how could they deny him? It was waiting for him when he arrived home. When he gave me the document, Edward had to steady my hands with his own; I could hardly read the pretty words staring back at me in bitter mockery. I went home with Edward to Avenhurst that same day."

I watched as Anne closed her eyes, attempting to recover from her unhappy tale. I was sick to my stomach for my friend. To love someone so and suffer such betrayal—the reader knows, it's a fear that lives inside all of us. I gently pressed her for the conclusion, knowing she needed to speak it more than I needed to hear it.

"What happened to Malcolm? What did Edward do?"

"Edward did not touch him, for my sake alone, I believe. Malcolm apologized sincerely. He told me that he had been estranged from his wife for some time and that he knew it was cowardice to keep his marriage from me, but he knew I wouldn't go with him if I knew the truth. He told me that I would always be *m'eudail* to him: I told him I could never be again."

I went to Anne. "I don't know what to say, except that I am sorry, Anne. You shouldn't feel ashamed, though. You were in love. Who could predict that?"

Anne wiped away her tears. "Still, it has cost me."

"You said Edward was full of pity when he saw you. Was he angry when you two left Scotland?"

"Only with himself. He told me he shouldn't have left me for so long. Edward tried to convince me to return to France with him, but I just wanted to hide from the world. Despite Edward's best efforts, the news that I ran away to Scotland with a married man spread quickly through our society. Edward stood by my side and remained with me here at Avenhurst."

"And George?"

"Yes, George. He came to visit Edward last year; I believe I told you that they went to the university together. Well George, despite being aware of my degradation, took a fancy to me. This pleased Edward quite well, and he agreed to the marriage. It was well for all of us. My status as a fallen woman was cleared, George married above his rank, and Edward was free of a burden."

"Anne."

"No, Vale. You think me harsh, but I caused quite the stir, and it deeply affected both me and Edward. I am just fortunate that Edward was as gentle with me as he was. Most brothers would not have been so. Honestly, I still wonder at his compassion. And I am grateful to George, I am. But I cannot pretend to love him, not to you."

I felt defeated for her. "It almost sounds like a business deal."

"Yes, in a way, it is. My marriage was a conscious decision that affected everyone involved for the better."

I took Anne's arm and patted it gently. "Let's go outside for a walk and get some fresh air."

✦

Anne and I walked towards the back of the estate and made our way over to a hayfield; the grass was overgrown here and, when sitting, provided us with some privacy. I reminded her of a previous conversation.

"A little while back, you told me that you had hoped that marriage in my time would have been based on love and mutual affection,"

"Yes, I did say that. That doesn't seem to be the case, though."

I thought about what I should say.

"We do marry for love in my time. That is normal: we don't tend to wed for the better good. It is too much to explain all at once, but even with this ability to marry whom one prefers based on love, it is not perfect. In fact, our divorce rate is very high in my time."

Anne's eyes grew large. "Is it? That's rather disappointing, to marry for love and then divorce."

"It is very disappointing." I began to play with the grass, attempting to make a braided wreath like I had as a child.

"Did you get a divorce, Vale?"

I looked up. Anne had the same look of pity that I imagine she'd seen in Edward.

A small, dry laugh escaped me. "No—I didn't get a divorce." I looked at Anne. "I wished for one, though. Maybe I would have eventually. I couldn't imagine being separated from my children, though, not for any length of time." The reality of being separated from them anyhow choked me.

"Was he cruel to you?"

I considered this question. "He wasn't cruel, not at first, but he wasn't kind, either. He was mostly indifferent towards me—at least it felt that way. I believe I represented what he thought he should want in a wife, but I wasn't what he really wanted."

"How can you be sure? I cannot see how any man wouldn't be taken with you."

Anne had more confidence in me than I did.

"I was never quite good enough for him, it seemed. I was expected to move with his every emotion, for better or for worse. When he was upset, I had to walk around him gently. If he was happy, I too was expected to be in a good mood, no matter how I was feeling or how my day went. He was more than capricious, though. If friends or relatives were around, our family image was all for show. The moment they were gone, his veil came off and his comments and innuendos began again. I never knew which mask he would have waiting for me."

I began to remember the anger I felt for him. I had been so grieved over what I had lost with my children that I hadn't allowed myself to think much about my husband.

"He did not hit me, nor call me names. Everything he did was understated. It took me a long time to recognize who he really was and what he was doing to me." Speaking with Anne was liberating, but it required me to admit my darkest thoughts. "Anne, the day I met John Emberley in the cemetery, I had been grieving my life with my husband. I wanted to be rid of him more than anything. And I got what I wanted, didn't I?"

"Oh, Vale."

"It's true. That first night, when you stayed with me, I woke up and realized none of this was a dream, I was no longer married; but that came with a price, a price I would not have willingly paid."

I could no longer keep from sobbing. I felt Anne put her arm around me.

"It's like I had this little light inside of me, and for over a decade he tried to blow it out. I would rather have been alone than spend the rest of my life guarding my little light." My eyes were stinging from the tears that now freely fell.

"My darling Vale, forgive yourself and dismiss those thoughts. You are not being punished. You—you are the very light you speak of. You have no idea of the happiness and love you have brought into our lives. You are the joy that has returned to Avenhurst. Let your little light shine again so that we may all enjoy its glow."

I held her arm tight around me.

"Perhaps—George isn't so bad," Anne teased. We both laughed.

"Perhaps your love for him just needs more time to grow."

"I hope that to be true. Maybe I should have him take me around on his horse. What do you think?"

My cheeks burned as I looked at Anne. "It helps."

◆

Anne left for Highgarden after dinner that evening, leaving Edward and me with Mrs. Miller. I watched the elderly woman work her sampler as I worked mine. I wondered what she would do with hers when finished. Mine had a purpose: I was embroidering little yellow and red flowers across a brown cardigan that Anne had given me. Despite her protests that it was out of fashion, I thought it was lovely, and I wanted to add my own touch to it. My mind kept going back to Mrs. Miller; she had seen so much of this family; the pains and the struggles. It made sense now, why she watched us so carefully. Anne didn't have to warn her about the capabilities of men; she was already far too aware.

Edward was engrossed in a book this evening, though I caught him looking at Mrs. Miller every so often. I believe he was hoping she would retire to her room early. Margot came for me before that happened, telling me she had drawn my bath. I said my goodnights and went to my room.

✦

I lay in bed with a heavy heart, thinking about Anne and her past. My past pained me as well, but thinking of Anne's helped me put my own struggles aside for the night. My curtains were open, and I could see lightning flashing in the distance. Light rain began to hit my window. I turned towards the fireplace, watching the embers flicker and burn lower and lower. I really should add some wood to it, I thought, but my eyelids were heavy.

"Momma! Momma!"

My eyes flew open as I sat upright in bed. I heard my son yelling for me. I could feel my heart beating in my chest as I jumped out of my bed.

"Momma's coming!" I yelled back.

I was disoriented. It was completely dark now, but I felt my way through the room. The storm was going strong, and the lightning flashed, allowing me to see to my door. I knew his voice; I heard it so clearly, as clear as the thunder bellowing now. I was trying to control my sobs as I made my way into the main hallway, groping at the walls, attempting to feel my way around.

"Damn it!" I cried.

I was distressed and frustrated that I couldn't just flip a light switch. I could see the door to Edward's study was open. The room lit up with flashes of lightning as I made my way inside. The curtains to his French doors were pulled back, allowing a clear view of the estate as the lightning continued in earnest. I looked around, calling my son's name. *I know what I heard*, I argued with myself. I stood there, staring outside at the storm raging on.

"I know I heard his voice." I sobbed.

I realized that this had happened in the past, before I came to Avenhurst. I had awakened once to my grandmother calling my name when I was a teenager, even though she had been sleeping in the other room. It wasn't quite a dream but a tired mind playing tricks on me. This trick felt unusually cruel. I opened the French doors and walked out onto the balcony. I let the rain hit my face and mix with my tears. The little relief I had felt from my grief was gone, now it was fresh and raw once more.

"Vale. Come inside—please."

Edward had come up beside me, putting a blanket around my shoulders. I let him lead me back into the study, closing the French doors behind us. He took me by the shoulders. I averted my eyes, knowing I would lose all my composure—or what little I had left. I knew myself well, for when Edward lifted my chin to meet his gaze, the flood of emotion was realized, and my tears were released. I felt him pull me into his arms, and then onto his lap as he sat down on the sofa. He held me for some time as I sobbed against him. Every repressed emotion—anger, grief, fear, even disappointment—I emptied into his chest. I cried until I was depleted, weary from my physical release. As my sobs finally subsided, I became conscious of our intimate position. Edward held me in a secure embrace, with one hand gently stroking my back. I could feel myself moving with his breaths, and I could feel his heart beating against my hand, which was resting on his chest. My head lay against his shoulder; I was spent. Edward cast his gaze down onto me. He used his thumb to wipe away a tear under my eye.

"What happened?" he asked kindly.

"I woke up—I thought I heard my son's voice. It was so clear, Edward. At least I thought so. I think I must have been somewhere between a dream and waking."

"The storm probably roused you. I'm sorry, I really am."

I leaned up to speak with him. We were now facing each other, closer in proximity than ever before.

"It broke my heart to hear you cry out for your son."

I fought back more tears as he spoke.

"And to see you in the rain, alone and distraught."

Edward leaned in, first kissing the tears on my right cheek, then my left. I closed my eyes as he did so. I could feel the heat of his breath against my skin as he moved. He placed his hand on the back of my head, stroking my hair softly—only waiting for my signal to proceed. I made to lean closer when the door swung open. It was Margot. I was momentarily stunned, and then I quickly moved out of Edward's lap, taking the blanket with me. Margot hesitated, but Edward was quick to demand her reason for coming in like a mad woman.

"Sir, lightning struck your stable. The men are moving the horses out. I happened to be outside speaking with one of the servants when it happened. I was sent for you—but didn't find you in your room." Here she blushed.

"Yes. Thank you, Margot. I will go to them now."

Margot went to leave.

"Margot—"

"Sir?"

"Mention nothing of what you saw."

"No, sir." She curtsied and then left.

I felt a little ashamed. I knew Anne wouldn't approve, and now Margot was uncomfortable. Despite this, I felt alive. Edward took my hand and led me back to my chamber door.

"Get some rest, my little bird—I must go." He gently wiped away my tears once more. "I will see you tomorrow."

And with that, he left down the hall.

Of God and Birds

# CHAPTER 18

I was unable to fall asleep again that night. For a long while I sat at my desk. I could see the smoke drifting from the stable, though it was not the fire that kept me awake. I knew they would rescue the horses and put out the flames—the fire burning inside me was much more difficult to contain. I could still feel Edward's soft kisses upon my cheeks. I wanted to kiss him and would have, were it not for Margot interrupting us when she did. As strong as my desire was for Edward at this moment, he was not the only one occupying my mind, nor my heart. The pain of hearing my son's voice again, even if it was false, was terrible to bear.

I lit the candle on my desk and took out two pieces of parchment paper; one for each of my children. I wrote them both a letter. I apologized from the bottom of my heart for all my inadequacies, my mistakes and, most of all, for taking the time I had with them for granted. I knew that time was fleeting—I was all too aware of it as I watched them grow—yet I still struggled. I had been tired, overwhelmed, and sad. No amount of knowledge about babies that do not keep and brief childhoods could remove the difficulties of motherhood. Despite everything, they were my world; my light, and now that light was gone.

I wrote to them about their day of birth; how I immediately recognized them as if I always knew how they would look. In each letter, I recalled their scent, their touch, the cuddles and naps we took together—how I loved to sing and rock them to sleep. I explained how through them, I understood God's love for His children. I told them that all I ever wanted was to be a mother, to be *their* mother; that I missed them, and how I could still hear their sweet voices as they called me momma. I doodled around their letters, drawing hearts and flowers for my girl and stars and moons for my boy. I was no artist, and a novice at using a steel pen—but I knew they would approve. I kissed the letters, leaving behind a few blots on the paper where my tears had escaped. I gently folded each letter and tucked them away for the moment.

✦

Early the next morning, before breakfast, I slipped from the house unnoticed. I walked towards the orchard. It was a cool, cloudy morning; I pulled my shawl tighter around me, hugging myself as I did. I felt the wind push gently against my body, encouraging me to continue on. For a while, only the nightingale's song could be heard as she anticipated the rain. As I continued, the soft rumbling of the river told me I was close. This river was not very large, but it flowed gracefully and would provide for those in need of it. I sat on the bank and closed my eyes. I could feel the breeze, which had grown stronger without the large grove to block it. The wind rippled through my hair, and it pushed the weight of my dress against my ankles. I did my best to imagine my children once more; to see their sweet faces in my mind.

I pulled the letters I had written to them out of my pocket and read them out loud, as if my children were there, listening. I told them how I loved them—that I would always love them; yesterday, today, and when I held them again. I folded each of their letters individually into a little boat, just as my grandfather had taught me, and placed them in the river. I watched the two little boats float away until they disappeared with the gentle current. I told them that this was not goodbye and I would see them soon, perhaps spoken only loud enough for God to hear.

✦

It was midday before I saw Edward again. I didn't join him for breakfast; I was mentally exhausted from our long night and my early day, so I fabricated a headache to Margot. Feeling guilty, I took my penance of a vinegar-soaked compress without complaint of the smell. I did my best to wash away the scent of vinegar before rejoining the world, but alas, I would be reminded of my sin for the rest of the day. I didn't see Edward inside the house, so I assumed he was either outside or had left for town. I saw no servant nearby to inquire, and then I considered it might not be appropriate; it was always difficult for me to make this call on propriety. It had been difficult enough to pretend that Margot did not see me in Edward's lap the night before, but the good maid kept anything she thought to herself and acted in her usual character.

Feeling anxious, I made my way outside. I both wished to see and to avoid Edward. Emotions I'd considered long dead were alive in me once more, and to see them reflected back at me in Edward's eyes was frightening for reasons I could not articulate, even to myself. I made my way over to the stable to see the damage from the lightning storm the evening before. The stable was a mess, but it still stood. I asked one of the boys where the horses had been placed and was told that Mr. Emberley had relocated them to a neighbor for the time being. I assumed that must be where Edward had gone. I busied myself for a short while by collecting some flowers. I had made it my occupation to replace them in the vases throughout Avenhurst. Mrs. Miller seemed to appreciate these small tasks of mine. As I was heading back to the house, Edward came walking through the front gates towards the house himself, calling for me to wait. I immediately felt a bundle of nerves, and a thrill of excitement coursed through me. I was determined to act natural and let him lead the conversation.

"Une petite fée des fleurs!" he said with a confident smile. "Where were you going just now?"

I couldn't help but to smile at his confidence. "I was going to place these *fleurs* in a vase, until I got distracted by a ghastly sight," I replied, changing my voice to a serious tone.

"Why, what did you see?" he asked, now concerned.

"An odd-looking creature, over there," I replied, pointing towards the front gates. Edward turned to see where I was pointing.

With his dark eyes back on me, he asked, "What odd thing did you see?"

"Some strange, forlorn-looking being coming through the gate—wearing a top hat and brown boots."

The tension in his forehead relaxed. "You're a wicked little sprite!"

"I can be." I laughed.

"Come! Walk with me before those distant clouds make their way over to us. Bring your bouquet."

Edward took my arm in his, and we walked around the estate in no particular direction. I asked him about the stable, and he said it would only take a few days to rebuild and that the horses would be well kept at a peer's home. I asked about his peer—Mr. Mark Adams—and how he knew him. Edward replied that they had grown in the same circle and went to the university together, and that he was one of the few people he still saw from his childhood.

"Then he knows George, too, from university?"

"Yes, my astute little friend. Though, they're not quite so fond of each other."

"Why is that?" I asked.

"Someone is in an inquisitive mood," Edward stated with a hint of humor.

"I suppose it would seem that way," I said more to myself, thinking about George.

"What's on your mind?"

"Now you're the one asking questions," I teased. "I guess I'm trying to piece together George's character. He's difficult to know, not that I'm very easy myself, but George is so quiet and reserved. The biggest reaction I have ever seen from him was that first night when you both hit John. I can hardly believe George is the same man."

"And what of me? Am I changed?" He was smirking, waiting for my answer.

"Not at all, Edward. You are just as beastly as I remember."

I was called wicked again and given a small pinch on the shoulder.

"George can be singular, it is true. I think he enjoys the quiet life. He was raised mostly through boarding schools, his father hardly sought him, and his mother he never knew."

"Did she die during childbirth?" I asked.

"No, she deserted him and his father both. He has scarcely known a female relative. George's character may be awkward at times, yet he has proven to be true to his word and helpful when needed. George has been a good friend to me."

I knew this to be true and felt guilty for bringing him up.

Edward continued, "Adams doesn't enjoy George's company because he delights in the gregarious and affable, believing life to be one large party. Adams is not so prejudiced as to reject George on his parentage alone, but with George being especially reserved, he does not fit into Adams's idea of a gentleman. You would never know, though, when they are together in the same room, as they are both very decorous."

I nodded my head. "Yes, you are right. At least I have seen that with George. And Anne thinks so as well."

"That I am pleased to hear. How was she when you spoke with her yesterday?"

Edward and I had made our way to one of the many benches scattered throughout the grounds of Avenhurst. He made room so I could sit next to him.

"She was well. We had a nice conversation."

I didn't say more than that. I tried to act busy with the flowers in my hand, arranging them in different ways. I felt Edward's prying eyes. I had no intention to reveal Anne's confidence in me, not on topics I knew to be unknown to him.

"Yes, sir?" I asked, smiling.

"Sir!" he exclaimed, entertained by the formality. "What did she have to say about our ride the other day?"

This inquiry caused a small blush on my part. "Never mind that," I stated coyly. "Besides, she mostly spoke of George."

"You said she spoke well of him?" The tension was back in his brow.

"I did," I replied, handing Edward one of my flowers, "and

she spoke well of you too." He eyed me curiously. "Anne told me about Malcolm and what you did for her. What you and George *both* did for her."

"Ah." He sighed. "Good, I'm glad she confided in you. What do you think of my sister's character now?"

It was my turn to look at him curiously; Anne's character was intact for my part. I told him so and explained.

"I felt very sorry for Anne. Sorry that she was deceived and even sorrier that she feels like she did something wrong."

Edward had his head cast down, turning the blue forget-me-not between his fingers gently, deep in thought. "It's not so simple, my little bird. Even when one is deceived, the shame still breathes inside you—always ready to remind you how far you fell."

I watched as Edward ruminated over some dark thought.

"You speak like one who knows."

Edward looked at me, even more solemn than I expected.

"There is something that I need to share with you. It is something that you may not approve of, nay, I know you will abhor it. Let us walk for a while."

I agreed, though my heart raced a little and my legs felt shaky. I hated the anticipation of bad news. Though I had no idea of what Edward would say, for his countenance to change so caused me much anxiety. We walked away from Avenhurst, beyond the gates, where we could remain alone and unheard. I stayed silent, letting Edward gather his thoughts while I regained my composure.

At last, he spoke. "Vale, I'm going to tell you a story, but please let me finish before you make any judgments on my character. It is not a story that I'm proud of, and it is not lost on me that this has likely affected everyone around me, including you."

He took my hand, looked at it, and gave it a squeeze before releasing it from his. Then he walked to a tree and leaned against it, resting his head and foot against the trunk, battling his thoughts, I could only assume. After a moment, he took off his coat, laid it on the ground, and told me to sit before resuming his position against the tree, this time facing me.

"I don't know if Anne ever told you, but my father was a rather melancholy man. This was especially true after losing my mother. Because of his bereavement, he hardly paid attention to his only child, forgetting that he did not grieve alone." Edward paused in thought. "To be fair, he was also occupied by my ailing grandfather, who was still battling his own demons.

"I had freer reign as a boy than my peers, though I was not completely set loose. Instead of boarding school, my father had me educated at home with a tutor, just as my mother preferred. As you yourself have seen, it can get lonely here without others around, so like you, I often took walks or rode around the county. This solitude left me solemn and sometimes unsympathetic and careless. My best form of entertainment came in the shape of someone you have been unfortunately acquainted with, my cousin John."

His handsome jaw set tightly at his cousin's name.

"Our fathers were not friends, but they were civil to each other. However, belonging to a second generation of discorded feelings, John and I were not so decorous to one another. We came into contact frequently throughout the years, his father's parish being nearby."

Edward watched my eyes glance over to the nearby church. "No, not this one. One day, John and I happened to meet in the woods, both of us riding that day. I had dismounted from my horse and was taking him to the stream for a respite when

John rode up to do the same. We exchanged a few choice words that were not very gentleman-like, I assure you, and never how I would speak in front of a lady—not intentionally. As it happened, we were overheard by a young woman. I was immediately struck by her beauty, having seen but few ladies at that age. Even more so was that she was alone in the woods; it was like seeing an apparition, yet instead of being frightened, I was enchanted. John took note of her as well, but he seemed less surprised to see her there.

"'Who are you arguing with, John?' she asked.

"'My worthless cousin,' was his less-than-polite reply.

"'Is this the cousin you speak so much of, the one from Avenhurst?' she asked him in a sweet voice.

"As she came near me, I felt my pulse quicken. John lost the color in his face and cursed at me once more. The girl chastised him for being rude and vulgar.

"'Excuse him, sir. John is naturally boorish.'

"I smiled at her. Her dark hair was only pulled halfway back, not unlike the way you wear yours so often, Vale. Her eyes were dark, too, full of mystery and knowledge to my own inadequate eyes. She was several years older than I, and perhaps a couple of years older than John as well, only adding to her appeal. Mind you, I had just turned eighteen, and I was new to the world of women. My father had shunned the gentry for some time, so my exposure to ladies of my rank was miniscule."

I shifted uncomfortably. I wasn't enjoying this story thus far.

Edward continued. "The girl introduced herself as Emilia Gheata."

I couldn't keep my eyes from meeting Edward's. Now I really dreaded hearing any more. I reminded myself that I had agreed not to pass judgment until I heard it all, though it wasn't judgment that was causing the ball in the pit of my stomach. I attempted a smile at Edward to encourage him to continue.

"It became apparent to me—very quickly—that I was not the only Emberley man enthralled by Emilia Gheata. John was overtly jealous, though Emilia did not seem too concerned. I assumed that he had no claim on her, else she would have acted more like his lover than she did. It became a habit of ours to meet in these woods, though it was always the three of us, John following Emilia around like a sad puppy. Concerning John, she seemed mostly indifferent, and the more he was discouraged, the greater my confidence grew. Towards the end of our walk one day, Emilia gently slipped a note into my pocket. In the note she confessed her love for me, declaring that she would rather die an early death than live without me by her side. I know it may seem ridiculous now, but to a young man with no life experience, it was maddening. To be loved so desperately by someone so beautiful and seemingly tender of heart—how blessed I considered myself. Her note included a time for us to meet alone, without the prying ears and eyes of John. And we did meet, that same evening. We met at the church gate, after nightfall, and I followed Emilia home. When I beheld the cottage, I knew my father would be angry. Naturally, I assumed she had been from the village. It was too late, though. I thought I was desperately in love, and I was determined to have her. It was her idea to elope to Scotland. I mentioned speaking to my father, but she hushed me with our first kiss.

"'He'll never allow our union. He hates my kind,' she said.

"I knew her words to be true. I told her to gather what she could, and we walked back to Avenhurst, where I gathered some belongings and money. We took the coach up north and were married."

I dropped the bouquet of flowers from my hand as the ball in my stomach hardened into utter disappointment and disgust. *No,* I acknowledged to myself, *I'm jealous.* And, perhaps, a little heartbroken. I could feel the burning sensation rising in me. Emilia! The one who showed such contempt towards me on the very night I arrived was Edward's wife. Now I understood Anne's disbelief in Gildi's words—I, too, doubted Emilia's ability to have any change of heart regarding me. I checked my emotions by keeping my face downwards, staring at little tufts of grass. After a moment of silence, Edward continued his story.

"I had no intention of living an outcast life amongst the highlanders, and so after a few days, Emilia and I returned to Avenhurst to face my father. I knew he would be upset, but I was positive that he would be moved by her beauty and sweet disposition once he met her. That was not to be. We argued for an hour. I had never seen my father so livid. This was beyond disappointment: he was disgusted and hysterical. My father may have been a solemn man, but he was always with reason, never acting with prejudice. I was appalled, to the extent that I began to accept that I might be without my inheritance. It struck me bitterly that John would inherit my land, but I thought only of my wife and her needs. I watched Emilia as I argued with my father. He did not even bother to send her out of the room, nay, he wanted her to hear it; her face was stoic and proud, a look I did not recognize in her. I was about to take my new bride and leave when we were interrupted by a great commotion from the butler and some guest who had just arrived. It was John. He was irate, cursing my name and Emilia's. My father, not usually one to entertain any of these behaviors, must have discerned the conflict and drew silent, allowing John to speak. John went to Emilia.

"'Days! You have been gone days! You said one night—damn it!'

"'Enough, John, you should leave—now!' Emilia attempted to send him away, but their discourse still struck me as intimate. John looked at me, contempt in his eyes.

"'Did you consummate the marriage?' he asked.

"'John!' Emilia exclaimed.

"'What right do you have to ask, man?' I replied, his question ridiculous to me.

"'Did you, Edward?' He then looked at Emilia. I could see her grow uncomfortable under his gaze, and not out of modesty—no—I could feel it was something else. My heart sank.

"'We are married now, John—of course we did,' I spat at him.

I felt defensive and insecure. John was momentarily frozen; then he spoke calmly and unemotionally to Emilia.

"'You were supposed to come back the next day, after feigning an illness.'

"John then became angry, calling her a derogatory name I will not repeat to your ears. It did, however, provoke Emilia, and there—in front of myself and my father, John and my bride had their lovers' quarrel, bantering back and forth about their failed plan to rob me out of my inheritance and punish the Emberleys." Edward became quiet. Though I wasn't looking at him, I knew he was lost in a rumination. "I have reflected on this moment many times. John has always disliked me and is a hateful man, but Emilia—she is cold and calculating. After your arrival, I then realized how deep their hate for my family runs."

I looked up with real pity in my heart. Poor Edward! I could never have expected this. I already disliked Emilia; now

I was on the verge of hate for the wretched woman. Edward was looking at me. His face was grave.

"You can imagine the extreme disappointment I suffered. After some time, I realized it was never love that I felt, but infatuation. Emilia knew what she was doing, and she exploited my naïveté, loneliness, and innocence in an attempt to both embarrass and rob me. My pride stayed bruised much longer than my heart."

I nodded, not having the words to say anything of merit.

"My father was much softer in his approach towards me afterwards. First, he banished John and Emilia from Avenhurst, then he explained the history between my family and hers. I had overheard some of the rumors about my grandfather before, but to hear the entire story and from my own father; it made a different impression on me. As for my marriage, due to the admission of adultery, I was able to get a divorce after some time, which is almost unheard of. It was very public, as they publish all court records, and I had to sue John to prove the act of adultery. Jealous as he was, he had no shame in admitting his guilt since he and Emilia continued their relationship—as you saw for yourself the night you arrived. Even with public humiliation, they were both proud of what little they did accomplish."

I hardly knew what to say.

"I'm sorry, Edward. They are both despicable."

He nodded his head. "Yes, they are, but my grandfather set the stage for this drama."

I watched in silence as Edward reflected a moment. Then a thought occurred to me.

"Is this the unhappy event Gildi spoke of?" I asked.

"Yes, I believe so. It wasn't long after this debacle that I saw Eldria in town. I knew she was Emilia's mother the moment I saw her. I was walking down the street, and as we were about to cross paths, she reached over and took my hand. It startled me. I went to pull away, but something like intuition stopped me. She gently patted my hand and mumbled a few words I didn't understand. When she walked away, I realized she had left something in my hand."

As Edward told me this, he pulled out something small and round out of his pocket; he handed it to me. I turned the small item over. It was a bronze lapel pin. One side had a small bird with a red face and golden feathers on its back; the other side was the pin with a closure. I looked at Edward.

"What kind of bird is this?" I asked, wanting to confirm what I suspected.

"A finch. A little goldfinch."

I thought of Eleanor. "That was eighteen years ago?"

"Yes."

"You've kept it all this time? You didn't know she had lifted the curse?"

He smiled. "No, I did not know. But I knew the symbolism of the finch and that she meant me well. I also kept it as a reminder that I would not marry so blindly if I ever dared to marry again."

*Who could blame him?* I thought.

"Edward?" He looked my way. "Is this why you were so good with Anne?"

"I understood all too well what Anne was to suffer. I was not happy with her situation. It ruined her reputation. But I knew the desire to be loved and to think someone loves you. For that, I had the utmost empathy for my sister. I felt guilty leaving her alone so long. Whilst I was out battling my demons, she was entertaining her own."

"You are hard on yourselves. You were both deceived."

"Yes, I suppose we were," he said after some consideration. "Though we both made what we knew to be poor decisions. Had I been honest with my father, I would have never married Emilia. Had Anne been honest with me, she wouldn't have been deceived by Malcolm. We both were unrighteous and willingly blind."

I admired him for his depth of accountability; that was a rare quality to find in a person, no matter the year or era.

"Have I disappointed you too greatly, Vale?"

I looked up at him, surprised at the question. I got up from the ground and went and stood beside him at the tree. I took his hand and opened it palm up, placing his lapel in the center. My jealousy had subsided, and my reason returned.

"You have not disappointed me. I am a little sad for you, though. You were a victim of an age-old ailment—loneliness. And like most before you, you believed another human being was the cure." I took a moment before I made my next statement. "And perhaps, you were a victim of your own pride. Was there no part of you that enjoyed gaining Emilia's affection when you knew John to feel the same?"

"Absolutely," Edward said with a scornful laugh. "And I received no less than I deserved. I knew that very night that as much as I would like to blame John and Emilia, callous people that they are, I also took a share in the blame. Deep down, I knew Emilia was not fully genuine. There were subtle signs, yet I chose to ignore them, out of loneliness and pride, as you say. It took me several years to stop being angry with myself. It was a hard lesson, with a few more that came afterwards, but eventually, I did learn."

I felt Edward eyeing me carefully. His face almost looked hurt—no, worried. He continued, "You do not believe a companion would cure my loneliness?"

I realized he misunderstood me, perhaps fearing a subtle rejection. I closed his hand gently around the lapel and kept both of mine on his. I gave him a small smile to prevent further injury.

"I meant that first you need to find some inner peace, forgive yourself, repent if you have not, and be glad of God's grace. This is necessary to be whole. Broken people seek those who, too, are broken, each hoping the other can do the mending, when neither has the skill."

I watched as his scowl relaxed and the confidence returned to his handsome face.

"Your words are comforting. So much wisdom for one so young." I inwardly laughed at the absurdity. Outwardly, I addressed it. "Well, I am not so sure about it being wisdom, Edward, but you forget, I wasn't eighteen in my own time."

"I do forget. It is impossible for me to imagine you any way but how you are now, standing so near me." He was gently squeezing each one of my fingers individually in a playful manner. "How old were you the day you met John?"

I collapsed his fingers with mine and squeezed hard—not causing a single degree of pain. "You know better than to ask a lady her age, sir. Besides, I was still younger than you are now." I gave him a sly smile. "But not by much."

Edward gave a small laugh before concluding our conversation. "Come, *ma petite vieille* I could use a cup of tea."

I asked him what *vieille* was, and only received another laugh. Before taking leave of our spot, Edward leaned down and retrieved the bouquet I had dropped, placing it back in my care.

We began walking back towards the house together when Edward stopped me once more and said, in a sincere tone, "I have repented, Vale, and I do believe I am a better man. I wasn't for a long time, but I am now."

Without saying another word, Edward took my arm in his as we walked towards home.

Psalm

# CHAPTER 19

I was restless and somewhat discouraged as I lay in my bed. I wasn't quite sure what was bothering me; something lingered on the edge of my thoughts, prodding and irritating. I listened to the crackling of the fire, hoping it would lull me to sleep. I had come to rely on a nice fire. It provided both warmth and sound, things I had previously obtained through modern means. It did not work, however; sleep abandoned me. I took my blanket and sat in a chair next to the fireplace; here, I could allow myself to ponder and wallow in my thoughts. I was mostly thinking of Edward. I considered the great amount of empathy he had shown Anne and how rare that was. Of course, in my time, few would have judged Anne for being deceived, but in this time, it was a different set of rules and vastly different expectations.

I traced my cheeks where Edward's lips had made contact. It was as though they had secretly burned an imprint that no one could see and only I could feel. I thought of what he said earlier that day, that he was a better man than before. As far as I knew, he was a good man. I could not see how he hadn't been one before; what happened with Emilia was not his fault.

Emilia—now I knew what was nagging at my mind and heart. Edward had belonged to her; for a short time perhaps, but he had been hers. My dislike for Emilia was beginning to leave a deeper impression on my heart. I was aware I needed to concrete these feelings, not water these seeds. I questioned how I could have such strong feelings of disgust and dislike. I found myself shaking my leg anxiously and curling my hair around my finger, the golden-brown tresses cutting off circulation. I was sick to my stomach, and then I understood: I was jealous again. *He does not love her,* I reminded myself, and I knew this to be true. I could see it in his countenance as he recalled his past. When I thought of all he had done for me and the friendship he had bestowed upon me, I felt ashamed for even entertaining the jealous spirit. I began to wonder at Edward's feelings for me. I remembered Anne's words: "A beautiful dream he did not know existed." I wondered if this was really true. I hoped so.

I knew Edward had a soft spot for me, but in this age, men needed but a few soft qualities to exist in a woman before they thought it enough for marriage. I could never agree to that. Even though in my own time I had still ended up in an unhappy marriage, I had kept to my vows and stayed committed, even if it was not the popular choice. If I could be that loyal in the twenty-first century, when I could ask for a divorce, what would happen to me in this century, when I lost all my rights to coverture? Though I had no property or anything of value, I valued myself and my happiness. I knew what it was like to live without it, and I would not make that mistake again. Yet there was a little voice inside, whether my head or heart I was not sure; it whispered to me daily, *you love him*. I felt the familiar burn work its way through my body.

"Yes," I said out loud, wanting the walls to know what I had known for some time and fought to admit. "Yes, I love him."

I began to weep. My love for him was deep and out of my reach. I had no control over it, and this frightened me. I did not want to love anyone; it cost too much. If I could be hurt so much by someone I was indifferent to, how much more painful would it be to be hurt by someone I loved? I fought being a shell of a mother for so long, it scared me to repeat that again, to be fooled again. I wiped my eyes with my blanket. *No,* I thought, *you were young and inexperienced before. He never did love you.* I had only fooled myself; the signs were all there, I just didn't know any better. My fingers made their way home to my cheeks. I felt flushed but calm. I wanted to seek Edward out, to allow him to comfort me again and cast away my fears. This was a great burden to place upon another being, I realized, but it was too late. Edward had sowed his roots too near mine, and every day I felt them intertwining together, becoming a single organism, a life force that relied on the other to live.

✦

The next few weeks were pleasant. Summer had come to England, a much cooler summer than I was familiar with, but the warm afternoons were welcome. Edward and I took many walks together, and he taught me to ride side-saddle—with assistance nearby, but I could ride. These were happy days, and with each passing one, my love for Edward grew stronger. Any doubts I'd had about Edward's love for me were fading. Jealousy may have stoked the embers burning within me, but Edward, he was as constant as the sun in the sky. When I felt downcast, Edward listened; when I wanted to be adventurous, Edward provided; and in those moments when my heart felt as though it would burst, yet words failed me, he was enduring.

Edward had returned from seeing his tenants one day and found Anne and me riding just outside of Avenhurst; he was pleased to see us in our new riding habits. Anne was lovely in purple; she insisted I wear blue.

Edward smiled as we trotted by, calling us, *"Belles dames."*

I was sitting by the fire that same evening, and Edward and George were to play a card game. On his way to the table, Edward paused at my side and whispered in my ear, "Behold, thou art fair." My cheeks burned deeply.

Avenhurst was lovely. The grounds were green and full of life: I had never seen so many different species of birds in one area or gardens as whimsical as those made for Catherine Emberley. Even the nearby woods were pristine and enchanting. The alteration at Avenhurst was not external alone. Inside, the servants seemed happier; of course, this was likely a reflection of a happy master. Edward was ever in a good mood, genial and pleasing, and always playfully vexing—it was his way.

I knew this to be a welcomed change, for Mrs. Miller remarked that she "hadn't seen this happy of a home in many ages."

Anne and George were getting on well; I caught Anne smiling after gentle words from George, and I could see he was attentive. George seemed more at ease; not so ambitious as to be the life of the party—Anne and Edward did that well enough for the four of us—but he was much friendlier.

I finally felt an inner peace I had never really known before. Life held a new excitement for me now, a new beginning. I quickly grew accustomed to having someone with me during the day. Usually it was Edward, and if not him, then Margot. I enjoyed Mrs. Miller sparingly. She was friendly enough, but she often dropped hints about propriety and the habits of young ladies. I did openly tease Edward. Little did she know, however, that I was my own best Jiminy Cricket, not her bourgeois ideologies.

✦

On a lovely, warm July day, I had been looking forward to having a picnic with Edward when he received a message from a neighbor a few miles away. This neighbor had wanted to gather some of the gentry together to discuss the prevention of cholera, to keep it from spreading to northern England. I told Edward I was interested to hear what ideas this Sir Hadley had and planned to have a science-based conversation with him when he returned.

"I doubt not that you will enlighten me greatly, my little bird. For now, I must harken to the rambles of a self-righteous middle-aged nineteenth-century man who doesn't know his head from his—well, never mind. I must go." With a tweak to my ear, Edward was off.

For the first time in a while, I had some time all to myself to do as I wished. Margot had taken half the day to go see some family visiting nearby, and Mrs. Miller was busy giving very specific orders to the chambermaids so that "their master would be pleased." I had wandered around the Avenhurst grounds for at least half an hour when I remembered that I hadn't yet visited the graveyard at the nearby church. I knew this graveyard would be older than any I had visited before, even if the graves were newer in 1847.

I made my way over to the little church as I meditated on the word *master*. The staff of the house often called Edward that, and even to me, they would refer to him as being "my master" or "our master." Initially, the word had a different meaning for me; gradually though, I had become accustomed to its use. Edward *did* master me, I admitted to myself. I wondered if he was aware of his effect on me. Even that tweak of the ear sent a thrill through me. I wanted to pinch him back, to squeeze him—oh, I wanted to kiss him. I hadn't found the courage yet. I could tease, and I did that well, but to make a move? I was hopeless.

I pondered these thoughts as I opened the small iron gate, grimacing as it creaked loudly.

The sound seemed at odds with the stillness of the graveyard. The day became overcast; it would be raining within the hour, I guessed. It was beautiful and solemn here. It looked so much older than the one I knew of in California, in my time. These were old graves, some as old as the seventeenth century. The information on the tombstones was different as well. Some just bore the person's name, while others had just that along with the year they died.

A tempestuous breeze pushed through the graveyard, awakening the large trees. The sound of the leaves rustling in the wind seemed to resonate throughout the solemn yard. The cool breeze lingered as I walked to the back of the church. I could see another building a little farther out. It was covered by many trees and was not visible from the road. I pulled my cloak around me. It seemed a warm picnic was not meant to be, with or without Edward. As I drew closer, I realized the building was a tomb. It looked like a small house. In the marble at the top was carved "Emberley," and in French underneath, it read, "*Seigneur, pour montrer ta gloire, pardonne ma faute qui est si grande. Psaume 25:11.*" I could only decipher a few words. Though my French was weak, I knew it to be a psalm. The tomb was hauntingly beautiful. It had a Gothic archway and a large cross on top with carved arch angels behind it, reaching for the heavens. On the side of the tomb were lancet-arched stained-glass windows. A large marble plaque listed the family names:

*In Memory Of*

*Catherine, wife of William Emberley, Master of Avenhurst Manor;*

*She died 26 Sept 1795. Aged 33 years.*

*Also of Elizabeth, their daughter in law, wife of James Edward Emberley; who died 18 Aug 1817. Aged 27 years.*

*Also of Eleanor Anne Bathurst, their daughter, wife of Andrew Bathurst; who died 21 June 1820. Aged 29 years.*

*Also of Thomas William Emberley, their son, who died 7 Feb 1825. Aged 41 years.*

*Also of William Edward Emberley, Master of Avenhurst Manor and husband of Catherine, who died 1 Oct 1829. Aged 71 years.*

*Also of James Edward Emberley, Master of Avenhurst Manor, who died 31 Mar 1834. Aged 54 years.*

*Here rests Edward's family,* I thought, *his grandparents, aunt, uncle, father, and mother.* I thought of their portrait. I could see their faces so clearly in my mind.

Nearby were smaller headstones, just as beautiful, though not as grand as the tomb. These held:

*Andrew Bathurst Died 1822. Aged 38 years.*

*Sarah Emberley Died 1832. Aged 41 years.*

*Charlotte Emberley Died 1824. Aged 34 years.*

I knew Sarah to be Anne's mother. Her monument was larger than Charlotte's or Andrew's, though theirs, too, were more magnificent than what most people would receive in my time. I felt a mixture of sadness and gloom as I studied the now-gone Emberley family. I wondered how often they were visited by those who remained behind; I had never seen Edward or Anne visit here. There were no fresh flowers in this graveyard; no balloons, no little reminders left on their graves by the living kin. I sat down by Charlotte Emberley's grave. It was small but elegant and easy enough to lean against. I closed my eyes. I could feel the breeze growing impatient. The wind was tugging at the bottom of my dress. I imagined the Emberleys alive and what life would have been like if I had been born to Eleanor; it pained my heart to learn she had passed at so young an age. I lamented not having the opportunity to meet her. I opened my eyes to this gloomy thought—and found I was not alone. I was so startled by this discovery that I was momentarily paralyzed and could not find it within me to react. Once again, I was alone in a graveyard with John Emberley.

Of Embers and Ice

# CHAPTER 20

Fear arrested me. I knew I couldn't get up quick enough to run, nor would I have the endurance to make it back to Avenhurst before he caught me, even if I was fast enough to make it out of the graveyard.

John must have known my trepidation, for he spoke it out loud: "If I wanted you, Vale, I had my chance. You've been out here, *alone,* all morning. Seeing how vulnerable you are, one would think you'd have learned by now."

I didn't know how to respond. He was right, but I would not validate this for him. I had grown comfortable and let my guard down. I cursed myself for leaving the Avenhurst grounds alone. My lack of response prompted another of his.

"I must say, I'm surprised that Edward let his *little bird* out of her cage. I would have thought him more careful with you."

Fear quickly faded into anger as I felt my chest and face flush with a sudden heat. I stood up. "It has nothing to do with Edward. I chose to come out here alone. A person should be able to take a walk without fear of being harmed, shouldn't they?"

Surprisingly, John nodded his head, and relented.

"I see you've met my mother," he said, gazing at the grave I had been leaning against.

John's clear blue eyes betrayed an emotion I hadn't seen in him prior—perhaps sorrow. As much as I disliked the man, my feelings of pity were evoked.

"I thought maybe she was. Your mother, that is—I wasn't sure. I knew Sarah was Anne's mother."

"Yes, and Andrew there, he was Eleanor's husband."

I thought about this a moment. Andrew would have been my father. I quickly pushed this revelation aside, not having the luxury to dwell.

"Only Edward's mother made it into the family tomb," John grumbled bitterly.

I thought of his pain. "I'm sorry, John. Your mother does have a beautiful grave, though, much nicer than most in my time." And then, with a little resentment: "You should know. You've been to one of our cemeteries."

John considered me a moment. I quietly chastised myself for intentionally pushing him; he could be capable of anything.

"Yes, you are right," he responded. "I have given that much thought, what I did to you. I visited my mother's grave last week, and it occurred to me momentarily that I took you from your mother, as well—until I recalled that she had already passed."

John's words stung. I hadn't shared that with him, or anyone here. I knew it was common to lose your mother at a young age during this era. It wasn't typical in mine; however, that was my experience. Even though it had been several years before, it was a wound that had never healed properly. I had concealed this grief for so long that it had become unnatural to speak of it, and I certainly did not want to practice now, with John.

"How could you know that?" I managed to say, trying to keep my voice steady.

"The same way I found you, Vale. Your DNA."

"My DNA?" I was dumbfounded.

John laughed, obviously proud of himself. "Yes."

"How?" I asked, somewhat disturbed.

John gave me a sardonic smile. "What do you mean, how? You've only been in the nineteenth century for three months, and you have already forgotten how technology works, have you? I did a DNA test on myself and it linked me to your grandfather, and then to you. You and I are about five or six generations apart."

I knew he had mentioned working on his ancestry with my grandfather. It never occurred to me that he had used DNA technology to do so.

I was perplexed. "So, I come from your line?"

"Yes."

"I'm trying to understand this. It's a bit baffling. Then you are my great-great-great-great-great-grandfather?" I had to hold up my fingers to keep count.

"There may be another great in there. I am not completely certain. But yes, technically, you are a direct descendant from my line." I was speechless; John was not. "Claudia knew exactly what she was doing when she cursed Aunt Eleanor and her child. You were placed in the least preferred Emberley line. The name dropped off along the way due to the maternal side. It made it a little more difficult to trace you, until I did the DNA test. After four years of struggling with research and learning *how* to research—*my God*—I found you in less than a year with the DNA test. It was easy once you did yours; we matched immediately."

As I listened to John, my mind wandered a moment. I remembered all the conspiracy theories about submitting one's DNA to the government, but never had I imagined that by submitting mine, I would end up in the nineteenth century.

I looked back at John, who was searching my face for a reaction, it seemed.

"You're not a very good grandfather, just so you know." I raised my left hand up. The scar was light, but visible enough for him to see what he had done.

John's face contorted. "I'm sorry about that. It had to be done, though. If I had asked, would you have submitted?"

"Of course not!" I exclaimed, the familiar heat rising in my chest. "You decided for me that I should come back. Gildi even said that the curse being lifted didn't mean that I had to come to this time. You made that choice. Do you even realize what you have really cost me, John? You speak of the loss of my mother, but…" I took a moment, unable to speak it out loud to him. "You can never know the extent of the pain you have inflicted upon me. The scar on my heart is much deeper than the one on my palm."

I wiped away the hot tears streaming down my face, mixing with the gentle, cool rain that began to make itself known.

"You are right, Vale—you are right. I gave little thought to how any of this would affect you. All I could think of was the goal I set out to achieve five years before; it's all I could see. I can only apologize."

I trusted him even less, if that was possible.

"How could you have so much conviction for your cause that you find a way to time travel, spend five years in the twenty-first century, and abduct me—but then you apologize as if it were an accident? I couldn't believe it even if I wanted to. No one has that much of a change of heart, John Emberley, no one."

I was breathing fast, and felt flushed. I wanted answers, and I suspected he was trying to deceive me.

"You're wrong." John took a step closer, so I backed up behind his mother's grave. He placed his hands up as if he were surrendering. "I really am sorry, Vale. You were never who I intended to hurt. You were a tool."

"A tool?" I felt almost lightheaded, I was so angry. "So you could hurt Edward?"

"Yes."

"You are a real bastard." My emotions betrayed me, and I sobbed, thinking of my children, the loss I still felt.

"You can't understand the hate I have for him. How much I have suffered at *his* hands. You only know kindness from him. I have only ever known disgust and hate."

"Yet *you* are the one who used me as a tool, as you just said. Just as you used Emilia."

I saw his countenance change; I'd struck a nerve.

"Edward has told you some things, has he? He made himself a victim, did he not?"

"No, he took accountability." I hated to revisit this particular topic, but I was defensive of Edward.

"So, then you cannot deny that he *too* used Emilia; he *too* used her as a tool—to hurt me."

I felt a knot in my stomach. I couldn't deny this; Edward as much as admitted so. I knew he had wanted to hurt John.

"Yes, Edward was guilty, just as you were. You both allowed your hate for one another to bring out the worst in yourselves."

Reader, I considered whether I should continue to argue, but to me, Edward had shown some remorse for his actions, and earned my empathy. John and Emilia had not.

"You two set him up, though, didn't you? You knew that once he was attracted to her, she could manipulate him. You both exploited him."

"Absolutely. It was our chance to get our revenge on the Emberleys."

"John, you *are* an Emberley!" I couldn't understand how someone could hold so much contempt for their own family.

"Yes, just as much as my poor mother lying in the grave next to you is. My grandfather never gave a damn about me or my father. He only ever loved James and Eleanor, and subsequently Edward. My father, mother, and I were naught to him. James taunted my father, then Edward taunted me. They had everything, but it was never enough. They needed to ensure we suffered."

I simply shook my head in disbelief. John was all emotion; it was difficult to take him at face value.

"Deny all you want; you were not there to live it. Why do you think I am in such sympathy with the Gheatas; with Emilia? They know all too well the suffering the Emberleys cause to those around them. The Gheatas accepted me and took me in when my father passed. I was done being a gentleman. I no longer cared for wealth and rank."

"Yet you tried to rob Edward of his inheritance."

"It was an attempt, yes, more for Emilia than me. It might have worked, had I not lost my temper. My little vixen wasn't supposed to consummate her temporary marriage."

"Temporary marriage? Do you hear yourself?" Now I was incredulous. "John, why did Emilia consummate the marriage if she knew how you felt about Edward? Have you ever really considered that?"

"Considered it? Yes, I considered it. She admitted her reasons. She used Edward much in the same way William used Maria. Emilia is not like the girls of this age; she is free spirited and wild, a child of the Earth, if you will. More like the girls of your time."

"I'm not sure you could ever understand the girls of my time, or your own. You don't think that a little part of her enjoyed being Edward's wife, not even for a moment?"

I watched John's face grimace as he deliberated on my

words. I regretted them, fearing I had pushed him too far.

Finally, John countered, his face relaxing. "Emilia is like ice: cold and dangerous—when she desires to be so. Edward was Emilia's opportunity to repay the Emberleys—to reflect their sins back at them."

"Claudia's curse was not enough?" I asked, feeling defensive of the Emberleys, their faces still fresh in my mind.

"No," he replied coldly, "not for Claudia and not for Emilia."

"I don't understand how you could trust her or forgive her, and I cannot understand harboring so much hate; I can't understand it of any of you."

"You have been removed from this. I don't expect you to understand. As for Emilia, it is as I stated: she can be cold when she needs to be, but I have known her most of my life and have loved her. Emilia protects her own."

I noticed John fidgeting with something on his hand. I realized he was twisting a small metal ring.

"Is that a wedding ring?"

"It is. We have been married—just recently."

I was unimpressed. "You two deserve each other; I truly mean that," I told him dryly.

"Do you, now?" he asked sarcastically. "You ought to, Vale. It is because of our union that you exist."

I regarded him in earnest. "Do you mean—"

"Yes." John took another step forward. "You are not only a descendant of the Emberleys, but the Gheatas, as well."

I squeezed the stone monument beneath my hand for support. I adored Gildi, but to share blood with Emilia—this was difficult to grasp. Then it occurred to me what Anne had told me about her and Edward, and the sensation they felt in their arms the day I came here. I had long wondered how the Gheatas knew of my arrival.

"Did you feel it? A tingling sensation, the day I came?"

John eyed me curiously before answering. "I did. Emilia felt it, too, as well as Gildi and her mother—the latter two, they knew what it meant. It is also how they knew the *anahex* had been completed and you were home." He placed a bitter emphasis on home. "Emilia was intentionally left out of her sister and mother's confidence. If she had known, she would have treated you with more kindness that first night."

I felt multiple emotions well up inside of me, but I held them steady, and I very much doubted his opinion. I started to rub my temple; I was getting a severe headache.

"You knew I was your descendant, yet you were wicked towards me the day I arrived here."

"Yes, I was. I was angry; once again, my plan was being foiled, and Edward was gaining much more this time. I spent five years suffering in that horrendous century just to take back to Edward what he desired most in this world."

This was the very issue I had pondered so many times.

"So why did you?"

"I didn't mean to. I had no idea the stone would bring us to Avenhurst. I had meant to go to London."

I felt a strange sense of calm. It was a relief to have some answers, even if I didn't like some of them. I thought of Edward and tried to pull some of his strength.

"Ah, I see. That does make more sense. Why London? What were you going to do once we arrived there?"

"Some of Emilia's relatives travel near and around London; they were the ones who assisted with the stone and time-travel spell. Naturally, I thought we would return there. As to what I would have done with you—it no longer matters."

"It matters," I replied, curious at my fate had John been successful.

John cast his eyes down. "Most likely, I would have married you to one of the Gheatas cousins. That was my plan. I knew you would need to be under a man's care, and you would have no choice but to consent. Once that was done, I planned on going to Avenhurst and revealing to Edward how I had found his fateful lover and bound her to another man. Fate, however, was on his side, not mine."

"Perhaps it was on mine," I replied, incredulous at the inner workings of this man's mind. "How much do they know about me, their family?"

"Everything. They had been waiting for us the entire time I was gone. They also thought we would return to the place where the spell was cast. It turns out, however, that the spell recognized the *anahex* and returned you to where you belonged: Avenhurst. Eldria always suspected this to be the case. Her cousin Revekah confirmed it when she visited in the spring. All who share your line felt your arrival." John deliberated a moment before he took a step forward and stated, "You are always welcome amongst the Gheatas, Vale. You would be accepted with open arms."

My mind was racing a thousand miles an hour. My headache was becoming more severe, and the rain had become steady, causing small puddles to form on the ground.

"I love Edward," I blurted out. "I do not want any issues with you or Emilia, or anyone else for that matter. I am a peaceful person. But I do love him, and if I must make a choice—well, it's not really a choice at all."

"Of course, you love him; it's unfortunate, but I expected you would," he stated grimly. "You don't have to make a choice about anything now. You do, however, need to be careful. You trust too easily; not everyone is always who they seem to be."

I began to get annoyed again at his ominous words.

"Edward is a good and honest man; he has only been caring and kind to me." I didn't argue but stated my opinion as a fact. "I'm going back now."

I began to walk away when John called my attention back. The rain was making it more difficult to focus.

"You said Edward told you about Emilia and me?"

"He did." I began to shiver.

"Did he also tell you about his time in Europe?"

I wasn't sure I wanted to know; I hadn't forgotten that Edward had alluded to his time there.

"Silence. I will take that as a no. Whilst I reunited with my feisty Emilia, Edward made his way through Europe, angry and bitter. From what an acquaintance has confided in me, he kept a mistress or two along the way. You see, he's not so much better than we are, is he?" John didn't smile but set his strong jaw. "It's satirical, is it not? That out of all of us, the only one who may actually have any virtue in her is the girl from the twenty-first century? Remember what I said. Be careful in whom you place your trust."

With his final, unhappy words, John threw his coat over his head and retreated back into the woods. I was now soaked by the rain. I held my cloak over my head as I ran back towards Avenhurst. I knew Margot and Mrs. Miller would be upset to see my hair wet: there was no convincing them that wet hair did not cause a cold, as they knew nothing of viruses.

The Grief of Love

# CHAPTER 21

Shortly after my wearisome conversation with John, I found myself sitting in the parlor room with my feet up next to a bountiful fire, its heat a soothing solace for my cold skin. Mrs. Miller and Margot went into a fit when they saw me running back to the house, wet and rattled, with the former calling me a "bedraggled-looking thing." Within ten minutes I had on a dry dress, a blanket around my shoulders, and hot tea in hand. Despite the nagging feeling in my heart, I felt at peace with my two fussing ladies, though they believed that I'd probably caught my death.

"Drink this, miss, and then take another cup. Mrs. Miller has gone to prepare some mustard plaster; she is sure you'll be in need of it by the morrow."

"Mustard plaster? What is that?"

"It's a sort of paste one makes out of dried mustard. We'll put it on your back and bosom to keep the chill from settling in your chest."

I merely raised my eyebrows and nodded my head. I knew better than to argue about the value of homemade remedies. My head still ached, but I was hesitant to say anything now. I knew they would provide a vinegar poultice, and between the vinegar for my head and the mustard for a cold I was yet to have, I was worried I would smell like a deviled egg.

I closed my eyes for a moment, reflecting on John's words.

Who was he to tell me whom I ought to trust? Him? That was laughable: he who caused everyone around him as much grief as possible. The only people I had any trust in were Edward, Anne, George, and the two ladies currently coddling me. The first three I knew I could trust with my life, for they knew my secret from the beginning and had only protected me since. Mrs. Miller and Margot had been nothing but kind, and though I wouldn't dare tell either the truth, this didn't negate my warm feelings towards them. Could he mean Gildi or Eldria? Certainly, I could trust them more than him or Emilia.

"Miss Leifman, are you feeling well, dear? Your face is crumpled in a painful way."

Mrs. Miller's question pulled me from my thoughts. She looked at me affectionately.

I yielded. "I have a horrendous headache, Mrs. Miller."

"Oh dear. Margot, go fetch some vinegar and a rag."

✦

A few hours later I was lying in my bed, listening to the rain hit the windowpane; for a while it was soft and romantic, then slowly it built to a passionate pattering that promised sudden release. My eyes were heavy, and they burned until I closed them; however, as soon as slumber was certain, my mind would suddenly awaken. My headache, which I knew was probably a migraine, had been relieved by the laudanum given to me upon Edwards's return. Having found me in pain, while reeking of vinegar and mustard, he ordered Margot to give me a small amount of the liquid opium and put me to bed. I had been in this sort of trance for a little while, not knowing how long I had slept, if I even did; I could not tell.

When I could somewhat control my thoughts, they continuously wandered back to Edward. I felt my face flush when I recalled proclaiming my love for him to John. I scolded myself for that. Not even Anne or Edward knew my feelings, yet here I had given John this intimate knowledge of my heart. Then there was the plaguing pull at my heart; that feeling which to ignore does nothing to relieve, but to acknowledge it only sends one further into a dangerous abyss. I knew which vice I harbored. I was becoming quite intimate with the emotion, and I hated it. My jealousy of Emilia was renewed, and now I was jealous of any mistress he may or may not have had in Europe. I argued with myself: What right did I have to feel this way? I felt the tears well up in my already burning eyes. I knew Edward had no idea of my existence at the time; in fact, I actually did not exist. With that thought crossing my high and exhausted mind, I began to laugh, and then cry, and then combine the two in some strange and fretful way that would have caused even the good Mrs. Miller to take a nightcap.

✦

I woke the next morning in a strange state of peace and calm. After my emotional breakdown, I slept well. Margot had let me sleep through the evening and night, so my bath was drawn in the morning. I was half-submerged in the warm water when the bustling woman came in, with a platter in her hands.

"Here is a little something, miss. I know you must be hungry by now."

I took a bite of the toast she offered me, the sweet butter

tasting better than it should as my stomach was sour.

"May I ask you a personal question, Margot?"

My kind-hearted maid looked at me rather curiously. "Why, yes, miss."

"Have you ever been married or in love?"

For the first time in my knowing Margot, I saw a shadow cross her generous face.

"I'm sorry, Margot. Never mind my question. The laudanum has left me in a strange mood."

I realized the mistake in propriety I was making. In my heart, I was still the nosy millennial woman who could carry on any conversation with anyone, so long as it wasn't shallow, but I needed to remember this would be very awkward for a chambermaid or anyone born in this century.

"No fuss, miss." Margot took a breath, then continued, "I was married once, lucky in love I was. Not many people in my station can claim that. My Tom was a gentle and kind soul. Tom had just started as a banker in London, and we had a small but nice little place just outside of town."

I watched Margot drift off for a moment before she looked back at me.

"Before we could save enough to maintain our home, Tom died of cholera. I had to go to work, and not knowing another soul in London, I came back north to live with my mother. We carried on well enough for a time, then she passed last year. I had just taken a position here as a chambermaid. Mr. Emberley has been generous and is a better master than most of the gentry in these parts. I was very pleased when he promoted me as your maid, miss. It has given me some pleasure to take care of someone, especially a kind little soul such as yourself."

Margot had taken hold of my hand, which I kissed and placed against my cheek.

"Thank you, Margot."

"Miss?"

I looked up at my gentle maid.

"Life is far too short to not spend it loving someone all you can. Even the poorest of us know that."

I smiled. "And the wisest too."

✦

Once I was dressed for the day, I made my way down to the parlor, where I found Edward sitting in his large armchair reading the newspaper. His eyes caught mine as I descended into the room.

"You look better; do you smell better?"

"I cannot promise that."

Edward smiled as he pulled a chair closer to him, beckoning me to sit. I received one of his piercing gazes, one that he liked to use when I was about to get a cross-examination.

I didn't wait for him to begin.

"Yes, sir. What thoughts lurk in that vast mind of yours?"

Edward rewarded my gratification of his ego with an even rarer expression, a smolder; I blushed in spite of myself.

Breaking the momentary tension, Edward rolled his newspaper and tapped me on the leg, letting out a small chuckle.

"What happened yesterday? Mrs. Miller said she almost mistook you for a beggar. You were described as such: 'wild-haired and sopping, like one of those women in the old tales.' I asked her why you were wild-haired and sopping, and she told me that you had been gone all morning, and that Margot had been out looking for you when you came in from the rain."

Though I know he meant well enough, I had the same feeling I did when I was a child being scolded.

"I didn't realize anyone was out looking for me. I had gone in the morning to the graveyard next to the little church. The rain was coming down rather heavily by the time I left."

"What drew you to the graveyard?" he asked gently.

"Honestly, I'm not sure. I have always been drawn to them. I spent a while walking around, looking at the old headstones and tombs. I know it's odd, but I find them comforting. Where I'm from, our graves are not as old as they are here. It was a lonely morning, so I thought I would spend it with the deceased."

"It is not so odd, Vale. Graveyards are a reminder that someday, we all find peace, which is especially comforting for those who cannot find it while living. I visit my mother and father every so often. I cannot say I find their tomb comforting, though."

"Why is that?"

He gave a slight laugh, "Because I know that's where I, too, will spend eternity—at least this mortal body will."

I nodded my head in agreement. "I had a similar thought when I was there, actually."

"Did you?"

"Yes, I did." I watched as Edward began to play with the tiny bit of lace poking out of my sleeve. "It occurred to me while I was there that in my time, I must now have an empty grave of my own."

Edward stopped his slight tugging and enveloped my hand into his. "I'm sorry."

I squeezed his hand back, rubbing my thumb against the gold ring on his middle finger.

"I know. It's all right. There's nothing to be done about it. I wanted to lapse into gloom, but it was a fleeting feeling. Too much has been outside of my control. It has left me feeling a bit lost at times. I was always in control of my life before, more than I think I knew. The unhappiness that I did experience, I could have changed if I'd had the courage. Now, many things are out of my control, so the little that is, I must manage carefully, especially my emotions."

I met Edward's gaze, still stroking his middle finger. His eyes were deep and empathetic. "I wish you hadn't visited such a gloomy, forlorn place by yourself. A leaden sky and old graves can dampen the happiest of spirits."

I smiled softly at Edward, unsure whether I should mention it or not. I proceeded.

"Well, I wasn't alone the whole time."

"No? Who was out there with you?"

I held my breath before speaking. "John."

I watched Edward's handsome face, which had been watching me as I spoke, go from relaxed and empathetic to hard and scowling at the mere mention of his cousin's name.

"You were alone in a graveyard with John Emberley?"

"Well, not at first, of course. I had been out there for a little while, wandering around like I told you, when he came in."

I could see every bit of my folly in Edward's expression. I knew I had been careless the day before, and now my own thoughts were mirrored in the eyes of the one I loved. I relayed what happened as best I could. I detailed all my wanderings throughout the graveyard; how I rested against one of the smaller headstones and opened my eyes to find John standing before me. I even explained why I didn't just run. I told Edward the conversation between John and me, everything short of John's mistress accusations and me proclaiming my love for him.

Edward leaned back in his chair, rubbing his chin with his hand. I sat and waited, dreading his words, knowing what he might say.

"My God, Vale. So many things could have happened. John could have gone off with you, and it would have been many hours before any of us would have known you were missing. Do you realize what that would mean? And even if he wouldn't harm you himself, which I would not count on, how many other men are out there? John could have done anything he liked with you, take you for himself or sell you to a high bidder. He told you as much, did he not?"

He shook his head, then he looked at me. I suppose seeing the look of terror in my eyes sobered his vexation a little. He moved to a crouch before me, taking both of my hands into his.

"I will never let that happen."

Tears of shame rolled down my cheeks. I was struggling with that familiar unease one gets when they become aware of how close they were to disaster and just narrowly averted it. The truth was, I was still afraid of John, and I knew what he was capable of. John attempted to convince me with his words, but I remembered his actions far better. My tears spilt until my lungs forced a sob. Hearing this, Edward stood up a little more, pulling me into his arms and kissing my forehead.

"I'm sorry, Vale," he cooed. "I didn't mean to upset you. It's just the thought of you, my little bird, being harmed again by that man is more than I can stand. John will do anything he can to hurt me. This you know. You have experienced its burden more than anyone else. It is a wonder he didn't do more yesterday."

Through my tears and sniffles, I asked him, "I told you what he said about me being his and Emilia's descendant. You don't believe him, then?"

"I believe that you are their descendant, certainly. I do not believe that this would alter their behavior and certainly does not mean you are safe with them so near," he replied sternly, taking a tone more often reserved for others. "In fact, it worries me more."

Edward stood up to pace the parlor floor. "That man has done nothing to garner any trust from this family, especially not from you. John can see your affection for Gildi and will use it. You are not so naïve?"

I promptly stood up. Edward's words and tone were sharp, and I felt the sting as they cut through my pride. I had never been called naïve, but I had been patronized, and often.

"Naïve! You might as well just call me ignorant, then," I stated as calmly as my quickened pulse would allow. "I have had to grieve my children, my family, my old life. I have learned to swallow my pride, repress my ego, accept that I no longer have the same rights and freedoms I was born with. I only wish that I were naïve—then maybe I wouldn't suffer so."

I did not wait for a reply. I opened the door and walked out into the morning.

The Pleasure of Love

# CHAPTER 22

I was fortunate that the rain had just stopped, but in my haste I didn't take a shawl or cloak, so I sat on the wet bench in the garden with my hands wrapped around myself, shivering. I hadn't realized how rain soaked the bench was until it was too late, so I took in every miserable sensation and wallowed in hurt feelings. Hot tears burned my eyes, falling faster than I could wipe them away. After a little while, my breaths became more regular and my heart calmed. I watched the birds appear and begin to peck at the wet grass and preen their feathers. Some remained hidden in the trees, chirping from above. I always did love to watch them play after a rainfall.

As I sat there, I started to reflect on my reaction—my overreaction. I had been defensive, it was true. I knew Edward would be upset I was out alone. He had warned me. Anne had warned me. I knew I was fortunate that John hadn't tried to harm me again, despite his testimonial of being changed. I was angry with myself for letting my guard down, just as I had several months before. With a cooler head, I realized Edward wasn't calling me ignorant—he meant I was too trusting—it was certainly a flaw of mine. Not that I trusted John, but I had a tendency to be swayed by wanting to believe others to be good. And Edward was right, I had a soft spot for Gildi, and John was surely aware of this. I was naïve—this time. Though I didn't like the tone Edward had taken with me, I felt I owed him an apology. He didn't deserve an outburst.

I finished drying my eyes on my sleeve, then stood up to go seek Edward. I turned around to find him there with me in the garden, leaning against the wall just after the entrance; he had been waiting. I walked over to him silently, not sure how I should begin. He offered me his hand. I took it in both of mine, placing it against my cheek; it was warm.

"I'm sorry you suffer," he said before I had a chance to apologize.

"No, Edward, please don't be sorry. I'm sorry, I really am. I don't suffer at your hands." I kissed his hand as I stated this. "My feelings were hurt, and I overreacted. You did not deserve that."

Edward's anxious face softened slightly. "I should have been gentler when I spoke to you. I should have explained myself better. I have told you about the history between John, Emilia, and me. It has affected me; hardened me at times. Since childhood we have been enemies. It is difficult for me to trust anyone because of him. And I trust no one with you. You are precious to me."

I felt more tears run down my cheeks, surprised I had any left. "I understand. I know what it is like to mistrust."

Edward held my face between his hands. "Your life is worth more to me than anyone else in this world my darling. *That* you can trust."

With my face still in his hands, Edward traced my temples with both his thumbs. I closed my eyes, indulging in the love I felt from him.

"When I found you in the oak tree, I was overwhelmed with the sudden urge to protect you. I knew then that it would pain me if you were to be removed from my presence. And when Gildi told us the story of Eleanor's bird and that you were restored to us, I understood. It was my soul that recognized yours. All those years—useless and wasted years—I was asleep. But you, my little bird, your song is sweet, and I have awakened."

I smiled at his words, before placing my hands on top of his and looking into his eyes. "There is a saying in my time—grief is the price we pay for lov—and Edward, God knows I have paid that price. Long have I been in a fog of sorrow, but I haven't felt alone. You are my solace. Warmth radiates from you like the heat from the August sun, and where you are, the fog ceases to be."

Edward placed his lips on my forehead and held me there against him. Before he had time to pull away, I found the courage to make my confession.

"Before I left the graveyard—before I ended the conversation with John—I told him that I love you. He had made me angry, but I didn't speak out of anger. I just needed him to understand. And I do love you, Edward. The fog has lifted, and I, too, am awake."

In a moment, I was wrapped in Edward's arms, his lips on mine. As he kissed me, I took in his scent, deep and masculine. I could feel his warmth as he pulled me closer to him. My body was memorizing his touch as my skin felt on fire everywhere his hands moved. I leaned in, allowing his lips to press against mine over and over, gently parting and closing. I ran my hand through his sideburns and up into his hair, my fingers learning him as they played. Finally, he or I broke our kiss. Probably he did; I was content to overindulge in his embrace.

Edward held my face once more between his hands, smiling at me.

"My little love," he said, "you are mine, are you not?"

I continued to run my hand along his jawline, feeling the

stubble as I did. "I am. I always have been."

I felt his lips on mine once more before he drew me to him again, gazing down at me.

"Then say you will be my wife. That you will let me love you and protect you." I felt his cheek press against mine as he whispered in my ear. "Let us pass through this life together as one. Your burdens shall be mine, and together, our joys shall be many."

I took the hand stroking my cheek and kissed it, several times I kissed it as I nodded my head.

"Yes, sweet man, I will marry you."

Edward lifted me into his arms with a multitude of kisses bestowed upon me. I giggled like the young woman I had become again, feeling youthful in my soul for perhaps the first time since I was a child. Edward carried me to the bench and sat down before I could warn him. I laughed as I recognized the cold chill he'd just encountered.

Laughing, he stated, "I had wondered why your backside was so wet!"

"Well, shame on you for feeling my backside!"

Edward squinted his eyes at me, most mischievously. "I took a liberty." Then kissing me again, he said, "And yes, I am shameful, just you wait and see."

He proceeded to tickle my waist, for which I pretended to chastise him, and when he stopped, I returned the favor.

✦

Some moments later, Edward was sitting in his large chair with me still in his lap, my head upon his shoulder. The rain had returned, and we were both cold, so we had made our way back to the parlor and settled near the fireplace. We stayed that way for a while, the pitter-patter of the rain and the crackling of the fire the only sounds besides our breaths. My hand rested on his chest, and I could feel his heartbeat in my palm as he stroked my hair. Occasionally I would feel him kiss the top of my head.

Finally, he spoke. "I cannot tell you what it means to me to have you nestled so close to my heart."

I smiled but said nothing. Edward lifted my chin to meet his gaze. His dark eyes had a twinkle in them. I couldn't help but smile again and was rewarded with another smolder. I pulled his face to mine and kissed him again, learning the feel of his lips against mine. I lay against his chest for some time, content and full of love, eventually drifting off into a peaceful rest.

Soon, I awakened to a nagging, griping noise from the hallway. Edward sat up straight as well. We could hear Mrs. Miller chastising one of the maids about dust in the upper rooms.

"Go, my darling, get ready for dinner. I will send Margot with something small right now. You haven't eaten today."

I nodded in agreement, just then realizing I was hungry. Still dazed from the morning's events and from sleep, I made my way to my room.

I closed the door behind me and then caught my reflection in the mirror as I passed by it. I smiled back at myself, with my wet and wild hair. I had worn my hair half-down, and now it was disheveled, with tresses flying every which way. My behind was still wet, and my eyes slightly puffy, yet I thought I'd never looked better. This was the real Vale; no makeup, no façade. This was the Vale Edward loved. I watched the door open through the mirror; Margot came in with a small plate of food.

Upon seeing my reflection, Margot's eyes widened. She exclaimed, "Another day as a vagabond! What will the master think, miss?"

I laughed heartily at her sobering comments and kissed the good woman.

"Make me beautiful, then, Margot, if you can. And please, let me have a sandwich!"

Can't Help Falling in Love

# CHAPTER 23

By midsummer, sunshine was in abundance. Though we had the occasional sprinkle, it had finally warmed up enough that I could claim to be hot every once in a while. The warmth was shared outside of Avenhurst as well as within it. The same evening on the day Edward proposed to me, he announced our engagement to the house. Mrs. Miller and Margot shed happy tears, and they both looked full of joy and relief. Edward allowed the housekeeper to make the announcement to the rest of the house, which she most certainly enjoyed doing. I took the most joy in telling Anne. When she and George had come, I had to meet her outside lest Mrs. Miller ruin my surprise. With her arm in mine, I pulled her out to the heather in the distance, explaining that a handsome man had taken me in his arms, kissed me, and then asked me to be his bride, and that despite myself, I could not say no. Anne gave me a quizzical look, causing me to laugh before confessing I spoke of Edward.

"You threw me off with 'handsome man,' my dear," Anne teased. Then she embraced me so tightly that we fell to the ground in a fit of laughter. We lay there together, heads touching, for a little while.

"I'm so pleased that he proposed. I honestly did not think he would for some time."

I turned my head towards Anne. "What do you mean?"

I could see Anne was preparing her next words. Turning to face me, Anne relayed the following:

"I have known Edward to be madly in love with you for quite some time, darling. I have watched the man pine and torment himself over you. Edward's love for you is more earnest than that of a shepherd with his most prized lamb. Since you first arrived here, Edward has ensured your every comfort, every need. No, don't look at me like I have known some hidden secret. I am not Edward's confidante, save for one time. Most of what I know is from his behavior, my own observations; and, perhaps, George has unknowingly dropped a word or two. Men underestimate our power of discernment; our sex are better predictors of behavior, of that I feel sure. Edward offered to provide for you because you are family, but I could see the immediate impact you made on his countenance. You gained his empathy—not an easy feat. When Gildi spoke of the future you and Edward were supposed to have, I could see his yearning. Edward and I have both lived such lonely lives, and for you to appear so suddenly and be so vulnerable, he did not stand a chance. Imagine my gratitude that we gained a friend, someone earnest and kind, not vain and inconsistent. I told Edward—a few weeks after you arrived, that is—that he should ask for your hand, that in your position it would be doubtful that you wouldn't accept. He refused and called me irritating! I thought perhaps that I had been mistaken in my judgment, but he admitted that he preferred for you to love him freely and of your own accord and that despite his feelings for you, he could live content enough as long as you found some peace. Watching you suffer so at first was almost unbearable, not just for my brother. My heart ached for you, Vale. I was angry with him when he sent me home, for both your sake and mine. Edward was right, though. I learned to love my husband, and you learned to live without me."

"I also learned I could not live without him," I interjected.

Anne smiled. "He took a risk, and it was well made. It was then I realized that Edward knew I was a barrier between the two of you. Not intentionally, but with my confidence so easily available, when would you turn to him?"

I smiled inwardly, knowing she was probably right. Anne would have been my crutch if she'd allowed it.

"I did, though. I was apprehensive of him at first. I have been rather timid around men my entire life. And then Edward is not just any man. What Gildi told me weighed heavily on my mind—that I would have been his lover, his wife. First, I was embarrassed, and then it seemed of little importance when all I could see was what I had lost."

I took Anne's hand and placed it against mine to see whose was smaller; they were the same size. "He was never completely away from my mind, though. I would not have told you before, but when he helped me down from the oak tree, I was immediately drawn to him. Initially, I assumed that my fear of John was lessened by putting my faith in Edward, since he had made it clear he was not on friendly terms with John. Before long, I realized it was more than that. Edward could be severe—I saw this in his reactions with others. But with me, he was always gentle. I know your brother has had his fair share of suffering, and I don't say this lightly, but in his case, I think it served him well."

"To have suffered?"

"Yes."

"How so?" She asked.

"Like you said, I gained his empathy. Empathy comes with experience; not necessarily sharing in the same sort of suffering, but to have been pained enough to understand that others do, in fact, suffer as well. Some of us are naturally empathetic; you and I for instance. Edward has shown me a great deal of empathy, and not only by providing for me, though I can't be thankful enough for that. I didn't have to worry about shelter, food, hygiene, or any other human need. I was allowed to wallow in my feelings; to be depressed for a time. My first husband would never allow me a morning to myself, sick or not, lest he must do something for someone else. You and Edward may have seen these things as very basic needs, but to me, it meant so much more. I needed to hide away, I needed time to myself to cry and be alone. I still do at times. By suffering in the way he did, Edward knew what I needed."

"What was that, darling?"

"I needed time. And I know how impatient that man's true nature can be, so giving me time was truly a gift."

Anne laughed. "He is impatient. And ugly too. Did I ever tell you how ugly he is?"

"He is not! Perhaps a little funny-looking though. It runs in his family."

"Ha-ha!" said Anne, feigning vexation. "I am serious about the impatient part, however. I had to put Mrs. Miller on alert. Mind you, all I merely said was that I thought Edward found you very pretty. My good old maid went into a state of agitation. You two having so much free and unsupervised time together, it was quite a breach of propriety. Mrs. Miller overlooked it the best she could while I was around, and still so when I left. But once I made that simple statement, I believe she thought Edward the devil himself."

My mind went back to the moment Margot caught me in Edward's lap, with only our nightgowns between us. *My God,* I thought, *had it been Mrs. Miller instead, I don't doubt that she would have died right then to spite us.*

"Well in his defense, he has been the perfect gentleman."

"Has he now? And by what standards do we weigh his behavior, those of this time or yours?" Anne asked facetiously.

I considered all the encounters between Edward and me. Yes, they usually broke propriety, but I did not care. What was propriety to me? A system that put far too much weight on decorum and not enough weight on true virtue. Not once had Edward ever made me uncomfortable, dismissed me, or treated me as an inferior. I internally weighed my feelings and thoughts and then chose my stance.

"Weigh his behavior by either century Anne, and still, Edward will ever be the gentleman I see him to be. Even if he did allow me to ride non-side-saddle once."

"You shameful girl!" Anne exclaimed and, thankfully, laughed. "I am no one to judge, Vale. You know this already. I just wanted to keep temptation from you. Despite what we tell ourselves—that it does not matter what society thinks or says—it still hurts to fall. If I could at least protect you, then I felt as though I'd done my part. I would have taken you to Highgarden if I could have. As you know, I lost that battle. It pleases me, though, that you two did find each other, after all, and that what Gildi stated about the future was not lost."

I thought of Gildi and the two visions she had shown me.

"No, I don't believe it was ever truly lost."

Anne and I lay there a while longer. The sun was moving across the sky, but the temperature had yet to fall. I caught her up on my conversations with Edward and John, and how Edward proposed to me. Then we poked fun at both Edward and George's expense for many reasons, tried to envision the perfect man for Mrs. Miller (unsuccessfully), and dreamt of babies. For the first time, I was able to speak about the topic without my voice faltering. Anne then reminisced about my first evening with her and made fun of my bra. This time I defended my twenty-first century underwear and the wonderful support they gave. Gradually, we both became quiet, enjoying the silence between us, a rare gift usually reserved for the best of friends.

After a few moments, I began to daydream about Edward and how I would tease him that night. I was then pulled out of my thoughts as Anne began to hum the tune of an old song, one my grandmother played often.

"What is that?" I asked.

"'Plaisir d'amour,'" she replied. "Do you know it? It has long been a family favorite."

"I know the melody. I have never heard the title. What does it mean?"

"'Plaisir d'amour,' The Pleasure of Love. *Plaisir d'amour ne dure qu'un moment, chagrin d'amour dure toute la vie.* It translates to 'The pleasure of love lasts only a moment. The grief of love lasts a lifetime.'"

"That is beautiful, Anne." The meaning of the French lyrics pulled at me painfully.

"You have heard it before, then?"

"Well, sort of. I recognized the melody from a song my grandmother loved. It was by a famous and handsome man named Elvis Presley."

"What is it called?" she asked, her voice slightly amused. Anne loved hearing about my time, though I was always careful with what knowledge I burdened her with.

"Can't Help Falling in Love with You." I smiled at the memory of my grandmother softly singing to the music as it played while she made dinner.

Anne and I still lay with our heads together; I could feel hers slightly brushing against mine as she moved about and spoke to me.

"Do you remember the lyrics of his song?"

I smiled. "Yes, I do."

I felt her grab my hand, "Please!"

"Oh, all right." I sat up and quickly looked around, making sure no one was coming. "I will sing it this once."

I put aside my shyness for Anne's sake and sang the song as I remembered it, perhaps a little more pensively.

Once I finished, I squeezed her hand back and asked, "Are you happy?"

I looked over at Anne, and she turned her head towards me, a big smile grew across her face. "That was beautiful, Vale. You have a beautiful voice. The lyrics are brilliant."

"Thank you."

I smiled to myself, proud that Anne would soon be my sister. Perhaps I should have told her so. Instead, I reached over and affectionately tugged at her hair, which was now half-down like mine.

"Should we see about some tea?"

"Yes, my little songbird, I think so."

We walked back towards the house, arm in arm. It must have been somewhere between six and seven o'clock. I could just sense the temperature readying to drop. Men were working in the back fields just outside of Avenhurst; I could see their brown hats and pitchforks bobbing here and there. The whole estate was in a midsummer glory, just like it would be back home, I thought. Yet, here, fall did not feel so far away. In my hometown, it would be at least three more months before a chill wind made its way back. I considered the city's current living inhabitants and felt sorry they would never know air conditioning.

As we approached the house, Edward and George must

have seen us coming as they came out to greet us. For the first time, I watched Anne give her brother a hug, a gentle quick embrace, and then she whispered something in his ear. George bowed his head as I approached, congratulating me on my engagement, and then Edward informed Anne and me that they were not to stay for dinner as George had begun to feel ill. Anne went to him.

"Ill? Have you a fever?" she asked him as she began to feel his forehead and neck.

George took her hands and carefully lowered them. "No my dear, and hopefully that will not be the case, either. I do not feel as well as I should like. If you would prefer, I could send the carriage back for you later?"

Anne studied him a moment. "No, that's unnecessary. Let's get you home. I will make a vinegar compress for you."

I caught Edward's eye; his lip twitched slightly, and I suppressed a laugh.

We said our goodbyes. I was sorry to lose Anne so soon, but we made plans to go to town for my wedding clothes. The wedding would be in a few weeks, with a small ceremony held at the little church next door. I was excited and nervous; the life I led felt surreal. Edward took hold of my hand, bringing me back to the present. Together, we watched as George and Anne's carriage made its way outside the gates.

✦

After dinner that evening, Mrs. Miller and I took to our samplers. She insisted on learning my French knots. Edward had taken up a book, but I could tell he wasn't reading it as he rarely turned a page. I would move from showing Mrs. Miller how I pulled the thread through after wrapping the string around my needle three times to glancing up at Edward, who was watching me. I attempted to hide my smile, but glancing back at him I saw that he knew he had succeeded in earning my attention. I raised an eyebrow at him but said nothing. *Little flirt,* I thought. I continued to inspect Mrs. Miller as she attempted her French knot.

"Yes, like that," I encouraged her.

I watched Edward stand up and make his way to the piano. I smiled in anticipation, expecting him to show off. I pretended not to notice and purposely acted more interested in Mrs. Miller's embroidery skills than I really was. Edward commenced his song on the instrument. I beamed as Edward began to play what I knew must be *"Plaisir d'amour."* We caught each other's gaze.

"Miss Leifman," the good gentleman stated, "I hear you can sing."

"Can ye, miss?" Mrs. Miller inquired.

I felt my face flush. I would kill Anne after my wedding, I decided.

"Just a little. Not very well."

"That is not what your sister-to-be told me," Edward quickly replied, proud of his discovery. He stopped playing for a moment and patted the empty space next to him. "Come, my darling."

And so I did. To Mrs. Miller's joy, Edward played the old tune while I sang new lyrics. Mrs. Miller thoroughly enjoyed our performance, save for the grimace on her face when I sang the lyric about sin, but still, she clapped when we finished. My Edward leaned over and gave me a kiss on the cheek, whispering that the pleasure of our love would last a lifetime.

Leifman

# CHAPTER 24

Over the next few weeks, Anne visited frequently, providing well-appreciated company. According to Anne, George had not been well. Not quite ill, she explained, but in a state of melancholy, it seemed. Anne was perplexed, and George, not wanting her to be affected, encouraged her visits to Avenhurst. I sent my regards to George, understanding despondent feelings all too well. I sincerely hoped that whatever ailed him would soon be relieved. I was not sorry to have more time with Anne, though, especially since I needed some guidance with wedding preparations; it was difficult enough the first time, when I had the internet to assist me. I was soon educated by Anne that it was not customary to have large wedding ceremonies, save for the Queen's, and usually it was done in the church with a couple of witnesses. Once the marriage ceremony was completed, breakfast ensued and then the bride and bridegroom left for their wedding tour. As for the small ceremony, I could not have been more pleased. I was never one for much pomp and circumstance. I loathed being the center of attention—even on my own wedding day. Anne, George and, of course, Edward, were all I needed on the blessed day. As to the wedding tour, this left me rather apprehensive. I had finally grown quite fond of Avenhurst and felt safe on the grounds. Departing from it for more than just a few hours left me anxious. Edward had mentioned France as a honeymoon, with a small stay in Paris and then a visit to the south in the Mediterranean. As lovely as it sounded, fear overshadowed excitement. I was careful not to express this to Edward. I felt I had been burdensome enough for a time, and here he was, both excited and happy.

The subject of the honeymoon had come up again one evening, when Edward and I happened to have the parlor alone and were enjoying the warm fire. Mrs. Miller had a cold and retired early. Without her watchful glances oppressing us, I ensconced myself on Edward's lap while he read to me. When the chapter ended, Edward laid it down on the side table and drew me near for a kiss. I usually kissed Edward surreptitiously but freely, yet when we were alone, I was more guarded with the affection I gave. I had made a deal with myself: I had remained innocent for my first husband in a time when it was little appreciated, though, I acknowledge, it had been for myself, not him. In this age, it would be no different, and it certainly helped that it was the expectation, especially as Edward stirred feelings within me that I did not have in such depth the first time.

Mrs. Miller, it turned out, was a safeguard, after all. I had little doubt that Anne had stirred her caution, and with Anne confirming it to be so, I could appreciate the effect this had. Flirting with Edward when Mrs. Miller wasn't looking made our courtship all the better. While she was distracted with her sampler, Edward would walk past us and tweak my ear; while she fussed over the arrangements on the mantle, I would pinch Edward, who feigned being scorned. On one occasion, I pinched his underarm a little too boldly, eliciting a small curse. I turned red with embarrassment, and Mrs. Miller turned her attention to her master in surprise. Edward quickly lied about stubbing his toe on the piano, while shooting me a mixed look of vexation and sheer amusement. When the good lady turned her attention back to the mantle, I quietly glided to him, attempting to soothe his wound.

"Away, wicked girl," he teasingly rebuked while giving me his arm freely. I gently rubbed the spot where I pinched him.

We had been carrying on like this, stealing kisses when no eyes were near us; occasionally he held me close, as he was now. To keep from encouraging him, I evaded his kiss with a small peck on the cheek and then lay my head upon his shoulder. I felt him begin to stroke my hair, my favorite small act of affection.

"Just think, in four short weeks, we will be able to enjoy each other's company freely, like this, without the fear of a meddlesome old lady." He spoke in a deep tone, almost music to my ears.

"Will you deny her access to the parlor?" I inquired, curious as to how he would prevent the barrier.

I had misunderstood.

"Well, no, my little bird. She will not be with us in France. I can see us already," he mused, "the parlor room in the house in the south is as comfortable as this one, though perhaps a little more open. We will lounge upon the sofa, windows open, the fresh ocean air breezing throughout the room, a generous fire, and the scent of orange blossoms to please my darling."

I liked the picture he painted. "Orange blossoms? They grow oranges there?"

"Of course. We own a couple of small groves. Does this please you?"

"Yes. I love the scent of orange blossoms, I always have. They remind me of home."

Upon hearing this, Edward tenderly tightened his hold and pressed his lips to the top of my head.

"You will love France," he said presently. "The climate sounds comparable to the one you have described of your home. You will have all the oranges, not to mention chocolate, your heart could desire. You will be a very spoiled lady."

I laughed lightly. "I believe you."

I hesitated for a moment but felt it best to keep to the honesty that existed between us. It was a new pleasure for me, to speak so freely to the man I loved.

"I am afraid. Frightened, really."

"Of what, darling?" He repositioned us so we could see each other.

"The idea of leaving Avenhurst—of traveling, especially. It's so different than what I know. How will we get there? What if we catch cholera? Are there bathrooms?"

My anxieties spilt out nonsensically. Edward merely laughed and hugged me again.

"You will be the safest woman alive! We will take a carriage to the train station and then use the railway for most of the journey, my love. We will then take a ferry to the continent and resume on a train. Then, perhaps, another coach to reach our destination." Edward looked at me, rather amused. "We will not catch cholera. I am now enlightened on the importance of handwashing, thanks to you, and we can take our own boiled water, if you please."

"I do."

"As for a bathroom, I am not quite sure what you mean. You will have to modify your toilette on the train, but you will certainly have access to a bath whilst at the hotel."

I sighed. All the vernacular I knew with regards to having to pee were not understood by this generation. I took a moment to explain to Edward my own version of a bathroom versus a restroom, and what a modern *toilet* was, indoor plumbing and all. Edward listened with the sincerest interest.

"The water actually runs into the house and is heated along the way?"

"Yes. That is normal for most people in my time."

"Truly Vale, I am surprised you have survived thus far. It is good you have Margot to heat your water, for you are, indeed, very spoiled." He smiled. "All will be well. Do not worry. Avenhurst will be here when we return. It will be an adventure, our first alone and as husband and wife; do not let your anxieties rob you of this pleasure."

I took his hand and kissed it. I must have encouraged him, for the gentleman took a liberty and began to outline my collarbone. "You have the prettiest neck, Vale, so slender and smooth."

I felt a familiar, deep ache at his touch. I knew all too well the risk I took if I allowed myself to engage. I took his wandering hand, playfully bit it, and then removed myself from his lap.

"Come back!" he called, proud and mischievous. "You'll drive me mad!"

"*Bonne nuit, mon cher vieux!*" I replied. I heard him laugh wholeheartedly as I closed the parlor door.

◆

Within a week or so, Edward had completed the arrangements for our honeymoon. I had my wedding dress and other items I would need for France, and the marriage license was secured. Upon seeing that lovely piece of decorated paper, I had another moment of surrealness; I could hardly believe I was marrying a man in a century I had not been born into. I had become so accustomed to the nineteenth century that, by now, these thoughts rarely disturbed me, yet occasionally, they broke to the surface, reminding me of who I was. This was one of those moments: seeing my name alongside Edward's was both thrilling and sobering. I still felt a sort of nostalgia to see my maiden name on paper, and to know that it would soon be Emberley; that I would formally be a part of this family, one I was supposed to have been born into. It left me with some feelings of ambiguity. It was not that I lacked pride in becoming an Emberley—quite the opposite was true—but there was a certain pleasure in being a Leifman once again. There was also a small feeling of loss. My name was the last part of me that I shared with a childhood family I no longer had. When alone, I often attempted to process this particular loss. John had reset my own time to 2003—everyone who was a part of my life after that point would not know me. I thought of my husband, who would likely meet someone else in college; colleagues; students, many of whom were yet to be born. None of them would ever know who I was. But for everyone who was in my life prior to and during this time, to them, I must have simply vanished. God only knows what horrific visions played through the minds of my grandparents and father. I'd pushed the ugly thought from my mind many times before, but staring at this rather beautiful half-sheet of paper, I finally engaged them. I knew in that same cemetery where John found me, I now had an empty grave. I also knew how the headstone would read:

Vale Leifman
March 12, 1985 – April 4, 2003

I was sure there would be a small note about being a beloved daughter, granddaughter, and friend; and perhaps even a "gone too soon" or "forever in our hearts" would be engraved.

I'd suffered through the loss of my children, yet knowing they would be restored to me was like lighting a candle in the darkness; it did not replace the sun but it allowed me to put one foot in front of the other and find my way home.

I knew my family must have suffered: to find their eighteen-year-old daughter vanished without a sign. And where did I vanish from? Even I could not recall what I was doing April 4, 2003. I thought of my father, and how he must've struggled: the loss of my mother had been almost more than he could bear. Alcohol had become his vice. I was ten when he deserted me and only sixteen when he came back into my life, full of remorse. I forgave him. It was easier than holding a grudge. It was not my nature alone, though, that allowed my clemency; that was a gift from my grandparents. My father's parents loved and raised me as their own after my mother died and father left. Most of what was good about me came from them. I felt tears gather in my eyes as I recalled their love for me. I could remember the feel of my grandmother's soft arms as she rocked me, calling me her sweet angel. I could still recall my grandfather's scent—a mixture of aftershave and musky cologne. Memories flooded my mind: sleeping in my Barbie sleeping bag at the foot of their bed when I was afraid, watching soap operas, learning to cook and embroider with my grandma, and reading the Bible with my grandpa. I was raised by a different generation than my friends were, allowing me to see the world through a lens rarely used by people my age. That lens, that love; it molded me and gave me the strength to survive life's greatest trials.

'Tis a Lie

# CHAPTER 25

After lunch, I went to my chamber to lie down. The warm down duvet was a welcome comfort as I pulled it around me as though I were in a cocoon. I felt tinged with a bit of gloom and hoped some rest would reset my mood. For some time, I lay there, hoping to drift into a blissful nothingness; instead, I dwelt on every little stressor my mind could create. Finally, I got up and walked about my room, checking drawers and assessing my luggage. Looking at my clothes for France helped build my excitement. With Anne's help, I'd chosen a few dresses made with a thinner material more appropriate for the southern French climate. My favorite was a soft cotton dress with blue flowers, leaves, and tendrils printed all over. The shoulders were pleated, and the bodice had gold buttons with mother-of-pearl in the center. I doubted this dress would be much cooler than my delaine ones, but I guessed it would be comfortable enough for the winter months.

I could already smell the orange blossoms and feel the heat on my shoulders. These thoughts provided me with some comfort, quieting my anxieties about traveling. I quit my chamber, hoping to find Edward in the parlor. Instead, as I was crossing the threshold into the hallway, I heard several distant voices. I retracted my steps and followed the voices down the hallway to the rarely used drawing room. I heard Edward's familiar deep tones amongst the rest and sensed one of them was unfamiliar. The door was open: I saw my husband-to-be first, then Anne, George, and a face I had never seen before. My bashfulness got the best of me, as well as the fact I had not been called for. I went to make my quiet retreat but Edward must have sensed my presence; he glanced in my direction and called out to me.

"Ah, there she is, my little darling. Come, Vale."

I tried to steady my embarrassment and took a deep breath before making my acting debut. As I walked over to the gathered group, it occurred to me—my God—am I supposed to curtsy? I felt a moment of panic and annoyance; I never thought to ask Anne. I hadn't met many people, and I would now proceed to humiliate myself. Perhaps it will not be formal, I hoped, and I could just sit. As I approached closer, all three men stood up, alerting me that this was, in fact, a formal greeting. *Of course,* I thought, *they always insist on so much refinement.* It was at times such as this when I felt discomfort most acutely, as though I did not belong.

Edward spoke first. "Mr. Cole, this is my beautiful fiancée I was speaking of, Vale Leifman."

Mr. Cole made a small bow and tipped his hat as he stated, "'Tis a pleasure to meet you, Miss Leifman."

Out of the corner of my eye, Anne caught my attention; I did not know if I should curtsy or not. As it felt completely foreign to me, I merely extended my hand and shook his as I would in my own time. Not knowing if that was correct or not, I didn't doubt the possibility of attending Anne Ellis's Finishing School for Millennials later that day. Regardless, my handshake sufficed as Edward took my hand and led me to the sofa to sit next to him.

"You are certainly every bit as lovely as Mr. Emberley said you to be, Miss Leifman."

I felt my face redden. "Thank you, Mr. Cole." It was all I could think to say.

The men quickly resumed their previous conversation, which sounded very matter-of-fact and businesslike. Anne was half-listening. She would nod her head here and there, but was mostly consumed by her sampler. I realized she was embroidering something white. As I eyed her work, she looked up and saw me. Smiling, she moved it lower into her lap, attempting to hide it from me. My dear Anne! I dreaded being parted from her for so long.

The conversation was picking up between the gentlemen. I heard a few words here about someone in Parliament. Mr. Cole said he feared more riots; Edward and George seemed to agree. Mr. Cole then went on about the smallpox and cholera coming from London. In short, Mr. Cole had nearly convinced me that I should never leave Avenhurst, even if I could hear the Mediterranean calling my name. Edward was in an astute mood, for he took my hand into his and squeezed it gently. Edward soon shifted the conversation to his tenants and what seemed to be the true purpose of Mr. Cole's visit.

"We need but to draw up the contracts, Mr. Emberley. The entirety of the business could be complete in two to three days' time."

Mr. Cole had dim blue eyes, but when he spoke of contracts, they lit up like a lamp with fresh oil.

"How soon can your office draw up the contracts, then? I am leaving for the continent in three weeks."

"Well, sir, I can have the contracts drawn by tomorrow evening, or Wednesday morning by the latest. It would, at this point, be a matter of the post and the urgency with which you are able to sign and then collect your tenants' signatures and have the documents notarized. If you were to leave for London by tomorrow, they would be completed by your arrival, and I could obtain your signature immediately. We would not have to wait on the post, and I could notarize the contracts myself. We would then only have want of your tenants' signatures, which shall be easy enough to obtain since they will see your own signature has been notarized. By traveling yourself, it does give us some time, in case we do meet any barriers from your tenants after the contracts have been made."

Edward seemed to reflect upon Mr. Cole's suggestions. "I would rather sign when I arrive in London. We will be departing for France from there."

"If that is your preference, Mr. Emberley, I will see that it is done. I can certainly work with George here to obtain your tenants' signatures. I—" Mr. Cole went to continue but George interjected.

"Edward, I think you must reconsider Mr. Cole's first suggestions. Consider your little bride and your wedding tour. You risk your tenants' refusal by not being present for their signatures, and then Mr. Cole and I will be writing and expecting your assistance in solving a matter that could have been completed before your departure."

I felt a slight irritation at George; though I knew his advice was sound, I felt a twinge of disappointment at the idea of Edward leaving for London for a few days. Edward felt the same, it seemed.

"I would rather not leave. I am sure my tenants will sign. I have been generous, more generous than many of my peers."

"'Tis true, sir, without a doubt," replied Mr. Cole.

George, much to my chagrin, persisted. "You are most generous Edward, I would never deny that, nor would anyone that knows you. However, the tenants, and not just those in Yorkshire, have recently gained an air of entitlement. The riots have perpetuated these feelings, and many landlords face these same disputes. Why delay? I know where your impediment lies." George looked over to me. "Vale will be cared for in your absence. In fact, I extend an invitation now for her to come to Highgarden with Anne and me. I doubt Anne will protest."

"Certainly not!" Anne stated enthusiastically. "Please, Edward. It will prevent a possible tenant issue for you, and give me time with *our* little bird before she is solely yours."

I couldn't help but smile at Anne's emphasis on *our* despite how disagreeable I felt internally.

Edward placed his attention on me. "How do you feel about visiting Highgarden during my absence, love? Having you under George and Anne's care is the only situation I can agree upon. If you wish me to stay, then I will stay, and will sign these contracts before we depart from England."

I knew Edward was letting me choose what I was most comfortable with, and I did struggle with what I wanted and what I knew to be best for Edward's situation. He was my whole world. The idea of him going to London alone, with cholera and smallpox all around him, terrified me. I had to acknowledge, though, that he had survived so far without my ideas of modern medicine. I could already see that George's idea had given him a reprieve.

"I think it would be lovely to visit with Anne at Highgarden, and I will feel better knowing this burden is removed from your mind."

With another squeeze of my hand, along with a slight pat, Edward continued with Mr. Cole.

"Then it is all settled. Mr. Cole, I will follow you to London tomorrow morning. I will take an early rail."

"'Tis wonderful, sir! I will make haste and see that all is ready for your arrival."

And with that, Mr. Cole stood up and bowed to us ladies, and then shook hands, thanking both Mr. Emberley and Mr. Ellis for their time.

"We will see you out, Mr. Cole. There is something more I need assistance with. This way please."

As the men walked out, I was left alone with a bright-eyed girl who had the most mischievously happy look if ever one existed.

"What *is* that look, Anne?!" I laughed.

"I am so excited for you to come to Highgarden." Anne came and sat next to me, pinching me with excitement. "Do you remember one of our conversations about your time, you mentioned—what did you call it? A bachelorette party?"

*Good heavens,* I thought. Mind you, Anne got a very mild explanation of these parties. In fact, what I told her was more akin to a bridal party from the 1950s, not the debauchery I had before my first wedding.

"What about it?"

"You and I are going to celebrate. George, bless the little old man that he was born to be, goes to bed rather early. And I happen to have been given a very nice bottle of wine from one of George's acquaintance's wives. I think we shall drink, be merry, tell ghost stories, and gossip after he retires for the evening! What do you say?"

Anne's eyes were shining like she had already consumed the bottle of wine.

"I love it!" I replied. Then I giggled as I thought of Anne inebriated. "I will write down my ghost story tonight, while I still have some wits about me."

With enthusiasm, Anne and I went in search of Margot to prepare my three-day stay at Highgarden.

Later that evening, I found Edward sitting at his desk, with several open letters in front of him. I admired the familiar scowl from the door and, not wanting to break his concentration, I went to leave unnoticed—unsuccessfully. Once he saw me standing there, Edward stuck out his arm for me to come to him. I kissed him on the cheek as I took my spot on his knee.

"Stay with me for a while, darling, unless I am far too dull for you to contend with tonight."

"Dull? Impossible. You're an Emberley. It is not in your blood."

Edward smiled, but there was something to the look on his face. He kept eye contact with me, forcing a smile.

"Yes?" I asked.

Edward placed his forehead against my own, "What is the matter with my little bird? Why is she so downcast tonight?"

"I am fine," I lied.

"'*Tis* untrue, as Mr. Cole might say. Your countenance has been gloomy since our conversation earlier today. I can send a message to Mr. Cole that I will wait until our departure date. It is only a matter of inconvenience if the tenants do not sign right away. George has a way of making the most trifling issues seem urgent."

I didn't doubt this to be true of George; however, Anne's happy little face came to my mind; I hated to disappoint her, and I told Edward so. "And yes, I am a little down that you'll be gone for a few days, and I do prefer my own bed, but I have survived more than these minor inconveniences."

"That is true. You have shown great tenacity, my darling. More than most men ever would."

I smiled at him and received a generous one back.

"Besides," he continued matter-of-factly, "you might as well get used to missing your bed."

I felt myself blush hard at his boldness, which did not go unnoticed by him.

Edward laughed at himself. "I only meant because of the hotel bed."

I took myself off his knee and walked towards the door, retorting, "'*Tis* a lie!" before leaving him to his letters. *Shameless man,* I laughed to myself.

Highgarden

# CHAPTER 26

The road to Highgarden had many more bumps and grooves than the one that led to town, giving me a new appreciation for rubber tires. Edward was no fan of this ride, either, which is most likely why we had not made a trip to Highgarden yet. I had never heard so many foul words, at least at one time, spill from my beloved's mouth. I teased him that such a dirty mouth could not possibly hope to kiss mine. At this, I received the most generous apology, and, "Would I oblige a wayward man such as himself with a kiss from an angel to seal his repentance?" I looked about the carriage in search of an angel, then told him I supposed I would have to do. As I bent near him to kiss his cheek, he turned his face and pressed his lips upon mine in a most scoundrel-like way. Though I quite enjoyed it, I called him the devil himself. When he tried to hold my hand, I pinched him and explained that he had already proved he is no gentleman, and that I was very disappointed; I'd had so much faith in the men of his era, and here I was, engaged to the wickedest one of all. Edward delighted in his chastisement, so much so that by the time we arrived at Highgarden, he had pulled me into his lap and was kissing my lips and neck again. I had not a care in my heart to fight him off. The idea of being separated from him depressed my spirit, so our feigned lovers' quarrel was the most welcome means of spending our last few moments together.

As the carriage crossed through the front gates of Highgarden, I was completely charmed by what I saw. Highgarden held no resemblance to Avenhurst. Whereas Avenhurst was the ideal Gothic mansion, old and desolate with an uncanny charm about it, Highgarden was the fairy-tale Victorian home I would've expected to see in a magazine. Made in a large cottage style, it was nestled between a bounty of trees, flowers, and flowering shrubs. The cottage had a large front door, with English ivy grown around it and the windows. It had the quaintest trimming and detailed woodwork all over. I loved it. I remembered Anne had said that it was recently built, but I never considered how beautiful and almost modern it would be. Anne and George came out the front door, with a maid following shyly behind.

Before leaving the carriage, Edward pulled me to him. His arms enveloped me, and he stated rather painfully, "I love you, my darling."

"I love you, Edward." I pulled his face to mine and kissed him.

Edward helped me out of the carriage, and I was quickly embraced by Anne, who offered me a kiss on the cheek.

Before pulling away, she whispered, "The wine is chilled."

I laughed to myself, catching Edward's eye; I was pretty sure he had heard her. The maid, Daisy, took my luggage, and stated she would see it to my chamber. Anne informed me they already had a fire going in my room so I would feel at home. This did please me, all the more so that Anne thought so much of me, and I knew George was putting himself out for Edward's sake. George did tease that they had prepared my cage well, so that Edward's bird would be in one piece when he returned; Anne gently scolded him for his dark humor.

The four of us walked inside the home, for home-like it was, and took a seat in the parlor room. Since this house was a good deal smaller than Avenhurst (though by no means was this home small, in my opinion), the drawing room and parlor were one and the same or, as I would have called it, a living room. The room itself was decorated nicely, with walnut wainscoting throughout and crown molding to match, complimented by a dark-green damask wallpaper. There were embellishments everywhere and a good deal of knick-knacks in various places, such as on top of the piano. I sat and admired the room as Edward and George spoke for a few minutes. Before leaving for the train station, Edward requested a moment alone with me.

"I meant to have this conversation with you on the carriage ride over, but as you couldn't keep your fairy hands to yourself, I must have it now before I leave."

I would have made several comments, but I knew him to be in a hurry, and I was already feeling the weight of his departure too heavily to tease him back. Even his jest was half-hearted. I took his hands in mine instead and listened.

"Stay close to Anne, please. Do not leave her sight if you can at all help it. As you saw, Highgarden is heavily covered with woods and other beautiful foliage. Its beauty is wondrous, but it is also great for hidden dangers."

I felt alarmed. "Do you know something, Edward?" I asked.

I must have looked distressed, for he pulled me to his chest. "No, darling, I am just being precautious. Truth be told, who could possibly know you are here? I just feel uneasy leaving you behind. George is here, and that is a comfort to me. I know he will keep you safe, but he can only do that if you two girls mind yourselves and stay near the house. If you and Anne must walk, I insist he go with you."

I nodded my head in agreement. "I will be vigilant and will not go out alone. I promise. Anne and I will be on our best behavior."

A wicked smile crossed his face. "Is that so? I believe my dear sister plans to be befuddled by the end of the night."

I laughed. "I will keep an eye on her, I promise you."

"I hope so! I warn you now, my little bird, my sister cannot hold her drink. Not wine, beer, or any other spirit, for that matter."

I considered what he said.

"Enjoy yourself. Just make sure she's got her maid near her before you go to bed."

"I will." I muttered as I made a mental note to watch Anne's wine consumption.

Edward kissed me once more and whispered that he'd written me a letter as he stuck it in the pocket of my cardigan. I was not to open it until tomorrow, the only day he would not see me at all; then he told me to watch for his carriage in two days' time. I walked with him outside, kissed him again, and reluctantly let him go. I watched the two-horse carriage pull him into the distance. I couldn't help myself; my heart felt heavy. A few tears rolled down my cheeks as I immediately felt loneliness creep in. I didn't stay that way long, though. Anne and George came to find me, and Anne insisted I do away with my melancholy as they had a great dinner being made in my honor—which meant there would be potatoes—and that George had planned a nice tour of the grounds, with my interests in mind. With that, George offered his arm to me, and the three of us made our way around Highgarden.

✦

The grounds of Highgarden were not as vast as those of Avenhurst, but they were certainly beautiful. Highgarden had a formal flower garden similar to Catherine's at Avenhurst, but it was not enclosed by walls. Several large English oak trees formed the perimeter, and they were surrounded by several varieties of large flowered shrubs. One species had large glossy leaves with a highly fragrant white flower, and the other was a lighter green bush with orange buds throughout; Anne called the latter Orange Glow. The whimsical garden, with its various roses, pretty biennials, and crawling English ivy, was spread within this boundary. I was certain if fairies ever did exist, this is where they would live. I could see Edward's concern, though: one could make one's way around unnoticed as the trees only offered a visual barrier. My first thought was not of the danger that could come within but the danger of a false sense of security, such as the ease of a toddler slipping away unnoticed. I made a mental note that should Anne become pregnant any time soon, I would insist on a gate being put up around this beautiful sanctuary.

After our tour, Anne showed me to my room, where her maid had already placed my belongings in a wardrobe and my toiletries on an oak table. My bed was small and quaint, with some down pillows and a soft throw folded on top. The small fireplace was alive with its fire, casting a happy glow, and the hanging oil lamps mounted on the wall were already burning. The whole room was domestic bliss. I lay back on the bed, and a peaceful feeling overwhelmed me. Even the scent in the room was pleasant as there was a bouquet of lavender on the table. Anne sat in the chair next to my bed, watching me with a smile on her face.

"I love your home, Anne. It is so cozy and beautiful. If you were a house, this is what you would look like."

Anne giggled. "Sometimes, you are nonsensical. Do you really like it? It is comfortable, but it is not grand and stately like Avenhurst. We only have a couple of servants."

"Anne! I should remind you that I had no servants in my time. I really do love it. It reminds me of home. *My home.*"

Anne got up from her chair to lie next to me. "Well, this is also your home for the next few days, and I am happy you like it. George is pleased with it."

"Does he really not mind my staying here? I know he has been struggling with his health. I hate to burden him."

"Oh no, darling, he is glad to have you here. It was all his idea, remember. I was so pleased when he offered. I am glad Edward has a friend like him."

"So am I," I replied.

✦

It must have been about eight o'clock at night as we three sat in the parlor. George was smoking his pipe, and Anne and I were playing with a deck of cards. I noticed Anne kept looking towards George, waiting and, perhaps, hoping. I glanced in his direction myself, searching his face for signs of weariness. *There, there it is*, I thought: *the double blink*. As someone raised by her grandfather, I recognized the first signs of fatigue anywhere. I looked back at Anne, who now had a smile on her face; I was not alone in my observations. We acted like we hadn't noticed and continued our game, slightly quieter than we were a moment before. After about five more minutes, George laid down his pipe and announced he was retiring for the night. Anne gave him a kiss on the cheek; George bowed towards me and told us to be good girls and not to stay up too late.

"Go change for bed, Vale. I will come to your room in a few minutes."

I went to my room, not needing a candle as this hallway was well-lit with oil lamps. My nightgown was folded in the wardrobe, so I quickly changed, excitedly anticipating my bachelorette party with Anne. I waited a few minutes, sitting next to the fire, when I heard a soft knock at my door. Anne peeked her head in to see if I was dressed. She walked in, wearing her gown and a small wreath of flowers around her head.

I was already amused. "What are you wearing?"

"My matron of honor crown. Here, put on your bridal wreath."

Anne had a larger wreath hidden behind her back. She placed the flowers upon my head; we looked like a couple of hippies.

"Thank you. I feel like a fairy princess." And I did. "Now, where is our wine?"

"Let us proceed to the parlor. I had Daisy hide it there."

"Won't George wake up? Maybe we should stay in here."

"No, no. The dead will rise before he does. Speaking of the dead, did you bring a ghost story?"

"I did!" I jumped up and went to my purse, a small sack I'd embroidered, where I had folded up a short story I had written the day before.

"Now come, Miss Leifman, and let the festivities begin."

We entered the parlor room, and Daisy had set out our wine and a pretty little charcutier board. I noticed she, too, wore a small wreath of flowers on her head. I just shook my head. Anne was too much, and I loved it.

"Who shall begin?" Anne asked as she took her first sip of wine.

"You. Since you are the matron of honor, you also have the honor of telling your story first."

I sipped my glass of wine. *My goodness, she should stay friends with whoever gave it to her,* I thought.

Anne began her story of wonder and mystery. I listened as she described a dark castle in a faraway place several centuries ago. There was a young maiden who was sought after by some tyrant, uncanny happenings, and a resolution where the maiden was reunited with her lover. It was a great story and not at all spooky, in my opinion. I now worried that my small and insignificant story might be too much for her.

"Now your turn, darling. Let us hear your story."

I had thought carefully over which ghost story to tell her that I could remember. I had gone over all the urban legends I knew. What made them difficult was that so many of them involved a modern vehicle. Lovers in the nineteenth century simply did not drive off in a carriage by themselves to make out. It just did not exist; so that excluded several well-known stories. Finally, I decided on a familiar story that involved no changes at all, and so I began my poorly written tale.

"There once was a lovely group of friends who just so happened to be telling ghost stories on a night just like this very one. These friends wanted to explore the graveyard nearby, but one of the young ladies was far too afraid. The friends teased and ridiculed her. Even her own sister laughed at her being so frightened. The young girl attempted to defy them and insisted that she, too, was brave. To test her, one of the young gentlemen gave her a small dagger.

"'Go and stick this into the grave that sits below the large tomb. We will wait here for you. Prove to us that you are not afraid.'

"And so, the young girl went. It was dreadfully dark, and the wind had an earnest chill. She walked slowly towards the graveyard. She knew it well, though she had never been there at night. The clouds broke apart in the sky, revealing a full moon; the entire graveyard seemed to awaken. The wind caused a moaning voice to murmur through the lonely graves. The young girl began to tremble; fear enveloped her completely. It was then that she decided to stand her ground; she could not return to her friends with the dagger in her hand, and she was a girl of great character. Nor could she drop the dagger and lie, though it crossed her mind briefly. So, she kept going, and finally came upon the large tomb with the single grave below it. The young girl took the dagger in both her hands and pushed it hard and fast into the grave. A smile broke across her face. She had done it. She had proved she could conquer fear! She stood up to leave, and suddenly realized that she was detained. Fear seized her once more, and though she attempted to escape, something held her to the grave.

"Her friends waited for some time. They made their small jokes and were surprised she would even attempt such a thing.

"'I would not dare go myself,' stated her older sister.

"Finally, the young gentlemen grew impatient. Knowing they could not return home without her, the young people made their way to the old tomb. Upon approaching the grave, the group stood horrified. There lay the young girl, dead. The ladies fainted, and the gentlemen lost their composure. She had driven the dagger into the grave—this is true. Unfortunately, she had caught her dress as she did so and pinned herself to the ground. The poor young girl had died of fright; fear had conquered her."

I looked up from the piece of parchment on which I had

written my story to see Anne, pale and wide eyed.

"Are you all right?" I asked, more tickled than I ought to have been.

Anne finished her wine, and I was pretty sure that was her second or third glass.

"That was amazing and terrifying. Bravo! How did you invent such a dreadful story, darling?"

I confessed to her that I had just elaborated on an old tale from my time and explained what an urban legend was. Anne was pleased. I noticed, though, that she was beginning to slur her words. Edward was not false; Anne couldn't hold her drink. I asked Daisy to use some discretion and assist Anne to her and Mr. Ellis's chamber. Daisy gave me a funny sort of look, and Anne noticed.

"Oh, never you mind, Daisy. I can get myself to bed. I do not share a chamber room with George, Vale."

Anne then dismissed Daisy for the night, determined to stay up a while longer. Anne explained to me that many married couples were not accustomed to sharing their chambers, and that she and George both preferred it this way. I asked her if she thought Edward would feel the same.

"I doubt that very much. Edward is so very much in love with you. Besides, you are so beautiful—Edward will want to wake up to that pretty face every morning."

And with this, Anne began to cry. My poor, sweet Anne. She was so very drunk. I knew when she became sentimental that I'd lost her. I tried to assist her to bed by placing her arms around me. We did well for several feet, then the grandfather clock chimed loudly and we both startled. Anne fell to the ground, knocking me over and causing me to hit my head against the wall. We were not quiet. This, of course, threw us both into a fit of giggles. Our good time soon ended, though.

George came out of his room, and he did not look pleased. I was immediately sober. Edward could be loud and capricious, but he was all bark. George had such a serious manner to him that it was unsettling. A man has such a way of affecting those around him with his temperament, that even the fair-tempered men are guilty by association. George looked down at Anne with such detest I almost started. Then, the unhappy man looked at me; I knew I appeared disheveled. Anne and I both had our hair down, our flowers were crooked, and both of us were in our gowns. We were the very scene of female impropriety. As George stared at me, his face reddened. I realized that my gown had come down my shoulder, and that I probably looked shocking to him. I pulled it up and quickly stood. I went to assist Anne up, but George came over and took her into his arms.

"She is secure, Vale. I have her now. Go to your room and get some rest."

I nodded my head and went to my own room. I placed another log into the fireplace so I would have some light, and then I crawled into my bed. I felt guilty and hoped I hadn't got Anne into trouble. Lying in bed thinking, I realized George seemed more like Anne's father than her husband. I knew there was an age difference, but so was there between Edward and me. Yet I knew that my soul was the same age as Edward's. Still, there was something more; age alone couldn't account for my uneasiness. I remembered how Anne had felt about being married early on. Perhaps George felt that resistance from Anne, or maybe he wasn't as comfortable with her *mistake* as he claimed to be. Whatever it was, I just hoped I didn't add to any troubles that might exist between them.

I sat with Anne at the breakfast table. Neither of us could pretend to be cheery. My coffee was especially important to me today, but poor Anne, she was having the harder time out of the two of us and couldn't stomach anything.

"Where is George?" I inquired, still nervous to see him.

"Oh, he went to collect the mail. He should soon return."

"Does he normally get it himself?" I was used to a servant bringing it to Avenhurst.

"Oh no, he usually sends Tom, but today he insisted on some fresh air, so he went. The post office is not far at all. We are closer to town than Avenhurst, remember."

"Is he upset?"

Anne looked at me with wonder in her eyes. "Upset, darling? About what?"

I felt like an idiot. "Last night, he seemed upset when he found us falling over ourselves in the hallway."

Anne laughed and rubbed her temples. "No, no, he wasn't upset. Perhaps a little surprised. We had awakened him, and he said it took him several minutes to realize where he was and who we were!"

"Oh." I laughed gently. "Good. I thought for sure we'd disturbed him."

I felt guilty for thinking so poorly of George. Soon we heard him come through the door, whistling a tune I was unfamiliar with. His soft brown hair was pressed against his face; he looked at me and gave a small smile. He proceeded to doff his hat and took a seat next to Anne. Upon handing Anne some letters, I remembered I had one from Edward waiting for me.

"How are you two feeling this morning?" George asked, seeing the answer with one glance at his bride. "Vale?"

"I'm fine. My head doesn't hurt, but I have felt better."

George gave a small chuckle. He looked at Anne and stated, "You could have at least extended an invitation to me, my dear. That was very good wine."

We all laughed. I felt relieved that George was in good spirits.

Dryad

# CHAPTER 27

Anne did not improve over the next few hours, and when George insisted she lie down and rest, she finally obliged. Before going to her room, Anne apologized, as it was our full day together, and she hated to miss it. I easily excused her and reminded her that a few hours of rest would give her a full recovery for the evening. I didn't mind Anne's short absence as Edward's letter was burning a hole in my pocket. Following Anne's example, I made my way back to my temporary room. I took a blanket, sat near the warm fire, and indulged in my lover's letter.

*My Darling Vale,*

*Any time apart from you must be of the most dreadful sort. As I write this letter, I see that you are attempting to read a book that you are either not interested in, or are too anxious to concentrate on its words—I assume it is the latter, as you are nervously wrapping your golden strands around that delicate finger of yours. My beautiful bird, it is not lost on me that we have never been separated since you first arrived here. It is a nervous state of mind that I also share. But remember, it is fear without substance. Before the end of the week, we shall be sitting here again by the fire, avoiding Mrs. Miller's watchful glances. I write you this letter to prevent you from engaging your most melancholy thoughts—I implore you, think only of happy things. We are about to enter the happiest stage of both our lives, to put the past away and dream of the future—it is such a lovely one. I love you, my darling, beyond what words my hand can pen. You are my dream come true. Until Thursday, I will envision my little bird sitting on my knee, your hair wrapped around my finger, and your little kisses to banish my own gloom. My anxious arms wait to receive you.*

*Forever yours,*
*EE*

I closed my eyes a moment to allow the blurry vision from my tears to subside. Edward's short but loving letter touched my heart deeply. Being understood by the one I loved was precious to me. I also missed him greatly. I laughed a little at myself as I sat there; I knew I would be with him again by the next evening, yet I still felt lonely. I'd struggled as a child to be separated long from my grandparents; I could hardly enjoy a slumber party with my friends. I knew myself well. Whomever I held a deep bond with, I struggled to be separated from. Before, it was my grandparents, then Anne—and now Edward. With my children, it was different. I didn't feel weak with them, no; I was their protector, their stone foundation. I knew too well the feelings of abandonment, and I did all I could to protect them from it, including remaining with a man who little appreciated me. He had been a good father, but a bad husband; how does one rectify it? How can mothers be expected to choose their own happiness over their children's? Some do, and perhaps they are right to do so, but in my situation, I felt I couldn't. My children went to bed with peace in their hearts, kissing mommy and daddy goodnight, knowing we would both be there in the morning. They didn't observe the relationship after they closed their precious eyes, the real one. Many bitter tears lulled me into sleep, but in the morning I got up, put away my regrets towards my other half, and remembered why I lived: for them.

I realized now, sitting in a new room, in a different century, with a new perspective, that I should have left. My God, I should have left. If I were that strong while I suffered so, how much stronger would I have been raising them without that deep oppression? I knew these were lessons one can only gain with experience. I pushed away these thoughts of the past. It was a life that no longer existed, and to dwell was exactly what Edward asked me not to do, even if it was in a different context. I had another chance; another life. Pain stabbed me at the thought of my children, and I recalled Gildi's vision, as I so often did. I went to my bag, where I kept small items, and pulled out another letter. This one I had written to myself. After Gildi gave me her visions, I wrote them down detail by detail. Whenever this life felt surreal or I felt too far away from my children, I read my letter. I kissed it, knowing they would soon be with me.

✦

I knew if I stayed in my room that inevitably I would become moody. I put on my brown leather boots and grabbed my cardigan, the one on whose left pocket I had proudly embroidered flowers myself. I desired a walk and thought I could convince Daisy to go with me, for I was still aware of Edward's instructions. I decided to go look for her myself as I hated to ring a bell for service; I did not like it in my own time, and I hated it even more now. Calling on a servant for a task merely to please myself seemed rather cold. A personal invitation felt friendlier. I didn't hear Daisy's voice anywhere close to the hallway, so I thought to check the parlor first. Instead of a buoyant Daisy, I found a gloomy Mr. Ellis. George was standing in front of a large window; I could see him in the reflection as the darkening sky made the glass a mirror from where I stood. I could see George was watching the clouds roll in. His occupied eyes moved from the clouds to engage with mine, holding me there a moment.

"Do you enjoy the rain, Vale?" he asked, turning to address me without the veil of the window.

"I do, most of the time. We get so little of it where I'm from that I can't help but appreciate it."

"Where you are from." George said this as a statement, as though reminding himself of something. "That is pleasant to hear. Most women, at least those I have been acquainted with, say otherwise. Mind you, they are all Englishwomen who have never had the opportunity to miss the rain. I have. I know we are supposed to prefer the bright, cheerful, sunny days, but I am guilty of preferring a mighty thunderstorm."

George's face had a slight rush of color.

"And it seems, you little bird-like creature, that we may have one tonight."

I gently laughed at his comment, not really knowing what to make of him. I knew some men couldn't help their awkward nature, and George was one of them.

"I came to find Daisy. Have you seen her? I thought I could take a walk before the rain or thunderstorm came in."

"I will take you; I was considering sending Daisy for you myself, actually. Women need their exercise; your faculties are accustomed to it daily, I understand."

I tried not to be annoyed. He didn't understand that he was patronizing. *It's just the era,* I reminded myself.

"Anne was asleep last I looked in on her. It is best to let her rest."

I agreed. George took my arm and led me out of the house and towards the enclosed garden.

✦

The trees were gently swaying and the large shrubs with small leaves were almost dancing when the breeze passed through them. I pulled my cardigan snugly around me, wishing I had grabbed a thicker shawl instead. I knew George and I would only walk around once before the rain forced us back inside; I could sense this was the calm before the storm. The sky had developed that eerie cast to it, and the surrounding foliage moved in anticipation, yet it was not unpleasant. George was lively; speaking of his university days, how he studied rhetoric and the classics, and his love of Greek mythology. This was a favorable side of George; I wondered how often Anne saw him this way. We were now at the far edge of the garden, and I could see that rain was imminent. George had stopped and was admiring one of his shrubs.

"Shall we go in?" I asked.

George stayed where he was but turned towards me. "Perhaps. I do love the scent of rain. I always hate to leave it."

I knew that feeling well; however, the temperature was beginning to fall, and I expected there would be hot tea and a warm fire waiting for us. I noticed a peaceful look on George's face; I couldn't help but think he could be a poet in secret.

His brooding temperament reminded me of several poets I had once studied. My Edward had mastered broodiness, this was true, but it was different with George. Edward desired a reprieve from his brooding. His nature was generally happy and calm, yet life had left its mark and marred some of his better qualities for a time. George, I felt, enjoyed indulging in his melancholy.

I felt a small raindrop hit my arm and extended my arms out to feel for more when Daisy presented herself to George.

"Sir, there's a man at the door for you. He is asking for the master of the house. I tried to turn the vagabond away, but he cursed at me and insisted I get you."

"We shall see about that now." George turned to me. "Vale, stay here under the arbor. There's enough foliage to keep you dry for a minute or so. It's best this man does not see you. I'll be back in a moment, once I dismiss him."

I nodded my head in agreement and watched George and Daisy stride away. I could hear George reciting something; it was Keats:

"'Tis not through envy of thy happy lot,
But being too happy in thine happiness,—
That thou, light-winged Dryad of the trees,
In some melodious plot,
Of beechen green, and shadows numberless,
Singest of summer in full-throated ease."

I smiled and thought, *A poet's heart indeed.*

**Caravans and Convents**

# CHAPTER 28

I could feel the temperature dropping as the clouds darkened. I saw a flash of light in the distance, and I began to count. I made it to seven seconds before the familiar boom of thunder sounded in the sky. I had my hand in my pocket, holding Edward's letter as a reminder I was not alone. The thunder, however, reminded me I was outside and still afraid of loud noises. I decided to abandon my post and go through the back door to the kitchen. As I turned towards the house, a dark object stood in my way. I ran into it, stunned to find a man standing there.

I didn't have time to fully accept the danger I was in before he covered my mouth, preventing a scream from escaping. I kicked violently, causing him to nearly release me before he gathered the strength to take me out of sight from the garden. I was forced through the large trees and shrubs, exactly how I had feared a child might escape if left out of sight. I had felt that the enclosed garden offered a false sense of safety, and I was sorry to have been correct. I could see approximately twenty yards away was a very old caravan; not an antique, but a busted old cart covered with thick white canvas. It reminded me of what the American pioneers might have crossed the country in. As the stranger forced me closer to the caravan, another man came running around from the side. I began to panic. I tried as hard as I could to scream and hit, but the second man came up to me and put a short dagger in my face.

"I hear you are acquainted with these," said the short man with a face like a common rat.

His hot breath reeked of liquor, and he smelled of cheap smoke. Upon seeing the dagger, I stopped struggling, more from shock than obedience. John came to mind, and I began to shake, maybe from the cold, or perhaps from anger.

"Throw her in the back," continued the rat man.

The taller man, who still held me against my will, took hold of my dress to throw me in the back like a sack of potatoes, but the rat man began to yell again.

"What the hell are you doing, Vie? Gag her and bind her hands before you do that!"

"If ya say so," he replied, as though this was a common order.

I felt a cold chill of terror, and as though I might faint. My heart thumped hard in my chest and ears, and tears blinded my eyes. *Where is George?* I wondered. Certainly, he would have realized I was no longer outside by now. I shook my head from side to side, attempting to loosen my gag so I could scream. Vie tried to hold my head and whispered in my ear that Pali, the aforementioned rat man, might actually stab me with the dagger if I didn't stop. I sobbed, not knowing what to do.

"Do not cry!" hissed Pali. "Vie, throw her in and get back there with her for now. It's time to go."

Vie lifted me up, and I went down with a nice drop into the back of the caravan, removing me from the steady rain. I felt someone sit down next to me, then pull me up into a sitting position. The man named Vie looked at me in wonder. I felt my heart skip a beat, the panic building again. I tried to stifle my sobs, but I couldn't. Vie brought his finger to his dry lips and made a shushing gesture. I closed my eyes and tried to breathe through the dread I felt. I felt the caravan pull away with a jolt, nearly knocking me over. I began to sob again, my moans loud enough for the insufferable Pali to hear.

"Shut her up, Vie! Hit her if you must! If we are caught, we don't get the rest of our money, you hear?"

"Yeah, I hear," he replied, now looking at me. "Quiet miss, ya hear? I don' wanna hit ya. I ain't so mean as old Pali, but I will hit ya if need be. You got us some good money, and we mean to get paid."

I was sick to my stomach. Why couldn't John just shoot me if he wanted me punished this badly? What had I personally done to him? I remembered how I had told him I would always choose Edward. I meant it, but now I wished I hadn't engaged with the man at all. It was too late for remorse now, I acknowledged. I closed my eyes again and tried to regulate my breathing. *Okay, Vale,* I thought, *this is bad, but there is nowhere really to go from here except to run or fight.* I knew I just needed to be smart about it. The most they could do was kill me, I decided, and as bad as that would be, wherever they were taking me was likely worse than death. If I must die, I would die trying to get away. I mused over these uncomfortable thoughts, rationalizing my options and debating on a course of action.

"You can take out her gag now if she promises to stay shut up," griped the rat man. "Hopefully she don't bite!" he added with a callous laugh.

Vie went to release the gag, then paused as he undoubtedly debated whether I would bite or not. Not quite confident, he took a corner and slowly removed it from my mouth. I took in a deep breath and bit down on my lip so as not to sob again, fearful they would replace the gag immediately. My tears flowed freely, however, and I could see this made Vie uncomfortable. *Good,* I thought, *guilty miser; you should feel bad.* The sun had gone down by now, and it was cold. The caravan provided minute protection from the wind and rain; I could hear the loose canvas flapping against the wood. Vie had attempted to tie it down, but the weathered material tore easily, creating gaps where the rain came through. I put my head down between my knees and sobbed as quietly as I could.

"Can I get up there with ya yet?" asked the uncomfortable Vie.

"Is she secure?"

"She ain't going nowhere, is ya, miss?"

I shook my head no and let out a soft sob. Vie moved to the front as fast as he could. Shivering, I began to move my hands about and realized that the binding was rather loose. I easily slipped one hand out and then another. It was my first success. I put my hands back behind me and kept the rope around in a faux binding, just in case they were to stop or look back at me.

The full strength of the thunderstorm came upon us, and I felt the caravan come to a sharp halt. I went over on my side, but quickly sat up, hands in the back. I heard a good deal of cursing, and then the rat man stated that the horse was spooked by the thunder. Both men got out of the caravan.

"We'll have to stay here until the storm passes. Half an hour, and it'll keep heading southeast. There, there, girl, shhh. That's a good girl."

I wished for the horse to kick him. It dawned on me; I knew we were heading west as we were traveling into the direction of the sunset. We would have to pass near Avenhurst, at least in the general direction, as Highgarden was about five miles east of the old manor house. Even if I couldn't see it, I thought, I was still moving closer *to* it than away from it. Not for long, but I still had time, I hoped. I was not sure what the men had planned, but they acted as though we had some traveling to do. I suddenly remembered Edward's words—the look he had on his face when he mentioned what some men were capable of. I knew very well what they were capable of. It was a fear that lived inside me; that lives inside all women.

"How far we got?" asked Vie.

"Perhaps two miles at best. Not far enough. Once this weather clears, we should be good on time."

"I hate this cold rain. Canna we make a fire?"

"And be caught? Use your head, Vie! And get used to the rain. There's more to come, especially once we get to Ireland. Lots of rain there."

"A small fire shan't hurt nothing. Right here under the tarp."

"And what are you going to do if Emberley should find us?"

"Right, right." He complained. "I shall freeze tonight."

"Oh, shut up, old man. It's not so cold to deserve so much grumbling."

The mere mention of the Emberley name made my heart ache. I wondered if they knew Edward was in London. I began to sob once again. The thought of Edward made me feel desperate. I lost my senses and began to make demands to be taken home to Avenhurst. I told them I could pay them well if they were to return me.

Vie was convinced. "Who could be richer than Edward Emberley?" he asked.

But Pali would not have it. "Too risky," said the little man. "Cannot guarantee our pay. We take her to Ireland as told. And you, girl, enough of that damn crying."

"Let me have some of that, Pali."

"Here, hopefully this shuts you up."

I leaned over just enough to see Pali offer Vie a glass bottle full of amber liquid. As the storm raged on, the horse neighed, and the men became merry and loud. Pretty soon, I knew the plans that had been made for my sake. I was to be taken to a convent in Ireland for fallen women. Vie argued that a lady like myself could be "naught but chaste," but the rat man informed him that the nuns would believe I was promiscuous, and he had a letter from his master attesting to the fact. I would have no choice but to take the veil once they accepted me, and there was no question that they would. My fear turned into mortification and then anger. I couldn't believe John; I would not allow him to do this to me.

While the men drank themselves silly, I gained my composure and devised a plan. When the rain stopped, they would be forced to move on, then I would make my move. Pali and Vie were already inebriated and, I decided, neither were very sharp to begin with. When the caravan moved, I would jump out the back. It wasn't a great plan. I would run as fast as I could and head northeast, getting as far away as I could from the caravan. I hoped it would be some time before they realized I was gone, and then it would be too risky for the duo to keep looking for me. I considered going back towards Highgarden, but I feared John would have someone waiting there for me, or even he himself might be waiting. If he was out there, he did have the skill to find me; he had proved that more than once.

My biggest fear now was not the escape but surviving the night. The temperature had dropped significantly, and though it was only late August, it was much cooler than where I was from at this time of year. Despite the possibility of my dying due to exposure, I preferred that end over being placed in an

Irish convent against my will.

After some time, the thunderstorm lessened; then the chance of more rain faded as the clouds cleared with a shiny bright moon above us. I felt tired. I had shivered for the past couple of hours, using up the little energy I had. The men finished their liquor and were preparing to leave. Pali was careful to keep an eye on me, which was wise of him as I might have taken the opportunity. I waited patiently, anyhow, and prayed for the time that I might be back at Avenhurst, warm and with the comfort of friends. As I laid my head against the wooden panels, I could smell the moldy scent of rotting wood. It did nothing to help my mood. My thoughts traveled back to Edward, then I worried my plan to escape would fail, or that it would work, and I might die out there by myself. The thought of never seeing him again tormented me. I also thought of my children. If I were to die, they could never exist. So much counted on my being strong and bold. My somber mind considered John's motivation in all of this. A convent: I wondered at his ingenuity. It was a great idea. Women hardly had any say in their lives as it was, and it would force me into celibacy. My thoughts were interrupted by Pali's croaky voice.

"Check on the girl before we go. Here, give her some of this."

Vie came over to the back of the wagon. I kept my hands firmly against my back to minimize the chance of him seeing the loose ropes. Vie looked at me, his gaze beginning at my face, then lingering on my chest, and then back up again.

"Poor little thing," stated the man, his eyes brighter than before. "Here, take a drink. It'll keep 'em bones warm."

Vie held up what smelled like whisky to my face. I didn't fight and took a small drink; I knew I needed the warmth from the liquor.

"Come, Vie, ride up here with me. I'll need your company for the journey, so stay awake or I'll push you off the wagon."

I sighed a breath of relief, knowing Vie was riding up front. I needed to escape without notice, and the way he looked at me gave me the impression that any little seed of humanity still residing in him had been overshadowed by the liquor. I felt the wagon hitch up again. My nerves were alive. I allowed the rope to fall away from my wrists, and as the wagon began to move forward, I quietly moved to the end of it. The canvas that kept me separated from the men was whipping back and forth. I took a deep breath and did not hesitate. I jumped over the back end of the caravan.

Amongst Friends

# CHAPTER 29

For a few moments, I was no longer cold. There was no doubt that adrenaline flowed freely through my veins, mixing with the whisky to encourage my hastened pace. I did my best to run northeast, in the direction of Avenhurst. I knew that even if I missed the estate, eventually I would come near a village, and most people in this area would know the Emberley name. As I ran, I prayed that my two inebriated abductors wouldn't notice my absence for some time yet. The landscape was somewhat wooded; not quite a forest, but many trees and foliage—enough to provide some cover yet let the moonlight in. I was glad the clouds had cleared so I could see where I was running, but without them, the temperature had dropped further. By now it was clear that summer was waning, and autumn would soon be here.

The beaming full moon provided enough light to allow my safe passage over the many rogue bushes and fallen branches that formed these woods. My heart was beating so hard I could feel my temples pulsating, and breathing in the cold air as fast as I did created a sharp pain in my chest. I must have run for half an hour before my senses, including those of pain and cold, came back to me. I slowed down to recover; I was out of breath and in a great deal of discomfort. My clothes were damp and heavy, making it more difficult to walk, and between the rain and my own sweat, my hair was soaked. I walked for a while, still praying and hoping I would find my way home to Avenhurst before being found.

I knew I would soon need to stop and rest, but this thought terrified me. I was beginning to feel exhausted, so anywhere I rested was likely to be where I stayed for several hours, asleep and vulnerable. The thought of coming this far only to be caught while I slept was enough to keep my fatigue at bay. In the distance, I began to hear a familiar burbling sound. My emotions welled up into a fountain of relief. I could recognize the sound of a river anywhere and in any time. Not long after my arrival, I came to understand that the earth, though similar in many ways, was perhaps most changed by sound. This was my own perception and perhaps the most protrusive in my mind because I had lived in an age when electricity drove every facet of life. It wasn't long after I arrived in 1847 that I realized the earth did not have the same hum as it did in the twenty-first century. Without electronics, large appliances, and heavy machinery, the humming I so often heard and rarely thought of was nonexistent. It had never occurred to me how loud the quiet could be. This burbling sound, though, was as old as the earth itself. It was a lively river, and I knew it had to be the one that ran past Avenhurst and the village.

The moon shone down as I made my way closer to the boisterous body of water; it was flowing strong. I was nervous to be so near it, especially after the rain, but I was thirsty and took the risk. I cupped my hands together and brought the freezing water to my mouth. The cool liquid was a welcome relief to my dry throat. Once I was sated, I moved away from the river, staying close enough where I could still see it. I needed it as a landmark to find my way home. I followed it for another hour or so before yielding to my exhaustion. I had been shivering the better part of the night and no longer had the energy to cry. I found a large tree to take shelter under. Though it couldn't protect me from rain or wind, should it come, it felt safer than sleeping directly under the sky. I folded up into the fetal position and held myself close as I tried to ignore the damp ground beneath me. As I lay still, I began to feel like I was spinning; I had to open my eyes to make it stop. As uncomfortable as I was physically, emotionally I was far worse. I thought of Edward and my children again. I feared my dreams would go unrealized. I felt the urge to cry but released a deep breath, almost a moan, instead. I closed my eyes again. The sounds of crickets emerged, an owl began hooting somewhere nearby, and I could hear the small clicking sounds of bats in the distance. This would be a peaceful way to die; nature holding me in her arms while her other children played. The dizziness I was feeling consumed me until my eyes burned, and sleep could no longer be avoided.

✦

I could clearly hear the rumbling of the river before I opened my eyes again; it seemed now that my ears were adjusted to my surroundings. The first thing I saw was the same tree trunk that had bade me goodnight. *At least I'm alive,* I thought, *or else I'm haunting a very remote area.* The pain I felt as I tried to stand reassured me I was indeed still a mortal. Though I had slept, it was not a sound rest, and my body ached. I braced myself upon the tree; the vertigo lingered. My throat was dry and scratchy, so I returned to the riverbank. I bent down to drink. The water was calmer this morning. I could hear many happy birds tweeting in the trees and brush nearby; for some strange reason, it gave me hope. I drank as much as I could, but my hands ached from the cold water. I placed my freezing hands in the pockets of my cardigan, doubting it would help much, when I felt Edward's letter and pulled it out. Upon reading it again, I found the energy to weep. I considered where Edward might be—boarding the train, I guessed. I knew he meant to return by this evening and would expect to see me waiting for him. This was his greatest fear, and I wept again at the pain it would cause him and that it had already caused me. I used my sleeve to wipe away my tears; then I looked down at my pale gray, paisley dress, now covered in dry mud. Though I was a mess, it was the least of my worries. I was anxious and afraid I wouldn't find my way home. Never, since my arrival in the nineteenth century, had I missed the convenience of a cell phone as much as I did at that moment. So much of this misery would be resolved with one call. It's easy to dwell on the what-ifs when one is cold, hungry, tired, and sore.

I made sure to walk at a distance from the river, relying on the woods and foliage to conceal me as much as possible. The two vulgar men could be anywhere. For all I knew, they might be well acquainted with this area, and I assumed they knew I was missing by now. I kept a watchful eye and listened for any sounds of human life. This was wise on my part, for I soon heard male voices and a horse neigh. I hid myself underneath the nearest bush, trying to conceal my fear as I began to tremble again. I put my face into my arms and breathed slowly, in and out. *Lord, please,* I prayed, *let them be good men.* I could hear their voices well from where I lay hidden.

"I cannot be sure, Mr. Smith, yet I am inclined to suppose that a young lady could not pass a night like the previous and live through it."

"No, Mr. Davies, I doubt that very much. I think we would be fortunate, if I can indeed call it fortune, to find her at all. What do we say to Mr. Emberley?"

"What can we? He will insist we keep looking."

"Then we shall."

I was terrified. John had more people searching for me. How could I get to Avenhurst now? I was beginning to despair. These men had horses, and they knew the countryside like the back of their hands. I wasn't even positive I was following the correct river. Tears flowed freely while I kept my face in my hands, praying they moved on soon. I could hear another horse trotting nearby.

"Come, gentlemen, any sign of the girl?" said a new voice.

"Nay, we have not. We had to rest the horses."

"Mr. Emberley has dispatched for help all over the county. He even requested help from the peelers down in London in case they went that way."

"Ay, that is good," said the first voice that began the conversation. "Let us be on our way."

Peelers! I knew John would never ask for help from the police. I pushed myself up off the ground as fast as I could. I was weak, but had a new burst of energy, if only for a moment.

As the men began to gallop away, I hollered as loud as my tired voice would allow, calling for help. One man looked back. I heard him halt his horse, and then stop the other men. Within seconds, the three gentlemen were dismounted and at my side, offering jackets, handkerchiefs, and their assistance. I quickly related to them the abridged story of my abduction. I was asked why I didn't come out of hiding immediately. I explained that I assumed they were speaking of John Emberley and could not risk my position. I was called a "very good and clever girl" by one gentleman and "quite a brave little darling" by another. It was completely patronizing and yet one of the happiest moments of my life; I was safe. If only all men could recognize how much of our safety and good fortune rests in their hands. It's a vulnerability placed on woman-kind. No matter the year—that vulnerability is always with us. Reader, I will add that one of the men, Mr. Davies, I believe it was, swore that I must be more resilient than most men he knew. I beamed at him.

✦

I held on the best I could as I sat side-saddle while Mr. Smith walked alongside me. It was an odd feeling making an acquaintance with these gentlemen. Though they were kind, I understood I had to be on my guard and abide by every form of propriety I knew of. As it was, I was beyond exhausted and uncomfortable, so saying very little came naturally and worked in my favor; it was expected of my sex. The gentlemen, however, were very polite, checked on me often, and promised to return me to my guardian.

As we began to pass through familiar fields, another horseman came towards us; this one I would know anywhere. If I could have thrown myself from the horse and ran to him, I would have, but I had neither the strength nor ability. Thankfully, though, he did. Edward pulled me into his arms and held me tightly against him for several moments. I didn't need to get any closer to Avenhurst to feel at home. Edward's familiar scent and loving arms were enough. I felt his kisses being spilt on top of my head as he loosened his embrace to get a better look at the mess I was. I could see it in his eyes that I looked as bad as I felt.

"My little darling, thank God you're alive," he choked out. He whispered in my ear, "Are you hurt?"

I shook my head, not wanting to draw any more attention. Edward gave a small nod of relief. I felt tears gather in my already tired eyes.

"Edward, I'm sorry. I wasn't alone long…" I couldn't continue.

"Nay, my darling," he consoled, "you are not at fault."

The gentlemen explained how they had found me while they accompanied us back to Avenhurst. I asked Edward how he'd known to come home so early, and he replied that he hadn't, but providence was on our side, and he would explain all he knew once I had rested a while. I squeezed his arm to acknowledge our good fortune, unable to speak clearly anymore. With my safety ensured, exhaustion set in, and I fell asleep against Edward as we rode back, only waking at the sound of the large gates opening.

We were quickly greeted by Mrs. Miller and Margot, both of whom seemed beside themselves. My body didn't easily recover from the little respite during the ride back to Avenhurst, and I believe I must have been in and out of consciousness. I vaguely recall Edward carrying me to bed, the ladies assisting me to remove my clothes, and warm blankets touching my skin, increasing the bliss I felt as I closed my eyes. With my good friends and Edward near, I drifted off into a contented slumber. Margot would later recount that she was certain I was near death, and Mrs. Miller continuously prayed over me.

✦

After several attempts, I was finally able to open my heavy eyes again. It was dark outside. The only light visible flickered from the fireplace. It took a moment for my eyes to adjust to the dim light, and when they did, I could see there was a sleeping figure in the chair near me.

"Is that you, Margot?" I asked, more a whisper than I intended. My voice faltered as my throat was still dry.

As she stirred, I realized it was my beloved Anne. "Oh, thank God. I was beginning to believe you were not to recover."

Anne came over and held both of my hands to her lips, copious tears streaming down her rosy cheeks.

"I'm just tired, Anne, and a little weak."

This was true. As I tried to sit up, I felt my head sway. Anne reprimanded me for attempting to get up. I asked for some water, which she hastened to give me. Once my throat was relieved, I asked about Edward.

"He was just here a few moments ago. He's been beside himself with worry. We all have. You have been almost lifeless and difficult to rouse. The doctor told us you might or might not recover from the extreme stress your little body experienced."

I closed my eyes, still overwhelmed with fatigue, and for the pain that I had caused. "I'm sorry, Anne."

"What for? You have done nothing wrong. But I guess that is little comfort. Even George—you should see him—is guilt stricken. He has hardly left his room since they found you. I hope you don't find me presumptive, but I told him that you would not have hard feelings towards him."

"Hard feelings? Whatever for? George did nothing. This was John's doing. Our only mistake was letting our guard down for mere seconds. John must have been watching my every move."

My voice gave out before I could complete my statement.

I had dreamt about John; he had tormented my mind while my body was catatonic. In my dream, I couldn't see his face, but I could feel he was always watching me; observing how I moved, and hating how I loved. Images and feelings such as these appeared and disappeared throughout the night, but one singular dream broke through. I was running, though I could not say why, but I knew I needed to get back to Edward and to my children. I could see Edward in the distance. My son was holding onto Edward's legs, and my daughter was in his arms. I knew instinctively they were his children now too. My heart leapt with love and excitement as I saw them. My desires were realized—then I was immobile. I could see a look of horror in Edward's eyes as I struggled against the net that had been cast over me. I called for him, but it was too late. I was being pulled away by an unfaced man, his voice familiar but altered beyond recognition. The dream left me haunted.

"Vale—are you well?" Anne's concerned voice drew me back.

"I'm sorry. I was lost in thought."

"No, I am sorry, my darling. And as I said before, so is George." Anne reached down and kissed my forehead. "Let me send for the doctor and find Edward. He will be so relieved that you are finally awake."

"I cannot believe I slept all day."

"All day? No, darling, it is nearly nine o'clock at night. Edward brought you home yesterday morning. You have slept away a day and a half."

*No wonder I feel so ill,* I thought. I was probably dehydrated. I managed to sit up a little by propping a pillow behind my back. I felt my head sway once again, but it resolved within a few seconds. I knew I needed hydration and to move about a little to hurry along my recovery. My knowledge of Victorian medicine was vague, but I knew enough to feel worried.

From what I could remember of the literature I had read, they expected ladies to convalesce in bed for weeks amongst other, more questionable, practices. I had to remind myself that fiction may not be the best lesson in history, even Victorian fiction.

My eyes were becoming heavy again when I heard the chamber door open. As I fixed my eyes on Edward, I fought the swell of emotion that poured through my body. I received a gentle kiss as he took my hands into his and sat near me on the side of the bed.

"I would not have left your side if I had known you were soon to wake."

I smiled. "I would rather you not watch me sleep. I'm sure I looked dreadful."

"Only because you resembled too closely a sleeping angel. I would rather you looked a frightening gremlin, so long as you were a living one."

I could not help but laugh, weak as I was. "Well now—you see, you have got your wish."

Edward ran his fingers through my hair. "A little wild, perhaps. Not quite frightening."

I saw his countenance change. He couldn't keep up with silly banter and looked graver than he had when he first entered. Edward's eyes were focused on my hair, which he had spun round his index finger.

"I think I failed you, my little bird." Tears fell from his lashes. With a somber voice, Edward admitted his fears. "I cannot shake away a feeling of dread, or maybe it is danger, that surrounds you. I have long been uneasy about you being alone, and still, I left you."

I took his arm and placed it around my shoulder so that we were in a half embrace.

"You left me with family, Edward. How could we have known? George had just walked away for a moment. John had to have been waiting. I heard the plans he had for me. How can we defend ourselves against an evil we can't see?"

Edward eyed me closely with a hint of some unknown insight shaping in his mind.

"What is it?" I asked.

"It is just something you said. I need to recognize evil—all forms of it."

I thought him peculiar at that moment. I wasn't trying to be profound, but for a reason unknown to myself at the time, Edward had been struck with something like discernment.

I found myself playing with the cuff of his sleeve, allowing him time to reflect before pushing the conversation forward. When I glanced back up, Edward was smiling in such a way— and he had such a way—that I could only respond back in kind. For this, I received a nice kiss on the mouth. Even in my invalid state, I could feel the heat of desire ignite across my skin and through my veins. I was still in an embrace and could feel his hand had slipped just under my gown and was resting on my bare shoulder. I smiled to myself, wondering if this was the Victorian version of first base, and at Edward for being so bold. Edward felt my smile through our kiss, and with his own guilty smile tried to question me, when Anne returned with the doctor beside her. Edward moved out of the way with a formal bow, attempting to recover his impropriety. Anne was not fooled. I saw the look of condemnation she cast at my lover as she walked past him. The doctor, a small, energetic man, did his examination with only Anne in the room: adequate rest, hydration, and sustenance was all I needed for a full recovery. I was impressed when he suggested I take a liquid diet before trying solid food. The good doctor also emphasized

I should have every comfort at my side, such as quiet company when requested and many warm cups of tea.

"Gentle little doves such as yourself," he stated, "must indulge in the luxuries of life if they intend to improve properly."

I smiled, knowing it was pointless to argue otherwise. I knew some IV fluids and Ibuprofen would do wonders, but I had neither of those twenty-first century necessities; warm tea and rest would have to do.

The Veil

# CHAPTER 30

As instructed, I spent most of the next few days in bed being very spoiled. I was able to convince Edward to let me sit in the parlor for a couple of hours in the evening; though he agreed, he insisted on carrying me there. In my room, however, I did manage to walk around with Margot at my side. The need to walk and move my legs was undeniable, and by doing so I recovered, at least physically, within a few days.

It was an internal battle to control my fear. The nightmare had tethered dark thoughts and dread to my mind, even when awake. It was well that I was indulged longer than required by the household, who worked to keep my spirits up, and it was a nice reprieve to spend so much time indoors, especially with Edward for company. While in the parlor, Edward read to me and played the piano, both activities that received Mrs. Miller's approval. Much to her disapproval, as her looks would show at times, Edward spent a good deal of time in my room. Margot was never too far away, but enough that Edward could sit near me in a chair, and we were able to piece together the incident without being overheard. With my own experience and Edward's, and the account given to us from those dwelling at Highgarden, the events unfolded as follows:

Our walk had been interrupted so that George would be intentionally distracted by a strange man at his door. This strange man must have been the same who I would come to know as Pali, while his companion, Vie, who must have been waiting for George to leave, took me against my will. Upon realizing this man was nothing more than a miscreant begging for liquor, George soon made his way back to the garden to escort me inside. Seeing I was nowhere in sight, George assumed I had sought shelter from the rain, and the loud thunder that had just begun. Once inside, Daisy asked George if the young ladies would be joining him for tea, and upon discussion, both realized I was not in the house. According to Daisy's statement, later confirmed by Anne, George realized the gravity of his mistake in leaving me and became immobilized with stress and fear. With Anne and Daisy reviving him to his senses, George took off in the storm to seek help by gathering a search party. I relayed my part to Edward, careful to keep my suffering to a minimum as he was already severely affected. Still, Edward listened with sorry eyes, rubbing his small lapel pin with the finch between his thumb and middle finger—he now kept it pinned to his left sleeve. Edward described his experience next.

"I made good time on signing the contracts in London as Mr. Cole had them promptly ready at eight o'clock in the morning, as he said he would. Fortunately, I was able to catch an early rail home the same day—I had no desire to loiter in the busy town, especially this time of year. As my train approached near home, I could see that the sky promised a thunderstorm, so I took a carriage directly to Highgarden. I expected to stay the night."

I held his hand tight then, knowing what anxieties must have taken hold of him that night. "Instead of finding a cheerful house to return to, my grief-stricken sister greeted me before I could fully descend from the carriage—she relayed what had happened. I took one of the horses from the carriage and went off in search for you whilst alerting the neighboring gentry of what had occurred. The storm had subsided by the time the party was pulled together. Anne mentioned that George and his party had gone towards London, so I stayed local and to the north. Something told me you hadn't been taken south."

I kissed Edward's hand as he finished. It was strong, even if the man himself was vulnerable. Piecing the story together in its entirety was emotionally taxing for both Edward and me. With no one to watch, I moved from my bed and into Edward's lap, taking my throw with me.

Edward held me against his chest. "All I could think about on the way home from London was the surprise on your face to see me returned so soon. But to find my sister in hysterics—I'm not quite sure I will ever recover from that. My happiness is completely dependent upon your existence, my darling."

I didn't fight back my tears this time. I gave into them and held Edward as close as I could. The beautiful sound of his heartbeat thudded against my ear.

"The opposite is true, Edward. Without you, my flame of life would be extinguished, and I would be nothing more."

I felt him move his lips near my ear. "No, my little bird, your flame shall always burn. This life is but a veil to another; and I plan on traversing with you through it. And when we are both gone from this journey, we will meet again, and we will walk together forevermore."

Upon further reflection, it became clear that John must have hired some of Emilia's relatives to take me; another attempt to punish Edward. After I repeated what I had overheard in their drunken conversation, Edward was even more convinced.

"It certainly could have worked. A gentleman removing a fallen girl, one said to be his beneficiary from his care, is not unheard of. The abbess would have felt it her duty to remove any stain from your character and would have insisted on your taking the veil."

"I would have refused!" I stated, indignantly.

"I do not doubt the obstinance you would have bestowed upon the unsuspecting sisters," he replied, looking rather grateful it had not come to that.

Imagining myself suffering through that mess was immensely irritating. "John is a real ass."

A little surprised at my outburst, Edward laughed. "Yes, my love, he *is* an ass."

✦

The rain kept us inside for the next few days. I watched as the house busied itself in preparation for the winter to come. Mrs. Miller even asked for Margot's help in the kitchen, where I learned they were organizing the canning they had done and were storing the nuts from the harvest. I hadn't even realized that harvest had been completed as I had never experienced it without loud tractors making their way up and down each grove. Between the doctor's instructions and the early autumn weather, Edward and I spent many hours alone, with just each other for company. Fortunately, mine was a resilient character, and with Edward's compassion and affirmations, my spirits were soon restored. I had come so far in reaching some happiness that I was determined to prevent the recent events from causing any more harm to my mental state.

For many, being cooped up alone for so long, even with one they loved, would become wearisome and lead to frustration; it was not so with Edward and me. For us, this increased the intimacy in our relationship. Being each other's constant companion and having little to do besides talk, we were able to acknowledge our own fears and anxieties, tease unabashedly, plan the future, and resolve the past. Edward always listened with great tenderness and offered his insight tactfully and with keen wisdom. Never did I feel small or disregarded—I was safe with Edward, and I was heard. The confidence between us was not just for my benefit. Edward shared with me his childhood; how his mother was the light of his life and how, when that light was extinguished, he had sought refuge by going inward, becoming stoic and hard. He admitted his hardness towards John, not excusing his malignant character but allowing that it did not help to foster benevolence in the man. The communication between us was remarkable and comforting. Every day with Edward was better than the previous. For the first time in my life, I felt complete. At night, I prayed for his health and longevity and thanked God for giving him to me.

Though I never felt lonely in Edward's presence, I did miss Anne, and I worried she would suffer being isolated at home. Anne was warm and affable, and she needed it returned in kind. I wasn't sure George could provide that for her. For George's part, I hadn't seen him since the incident at Highgarden. He did write me a nice letter, apologizing sincerely for what had transpired and declaring it was his fault and that he would never forgive himself for allowing such a risk at my expense. I showed Edward the letter, thinking it was unfair for George to blame himself; oddly, he didn't outright agree with me. Edward did not blame George, but I thought perhaps he did think him more careless than he should have been. I didn't argue for or against Edward's thoughts, but instead reminded him it was behind us, and with that he agreed completely.

During this time together, Edward and I discussed staying in England for some time as neither of us felt compelled to travel any time soon. Knowing I was looking forward to a Mediterranean winter, Edward promised I would not go cold, and he would see I was always near a fire on the chilly days to come. I also resolved to wear as many petticoats as needed to keep warm, which Edward declared would be unnecessary.

**My Beloved, My Friend**

# CHAPTER 31

Another week had passed since my unfortunate adventure when summer returned once more for her final farewell. It was early September, just days before our wedding was scheduled. I found Edward staring out the window at the bright day, watching the sun dance across the water that remained from the previous day's rain. The man had a serene aspect to him. I couldn't help but note how much the weather affects us as humans, no matter the time or place, or how young or old we are; a storm excites us, and a disappearing summer day calms us. Edward insisted that we go for a walk. I wore my cream-colored muslin dress with the floral print and its array of autumn colors. The long sleeves were warm enough that I didn't need my shawl.

I took his hand into mine, and together we made our way outside. As we walked, Edward moved his arm around me. I could feel him stroking my long hair, which I wore unfashionably down. Even with the change in scenery, Edward remained in a singular mood. He had left for a short while after breakfast, and since his return, he had been in this curious state—not upset nor melancholy, but as though he had found some peace. Edward noticed me watching him and smiled.

"You have that look on your face."

"Which one?" I asked, smiling at his presumption.

"The one that is questioning my thoughts."

"I am. You have been quiet since you left this morning."

Edward only smiled. The sun was behind him, and I could see that he had some red undertones in that raven hair of his. As we walked, I noticed he was leading me outside Avenhurst through the large front gates. Abruptly, Edward pulled me to him, pressing his lips upon mine.

"I have been reflecting on my final moments as a bachelor."

"Final moments?" I realized then he was leading me to the church.

"I came here this morning to speak with Mr. Kent, the clergyman. He agreed to marry us today. What do you think, my darling? Have we any reason to wait?"

I felt my heart swell.

"There is no reason I can think of that could convince me to wait another moment."

With my hand in his, I walked to the little church one last time as Vale Leifman.

✦

It was a small and quick ceremony, with only us, the clergyman, and his witness. Edward had our wedding bands in his pocket; as he later admitted, he woke up to a pleasant sunny day with the intention of ending it with his bride at his side. Our vows were simple, the same Christian vows my grandparents recited and later displayed on their wall back home. As for our kiss, it lasted maybe a moment longer than the good vicar would have liked, but to me, it could have lasted forever and not been long enough. Mr. Kent pronounced us man and wife, and with giddy steps we left the small church.

I felt my heart beat a little faster as I walked out with my new husband. Reader, I remember many details about my Edward that day, but it is his face that lingers in my mind. I could detect no signs of anxiety, nor did I sense any trepidation or impatience. The peace I saw moments earlier was displayed across his smooth and happy brow. Edward didn't wear his top hat. His dark tresses were swept to one side, allowing his brilliant brown eyes to shine. He eyed me from the side with a sly smile, pulling me closer to him and embracing me tightly. We had barely made it to the churchyard, and I reminded him that the vicar could still see us. Edward smiled; he couldn't care less what the old man thought, he informed me.

"You are my most precious jewel, my little lamb to love and protect." He took both my hands and kissed each one gently. "I think I little deserve you, who are so virtuous and good. But know this, my darling: every day since you arrived, I have thanked God for your presence, and I thank Him more now than ever for your love for me."

Moved by his words, I pulled him into my arms and kissed him with all the freedom allotted to my own generation. The kiss ignited some passion in his person, but I wasn't ready to leave the church just yet. I took Edward gently by the hand and walked over to his family tomb. Where his mother's name was inscribed, I placed my hand and closed my eyes for a moment. Edward waited to question my action until we approached the front door to Avenhurst.

"Did you say a prayer back there, Vale?"

"Not exactly," I confessed. "I told your mother I would take care of you."

Edward showed a soft smile. "It is my job to take care of you, is it not?"

"It is, I believe, our job to take care of each other."

Without saying another word, Edward lifted me off my feet to be carried over the doorstep. I laughed that the tradition existed here and wondered for a moment when it first began. To my surprise, Edward didn't put me down once inside. Instead, he carried me through the parlor and into the hall, where we met an aghast-looking Mrs. Miller. I put my face into his neck in comical shame, knowing she was stunned. Edward did not let her suffer long.

"Mrs. Miller, we have just been married. Mrs. Emberley and I will take our tea at a later hour."

I felt a thrill at his words.

"Yes, sir, well—certainly, yes. I will inform the house if you prefer."

"That will do fine, madam."

And with a quick curtsy and congratulations, Mrs. Miller was off to share the good news.

Still in his arms, Edward and I made our way down the hall to his chamber room. Refusing to put me down, Edward held me tightly against him to reach the doorknob. His scent engulfed me, and I was more infatuated with his person at that moment than ever before. When I looked up at him again, he had closed the door, and it was just him and me. I felt myself blush under his gaze; his eyes were so deep and full of desire. I knew my own must have matched his. Edward bent down and kissed me, before setting me gently down on my feet.

I felt his fingers comb through my hair and rest there as he whispered, "Behold, thou art fair, my love; thou hast doves' eyes within thy locks."

I owed Mrs. Miller and my grandmother for making me study scripture. I ran my hands through his hair, likewise, leaving small, soft kisses along his jawline as I did so.

"His head is the finest gold; his locks are wavy, black as a raven."

Edward touched my nose with his. His coat was removed. Both of his hands ran down my back, pulling me closer to him. I felt his mouth move to my neck, causing blood to rush to my chest with so sudden an intensity I almost felt dizzy. I placed both of my hands on his shoulders to steady myself, then allowed them to explore his chest as I removed his vest, then his shirt.

With another kiss, Edward continued. "Thy lips are like a thread of scarlet, and thy speech is comely."

He had released my dress and unfastened my petticoats. I managed to lose my shoes as he kissed me. My love for him was ignited with such an intensity of longing that I hardly knew myself. With each kiss and touch from Edward, a current of electricity rippled through my body. I broke our kiss to see that all that was left between Edward and me was my shift. My lover was bolder than I, but he was patient. He pulled my shift down to reveal one shoulder, which he kissed with tender affection. I kissed his chest, his neck, and then his mouth.

"His mouth is most sweet, and he is altogether desirable. This is my beloved and this is my friend."

Edward smiled with his lips still pressed against mine, and then my shift was no more.

Birds and Fairies

# CHAPTER 32

I had been Edward's wife for four days when I saw Anne again. Edward had left all but the inhabitants of Avenhurst in the dark about our marriage so we could have a few uninterrupted days together. As Anne and George descended from their carriage, I was surprisingly nervous to see my friend. I walked out to greet them, getting a warm embrace for a welcome. Anne kissed my head before placing me at arm's length to look me over.

"My sweet Vale, you look better than I imagined. I had dreaded finding you out of sorts and severely affected."

Anne's soft brown eyes revealed her worry.

I held her hands. "Your brother has kept me well enough. And as it turns out, being taken by those men is not the strangest thing to ever happen to me."

Anne gave a half-laugh, still too disturbed to accept my facetious humor. She was patting my hand with affection when she glanced down and saw my new ring. Taking my ring in between her thumb and middle finger, Anne rolled it in disbelief.

Glancing up at us, she said, "Married?"

"Four days ago," Edward replied.

I braced myself, afraid she would be upset; Anne had intended to be our witness. I had nothing to fear. She kissed my cheeks repeatedly, exclaiming she had a little sister.

"Oh, George! You have a little sister-in-law!"

I looked over at George, anticipating his happy expression; it was not to be. His round face was contorted, his soft features hard. I could see he was in pain.

"George, are you all right?" I asked. He recoiled as I touched his arm in sympathy.

I looked to Edward, who seemed as confused as Anne and I were.

"What is the matter?" Anne asked.

"My apologies to you all. I am…ill. It has been a struggle, and I do not wish to be a dark cloud on this happy day." George took his handkerchief and rubbed his face. "Vale, I am sure you were a lovely bride."

I thanked him as Anne offered her arm to him. Edward asked him to go inside and rest a while, which he accepted graciously.

✦

What illness inflicted George, I did not know. But whatever it may have been, he was fully recovered for the rest of the lovely evening. I watched him from time to time. His face remained pleasant, and what was most pleasing was that his attention remained fixed on Anne. Rarely did he remove his eyes from her. I had never seen George so engaged with Anne, so full of adoration; it was pleasing for her as well. Anne was in the most splendid mood of all, teasing the men and telling her little jokes that weren't all that funny, which of course made her all the more charming. Together, Anne and I accompanied Edward at the piano as he played. Anne had a lovely voice, smooth and whimsical. She had teased before that she could hold a tune but didn't have a beautiful voice. She was wrong; it had a slight edge, one that would have been appreciated in a later time.

During the evening, when Anne and I chanced a moment alone, she reminded me I was their little finch returned to them.

"Look at what you have done, my darling. We are a family, and not just in name. When I first beheld you, I just knew that you belonged to us. I thought it unwise to confess that to you then, but I could feel it in my heart."

I kept my arm in Anne's much of that evening. *My dearest friend*, I thought, *I owe as much of my current happiness to you as I do my Edward.* A room was offered to Anne and George to remain for the night, but George thought it best they return home; he believed that his health improved more rapidly when in the comfort of his own bed. Anne could not argue against his opinion—few would—but I could sense her disappointment. I wondered at George's ill health. I knew that by my time's standards George was fine, at least physically; however, I suspected something ailed him mentally. I kept my thoughts to myself.

✦

Later that night, I lay awake; both my body and mind were restless. I watched Edward as he embraced a sweet retreat from the world. His breathing was slow and regular, his face tranquil and content. I perched myself up on one arm and admired the sleeping man beside me. I was anxious and had no reason to be; it was altogether frustrating. I placed my hand on Edward's chest to see if he stirred—he did not. My mind drifted between thoughts of a man in my past whom I desired to forget and George, though I didn't know why. I moved closer to Edward, resting my head on the small of his shoulder. George seemed to love Anne; did he doubt her love for him? It could explain his perpetual gloom. Perhaps he just struggled. Many people did, I considered. George's childhood had been difficult. He had been abandoned; I understood this and the pain that remained. In my case, my grandparents had been more like my parents. George didn't seem to have been so fortunate.

My mind wandered back to Edward. I could not help myself; I began to nibble on his jaw. His stubble always pleased me. With my attention on the sleeping man next to me, I decided to let sleeping dogs lie and forget about the troubles of others. As for Edward, I had succeeded in disturbing his peaceful slumber. His eyes fluttered open, and a knowing smile crossed his face. I quickly feigned sleep, but he was not fooled. Edward rolled over, propping himself up with me under him, nudging his head in my neck.

"Is this my little fairy who is prodding me out of my sleep?"

Feigning a jealous tone, I whispered, "And who else would I be?"

"Well, little sprite," said he, kissing me between utterances, "that depends on the form you choose to take. Sometimes you are a little bird: lively, independent, yet vulnerable. Other times, you take on the form of the fae folk: feisty and fierce, awakening gentlemen from their rest."

I laughed as he kissed his way from one shoulder to the other, with a short pause at the hollow of my neck. I smiled at him and took his handsome face into my hands as I gave him a firm kiss.

"In this moment, I am simply your wife."

With a meaningful smile, Edward wrapped me in his arms and pulled me to him. "And that is my favorite version of you, my darling Vale."

✦

We made our way to breakfast a little later than usual the next morning. As Edward pushed in my chair, a servant handed him a letter, stating it was from Highgarden. I took my coffee as Edward read the letter in silence. I watched him frown as his eyes took in some unpleasant news.

"I suppose it could have been worse," he said at last.

"What could have been worse?"

"This was from George. There was a fire at Highgarden last night." Seeing my anxious face, he added, "The stable. It burned to the ground. They lost a horse, but everyone is safe."

"That's terrible. Does he know how it started?"

"Yes. He says it must have been his servant, Tom. Apparently, he takes to his drink too late at night."

Edward folded up the letter and started on his breakfast.

"Well, I'm glad they are all safe. That's too bad about the horse, though, poor thing."

"Yes, she was a good mare. I'm sure Anne is upset. George said the steeds broke through their stables, but the mare stayed."

Edward drank his coffee and nibbled on his black pudding, lost in thought. I pitied the mare, knowing how frightened she must have been. Endeavoring more pleasant thoughts, I took my fork, attempting to grab a potato. I thought how pleasant a meal this was: bacon and potatoes. I had learned to enjoy most of the food presented to me, jellied eel aside, but this would always be my favorite meal.

"What do you think?"

I looked over at Edward, my fork suspended in air. I had not heard a word he'd said and told him so, apologetically.

"Nonsense—don't apologize. I was thinking out loud, really."

"I was very focused on my breakfast," I said with a smile.

"Good! It is pleasing to see you eat, especially with autumn here. Imagine, a gust of wind and you would be swept away, little as you are."

I gently kicked him. "Not with all of these petticoats—impossible!"

At this, Edward attempted to lift my dress and count my petticoats for himself. I took his bacon as penance.

"I will take more," I stated, as he called me a thief. "Now tell me, what do I think of what?"

"Never mind, my love. It was a fleeting thought. I am going to invite my sister and George for dinner again, unless you mind."

"You know I do not," I stated with a smile, thinking him so handsome in his black coat and patterned vest.

Edward caressed my cheek before taking his bacon back.

Here to Stay is the New Bird

# CHAPTER 33

The next several months were spent in newlywed bliss. Edward and I were yet to tire of each other's company, which was well as we were constantly together. Autumn passed quietly, with many colorful walks under the changing trees. Now and then the sun would appear and show off the splendor of nature; I had never seen anything quite like it, certainly not where I was from. Of course, back home in California, some leaves changed and fell from the trees, but not in such a vast and vibrant way as they did up north at Avenhurst. Everywhere I looked, I was met with the vibrant red maple leaves that covered the ground and were intertwined with the oval-shaped leaf in remembrance of the beech. The ubiquitous orange and yellow oak leaves, mixed in with this festive lot, enhanced the beauty and wonder of autumn.

October passed without candy or trick-or-treating, though I did show Edward how to carve a pumpkin. Mrs. Miller was surprisingly amused by my jack-o'-lantern. I traded Thanksgiving, which was almost unheard of at this time, for Bonfire Night for my November holiday. Then came December with her snow flurries and yuletide greetings. The little village near Avenhurst was as festive as it might have been in my time. Every door and lamp post had a wreath with holly berries hanging from it. People caroled in the streets, and Christmas geese were advertised in little pamphlets by the butcher; it was like walking into the world of Dickens. Back at Avenhurst, Christmas cheer had enveloped the entire estate. I had mentioned once to Edward that I loved Christmas. With great patience, he listened as I explained how Christmas became commercialized, which I both abhorred and loved—I was only human after all—and yet it still, somehow, brought families and friends together. I learned that Christmas still held all these qualities, especially during this time. According to Edward, Christmas had been on the resurgence after falling out of popularity around the beginning of the century. The queen and Prince Albert had popularized Christmas, and the middle class embraced every cheerful aspect of it; I fit right in.

The servants were as excited as I was to decorate Avenhurst. There were no plastic Santas or reindeer in this era, so all our decorations were homemade. We had garlands of pine and holly placed about the house. There were advent wreaths with candles on every table, and Edward hung mistletoe in every door frame where he thought he might catch me. I warned him that with so many opportunities, he might just find himself under one with Mrs. Miller instead. The scent of pine permeated the house and brought forth an array of memories. In my time, I would have burned a scented candle to add to the Christmas ambience, but here, candles were a necessity, not a novelty. I did manage to find cloves and cinnamon sticks in the pantry, and with Margot's assistance, we placed them in pretty little bowls of hot water, which were strewn around the parlor and breakfast room; the scent of Christmas was in the air. I delighted in making Avenhurst feel like home, not just for myself, but for those who had dwelled there the longest.

The Advent season was lovely, but not without its trials. As much as I enjoyed the nostalgia that comes with Christmas, it inadvertently reminded me of what I had lost. I thought of my children and the eager looks on their faces when they saw Christmas lights; I realized these were only memories now. Even if Gildi was right, and I prayed she was, I still would not live those same memories with them. This was a bitter draught for me, to remember something so wonderful so clearly and to know that I alone would carry the memory. I would never again fight to find that perfect gift to have under the tree or drive them around town looking at all the festive and illuminated homes. I would never hear the various versions of the same songs in the department stores, nor would I bake cupcakes for my kid's class party at school. That life, my previous existence, reminded me of a picture drawn with a pencil; no matter how well you erased it, there would always be a soft outline left behind. I was living in that soft outline; most of the time it had become hardly perceptible, but there were moments when I could make out the picture in its entirety.

I had been absorbed in my thoughts as I was adding some fresh garland to the mantel when Edward found me. He kissed my cheek before inquiring why I had looked so downcast. By now, I knew better than to hide my feelings, and never having a reason not to, I shared openly what was bothering me.

"I just miss them. It's so different here—not that I'm not happy—but it *is* different, Edward. There are so many things they will never see, so many memories they will not have, yet I can never forget."

Edward caught my tear with his thumb before pulling my locket into his hand and opening it. We both admired their beautiful faces.

"Those memories are a part of you. Even if you alone can see them, they will exist as long as you do. Someday, and soon I would imagine, you will hold them in your arms again. You will be so content and joyous that those memories will serve as a happy tribute to all you have."

I dropped my garland and wrapped my arms around my husband, kissing him as I did.

"If you feel like following me, I have a happy surprise for you!" Edward looked rather proud of himself, so naturally, I couldn't wait to see what his surprise was.

Edward led me from the drawing room, where I had added a few extra touches in case we had company, to the parlor, where we spent most of our time. I could smell it before Edward opened the door: there, at least nine feet tall, stood a fir tree in all its majestic glory.

"I saw how you looked at the pictures of them in the newspaper. I would have had one for you sooner if they had cut some in the village, but they did not. I had to send out *three* men to bring back this beast!"

I couldn't help but laugh. I knew Edward had gone through some trouble for it, which was why I hadn't asked for one to begin with. The Christmas tree was still a new trend, so Christmas tree lots were yet to exist, at least where we were.

"Come here!" I gave Edward a kiss. "You didn't have to do this."

"I know, my love, but you did not have the pleasure of seeing your own face as you spoke of them with genuine childlike happiness. When I showed you that picture of the royal family, thinking it was a passing fashion, you declared that these dead woods were as vital to Christmas tradition as eggnog and brandy. I could not deprive my bride."

"Well, I love it. More than you know."

✦

Christmas arrived, and we were to spend it with Anne and George, who were expected to arrive late afternoon. I was with Margot in my old chamber room, which now served as my dressing room, where she was arranging my hair in the latest style—of 1847. I had several braids all over my head, wrapped in a bun with some little holly berries placed prettily throughout my hair. As Margot made her finishing touches, Edward let himself in.

"You are so beautiful, my darling. Your red dress brings out your rosy cheeks."

"You look rather handsome yourself," I replied.

Edward wore a brilliant red vest under a formal black coat.

"Can you spare her a moment, Margot?"

"Of course, sir," she answered.

"I will return her to you momentarily."

Edward and I returned to the parlor and arrived at the Christmas tree. I looked at him curiously.

"Look closely."

I looked the tree over. I could see the beaded garland we'd strung, the little cakes with raisins that the servants had made and placed upon the tree, and the little candles we would light for the first time that evening. My eye caught something new placed on one of the branches. There, tucked carefully in the pine, were two paper birds. I touched them gently, careful not to disturb the delicate pair. The two little birds were created beautifully out of what looked like embossed paper with a leafy pattern.

"They are so lovely, Edward; did you have these made?"

I had told him of the ornaments of my time; it seemed he was full of surprises.

"No, my darling. I made them myself."

I was impressed and moved. "Are they love birds?" I asked, thinking him romantic.

"Not exactly. I have had a heavy heart for you since our conversation a few days ago. I made one for each of them."

I closed my eyes to steady my emotions. "I do not believe I have ever had—so precious a Christmas gift, Edward."

No diamond or gold jewelry could ever mean more to me than the two little paper birds, one for each of my children, that Edward made with his own hands.

◆

The rest of Christmas was spent in lively fun. When Anne and George arrived, Edward called on all the servants, giving each one a Christmas bonus. Then we played a couple of games with them, as well as one I considered to be traditional, Yankee Swap. Edward and I provided the gifts, which the servants took turns taking from each other before everyone had their own to leave with. Edward was naturally a generous man and, when in good humor, even more so. The cheery fellow had ensured that the cook had plenty of turkey for everyone in the house that we could box up for the next day, and Anne and I had created gift baskets full of fruit and nuts grown here at Avenhurst for all to have. Altogether, the servants were pleased, and so were we. Mrs. Miller remarked that this was the happiest Christmas she had witnessed at Avenhurst since Edward was a little boy.

During the latter part of the evening, Edward, Anne, George, and I all exchanged little gifts, and then spent the remainder of the evening playing the piano and singing Christmas songs we knew. Mrs. Miller and Margot stayed with us for company, both pleased at what they saw and heard. I came to realize that many of the Christmas songs I was most familiar with were not yet written. I inwardly apologized to the creator of "Jingle Bells" and hoped it didn't take off in popularity before its time. Luckily, "Silent Night" had already been written and was Anne's favorite.

The whole evening was joyful. Edward had brought out the best wine, and Anne and I both watched in good humor as Mrs. Miller's cheeks grew rosier by the minute. I had enjoyed a glass of wine and went to get a second when I found George lingering next to the mahogany liquor table by himself. I noticed he was standing right under the mistletoe and, finding myself in quite an affable spirit, I couldn't resist giving him a kiss on the cheek. Next, I found my Edward and gave him two.

✦

Christmas passed in splendor, and the new year followed promptly. New Year's Eve was uneventful; I was informed this was typical. As for me, I had been used to spending my New Year's Eve at home, putting my little ones to bed, and doing my best to stay awake as I waited for the ball that had already dropped three hours prior to make its way down in Pacific Time. This New Year's, though, was of considerable interest to me as it would be my first time welcoming in a year that began with eighteen; it was even more surreal than when I welcomed in the new millennium.

Winter continued to pass peacefully at Avenhurst. The wintry landscape might have looked bleak to some, but sitting next to a warm hearth in the arms of the man I loved, it seemed to me a winter wonderland. Though we had the occasional snowfall, rain was far more common, and this rain was cold. Our walks were few, and when we did venture out, I could only bear the cold for so long. It was, for a time, a sleepy estate. We had few visitors besides George and Anne, and even their visits were sparse. Mostly, it was just Edward and I for company, and neither of us minded. I reveled in his attention, asking him question after question. His mind was so deep and vast, to explore it was a pleasure. Together, we could discuss anything: we both had a natural desire to learn, to question, and to arrive at an answer, even if we got there by different methods. Edward's analytical ways fascinated me. I felt stronger of mind because of him, something I rarely gained from others. I sometimes doubted that Edward gained anything from me, but he had a way of quieting that doubting voice of mine.

"How could one person have such an old soul yet such a joyous personality? To feel and love so deeply yet be so logical and understated? You are a paradox, my little bird. One could read a chapter from your book of life every day and still never learn all the secrets of your soul."

Every day with Edward was a blessing. Of him, I could never tire.

By the time spring began her descent into England, Edward and I had only grown closer as husband and wife. Together we began plans for the upkeep of Avenhurst. Edward mentioned that it had been some time since any real attention had been paid to the old establishment, and he could not let his wife and our future children live in a desolate place. I had never considered Avenhurst as such; however, my expectations for old homes were substantiated in the house: dark halls and large vacant rooms around every corner. It wasn't until I stayed with Anne at Highgarden that I understood the importance of cozy small rooms and carpeted living areas.

Edward began making more frequent trips to town, hiring workers to assist with the fields and orchards, and the renovations inside the house. Knowing I preferred some kind of occupation, Edward put me in charge of the horticulture of the estate, besides the task of choosing carpets and wallpaper. Deciding on what made Avenhurst pretty was enjoyable, but needing something more, I asked Edward to help with the business somehow. With gentle veracity, Edward explained that few men would work with a lady, or a woman at all. Despite this, Edward included me in all plans in and outside of the estate and had me write his letters as he dictated. This was especially important as this way, I learned how he managed Avenhurst and his tenants. I stayed away from meetings with his associates and agents; on those days, I enjoyed my role as woman of the house. I made sure the servants followed Mrs. Miller's instructions and that they were well and content working for their master. A woman from my time might find herself offended at my position; I, however, understood that my husband did value me, and that was worth far more than recognition from his peers. I didn't have the ability to change the ideologies of this age, and I could either let it burn me up inside, or I could remember that change was inevitable. I smiled inwardly, knowing our time would come.

Even with the remodel and Edward's work, very busy days were rare. We were often left to our own devices to find something to keep busy with; with this, we had no issue.

✦

Before we knew it, it was mid-March, and though it was still cool throughout the day, the earth was warming, and the trees and orchards were once again in bloom. I was standing at the window in my and Edward's chamber, watching the happy birds fly from tree to tree, hopping around the budding branches while chirping their sweet tunes. I was lost in thought watching the little creatures when I felt strong arms wrap around me.

"Those are your kind, you know—the goldfinches."

"I thought they might be—finches, that is. I had finished my toilette and was going to head downstairs when I heard a burst of twittering coming from outside."

Edward bent down and kissed my cheek. "They are wishing you a happy birthday."

I smiled at him. "I can hardly believe it's my birthday already."

"Because time passes so swiftly?"

"That—and because I'm turning nineteen for the *second* time."

Edward laughed. "Yes, that does not seem quite possible, darling, but we know it to be true. Don't allow your thoughts to linger in the supernatural too long. What was meant to be—is."

I knew he was right. Mostly, I didn't wallow in what was unusual, or I would never have peace. But days like today—or bringing in the new year—were surreal and harder to ignore.

Like a Flame

# CHAPTER 34

That evening, Anne and George came over for my birthday dinner. Afterwards, Anne and I took a walk alone. I watched her closely that night: so many forced smiles, except when she wished me a happy birthday. I watched my dearest friend fiddle with her wedding ring, twisting the gold piece back and forth absently as we walked. I had previously kept my thoughts and worries to myself, knowing that much of what I could offer in the form of advice was probably pointless. I stopped walking and asked her to sit with me.

"What weighs so heavily on your mind?" I questioned as I began playing with her hair.

Anne had worn it half-down, more like my style than her own. She took some time to gather her thoughts; I braided and rebraided her hair patiently.

Anne turned towards me, taking my hand. "Remember when you spoke of your little light, Vale, the one inside of you?"

"I do."

"How does it burn now?"

"Like a flame. Every day I feel it burn hotter inside of me."

"I can see it—I can see it in your aspect, hear it in your voice. You *are* that light now; it illuminates and glows about you. It has guided Edward, and I need it to guide me now."

I took Anne in my arms and let her sob a long while. I

knew too well the emptiness she felt and was sorrier than words could express. I held her head in my lap, and was stroking her hair when she finally spoke again.

"He does not love me. I can feel it. Not like Edward loves you—" Anne stopped, unable to continue for a moment. "Not like Malcolm loved me. What Malcolm did was wrong, and I know that. Good God, it was so wrong, what he did—but to wake up every morning to a husband who barely knows I'm alive, or perhaps wishes I was not. You looked at me just now like I exaggerated that last point. Maybe I did, but I'm not so sure."

"George seems happier than ever, though. Why do you suppose that is?" I asked.

A solemn, bitter look crossed her soft face.

"That is a good question, darling. That affection—it seems to be reserved for his visits here. I often wonder, had I loved him better in the beginning of our marriage, would that have saved him some grief? Is he indifferent now because I took too long?"

"You keep questioning if he loves you, but do you love him?"

Anne did not immediately answer. That struggle was so inherently familiar to me. *Do I love him?*

*No Anne, you do not,* I wanted to say. *You're supposed to love him, you should be grateful for him, that is what you have been told your whole life. Be a good little girl. Accept him as he is. You're being too sensitive. All lies we've been taught as young girls—put them before ourselves. But the hitch is, you cannot make yourself love another; not without losing the love for yourself first.* I thought all these things while Anne deliberated internally. I didn't press or tell her what she might or might not know already. To be told what and how to feel by me would be more detrimental to her sense of self than what others might say.

"It does not matter," Anne said at last.

"What do you mean? Anne, everything you are feeling and thinking matters. Especially to me."

Anne looked defeated: "I know I matter to you, and that will have to be enough. I am married. My life is fixed. Don't look at me like that. You are wrong, I tell you. I see it in your eyes. When you have a problem, you take some time to decide on a plan, and then you act. It has worked for you in the past, I believe. You forget you were allowed to be independent; you were encouraged to go to school, to work. I never had those options. I realize now you don't, either; fortunately, Edward would move heaven and earth to please you. You deserve that. It was a long time coming. As for me, I have George. Whether he loves me or not, it is a burden I must bear—my penance, I suppose. I have a comfortable life, though, do I not? Am I not provided for? Am I not comfortable? I have you, my most darling sister, and Edward, a brother who I have never been closer to. I am grateful."

I knew not what to say. I agreed with her final points. I'd reasoned those myself before. But I knew she would linger in self-doubt and misery until she met with the grave. I wanted to tell her that she was not stuck, but how could I? Anne could not file for divorce; that particular right was yet to exist. She could leave him, but go where? Her only option was Edward, and with that, I was sure I could assist. To do so without her permission, though, would ruin our relationship. That I was also certain of.

"What if you came home to Avenhurst? To live with Edward and me?"

Anne did not hesitate. "No, Vale. Push that thought from

your mind. I have already been a fallen woman; I don't need that again." She looked at me and smiled. "I know you mean well, my love, I do. Please just recall your own feelings with your first husband. I know you hate to. Did you leave? You did not. Maybe you would have, but you know better than anyone what it is when the stakes are higher than your own happiness. I know I don't have children, but I have a family, and that family does not need my shame to blight it again. Promise me, Vale, that you will not approach Edward with my marital woes."

I hated to do it. "I promise. But before you walk away…" Anne had got up to walk back. "Hear me once, and I will not speak again unless you broach the subject."

"I am listening," she replied.

"I wholeheartedly believe that you do not have to suffer. God didn't create you to self-sacrifice and bear a burden that's not yours to bear. You imply you have shamed this family. You have not. And if so, what does it matter? Who is this family but Edward and I now? We love you. Edward arranged your marriage to protect you, not to harm you. I am sure this is not what he intended. But even then, Anne, do not ignore your pain. You ask me to recall my feelings about my first husband, and you are absolutely right—I hate to do so, but I do it often. And every single day I am grateful that I can refer to him as my first, not my current. The stakes were high, and I paid dearly. Even if leaving him and my whole world behind was out of my control, the fact that I was unhappy and wished to leave remains true. I never told you, but the day I stood in that cemetery, just a few moments before John Emberley made his presence known, I had removed my wedding ring. I decided that day, in front of all those souls who had come and gone before me, that I was done. I had endured enough.

Did that momentary mental strength matter when—well, you know the rest. I think it matters still. I made a choice, which is why I long felt that I had been made to suffer. But those thoughts are folly, Anne, are they not? Could I have helped my circumstances?"

"You could not have. Not with John."

"No, not with him, or my first husband; and you couldn't with Malcolm, just as Edward couldn't with Emilia. Just because we are not perfect, or we have fallen short in our human ways, that does not give others the right to use us, deceive us, or mistreat us."

I took Anne back into an embrace.

"That is the lesson I've had to learn. Edward had to learn it. Now you do as well." I released my embrace to look her in the eyes. "George may not be intentionally hurting you; you would know better than I. I'm not saying leave him or abandon your marriage. I am saying Edward and I are here and will support any decision you make now or in the future. Edward needn't know your feelings just yet, but he will support you. I am also saying you should speak with George. If you feel you could love him, then let him know what you need. You have many thoughts you need to sort; I recognize it. But you're not without options, even if divorce isn't one of them."

Anne held me in a long embrace and then ended it with a kiss on the cheek.

"Come, my wise little bird. I can see Edward. He keeps peering out the front door at us in anticipation. Let's go to our supper."

Anne took my arm to walk and then, before departing, stated, "I will think on all you have said."

Our spirits lightened as we watched Edward and George play a hearty game of billiards. I never learned. Anne could play well, but she preferred to watch the two gentlemen, who were highly competitive, grumble and vex each other. I even heard a curse or two under George's breath, unlike Edward, who had loudly sent him to the devil several times already. I was highly amused. It just was not in my nature to get frustrated over a game like this—except Monopoly, which I was glad was yet to be invented. A victorious Edward came and sat next to me on the sofa, pulling me to him for a congratulatory kiss. George walked towards the brandy table, licking his wounds at his loss. Anne went to him and stated that Edward had always been boisterous in his wins, to which George pinched her cheek and agreed.

"You will not always be the winner, Edward; your day will come," George remarked.

Edward laughed. "We shall see about that! But not anymore tonight. It is late, and I have a long day tomorrow."

"How is that?" George asked, after he took a drink.

"I must go see a tenant before I make my way to town. I have an errand there. My little darling here wants a hot house for her oranges and lemons. Don't blush now," he stated, smiling at me. I hated asking for anything, but Edward loved providing. "You shall have what you want. Just know, I do expect lemonade."

I held the hand that was wrapped around my shoulder and then kissed it. "I will see to it."

George was watching us when he interjected.

"I will see that tenant for you, Edward. No need for you to

tire out your horse, covering the entire county. Go to town. Let me handle this business."

"If you don't mind, I think that would be well. I would rather not be gone the entire day."

Edward placed his attention back on me. "Do you want to accompany me tomorrow?"

I was about to reply yes when George interrupted.

"What if you took Anne with you? I could bring her early before I set out. It would do her good, unless it would be a burden."

"Of course, she should go. Anne, what do you think? Do you want to spend the day with us? There are a few nurseries that have become popular."

I saw the relief on Anne's face as Edward so easily accepted her companionship. I saw my moment and took it.

"Edward, you and Anne should go. But I would rather stay home." Edward looked at me in surprise; I never intentionally parted from him. "The mornings are very cold for me, and I quite enjoy being home next to the fireplace." Edward ran his thumb along my bottom lip. His eyes were both playful and knowing.

"If you insist, my darling. Anne and I shall go."

Turning his attention back to George, who seemed rather pleased, Edward stated, "Bring Anne around ten. We will leave for town about the time you leave to go see Mr. Hodge."

The plan was agreed on. I would have preferred to go with Edward and Anne, but it was a small sacrifice on my part. I secretly hoped Anne would work up the courage to speak with Edward, but I intended on keeping my promise and staying out of her affairs. At least Anne had tonight to think, knowing she would be alone with Edward for much of the day.

Anne and George arrived promptly at ten. Anne looked lovely in her green dress, with her hair pinned back with little buttons. She was in a lively spirit, just like her old self. I wasn't sure what it meant; perhaps she had come to a decision, one way or another, I considered. Edward and George briefly discussed some documents George had brought with him and then the concern with the tenant. Apparently, one of them had been out gambling, and then fighting with his wife upon return. I was surprised that Edward would intervene, being his landlord, but according to Anne, since it was Edward's property and he was a member of the gentry, he was liable for all negligence and impropriety on his own land. There were still times I felt ignorant of their ways.

The carriage was pulled around, and George and I walked our spouses out together.

"Are you sure you prefer to stay home, where it is comfortable and warm?" Edward asked teasingly.

I had mentioned to him in bed that I wanted him and Anne to spend some time together. I did so without explaining why, but Edward's intuition rarely failed him, and he agreed that it might do her well.

"Absolutely. Besides, I have a book calling my name." I kissed him as I said this.

"Very well, my little darling. Stay inside and enjoy yourself." Edward returned my kiss and then whispered in my ear, "Don't get any ideas about becoming a governess. You would hate it."

I laughed as he helped Anne into the carriage.

George remained at my side as he and I watched the carriage depart to the front gates of Avenhurst. I could hear the sound of the wheels change as they moved from the cobblestone path onto the dirt road. I turned to George to bid him a good day before going back inside. He proceeded to take off his hat and run his fingers through his wispy fine hair before replacing it again.

"You'll be around then, George, later today?" I asked, in my feeble attempt to break the awkward silence.

"Yes, yes. I am going now to get this business done. Shan't take too long. A couple of hours perhaps, depending on Hodge's response."

"Indeed. Well, have a good day and ride carefully."

And with that, I made my way to the parlor, where I'd left my novel, chastising myself for my innate awkwardness. I found my book between the back of the sofa and the bottom cushion, right where I had left it. Edward, though he knew me well, was incorrect in my choice today. Though I loved that little governess and gladly read it over and over, it was a new book to him, not to me. Today, since I was all alone, I took the opportunity to explore more deviant characters with looser principals. I was several chapters into M.G. Lewis' *The Monk* and beginning to understand why Edward preferred I not read it, when George reappeared. It could not have been a full hour.

"Already back, George?" I asked, letting my book slide from my lap, back to the couch by the arm rest.

George was toying with his cravat as if it were too tight.

"Yes, Vale. Unfortunately, Mr. Hodge's wife reported him gone. Apparently in town somewhere. I think I know where, perhaps, but I would rather not have an altercation with a drunkard so early in the day."

I smiled, having little to add. "I doubt anyone could blame you."

"I should hope not," he responded.

"Would you like some tea or coffee? I can ring for some."

I stood up, pushing my book down as I did so, hoping it wasn't too obvious. As I went to approach the bell, George arrested my hand.

"I think I would rather take a walk first, if you don't mind. I can understand if you would prefer not to. I have broken your trust once already."

"George, that's rather harsh. I have never felt that way—you couldn't help what those men did. You're my friend, and all is well between us."

George offered a small, sad smile. Feeling sorry for him, I agreed to the walk. I mentally bade the shameless Ambrosio farewell for the present, hoping to return to my novel before Edward and Anne returned.

"I will grab my shawl."

**Reprobation**

# CHAPTER 35

George led me down the old familiar orchard. It was easy to see the cloudy spring sky as the branches were still forming the small buds that were just beginning to wake. The sounds of birds filled the grove. Many were making their nests here. I followed George, who seemed to be walking without purpose as we kept going farther away from Avenhurst. George was quiet and composed; he paused to examine a branch with multiple pink buds sprouting out. I was content in the silence, so I waited patiently with him.

"You hid in this very grove when you arrived. Do you remember?"

"Of course, George. I remember all too well."

"As do I," he stated somberly.

This bothered me. I began to question whether or not George lamented my arrival. I had long feared that to be the case.

"Are you all right? Is anything the matter?"

George snapped the twig from the branch. We were a few yards away from the far end of the orchard; I could hear the river from where we stood. George looked down at his feet, obviously thinking of what to say. I had never been able to read George the way I could Anne and Edward. Even Mrs. Miller was more of a conversationalist.

"Everything is wrong, Vale. All of it, all of this."

George turned towards me, no longer avoiding eye contact. In fact, I wished he would, for now his gaze was so intense that I felt it burning through me.

"How? How is everything wrong?"

"I'm a sinner, Vale. I believe my soul is damned."

I felt my heart drop and a knot weave tightly in my stomach. I anticipated a confession, fearing for Anne.

"We are all sinners. Why do you believe your soul to be damned? You're a good man."

George just gazed at me, never breaking eye contact.

"Have you done something?" I asked, beginning to worry.

"I haven't done anything—yet. But I am going to. I've already accepted my fate. I have desperately tried to prevent my iniquity. It has been in vain."

I couldn't grasp his meaning. He had called himself a sinner. I considered that maybe he wanted a divorce.

"What fate have you accepted?"

George relaxed his gaze and his stance. I watched him walk over to one of the trees, where he rested his hand on the bark.

"I have always favored this orchard. I have made it a point to walk it as often as possible ever since I first visited Avenhurst. I could never say what drew me in, yet since I was a young man, no matter the time of year, I have felt a calling to walk up and down, examining each tree and its foliage. Edward would insist that I must have the heart of a poet, yet I have no talent for the art. I knew it was something more." George turned back towards me. "Have you ever felt called to an object before, Vale?"

I had, not to something, but someone. I was not going to tell that to George, though. His manner disturbed me.

"She doesn't respond." George smiled, then grimaced. "Well, it matters not. You see, I knew the day you arrived that my life was condemned. It is no coincidence that you sought refuge in this same orchard. When I saw you walk out with Edward, in that blue dress and with your long and free hair, I knew then why it had always called to me. Edward calls you his bird. He thinks you sing a song only he can hear, but that is false. For me, you are a siren; my temptress, my Delilah. Desire planted its seeds in my soul and laid deep roots there. What began as a slow-burning ember has become a flame, fanned by hate and jealousy for someone I once loved. I have reasoned with myself, God, and his angels, but it is no use. I no longer have a desire to fight it—I have chosen reprobation."

I did not know whom I was looking at. I felt like I was seeing George for the first time. His soft features were contorted and hard. It was worse than John Emberley. John looked at me with contempt and annoyance; with George, it was something worse. I was afraid, but I was too far away from the house to yell for help.

"Whom do you hate that you once loved?" I asked, quite conscious of the answer.

"Edward was a brother to me, but he stands in my way. I have battled grief and guilt. I have repressed my feelings, only for them to be reignited painfully. With each passing day, I watched you draw closer to Edward, and coincidingly I drifted, resentment taking the place of tenderness. The more of you he had, the more I wanted."

It felt as though someone had died. The man standing before me was not shy nor feeble; his melancholy subsided, he had made a decision and meant to see it through. Even in my current state of fear, I could see that. My heartbeat drummed loudly in my ears, and I began to shake. I knew I only had one chance. I grabbed my dress and began to run back towards the house as fast as I could. George soon overcame me. I felt a sharp pain as he grabbed my hair from behind, and more pain still as I went down hard on the ground, pinned with his weight on top of me.

I was panting and sobbing. "Please God—George, please let me go! We are friends—family! This is not you!" I cried and struggled to get him off me.

George pushed my head firmly against the ground, applying so much pressure my head began to ache. I stopped struggling, and he relaxed his hand.

"Quiet now," George whispered in my ear.

He began to stroke my hair gently; I felt my skin crawl.

"Think of Anne—George, what this would do to her, what this will do to our family?"

"I have already told you, Vale, it is all I have thought of. I tried to be happy for Edward, but it wasn't possible. When I first saw you, my fate was set. I had never seen a creature so lovely, so interesting. I should have been terrified of a stranger from another time, yet I was enchanted. I knew Edward felt the same. Upon seeing your face and hearing you speak, gentle as your voice was, I instantly regretted that I was bound to another being. Then Gildi told us of your fate with Edward; my envy was ignited then. I feared my own feelings as they were so strong."

I began to resist again. My nature wouldn't allow me to submit to him. I tried to scream. George grabbed my hair and forced my head back down on the ground.

"Stop resisting, and damn it, stop whimpering. I cannot stand it. I don't want to hurt you."

This time he laid his cheek against mine. I did my best to refrain from sobbing, fearing more violence, but I couldn't control the tears escaping. I noticed the orchard was silent. I could no longer hear the birds. George began to slowly run his free hand up and down my side as he continued speaking his disgusting thoughts.

"I need you to know that I tried, truly I did. I did not want any of this. Why do you think I sent those men? You would have been safe in Ireland, away from the desires of men. You think Edward an innocent man—I know better."

I wept bitter tears at his words. I had been a fool. It was so easy to blame John. He was a clear villain in my eyes after all he had done.

"You don't believe that! Let me go, George. No one has to know—please."

My pleas were ignored as if I hadn't spoken a word. George was finally confessing his true self.

"After that debacle, I considered myself lucky that I was not the accused, for in my own eyes, my guilt was blatantly clear. I will also admit I was relieved to know I would get to see you again. I tried to cut off the hand that offended, and through fate, she was restored. Then I learned that she was not restored to me, but to my best friend. I lost control the night I heard of your wedding. Anne seemed at peace now that you and Edward were married. I could not understand how she could be so pleased about your marriage. For me, it was naught but misery. I was sickened knowing Edward had learned your body, felt your smooth skin beneath his. I got drunk and set my stable on fire, nearly killing all my horses in my heat of fury. It was then that I decided that if ever I felt my need grow so strong as to hurt you, I would end myself. And I meant it—I did my best to suppress my feelings for you. Then one day I saw you and Edward. I had come alone to Avenhurst to bring him a letter, but he wasn't in the house. I walked out towards the garden and saw you and him there; you were sitting in his lap. I watched you run your hand up and down his jaw, whispering something tender in his ear. I knew by his smile that he was entertained. He pulled you closer to him, kissing your neck as you giggled and cooed, before kissing you with the full force of his mouth. You didn't restrain or pull back; you embraced him, pulling his head closer to yours with desire. I had never seen a woman be so willing or having the same need as a man. I knew then I was lost, Vale. My next step was to end my life, so I began that process. I bought life insurance and adjusted my will. I planned for it to seem like an accident. Anne would be left with everything, and she would have Edward; he is a generous brother. I made peace with my fate for a time. But then you would visit me in my dreams. You were taunting me. I would wake in a passion, only to be disappointed and alone. That is when I realized the fate of my soul was already damnation. If I can't be forgiven for taking my own life, what then do I lose by having you first?"

George began to kiss my neck, nearly driving me to madness in disgust. I screamed as loud as I could for help once again, throwing my body against him as hard as I could, hoping to break free. I paid dearly with a hard thump to the back of my head. I didn't lose consciousness, but it did leave me momentarily stunned. I just wasn't strong enough. No matter how much I fought, it only caused me more harm. With the throbbing intensifying in my head, I thought of all the women in my time and throughout history who had been in this same place: powerless, scared, and alone. Dearest reader—I was so sorry. I had always felt empathy for others, but I could never have known the helplessness of it all. Against everything I wanted, I knew I would have to submit and bear it. I no longer sobbed, but I allowed my tears to flow freely. I knew only God could hear them. I felt George fumbling with my laces, attempting to free my dress. I felt my corset loosen. He took his time rubbing my back. I supposed he was trying to learn my body the way he thought Edward had. The thought of Edward brought fresh tears that stung. I prayed he would forgive me for giving up the fight.

I could taste a mixture of blood and dirt in my mouth, and I was acutely aware of George running his hands up and down my legs. I was being held down by what must have been his knee in my lower back, keeping me in the prone position. George was now back at my neck, kissing it and breathing heavily. I felt sick. I closed my eyes and started to recite the Lord's Prayer in my mind to block out my senses as much as I could. When I felt his leg shift with mine, one last plea escaped my lips.

"Not like this, George, please. I'm not an animal."

George paused for a moment, considering my request. Instructing me to keep my eyes closed, lest he change his mind, he rolled me over onto my back. As I obeyed, I could see myself back in ninth-grade gym class. I was smaller than the others and teased often for it. My teacher, however, warned the other students that small did not mean weak. That day we had practiced self-defense, an art I had yet to put to use. I opened my eyes and looked straight into George's—they were now wicked to me.

The strike was sudden and severe, with all the force my small hand could give. It was enough. I was certain I had broken his nose as George fell back, blood gushing all over him. Before he had a chance to recover, I fled. If he caught me now, my fate was sure. Adrenaline coursing through my limbs, I ran as fast as my legs allowed. The trees flew past me until I came out into the open, with Avenhurst in view. To my surprise and great relief, Edward was home, and not alone. Running towards me beside him was John. Within seconds,

I was in Edward's arms, just in time for George to make his appearance; he, too, was surprised. I watched his face falter as he made eye contact with Edward. I had seen enough. I burrowed my face in Edward's chest, attempting to recover my breath. I was shaking uncontrollably. I heard John curse and looked in time to see George take several steps back before attempting to flee, but John was fast and aimed his pistol at him.

"Take her home, Edward. I know what I need to do with Mr. Ellis."

I saw Edward look at John, almost uncertain. George looked neither scared, nor angry. In fact, he looked relieved.

"Take her inside, Edward. I brought her here. I will make it safe for her the only way I know how."

"Very well," he agreed.

Edward hesitated, still holding me tight and looking at his friend.

"You were my *brother*. My family!" I had never heard such raw emotion in Edward's voice, such grief. "How could you do this to her, to Anne? My God, how could you?"

George would not look at Edward or address him.

Seeing this, Edward turned to John and asked, "Where shall you take him?"

"Never mind that. Go on, before she faints," John replied with gentle authority.

Edward nodded his head at John, who I saw force George back into the orchard with the end of his pistol. Edward lifted me into his arms, kissing me on the forehead and telling me how sorry he was. We proceeded slowly to Avenhurst. As we approached the large front door, a gunshot echoed through the grove, and a large flock of birds fled the trees. I startled, still in Edward's arms, and then cried. Edward paused for a moment, tightened his embrace, and opened the door.

A Charm

# CHAPTER 36

It was difficult for all of us. Betrayal and disappointment, if allowed to grow, will flourish, as all weeds do. For my own part, I had already learned about myself that if I stayed in my own head, those weeds would choke out all the joy and happiness that dwelt within me. When Edward asked me to lean on him and trust in his confidence, I chose to do so, as long as he could do the same with me. To trust another with your fears, especially in so delicate a situation, is quite simply difficult. I had nightmares for several months following my walk with George. The dreams all seemed to have the same theme: I would find myself running as fast as I could while making no progress. I would grow anxious as I knew George was closing in, then I would feel him grab me, and as I heard the gunshot, I would wake from my sleep, tormented and afraid.

I did my best not to dwell and give free rein to my emotions. I remembered all I had been taught in my own time about taking care of oneself, and so I began to write it all down. I allowed myself to feel my emotions, to see them written on paper—as a reminder to myself I would once again, be whole. It was a wonder that in my entire thirty-seven years of existence, I had never understood how therapeutic writing could be. In some ways, it saved my life. I no longer had to live inside my head; I had found a way out.

Though my suffering was great, I worried more for Edward

and Anne; they had loved him longer and had already trusted so few people. The pain they both felt was insurmountable at first. My dear Anne, she had worked so hard to deny herself, to grow to love a man with whom she had so little sympathy—but he had long been part of her life before they were lovers. Anne was rewarded with treachery in its worst form. I worried at first that she would find some fault with me, but those fears were unsubstantiated. Anne placed the blame on herself, and I worked hard to relieve her of that unnecessary guilt.

Edward wasted no time in bringing Anne home from Highgarden. He let the place out, hoping to remove as many negative associations with it as he could. Having Anne home was good for all of us. After our initial conversation about that day, Anne rarely spoke of George and usually kept herself busy with Mrs. Miller. My role inside the house took a backseat while Anne was there, and I didn't mind, as long as she felt some peace.

A few months after the incident, I happened down the old hall, where the portraits were kept, when I heard what sounded like sobs coming from one of the rooms. I knew the sound of Anne's tears far too well to fear any otherworldly creature. I opened the door to find my dear friend sitting in a chair, distressed and weeping. Between gasps, Anne declared she was a bad person who deserved no happiness.

"Why is that?" I asked tenderly, my heart heavy.

Anne considered me a moment before confessing her relief that George was gone.

"I did not want him to die, please do not misunderstand me. I had become so miserable, though. Had I allowed you to speak with Edward sooner, when I first knew how unhappy I was, I could have spared all of us. Even George. He might have moved on instead of descending into madness."

"None of this is your fault, Anne." I turned her face to mine. "Look at me. George was a broken man; he had been for some time. None here are to blame. Not you, me, or Edward."

"Edward may need reminding of that, as well."

I nodded my head. Anne was correct.

✦

My darling Edward! I could see his pain better than my own. In fact, worrying about him was a great distractor for me; my energy was easier spent on others. To him, George had been friend, brother, school mate; a companion through so much of his own unhappiness in his youth. The day it happened, we held each other all night. It was the first time I had witnessed Edward sob without restraint. Edward, who understood betrayal so intimately, could not fathom that his friend, with whom he trusted his own life and that of his sister and wife, coveted the one while married to the other. As Edward held me, he explained how he and the others had known to find me.

"Anne and I had just left the first shop whilst in town. You had stated how down she had been feeling, and being her brother with but little knowledge on how to please her, I insisted she have a new bonnet. Her face was a little brighter afterwards, and she admitted a gift from me was the gift in and of itself. Happy people we were as we headed to the nursery to retrieve the plants you had requested. That is, until I happened to see John across the street from us, admiring the market poultry. I, against Anne's disapproval, went straight towards him with the full intention of brawling. I was still seething from what he had done to you and planned on giving him a good blow to the head. On approach, however, I saw that Gildi and Emilia were with him and that Emilia was with child; I thought it highly improper to hit him in front of the women at this time. Instead, I told him what a coward he had been to treat you so, after bringing you here in such a ghastly way and then attempting to place you in a convent. I felt the rage burn from my toes to my ears; I exaggerate not, I could quite literally hear my own heartbeat pulsating in my ears. I half-expected him to attempt to hit me first. To my surprise, John never lost his composure. Instead, he offered knowledge I did not expect. I didn't care to listen initially, but with Anne's persistence, I relented. Thank God I did.

"The two men who were hired to take you to Ireland were not hired by him. In late August, John had taken the Gheatas south to London, where they were to visit family for a few months away from our northern weather. After the incident, and, by the sounds of it, after they realized you were no longer in their custody, the two cowards who took you also went south to hide. Gildi sensed them at one of the campfires near their bivouac. There had been rumors that they had attempted something illegal up north, something they had done to a lady of the gentry. Gildi, being the sibyl she is and having the familial connection to you, knew to whom they had caused harm. The miscreants, though, were loyal to whoever hired them, as much as they could be. Neither Gildi nor John could get the name of their employer. John assumed they were counting on payment if they kept the man's secret. John only learned that much because the two enjoyed their drink, and one of the men felt slightly guiltier than the other and provided more information than he should have. I asked John why he didn't inform the authorities or at the very least inform me, but he stated it was unnecessary; he took care of them himself with help from other members of their clan. I struggled to believe John initially; it was only when Gildi persisted and explained for him that I became convinced.

"'We have not been home for months, Mr. Emberley. John has no reason to cause Vale trouble. Vale is a Gheata as much as she is an Emberley. Emilia has insisted that John let you two be.'

"Emilia confirmed Gildi's statement before Gildi continued.

"'We have only been home two days, Mr. Emberley. I planned to request a visit with Vale tomorrow. I still sense a dark presence near her.'

"I told her how you were fine now and how we had been married. Gildi seemed pleased, but still uneasy.

"'Sir, I dreamt of Vale last night. A net was thrown over her, and then her body was broken. I could not see the man's face, but I know it to be a man who hurt her.'

"'How could you not see the man's face?' I asked. 'You are a clairvoyant, Gildi.'

"I did not mean to sound frustrated, but now I felt fearful for you once more. Thankfully, Gildi does not offend easily. The good woman explained that her visions about you were clearer when those you loved were a part of them, your children for instance. They were a part of you; therefore, she could see them without any issue. And as for the one of me, she stated that we also shared a familial connection, through John, so that vision lent itself freely. Mind you, you have never told me of this vision."

"And I'm not going to tell you tonight, either, my love. Continue with your story."

"So, you see, Gildi's visions about you are only complete if you share a lineage. Gildi made it clear she could not see his face, but felt that you most certainly knew the man. Gildi believed this man to be the same one who attempted to have you sent to Ireland. I cannot tell you what fear took hold of my heart at her words. As much as I cursed myself in the moment, George's face was the first to surface in my thoughts. It had been a shadow in my mind, one that had caused me great discomfort. I had told myself that I must be insecure or jealous. Outwardly, George carried on like all was well between him and Anne, but I could see it was not so; it was a farce. For a long time, I assumed that they just needed to understand each other and that their love would grow, but then I recognized the way he acted around you. George tried too hard to avoid you. I thought him awkward at first. You were from another time, after all, and foreign, and beautiful. I could not blame him, of course; I thought it natural for him to be so shy. He *was* shy with most women."

"When did you first begin to doubt George?" I asked, mystified to hear Edward admit so much.

"When Anne realized we had been married, astute little woman. George's face, it was as though the very life had drained from it. He made his excuses. You were there, you heard. I fought my own instinct then, as well. I could not deny the unhappy look on his face, but I did convince myself that he was merely a little envious of our relationship. I never considered that he coveted you. When Gildi said that in her vision, it was someone you knew, I think I must have muttered his name out loud, for Anne grabbed my arm in alarm, reminding me that you were at Avenhurst alone with him. I looked at my sister with dread. What unease did she carry with her that she immediately feared you being alone with him, as well? Hindsight is so clear, is it not, my love? All of the signs were there, surrounding us."

I rubbed Edward's back, pulling him nearer to me. "It always is so clear after the fact. All of us were deceived by him."

"Yes, we were. When Gildi heard his name, it was like the last piece of the puzzle had been delivered to her. 'It is, Mr. Ellis, sir; I can feel it, and I can see it now.' She then insisted we make haste, that George planned to end himself after he..."

Edward could not finish his statement. I placed his head on my shoulder and held him there for a while. I reminded him that once again, providence had been on our side.

✦

Some time passed, and I did see Gildi again, this time with Emilia and her baby. I held the small child in my arms for a while, knowing that I came after her. As much as I felt a connection with the Emberleys, I couldn't deny the connection I felt with the Gheatas, as well. I could never love Emilia, not like I loved Gildi, but I liked her better than I had previously. I felt no jealousy towards her. Edward was completely mine in body and spirit. I knew that because of Emilia, Edward could only appreciate my love all the more—for she had once shown him what love was not.

Edward and John made their peace. Neither walked away liking the other better, but I knew their hate for each other was ended. Secretly, I wondered if the now-gone Emberleys rested better. As for the kind old woman who foresaw so much of what came about, I saw her once more before she passed the following year. Eldria held my hand in her weakened one and gave me a blessing in English. With their mother gone, John and Emilia went back south with their child, and Gildi decided to go with them. Before she left, I told Gildi how important she had been to me, even if I had never been able to express it before.

"I know, Vale. I felt it."

I noticed that Gildi wore a necklace. The ornament was under her dress. Upon lifting it out to see what it was, I recognized it as the amulet John had used to bring me here.

"I keep it as a reminder," she stated, smiling at my apprehension.

"Of what?" I asked.

"That restoration is always possible for those who seek it."

Gildi and I write to each other frequently. The last I heard, which was a month ago, she, Emilia, John, and their child are moving to the United States. Apparently, John wants to invest in some real estate he knows will one day be popular.

✦

Our healing did not happen overnight, but over many months of patience and love for one another. One warm summer day, it was just me and Edward. A few weeks before, Anne had gone to London with some old family friends at Edward's insistence. From a letter she had sent, it sounded as if she had met a gentleman she fancied. I asked Edward to walk with me this day. I had been determined not to allow my walks to be haunted by what happened, so I brought Edward to the old oak tree he had pulled me from, asking him if he remembered it was here that we first met.

"How could I forget where I rescued my little bird? You were so timid and afraid at that moment." Edward pulled me to him, kissing my lips, then my forehead. "Little did I know, she would be the one to rescue me."

I returned his kiss. "I have something for you."

I gave Edward a small box. He opened it to find one of the small paper birds he had made for me the Christmas before. I watched him carefully pull that tiny bird out of its box and press it to his lips. I knew he understood.

"I have done very little to deserve you, my darling," he said, holding me against his chest. "Just know Vale, I thank God every day for you."

✦

Sitting in the enclosed garden, I can hardly believe it is spring again. The fragrance of the jasmine surrounds us, as do the happy chirps of birds. It has been two years since I first came to Avenhurst. The garden is more beautiful today than when I first beheld it, if that is at all possible. The flowers have spread, and the cherry trees Edward planted that first spring have begun to mature. I cannot help but smile as I lean back into the warmth of my husband, who is sitting behind me. We are having a picnic today, just the three of us. As sweet as the flowers are, none compare to the rosy cheeks of the babe in my arms. I am mesmerized by him. I never admitted it outwardly, but I had feared for some time that he would not look or feel like the little one I remembered. When my son was first placed upon my chest, I recognized those large eyes at first sight. I knew his scent, and I remembered his sweet coos and gurgles. The pride in Edward's eyes was a vision to behold, and seeing him so gently hold his tiny son, my heart won't soon forget it.

My dear Anne had come from London about a week before his birth to welcome her nephew, with her new husband and round belly.

The proud aunt doted on him. "He is so beautiful, Vale." Anne watched him with gentle eyes before her old, wicked smile returned. "Thank God he looks like you!"

The world here is so quiet at times, especially days like today. As I close my eyes, all I can hear is Edward's light breaths and my son's little gurgles, only interrupted by the chittering birds playing in the trees.

"Look, my darling. Do you see them?" I look to where Edward is pointing.

There in a cherry tree sit a little group of English goldfinches.

"I do," I reply softly.

"Do you know what a group of them are called?" he asks, with that knowing smile of his.

"No, I do not. Tell me."

Kissing my cheek softly, he says, "A charm."

I smile back at my love, then down at my sleeping boy. Yes—a charm. How much lovelier that word is than a curse. I now believe I was never really cursed. My whole life, in both times, served a purpose. I had been discontent, disappointed, and depressed; but I also knew the meaning of unconditional love, hope, and faith. I would always miss those I lost in my former life, but I know that this separation is only temporary. I hold my son up to watch him closely as he sleeps. Edward wraps his arms around us, whispering his love. With a heart that feels truly blessed, I recall that warm spring day in the cemetery in California and what I had read:

*"God shall wipe away all tears from their eyes; and there shall be no more death, neither sorrow, nor crying, neither shall*

*there be any more pain: for the former things are passed away. Amen."*

# ACKNOWLEDGEMENTS

Writing a novel, especially one that has haunted the author's mind for many years, can be a lonely endeavor. Turning that novel into a book that can finally be read and perhaps, even enjoyed by others, requires collaboration and to risk vulnerability. Fortunately, I couldn't have asked for better support for this story of mine.

I must begin by thanking my early readers, Larissa, Nicole, Richard, and my mother, Melodie. I didn't know at the time you each had a label of Alpha or Beta reader. What I did know was that you each brought a different skill set as readers and what you said, and often, what you didn't say, gave me imperative feedback that has enriched this novel.

My editors. Jessica Knauss with The Historical Novel Society. Your astute knowledge of historical details and editing abilities while discerning the author style is invaluable to me. Edward Crocker, I am still amazed at your keen judgment, kind words, and beautiful editing work on my novel. You truly understood my technique, author voice, and themes that I so hoped readers would. From the bottom of my heart, thank you.

To my family and friends, here at home, across the country, and in the UK who have lent me your thoughts, opinions, and most importantly, your encouragement, I thank you.

And finally, to my children. Perhaps I owe each of you an apology; these characters have, at times, consumed my thoughts.

My darling boys, you have only ever been encouraging. I am forever thankful to God for allowing me the privilege of being your mother. As you grow, I wish for each of you to follow your heart. I love you.

# TESS BENTLEY

Tess is a writer of historical fiction with a touch of speculation and the Gothic.

Tess has loved books—their scent, feel, and the world held within their pages—since she was a young child. That love of reading was vital in her development as a woman and mother. After spending ten years working as a registered nurse, Tess found herself *in extremis*, and returned to her first means of escapism: books. Tess has since written her first novel, Vale and has recently received her MA in English with a specialization in Gothic Studies with Distinction. Women's issues—now and historically—hold a tender place in Tess's heart.

Tess lives with her family near the foothills of the Sierra Nevadas in California. When she is not writing, Tess is likely reading something Brontë related and imagining herself somewhere in Victorian England. Follow Tess and her blog at tessbentley.com

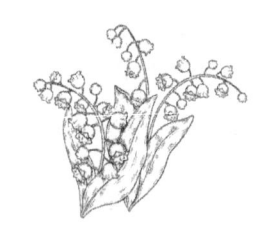